A
PATCHWORK
PAST

Books by Leslie Gould

THE COURTSHIPS OF LANCASTER COUNTY

Courting Cate
Adoring Addie
Minding Molly
Becoming Bea

NEIGHBORS OF LANCASTER COUNTY

Amish Promises
Amish Sweethearts
Amish Weddings

THE SISTERS OF LANCASTER COUNTY

A Plain Leaving
A Simple Singing
A Faithful Gathering

An Amish Family Christmas: An AMISH CHRISTMAS KITCHEN
novella

PLAIN PATTERNS

Piecing It All Together
A Patchwork Past

A PATCHWORK PAST

PLAIN PATTERNS • 2

LESLIE GOULD

BETHANYHOUSE
a division of Baker Publishing Group
Minneapolis, Minnesota

© 2021 by Leslie Gould

Published by Bethany House Publishers
11400 Hampshire Avenue South
Bloomington, Minnesota 55438
www.bethanyhouse.com

Bethany House Publishers is a division of
Baker Publishing Group, Grand Rapids, Michigan

Printed in the United States of America

Library of Congress Cataloging-in-Publication Data
Names: Gould, Leslie, author.
Title: A patchwork past / Leslie Gould.
Description: Minneapolis, Minnesota : Bethany House, [2021] | Series: Plain
    patterns ; 2
Identifiers: LCCN 2020046126 | ISBN 9780764235238 (trade paper) | ISBN
    9780764238147 (casebound) | ISBN 9781493429967 (ebook)
Subjects: GSAFD: Christian fiction.
Classification: LCC PS3607.O89 P38 2021 | DDC 813/.6—dc23
LC record available at https://lccn.loc.gov/2020046126

Scripture quotations are from the King James Version of the Bible.

This is a work of fiction. Names, characters, incidents, and dialogues are products of the author's imagination and are not to be construed as real. Any resemblance to actual events or persons, living or dead, is entirely coincidental.

Cover design by Dan Thornberg, Design Source Creative Services

Author represented by Natasha Kern Literary Agency

21 22 23 24 25 26 27   7 6 5 4 3 2 1

In memory of my mother,
Leora Houston Egger.
A woman who was always of good cheer
and knew, without question,
that Christ overcame the world.

These things I have spoken unto you, that in me ye might have peace. In the world ye shall have tribulation: but be of good cheer; I have overcome the world.

John 16:33

PROLOGUE

·····❖·····

Jane Berger

August 25, 2017
Nappanee, Indiana

Five months ago, planting a large garden on the property of Plain Patterns seemed like a good idea to Jane Berger. But as she stood in the middle of it now, a basket on her arm, she wasn't so sure.

She still had her monthly historical column to write for the *Nappanee News*. She'd finished and mailed the one for September, but now she needed a topic for October. Between her writing, running her quilt shop, and trying to find time for her gardening, she was feeling overwhelmed.

She'd made watering a priority, but she couldn't keep up with the weeds. And now she couldn't keep up with the produce either. Spinach had bolted, fallen tomatoes were rotting on the ground, and zucchinis had grown into the size of baseball bats. Six months ago, she'd imagined hosting preserving classes in the kitchen area of the quilt shop. She'd hoped they'd draw more Englisch customers to Plain Patterns. Maybe they'd be interested in quilting too.

She'd also imagined the quilters sharing the produce with neighbors and kin. Miriam, the young single mother who was living with her, had planned to set up a vegetable stand on the highway to sell the produce. However, her three-month-old son was taking up all her time.

At this point, Jane doubted she could pay people—let alone charge them—to take away the produce.

Today, before the quilting circle began, she'd concentrate on picking what was ripe and hope someone from the circle without a garden would take some of it home.

She began with the cucumbers, twisting one after another off the vines. As much as she worried about the garden, she had more pressing matters to be concerned about—Miriam and baby Owen, to start with. None of them had gotten a full night of sleep since the little one had been born. She didn't regret having Miriam and Owen live with her, but she'd underestimated how much help Miriam would need. More so, she'd underestimated how much work a newborn was. She'd never married and never had children of her own, but she'd been active in the lives of her nieces and nephews—just not in the middle of the night.

She yawned as she transferred the cucumbers into a cardboard box on the grass. After swiping the back of her gloved hand across her forehead, she started in on the beans, dropping them into her basket. It was only seven in the morning and already growing warm. It would be another scorcher of a day. She reached the end of the row of beans and then dumped the basketful into another box.

She stepped back into the garden, through the weeds. She had to find some help. Her great-niece whom she'd hired to weed at the beginning of the summer had taken a job as a mother's helper last month. How could the weeds have grown so much since then?

Jane stepped over to the zucchinis and began pulling the medium-sized ones—perfect to be stuffed with meat and rice and then baked—from the vines. The large ones could be grated for zucchini bread. The smaller ones were better for stir-frying.

She paused for a moment and straightened her back, thinking again of a topic for her October column. She had a vague memory of her great-grandfather, *Gross Dawdi* Vyt, telling her a story. It had to do with a long drought. She yawned again. If only she wasn't so sleep deprived. She shook her head, as if she could clear the fog in her brain.

Gross Dawdi Vyt had been born in February 1865, right before the Civil War ended. He'd lived to be ninety-eight, dying when Jane was eleven. He'd been lucid until the end, frequently telling stories from his childhood. Jane had loved sitting at his feet, soaking up his every word. She attributed her love of history to him. By the time she was ten, she'd started writing down some of his stories.

He had two children, a son who'd died in 1918 and Jane's grandmother, Katie. She and her husband inherited the Landis farm and then passed it down to Jane's father.

As Jane bent down to pick the next zucchini, the growing heat of the morning sun rippled up her back and the thought of a fire startled her. She inhaled sharply. Dawdi Vyt had told her about the Great Chicago Fire. Members of his family had been in the city the day the fire broke out.

She stood up straight and tried to remember his story. But she couldn't recall the details, not even what year the fire occurred. It was definitely in the 1800s. Maybe the 1880s? Had she written down what he'd told her about the Chicago Fire?

Could she trust the notes of a child? Or was that story, like so many others, now lost forever?

She finished filling the basket with zucchini and carried it into Plain Patterns, placing it on the table by the door. Then she returned to the garden for the cucumbers. She felt a twinge in her back as she lifted the heavy box. Her age—sixty-four—was catching up with her. She took a last look at the garden. She'd hardly made a dent in picking the ripe produce, and she hadn't weeded at all. She'd come back out after supper to do that.

After she took off her gloves and washed her hands, Jane walked through the inside of the shop, closing the windows and pulling the shades, hoping to keep it cool as long as possible. Then she started to tidy up, which she'd been too tired to do the evening before, putting away bolts of fabric, straightening the thread display, returning patterns that customers had left out on shelves, and straightening the display quilts.

Each year her shop grew busier. More and more tourists were finding their way to Plain Patterns, along with both her regular Amish and Englisch customers. She delighted in every single person who entered her shop, even the rushed tourists trying to get to their next destination as soon as possible, but she especially loved the women who were part of her quilting circle. Phyllis and Betty. Arleta, who was Miriam's mother. Regina Smucker, who was confined to a wheelchair, and her daughter, Tally. Catherine, the bishop's wife. And Dorothy and her granddaughter, Savannah, who had moved to Nappanee last winter.

There was a comradery among the women that encouraged Jane. All were very different, and yet they supported and loved one another. All had some sort of heartache. Arleta had lost her first husband. Savannah's fiancé had dumped her the week before their wedding. Catherine's youngest daughter, Sophie, had left the Amish and now lived in Elkhart. Sadly, Catherine wouldn't talk about her at all, sharing about her five older children and fourteen grandchildren instead.

Jah, each woman had some sort of heartache in her life.

Once Jane had everything in place, she sat down at her desk at the back of the shop. In front of her was her trusty typewriter. But it wasn't time to start writing yet. It was time to do some research.

On her bookshelf was a set of encyclopedias. She took out *C* for Chicago and quickly skimmed until she found the entry for the Chicago Fire. It had started on October 8, 1871. Why in the world would any of her ancestors have been in Chicago in 1871? It was one hundred miles from Nappanee, a town that didn't even exist in 1871. It wasn't until 1874 that the train came through and the town was developed. Of course, they could have taken the train from Elkhart. But why would they? What business would Amish farmers have had in Chicago?

This coming October would be a great month to feature a column on the fire. But as she quickly did the math, she realized that the fire was 146 years ago. Should she wait four more years and write it then?

She remembered her editor had told her to "never hoard a story." She might not even be writing for the newspaper in another four years. If she didn't tell the story now, she might not have another chance.

But first she had to figure out if she even *had* a story. Had one or more of her relatives really been in Chicago at the time of the fire? Had there been a connection between the people in the area that was now Nappanee with people in Chicago? She felt an ache in her heart for Gross Dawdi Vyt, and for her *Mammi* Katie too.

She opened the bottom drawer of her desk and took out the notebook that held her grandfather's stories, ones that she'd written in her childish hand. But before she opened the notebook, she stopped, folded her hands, and closed her eyes. She prayed the Lord would see to her needs concerning the garden and to guide her as she researched and wrote her next story. And then she prayed for the women who came into the shop.

There was someone specific who needed to be cared for. Perhaps someone besides Miriam. Perhaps someone who was struggling right now—someone Jane wasn't even aware of yet. She prayed, in the midst of her exhaustion and own problems, that the Lord would open her heart—and her story—to minister to a woman who needed it most.

CHAPTER 1

———◆———

Sophie Deiner

August 25, 2017

The doctor, an older woman with short gray hair, stepped into the office and extended her hand. "Hello, I'm Cassie Jones."

I shook her hand. "Sophie Deiner."

"Pleased to meet you," Dr. Jones said. "I'm taking over your case."

I nodded. The receptionist had informed me of that when I'd checked in. My last rheumatologist had taken a job at the Mayo Clinic and had left a month before, just in time to miss my latest flare-up.

"Tell me about yourself." Dr. Jones sat down on the swivel stool but didn't turn toward the computer.

"I was diagnosed two years ago . . ." I paused.

She nodded.

"My last flare-up, before this one, was eleven months ago."

She nodded again. Perhaps she'd actually read my chart. "Any fatigue? Have you been running a fever?"

"Yes and yes."

"Hair loss?"

"Some." Although I had so much hair that to lose some wasn't noticeable, or at least that was what my friends told me.

She peered at me closely. "How about a rash?"

"I haven't had one this time. Mostly I'm just exhausted, and I'm having a lot of joint pain, primarily in my wrists and knees. Some in my fingers."

"Tell me about how you spend your time."

"I work at the co-op," I answered. "And I'm also involved in overseeing the community garden up at Union Park."

"How physically demanding is your work?"

I stifled a yawn. "Both are definitely physical. Unloading crates of vegetables. Weeding and watering at the garden. That sort of work. But nothing too strenuous. Weeding has exacerbated the pain in my hands, though."

"Activity is good as long as it's not exhausting." She asked me a few more questions and then said, "Your blood test shows you're in the early stages of lupus nephritis."

My heart began to pound. Inflammation of the kidneys. I knew that was a possibility but didn't expect it, at least not so soon.

"Diet and exercise are two of the most important treatments. Walking, swimming, and yoga can all help. Avoiding sodium and processed foods can too. We'll try you on a new immunosuppressant drug and also a prescription to protect your kidneys."

I nodded numbly.

"Can you take time off work and have someone take care of you?"

I shook my head. I lived in a house with four other girls. I had rent and bills to pay. I could barely afford my life as it was.

I stifled another yawn. My roommates had been up half the night playing beer pong in the living room, so I'd hardly slept the night before.

"What about family?"

"Pardon?"

"What about family?" Dr. Jones asked. "Can they help you?"

I shook my head.

"No family?"

I sighed. "I do have family. I just don't have a relationship with them."

Her dark eyes met mine. "Did you grow up Plain?"

"Why do you ask?"

She shrugged. "Your last name is *Deiner*. You speak with a bit of an accent."

I'd hoped my accent wasn't obvious anymore. Apparently it was.

"Amish or Mennonite?" she asked.

"Amish."

"When did you leave?"

"Three years ago."

Her expression filled with kindness. "When you were only nineteen?"

I nodded.

"I grew up conservative Mennonite." She leaned forward a little. "When I left to go to college, most everyone thought I'd left to go to hell."

I could empathize but didn't say anything.

"I don't know why you left your community, although I could make a guess from your chart."

Again, I didn't respond.

She smiled a little. "It seems like going back might not be best for you."

I nodded.

For the first time during the appointment, she turned toward the computer. "I'll send in your prescriptions. And I want you to come see me in about a week."

"That's a little soon, isn't it?"

She swiveled back toward me. "It's imperative that you take this seriously. If the lupus nephritis continues, you will probably need chemotherapy sooner rather than later. And eventually, you may need to go on dialysis." Her eyes were kind but serious. "Take time off work. Rest. Exercise. Watch your diet. That's what you need to concentrate on for the next two weeks, at least."

I hesitated. She'd grown up conservative Mennonite. She'd guessed at my past. She seemed to want to trust me to take care of myself. "I'll take another look at my budget, see if I can cover rent this month if I take time off work."

"Good. Call if you're not feeling better in a couple of days," she said. "Call immediately if you're feeling worse."

"I will." I stopped myself from jumping off the table and running from the room. I needed to be back at work at the co-op ASAP and then at the community garden by five. Gardening counted as exercise, right? And the vegetables I grew kept me from eating processed food. Those were both good things, right in line with what the doctor had just prescribed.

Dr. Jones held up her hand. "Don't go yet. I think an injection is in order, as long as you don't overdo it just because you're feeling better." She extended her hand. "It's been a delight to meet you, Sophie. I look forward to seeing you again in a week or so." She seemed so caring, so empathetic. I was more than an interesting case study to her.

Tears stung my eyes. "*Denki*," I managed to say as Dr. Jones left the room.

I WORKED in the produce department at the co-op and was an expert at displaying the produce so it moved quickly out the door, at training customers on how to pick a ripe watermelon, and at sharing tasty recipes to entice people to try fruits and vegetables they might not otherwise buy. *Waste not, want not* was what *Mamm* always said to me, and that was one of my goals when it came to the produce at the store. And if I failed to sell as much as I possibly could, I whisked nearly overripe items out the door and to the downtown shelter while they were still salvageable.

I'd come straight to the co-op after the doctor's appointment, and now I had fifteen minutes left on my shift. It couldn't end soon enough. I felt a little off. A little nauseous. A little lightheaded. More than the constant fatigue I'd been working through.

Maybe it was because of my rough night. In the middle of the beer pong game, my roommate Bri's boyfriend, Mitch, showed up. His voice boomed through the entire house. Bri giggled and said, "Shh. Sophie's trying to sleep." For half a second his voice fell to a normal level, but then grew louder again with each word until, even with my pillow over my head, it felt as if he was shouting above my bed.

Besides Bri, I shared the house with three other women. Haley was a social worker, Paige waited tables at a restaurant downtown, and Ivy was a dispatcher for the Elkhart County Sheriff's Office. I had heard all their voices, at one time or another, throughout the night.

And once I finally did fall asleep, I woke in a panic. I'd been dreaming about Lyle.

I took a deep breath, trying to rid myself of my dizziness and my thoughts of the night before.

I started to stock the blueberries. As I did, Mr. Immigration Lawyer stopped near me, in front of the eggplants. He had dark curly hair and big brown eyes. He always wore a suit, usually a little wrinkled. Today his blue tie appeared as wilted as week-old spinach.

One of the women at the community garden had pointed him out one day as he walked by. She was an Iraqi refugee and said he'd been her oldest son's lawyer.

I'd given her a questioning look. "Why did your son need a lawyer?"

She'd laughed and said, "Immigration, of course." She'd turned toward the man and called, "Hi, Mr. Jasper!"

He'd turned around, a befuddled look on his face, but then brightened and called back, "Nadine, how are you?"

"Wonderful!"

He'd strolled toward the fence. He was young, maybe in his late twenties. "How are your kids?" Their conversation was friendly and brief.

After that, I had thought of him as *Mr. Immigration Lawyer* or *Mr. Jasper*, although I had no idea if Jasper was his first or last name. When Nadine rejoined me in the garden, she explained how he'd spoken at a meeting she attended for refugees and then soon after took on her son's case. Mr. Jasper had also helped a couple of her friends who needed a lawyer, and he'd given her oldest son good advice to help him adjust to life in America. Nadine went on and on about the man.

He was a regular at the co-op, but he was earlier today than usual. And typically he headed straight to the deli, avoiding the produce altogether.

"May I help you?" I braced myself against the table.

"I need an eggplant." He pointed toward them. "Are all of these good?"

"Yes." I took a step closer and picked up one. "You want one that's firm and shiny." I flipped it over, examining it. "And free from cuts or blemishes." I pressed my thumb against it. "See how the flesh springs back? That means it's good."

He nodded seriously. "Thank you," he said, taking it from my hand.

"New recipe?"

He shook his head. "I'm using it as an object lesson in court on Monday."

"I see." I didn't, though. Why did it matter if it was good if he didn't plan to eat it? I watched as he strode to the back of the store, toward the deli.

"There goes Mr. Cute Suit," Bri said. Besides being one of my roommates, she also was a co-worker.

I smiled. "You mean Mr. Immigration Lawyer."

She cocked her head. "Really? He's a lawyer?"

I nodded.

"So, he's rich?"

I wrinkled my nose. "I think you're thinking of a corporate lawyer."

"Then he could be rich if he switched jobs?"

"Maybe." I shuffled back to the blueberries. My fingers ached from the repetitive motion of stocking the tables, and my knees hurt too. I pulled my phone from my apron. Eight minutes until quitting time.

The next thing I knew, Mr. Immigration Lawyer's face was much too close to mine.

"Are you all right? Can you hear me?" He turned to Bri, whose face swam into view. "Call 9-1-1."

"No, I'm fine." I realized I was flat on the floor and started to sit up, but then the ceiling started to tilt.

"Give yourself a minute," Mr. Jasper said.

"I'm probably just dehydrated." Had I had anything to drink with lunch? Did I even eat? I'd gone to the doctor over my break and couldn't remember getting anything to eat before I resumed my shift.

Hopefully that was what was wrong. But what if one of my kidneys was failing?

"Sophie, do you want me to call for an ambulance?" Bri asked, holding her phone up.

"Yes," Mr. Jasper said at the same time that I responded, rather forcefully, "Definitely not. I can't afford it."

His eyes softened. After a long pause, he said, "How about a bottle of water? And a granola bar."

"I'll get something." Bri disappeared.

A crowd had gathered, and Mr. Jasper waved them all away. "Give her some room." He stood so that he was positioned in front of me. I managed to sit up and scoot against the berry table, ducking my head under the overhang, hoping no one would notice me.

Our manager, Don, followed Bri back. She bent down and handed me the water and then a chocolate muffin, saying, "I thought this might be easier to eat."

"Denki," I said.

She laughed. "What?"

"I mean, thank you." I took the water and drank half of it in a long swig. Why had I spoken in Pennsylvania Dutch? Maybe something was wrong with my brain.

"I called 9-1-1," Don said.

I groaned. "Call them back. I don't need an ambulance. I just went to the doctor this afternoon."

He frowned. He was worried about liability most likely.

"I'm fine," I said. "Really."

The manager looked at Mr. Jasper, who shrugged and said, "You can have them check you out—blood pressure and whatnot—and then refuse to be transferred."

Bri whispered, rather loudly, to Don, "She has lupus."

"Which is why I was just at the doctor." I glared at Bri. "Please, I don't want to be checked out. I'm fine. I just need to rest."

"Okay," Don said warily. "But you shouldn't drive home."

"I get off at five too," Bri said. "I can take her."

"Cool." Don took a step backward. "I'll wait outside for the ambulance and let them know they're not needed."

Mr. Jasper met my gaze. "What else can I do to help you?" His eyes were bright.

"Nothing," I said. "But thank you."

He smiled kindly and then walked away.

BRI WASN'T USUALLY VERY FIRM, but no matter how much I begged, she wouldn't take me to the community garden. "Don would be upset," she said. "I promised to take you home."

"But no one will do the watering."

"I'm taking you home, where you are going to get something to eat and rest." Her voice was full of conviction.

After I ate leftover vegetarian lasagna and drank two full glasses of water, I sprawled on the couch and scrolled through social media for fifteen minutes in a blatant attempt to escape my fears. Should I call the doctor? Were my kidneys worse than she thought?

But then Mitch arrived and distracted me. I liked him well enough, but I didn't like the fact he didn't know how to use an inside voice.

"Sophie!" he boomed. "How's it going?"

"All right." I sank back against the cushions.

"She's not all right," Bri said. "She fainted at work today."

"Oh." Mitch took a step back. "Do you have something contagious?"

I shook my head. "Absolutely not. You're safe as can be."

He smiled and then boomed, "Well, I hope you'll feel better soon."

After they left, I felt a little better. Maybe it was just the quiet or the fact I had some food in my system. Or maybe the injection was kicking in.

Whatever it was, it wouldn't hurt to go to the community garden. I liked my job, but I loved working in the garden. My Amish upbringing had served me well when it came to coaxing seeds to germinate into plants and then to bear fruit or vegetables. Growing up, I begged to work outside instead of cooking, cleaning, or doing the wash. Mamm liked working in the garden best too, so when my older sisters left home, I ended up working in the house far more than I wanted to.

But now I could garden all I wanted. As long as my health cooperated.

I walked back to the co-op, got my car, drove up the hill, and parked.

I slowed my pace once I was on the pathway to the garden. The lavender, purple, and orange dahlias bloomed in the bed that bordered the garden fence. On the west end of the garden, the rows of sunflowers swayed slightly in the evening breeze. In between the dahlias and the sunflowers were rows and rows of raised beds, with plots assigned to a person or family.

When I reached the gate, I caught sight of Nadine and her thirteen-year-old daughter, Yani, who were working in their plot.

"Sophie!" Yani said, tugging on her hijab as she spoke. "You're late."

"Better later than never," I called back.

"What?"

"It's an expression."

"Ah, an idiom." Nadine grinned.

Was it an idiom? I wasn't sure. She was probably right. Nadine, who had studied English in Iraq and continued to take classes now, knew the parts of speech better than I did.

"How is your okra coming along?"

"Better." Nadine pulled some bulbs of garlic from the ground. Her family had four of the raised plots, one that included rows of herbs—sage, mint, cilantro, parsley, and thyme. Then cucumbers, tomatoes, eggplants, peas, onions, spinach, okra, and beets. Gardening, I'd come to realize, was a universal language.

But it never ceased to amaze me how we could grow the same ingredients and come up with vastly different dishes. Ingredients were like musical notes or the letters of the alphabet. The possible combinations were endless.

Nadine had brought me beet soup with spinach one time. It also had split peas, lime juice, cinnamon, and cilantro in it. Never in a million years would I, or anyone else who grew up Amish, combine those ingredients. But it was absolutely delicious.

The food was just the beginning of my connection to Nadine and her family. We'd all arrived in Elkhart around the same time and met at the community garden about six months later. Nadine invited me for tea at their sparsely furnished apartment not long after we met. Over fruit, date-filled pastries, and the strongest tea I'd ever had, we talked about our pasts.

Nadine was the widow of an Iraqi professor who had been murdered, along with her two youngest children and driver. After a two-year vetting process, Nadine and her two middle children had received refugee visas to the United States, but her oldest child, Mo, was twenty-one and had to apply and be vetted all over again. At his insistence, Nadine had to make the impossible choice to leave without him and hope he could get out later. At the time I met her, Mo was still in Iraq, in hiding. Thanks to Mr. Jasper, Mo finally made it to Indiana.

After Nadine had finished telling me the story, she asked if I would look at a piece of mail for her. The envelope, which had *Important* stamped across it in red letters, confused her. It turned out to be a credit card application.

Puzzled, she asked, "So I don't need to do anything?"

I assured her she didn't. "It's junk mail."

"Junk?" Obviously that was a new word for her, most likely one not covered in her English classes.

"It's unnecessary," I said. "Advertising, essentially."

"But it says *Important*."

I nodded. "It's just a trick to get you to open it."

She rolled her eyes and shook her head, letting me know she understood.

As soon as I'd left her apartment, I'd gone straight to the library and checked out some books. Because of what the Awad family went through, I ended up educating myself about refugees, and then some about immigration to the US in general too. I'd also read about the recent reduction of refugees allowed to come to our country, even from places where the US had contributed to thousands and thousands of displaced people through years of war.

Another time, as Nadine and I weeded among the rows at the community garden, she shared her worries for her children. Yani was eleven at the time, and her second-oldest son, Zamir, was eighteen. Would they be influenced by the negative aspects of American culture? Was Yani safe walking home alone? Would she want to stop wearing her hijab? How could Nadine continue to teach her children the values of their culture in this new world?

I listened, realizing her fears were the same as my Amish parents, and that in many ways, I identified with Yani. I too had grown up wearing a head covering and feeling different around Englisch teenagers. But I had been around other Amish girls in the same situation, while Yani was very much in the minority in Elkhart.

I didn't have answers for Nadine, except to encourage her to keep instructing her children—and to listen to them, no matter what they had to say.

I knew Nadine had financial worries too. They'd had a housing allowance for four months to give them time to find jobs and get settled, but by the fifth month, they were on their own. Nadine, who had a degree from the University of Baghdad, found a part-time housekeeping job at the hospital, and Zamir found a job at a fast-food restaurant. Their incomes barely covered their expenses. I made sure they knew about the food pantries in town, but they didn't have a car then and had to take the bus. When I could, I gave Nadine rides.

She often thanked me for my friendship, for how I'd helped her. But the truth was, she'd done as much for me, if not more. She'd expanded my small world by showing me an entirely different culture. She had helped me see my own upbringing more clearly and helped me understand the worries my parents had for me. And above all, she'd made a connection with me when I truly needed a friend.

With the garlic still in her hand, Nadine touched my shoulder, redirecting my attention back to the garden. "Are you weeding tonight?"

I shook my head. "Just watering." When people were out of town, I often watered their plots for them, especially if rain wasn't in the forecast. "I can't stay long."

"Oh?" Yani grinned. "Do you have a hot date tonight?"

Nadine smiled too. It was amazing what Yani had picked up in such a short time.

I laughed and just shook my head.

As I watered along the north side of the garden, a figure appeared on the sidewalk.

"Mr. Jasper!" Nadine yelled. "Hello!"

Mortified, I continued watering but turned my back to him. A wave of dizziness swept over me at the sudden movement. I certainly didn't want to faint in front of him again.

"Nadine!" Mr. Jasper yelled. "How are you? What are you harvesting today?"

I stepped to the far fence and lowered myself to the ground, tossing the hose behind me into a patch of corn.

Nadine and Mr. Jasper kept talking. "My eggplants are coming on."

"Eggplants? I just bought one today."

"I'll give you a basketful in a few weeks," Nadine said. "I wasn't sure if the weather would be warm enough, so I started the seeds inside. This hot stretch has helped."

"Fascinating," he said. "I grew up in the city. That's why I always walk by here. The garden is so peaceful."

I imagined Nadine's face beaming with joy. She had the kind

of adoration for Mr. Jasper that other women had for their OB doctor or midwife. It was as if he'd birthed her son into this Midwest town of fifty thousand people and made her family as whole as it could be again. She would be eternally grateful to Mr. Jasper for taking on her oldest son's case, preparing the paperwork and appealing to state senators and INS. He had played a huge role in getting Mo to the US and reuniting Nadine's family, at least what was left of it.

After a few minutes of conversation between the three of them, Mr. Jasper said, "Good to see you again, Nadine. And you too, Yani. Tell Zamir and Mo I said hello." Nadine's sons were now twenty-four and twenty-one. Both worked at the RV manufacturing plant outside of Elkhart.

A minute later, Yani called out, "Sophie! Where are you?"

I winced, hoping Mr. Jasper was farther down the street by now. He probably wouldn't remember my name, anyway. I grabbed the fence and started to pull myself up. But another wave of dizziness swept through me.

I waited a minute, my thoughts falling on what I'd read about kidney failure. When I was first diagnosed with lupus, I was determined to beat it. It took me a few months to realize that was impossible. I had to learn how to manage it. It seemed I hadn't been doing a very good job of it lately.

"Sophie?"

I grabbed the hose and then pulled myself up with my other hand. "Over here."

Nadine and Yani both started toward me. "Are you feeling okay?" Nadine asked. "You are pale."

"I think I better go home."

"To your mother's place?" Nadine had been dumbfounded that I was a single woman living away from my parents.

I shook my head as I handed her the hose. "I know this is

a lot to ask, but would you mind finishing the watering? And could you and Yani do it for the next two weeks or so, along with the weeding? But if you can't, I—"

"No problem," Nadine said, pointing the hose toward a group of blueberry bushes. "We are happy to help." She grinned. "No reason to beat around the bush."

I couldn't help but smile. Not only did she understand idioms, but she could use them too. Maybe not perfectly, but almost.

CHAPTER 2

◆

The next morning I literally couldn't get out of bed. It had been another noisy night. A movie at top volume in the living room. A midnight meal in the kitchen. Shushing followed by laughter, whispers, and then a return to normal volume. I knew my roommates didn't do it on purpose. They just weren't wired to be quiet. And it was their house too.

I stared at the ceiling, feeling the early heat coming through the window, knowing I needed to get up and close it. But I couldn't move. I was due at work in half an hour. Usually when I had an injection, I felt better by the next day. That wasn't the case this time.

I could hear some of my roommates getting ready for the day, even though it was a Saturday. We all had different work schedules, but my roommates could party half the night and still get up early.

After another five minutes of feeling paralyzed, I managed to roll over and retrieve my phone from my nightstand. I called Don. He sounded grumpy when he answered.

"Hey," I said. "It's Sophie. I need to take today off."

His voice softened. "Sophie, hey. I'm glad you called, actually.

HR told me you need to take more than a day off. Per company policy, we need a doctor's note before you come back to work."

"What?"

"You fainted. You could have seriously injured yourself. We need a medical clearance."

"I have an autoimmune disease," I said. "That's why I fainted."

"Regardless," he said, "I need a release from your doctor clearing you to come back to work."

I hesitated. "I'll . . . see what she says and get back to you."

"Seriously, Sophie," he replied, "consider taking some time off. We don't need any more incidents like yesterday."

I hated to use PTO, but I couldn't pay my bills if I didn't. And I was paranoid enough about long-term kidney damage that I knew I needed to get this flare-up under control. And it was a blessing that at least I had PTO now, plus health insurance. I didn't work enough hours the first year on my job to qualify for either.

"Sophie?"

"I can use some vacation time. Two weeks?"

"Sounds good," he said, "I'll mark you down for it. If you're not feeling well after that, give me a call. Otherwise I'll see you in two weeks from Monday."

"All right."

"Take care."

"Thanks." I ended the call and then rolled over. My thoughts fell to my parents' farm, which I'd been dreaming about before I woke up. It was quiet and peaceful. Well, the physical environment was peaceful. The emotional one? Not always.

I fell back asleep. When I glanced at my phone again, it was 9:30. Still feeling as if I'd been hit by a truck, I fell back asleep a second time.

I awoke an hour later, realizing I'd forgotten to pick up my prescriptions the night before. I sat up, finally swinging my feet to the floor. Could I go home, back to the farm?

I stood slowly, shuffled to my closet, and stared at my duffel bag. *God, what should I do?* I needed a place where I could recover physically, but I still hadn't recovered spiritually and emotionally from what forced me to leave home in the first place. Now I was a physical mess too. Would going back help . . . or hurt?

All I needed was a place to sleep. Somewhere quiet. A place with healthy food and someone to pay for it and cook it too.

People assumed the Amish ate healthy because many have large gardens. But those vegetables were often accompanied by lots of red meat, heavy gravies and sauces, and sugary desserts. Overall, the Amish diet was high in sugar, calories, and unhealthy fats.

However, my Mamm had changed our family's diet years ago. We ate more chicken than beef. She stir-fried and roasted veggies instead of boiling them to death. She used whole wheat flour when she baked. She even made her own whole wheat noodles. She cut out most added sugar. Fruit was considered dessert in her book. An occasional pie, with less sugar than called for, was a real treat in the Deiner household. Mamm and I didn't have much in common, but the one thing we shared was a love of fresh, good food.

I needed rest and meals I didn't have to shop for, prepare, or cook. Would Mamm be willing to provide that for me, so long as it was temporary?

Healing physically was what was most important right now. If I stayed close to home and didn't engage with Mamm about the past, I doubted being at home would hurt me. And it might help.

After I showered, I sent a group text to my roommates, explaining what was going on as concisely as possible. Then I pulled on jeans instead of shorts and a scoop-neck T-shirt instead of a V-neck one, trying to be as modest as possible. I grabbed the duffel bag and dropped it on my bed, quickly packing a few essentials. I also grabbed a few books off my shelf.

I managed to drink a glass of orange juice and eat a handful of almonds, but that was all I could get down. I filled my water bottle, grabbed my purse and bag, and climbed into my car, a fifteen-year-old Honda Civic. After picking up my prescriptions, I headed for Nappanee.

It was only twenty miles away, and yet I hadn't been there in three years. Not once. I'd left a couple of messages on the phone out in the shanty, but that was all. One time, *Dat* called back and left a message on my phone. I'd sat there and stared at the buzzing phone, too afraid to pick up. I still had the message and listened to it from time to time. *"Sophie, we were happy to hear from you. You are in our daily prayers and always welcome to come back home and join the church."* That was all. He said it with no emotion and no inflection. It sounded as if he had read it—and seemed as if Mamm had written it.

I turned onto Jackson Boulevard and crossed the Elkhart River, right before it joined the St. Joseph River at Island Park, and headed west, driving along the river as I did, until I turned south. Then it was an absolute straight shot to Nappanee. No hills, no turns. Not even a curve in the road.

I turned right and drove around the town, and then headed south again, crossing the train tracks. Finally, I turned down the lane to Mamm and Dat's place.

Dat had inherited the farm from his father. The white two-story house with its wraparound porch had served our family well when all seven of us kids were home. I was the youngest, and by the time everyone else left, the house felt too big. I was just an echo bouncing off the walls.

Now there were grandchildren. The oldest was fifteen. I had no idea the age of the youngest, but probably a newborn. I didn't get much news from my siblings. All had joined the church. All had married. All were bearing children.

And then there was me.

I pulled into the driveway and parked my car in front of the house. Mamm's garden was as big—and tidy—as ever. There wasn't a weed to be seen, and judging by the drops of water on the gigantic pumpkin leaves, it appeared she'd watered that morning.

She'd lined the outside of the garden with marigolds, as she always did, to keep away aphids. Her corn was shoulder-high, and her green bean plants hung heavy with beans. The heirloom tomatoes were the size of tennis balls, and her pumpkins were as big as basketballs and just beginning to turn orange.

I climbed out of my car, leaving my bag in the back seat. Immediately, sweat began rolling down the back of my knees, under my jeans. I wished I could wear shorts, but my parents would already be horrified by my attire.

Deciding I might startle Mamm if I walked straight into the kitchen, I started around the side of the house toward the front door.

"Sophie?"

I turned around.

"Sophie!" Dat hurried toward me, coming from the barn. "I heard a car, but I didn't expect it to be you."

Besides saying *Denki* the day before, it had been years since I'd spoken Pennsylvania Dutch. "Hallo, Dat!" I said, my heart racing as my tongue wrapped around the foreign words. "*Sis mich.*"

It's me.

I FOLLOWED DAT through the back door and into the house, not sure of how to tell him why I was there. He went straight to the refrigerator and poured us both glasses of lemonade.

He carried the glasses toward the kitchen table. "Let's sit in here."

"Where's Mamm?" I asked, sliding into the seat on his left, where I'd always sat as a child.

"At her quilting circle over at Plain Patterns."

"Jane has a quilting circle now? In her house?"

Dat shook his head. "Her brother built her a shop a few years ago, right around the time you left. It's across the road. It has a large area for the fabric and supplies, then a quilting area, and even a small kitchen. She's got a parking lot and a stable for horses. She has quite the business with both Amish and Englisch, and lots of tourists shop there too."

"How nice." I'd always liked Jane. She was one of the few adults in our district who continued to treat me as she always had when I was on my *Rumschpringe* and the rumors about me started.

"She has a young woman living with her, a single mother who is new to the area."

That didn't surprise me either, that Jane would reach out to someone in need. A wave of sadness washed over me.

Dat took a long drink of his lemonade, which gave me a chance to stare at him for a moment. He was sixty-five and still farming full-time, growing silage and soybeans. And sometimes lentils. His beard and hair were mostly white. He'd put on a few pounds, even with Mamm's healthy cooking, and had more of a belly than I remembered. He also had more wrinkles, and his gray eyes appeared tired.

Being a bishop to thirty families was most likely the reason behind that. Although there were several ministers and a deacon, Dat held the most responsibility. I wanted to tell myself that it was everyone else's problems that were wearing on Dat, but I knew that my running around, my middle-of-the-night move to Elkhart, and my lack of communication over the last three years hadn't helped.

With a pang of guilt, I took a long drink of lemonade too. It was made with fresh lemons and tasted extra tart. Just the way I liked it.

Dat wiped his hand across his mouth and said, "So, daughter, what brings you home?"

"I'm ill," I answered. "I was diagnosed with lupus two years ago, and I've had a flare-up."

He gave me a questioning look.

I explained that lupus was an autoimmune disease that can affect the blood, joints, kidneys, heart, lungs, and even the brain. And that usually it wasn't a problem, but at other times it would flare up and leave me quite sick. "My kidney function is down," I explained. "My doctor gave me new medications, but she said I needed rest."

He wrapped both hands around his glass. "I see."

"Would Mamm be okay with me being home for, at the most, two weeks?"

He lifted his head and met my eyes.

I cleared my throat. "Would you?"

"Jah," he said. "I am fine with you staying for two weeks. It won't be easy for your Mamm though. . . ."

Theoretically, by the mandate of scripture, Dat was the head of the house, and his decision should have been the final word. To those not in the family, it probably appeared that was the way my parents' relationship worked. But their children, me more than anyone, knew how much influence Mamm had on their decisions. I had no quarrel with that, and I respected

Dat for valuing Mamm's ideas. In scripture, the Apostle Paul admonished wives to submit to their husbands, but then he immediately said husbands and wives should submit to each other.

"Sophie." Dat interrupted my thoughts. "You can stay. You look exhausted. Rest until your Mamm comes home. We can all talk then and sort out the details."

I finished my lemonade, thanked Dat, and then curled up on the couch in the living room, under the west-facing window that looked out over the front pasture and the poplar trees that lined the lane.

My older siblings had followed Mamm's plan for their lives. My four older brothers and two older sisters lived nearby. All had joined the church by the time they were twenty-one and married by the time they were twenty-three. One of my brothers worked in an RV factory on the outskirts of Nappanee. Another worked for a landscaping company, another at a feed store, and the last one had, fortunately, married the only child of a farmer who needed his help. One or two of my brothers would inherit Dat's farm, although I had no idea how it would all work out.

My sisters, twins Ruth and Beth, were eleven years older than me. I'd never been close with either of them, and they were especially critical of me during my teenage years.

I'd always been a wild child. Disruptive during church services. Challenging everything. Inattentive at school. I wasn't purposely being naughty. I just had so much energy, combined with a lot of questions. Why could Englisch girls wear pants and I couldn't? Why could they play soccer? Why did I have to learn to bake when I hated it? Why did I have to work in the house while my brothers got to be outside farming all the time?

I was constantly being reprimanded. And once Dat became bishop, Mamm seemed more horrified by me than ever.

"Your Dat is in a position of leadership," she would hiss. *"Our children, according to scripture, must be obedient. Do not embarrass us."*

It was a useless command. I couldn't help it, no matter how hard I tried. And I did try for a while.

But by the time I was eighteen, I was going out with Lyle Stauffer. Jah, he'd grown up Amish, but he was three years older than me, drove a fast car, and partied a lot. My parents adored Lyle, so they weren't concerned. Sure, he was on his Rumschpringe, but he had always been a golden boy in our community. Tall, handsome, and gregarious. Polite and helpful. A charmer, through and through.

Up until the night I left, my parents believed Lyle would be my saving grace, that he would lead me to join the church and all their worries would cease.

However, Lyle had a secret side my parents never saw and a mean streak that he hid well. In school I'd seen him trip a younger boy and make it appear as if the boy had stumbled. I'd witnessed him mock a clerk who stuttered and taunt a young man at a party who clearly had learning disabilities. Those should have all been red flags to me, but I was young and adored him too. I didn't adore him as much, however, when I was the target of his taunts, mostly when he'd been drinking.

I'm not sure what went wrong with Lyle. His Dat had retired from working at the RV plant when Lyle was eighteen, and his parents moved to Ohio, where his oldest brother lived. Lyle moved into a trailer on an uncle's property. Looking back, perhaps it was too much freedom for a young man, especially one who had grown up Amish and had character issues. Maybe he still needed the direction of his parents instead of being left, essentially, on his own. Or maybe he would have ended up that way no matter what his parents did. Clearly, he had been a bully since childhood and continued with the behavior into adulthood.

Still, Lyle always planned to join the Amish, and I did too. Even so, it wasn't as if we were courting, meaning we had marriage as our end goal.

No, we were definitely dating. Having fun. Living for the moment.

I rolled against the back of the couch. I didn't want to think about Lyle. About my late-night flight from my parents' farm. About what happened next. There was a reason I hadn't come home in over three years.

I closed my heavy eyes, willing myself to go to sleep.

"WHOSE CAR is out by the garden?" I awoke to my mother's voice. "Who is here?"

"Sophie," Dat answered.

I waited for her response. It didn't come. I rolled over so I was facing the archway to the kitchen. I could see the table but not my parents. I closed my eyes again.

After a long pause, Dat said, "Catherine. She's ill."

"Well, she doesn't think she can stay here, does she? She has Englisch friends. Someone else can help her."

I heard the sound of dishes clanking and water running, but no voices. Were they whispering? Or at an impasse? A pot clanked against the stove.

Dat said, "Now, Catherine. Listen." There was another pause. "She needs a place for two weeks, at the most. I told her she could stay."

There was another pause and then the sound of the back door slamming.

I knew I needed to get up. Check in with Dat. Talk with Mamm. But I was so tired. So paralyzed.

When Dat's footsteps retreated out the back door, I rolled against the couch again and drifted back to sleep.

I awoke a second time to shadows in the living room. I pulled my phone out of my pocket. 3:05. I listened but didn't hear anyone in the house. I rose and shuffled into the kitchen. After I downed a glass of water, I walked to the window that looked out over the backyard.

Mamm stood in the middle of the garden, her hand on her lower back, staring at the house. I stepped backward. Could she see me?

She wore her white *Kapp* and white apron instead of the scarf and gardening apron she usually donned. I squinted. Her apron was covered with soil. A pile of weeds that she'd purged from what had looked like a weedless garden sat on the edge of the lawn.

I put my glass in the sink and headed out into the heat.

Perhaps she sensed me coming because she attacked another weed, yanking it up and flinging it into the pile.

She had sweat dripping down the side of her face, and her Kapp was stained with soil too. She'd have to bleach it, along with the apron, to get it clean.

"Hallo, Mamm," I said. "How are you?"

She turned toward me, shading her steely eyes with her hand. Gray strands of hair had wriggled their way loose from their pins. She had a streak of soil across one cheek, and she also had more wrinkles. Without answering my question she said, "Go talk to your father. He's on the front porch, trying to recover from the shock of your showing up here."

I pursed my lips together, tempted to head straight to my car and right back to Elkhart. But then what? I truly believed my roommates cared about me and that they would say they'd help, if I asked. And they would say they'd be quieter so I could rest. But I couldn't imagine them actually following through. Their intentions were good, but most of them could barely take care of themselves, let alone me.

I pivoted, aiming toward the side of the house. As I walked, I was overcome with fatigue. Was I getting worse? Or had coming home allowed me to admit just how horrible I felt?

"*Guder Nummidaag,*" Dat called out.

"Good afternoon," I answered in English without meaning to.

"Come sit."

I obeyed him, climbing the stairs slowly and sitting down in Mamm's rocking chair. He looked even older than he had a few hours before. What had he and Mamm wrestled with while I was sleeping?

He rocked gently. "These last few years have been especially hard on your Mamm. She was deeply hurt when you left."

I nodded. I could see that. I had guessed she would take it personally, that she would internalize it.

He sighed. "We decided—together—that you can stay. Your Mamm will cook for you, and we want you to rest as much as you can. However, we want you to wear your dresses, aprons, and *Kappa* while you're here."

I nodded, too tired to argue.

"And if you're feeling up to it, you need to go to church with us."

I wasn't expecting that. I figured they wouldn't want anyone to know I was home.

"All right." All I had to do at church was sit.

"Two more things. No cell phone in the house and park your car in the shed."

"Done." As I stood, I said, "Denki, Dat. I appreciate your help."

He looked up at me, his faded gray eyes brimming with tears. "I pray that good will come from you being here. That is what I am asking of God." He met my eyes. "Please be open to that."

Before I realized what I was doing, I nodded in agreement, without really knowing what he meant. Or what good could possibly come from me being sick and stuck back home.

CHAPTER 3

❖

As I headed toward my car, I stopped at the garden. Mamm was on her hands and knees in the loamy soil, weeding between the strawberry plants.

"Mamm," I said, "may I speak with you?"

She shook her head. "You've spoken to your father. That's enough for now."

Stunned, I didn't respond. Perhaps on her own accord, Mamm would have sent me back to Elkhart. Perhaps she had submitted to Dat after all.

I grabbed my bag out of the car, hauled it up to the back porch, and then drove my car toward the shed. The driveway ran parallel to the highway for twenty yards or so. A white pickup came toward me on the road. As it approached, I was pretty sure it was Derek Raber in the driver's seat, a boy I'd gone to school with, who was a year younger than me. I was surprised he hadn't joined the church yet.

As I neared the shed, Dat strolled toward it. He yelled, "I'll open the door for you."

I slowed down even more, giving him time to arrive first. He entered through the side door and then lifted the garage door for me, and I eased the car inside. Two buggies were on the other side of the shed, and the field dragger was in front. When it was my parents' turn to host church, Dat would empty the shed out and clean it from top to bottom, to make it ready for the benches for the service.

After putting the car in Park and turning off the motor, I pulled my phone from my back pocket, turned it off, and put it in the glove box. Dat still stood at the door, ready for me to walk underneath it so he could pull it down.

"Was that Derek Raber who drove by?" I asked.

"In the white truck?"

I nodded as I stepped through the opening.

"Jah." Dat pulled the door down. "It was."

"What's he doing these days?"

"Working at Mill Creek Farms, with . . ." Dat's voice trailed off.

"With?"

"Lyle," Dat said. "He's the foreman, and Derek is on the crew. The owner has been ill for the last year, and Lyle is pretty much running the place."

"Oh." I turned and pointed toward the house. "I'm going to go check out my old room." I'd need to wash my dresses, which would mean I would need to ask Mamm if she planned to do laundry soon. I already dreaded talking to her.

I walked wide around the garden, avoiding her altogether. Once I reached the porch, I grabbed my bag and headed into the kitchen. On the table was a piece of paper that I hadn't noticed earlier.

Sophie—there's a salad in the refrigerator for you. It was written in Mamm's handwriting. Englischers were always so surprised we had a fridge, thinking my family was on the grid.

We weren't. It was powered by propane. So was the stove, while the old wringer washer in the basement ran on gas.

I put my bag down on a chair and opened the fridge. A chef's salad filled a big bowl. There was a wide variety of greens, cucumbers, cherry tomatoes, hard-boiled eggs cut in quarters, and cubes of home-cured ham. My mouth watered.

Mamm had made a meal for me. She might not want me home, but she'd left me food to eat. I grabbed her homemade vinaigrette, the salad, and a fork and headed to the table. I ate half of the salad and then put it back in the refrigerator. Perhaps I'd have the rest for supper.

I picked up my bag and headed through the living room to the foyer and then up the staircase to the landing. I stopped at the window. Mamm had gathered up the pile of weeds and was tossing it an armful at a time into the wheelbarrow. Dat stood on the edge of the lawn, his hat in one hand while he wiped his forehead with a handkerchief.

I continued up to the second floor. Mamm and Dat's door was closed, and I didn't open it. The next room was Mamm's sewing room. The door was ajar, so I peeked inside. Her sewing machine was under the window, and her cutting table had several pieces of fabric folded and stacked on it. Everything was in its place. There was no clutter in Mamm's life.

I eased open the door at the very end of the hall. The afternoon light came through the open blinds and spilled onto the polished wood floor. The single bed had the same quilt on it as it had when I left, a log cabin design Mamm made and gave to me for my thirteenth birthday. I'd toyed with the idea of taking it with me when I fled but decided it would be an insult to Mamm.

I placed my bag on the bureau and grabbed the single pillow on the bed, hugging it close. The case smelled as if it had been freshly washed and line dried. I walked around to the window. The sill was completely free of any dust. I stepped to my dresses, hanging on pegs along the far wall. I lifted the fabric of the lavender one to my nose. It smelled freshly laundered. Puzzled, I smelled the blue one on the next peg. It had been washed also.

Mamm didn't want me to come home, and yet she'd been keeping my things as if she expected me to return at any moment. And stay.

Had Mamm hoped I'd come home?

Instead of putting on one of my dresses, I curled up on the bed to rest. For just a minute.

The next thing I knew, Dat was knocking on my door. "It's time for supper."

I didn't respond. I just wanted to sleep, but the room was warm. I needed to open the window. And at least get something to drink. The last thing I needed was to get dehydrated.

But if I was going downstairs, I should put on a dress. The thought exhausted me. I caught a glimpse of the water bottle in my bag and managed to say, "I'm going to keep on sleeping."

The door inched open. "Everything okay?"

"Just tired is all."

"This isn't like you," he said. "You slept all day. You were the one who would never nap—not even when you were a baby."

I muttered, "It's because I'm sick."

"Oh." Dat may have said something more, but his voice trailed off as I fell back to sleep.

The next morning, after I showered, I put on one of my dresses, a pink one that Mamm had made when I was seventeen. I pricked myself as I fastened the front with straight pins. Then I twisted my hair into a bun at the nape of my neck and covered it with a white Kapp, the motions feeling as familiar as brushing my teeth. There wasn't a mirror in my room, but there was in the bathroom.

The sight of myself made my heart race. Dark eyes with dark circles underneath. A strip of dark hair, parted in the middle, and then covered by the white Kapp. My pale face made my lips look extra red. I could imagine what the gossip after church would be. It would most likely include that my illness was a punishment from God for my sins. Or that I was faking being sick. Chances were high that most would never have heard of lupus.

When I reached the kitchen, Mamm was scrambling eggs with peppers, onions, and spinach. "We'll eat in a couple of minutes."

"Denki." I had absolutely no appetite but knew I needed to eat something.

"Dat will be in soon."

I nodded.

"How about some coffee?"

"No, thank you." I stepped toward the counter. "Do you have any herbal tea?"

"Herbal tea?" She turned toward me.

"Caffeine isn't good for my condition."

She shook her head as she turned back to the griddle. "Dat mentioned you have something."

"Lupus," I said. "An autoimmune disease."

She shrugged.

"I'm having a flare-up right now. I'm running a low-grade fever, my joints are achy, and my kidney function is down. The symptoms come and go, so sometimes I'm fine and other times I'm ill and exhausted."

She turned the burner off. "Is this one of those new diseases?"

Although I wasn't quite sure what she meant by "new diseases," I guessed she was lumping lupus in with fibromyalgia and Lyme disease, which she also probably didn't understand. I'd done research on both when I first became sick, trying to figure out what was wrong with me. There were a lot of people in the world who had "invisible diseases" that they suffered from. In fact, there were eighty different autoimmune diseases, and nearly any body part could be affected.

"No, it's not a new disease," I answered. "It was first recognized centuries ago."

She turned toward me. "Really?"

I nodded. Did *she* think I was faking it? I poured myself a glass of water as Dat came through the back door. As soon as he washed up, we sat down to eat.

An hour later, we were on our way to church. I rode in the back seat of the covered buggy. Already it was hot and humid. I took my lip balm out of my purse and slathered it on my lips. Mamm turned around and stared.

"What?" I held up the stick. "It doesn't have any color, I promise." As a teenager, I used colored lip balm and mascara, and sometimes eye shadow and blush. I nearly drove her crazy. But once I left the Amish, I hardly used makeup at all.

Church was at the Lehmans' home, which was three miles down the road. We passed the one-room school where I spent my days as a scholar. It was painted white and was the size of a small house. Inside, it had tables and benches, a chalkboard, and a woodstove in the back to heat the building. Thirty to forty scholars studied in it at a time, all taught by a young woman in her twenties, usually. We studied reading, writing, and math, along with some German and basic science. Amish children were considered done with school after the eighth grade.

As with most things concerning my growing-up years, I had mixed feelings about school. I loved being with the other children and interacting with them. I hated sitting still and the shame of never being a "good student." I struggled with math and writing, although I was a great storyteller. Of course, some people, including Mamm, called my stories "lies."

My favorite subject in school was recess. The grounds included a baseball diamond, a volleyball court, swings, and a slide. I excelled at volleyball and softball. I was always one of the first chosen for teams when I wasn't the captain doing the choosing.

We soon reached the Lehmans' place. From the parking of the buggies to the clean-up of the meal and the loading of the benches back into the church wagon, Sunday morning services were a well-oiled machine that rolled along nearly to perfection.

Mamm and I walked toward the Lehmans' shed while Dat unhitched the horse. Because Dat was a bishop, we arrived early. It was a quarter after eight, but the service didn't start until nine a.m. Dat wasn't preaching this morning, but he would be reading scripture and leading prayers. I was relieved he wasn't preaching. Would he feel compelled to mention me if he was?

Everyone loved the story of the prodigal returning home, but I hoped the congregation wouldn't get their hopes up about me. Perhaps Mamm had already gotten the Amish grapevine started about my return.

Flower beds of red geraniums lined the outside of the shed, and wisteria climbed up a trellis next to the open door. The church benches were all set up, and I slipped onto the back one on the women's side. I was supposed to sit with the other women my age, but I decided I wouldn't leave the back row, in case I needed to leave the service to find a place to rest.

An hour later, the singing ended and the preaching began. My back began to ache and soon the space between my shoulder blades burned. Sitting on an Amish bench for three hours twice a month was one of the best core workouts there was. I was definitely out of shape.

An hour into the sermon, I couldn't handle sitting any longer, so I slipped out the side door and into the bright August sunshine.

There was a young woman sitting under the oak tree in the backyard. She was younger than me and wore an extra-plain brown dress. Next to her was a baby, probably three months old, on a blanket. He had a head full of curly hair and big brown eyes.

I approached her. "Could I join you?"

She squinted up at me. "Sure."

I sat down with my back against the trunk. "I'm Sophie."

"The bishop's daughter?"

I nodded.

"Welcome home," she said. "I'm Miriam." She gestured toward the baby. "And this is Owen."

"Your little brother?"

"That's what everyone thinks." She smiled. "He's my son."

Pained, I missed a beat but then managed to say, "He's darling."

"He was screaming five minutes ago," Miriam said dryly.

"So was I. On the inside."

Owen smiled up at me, as if on cue.

"What brought you home?" Miriam asked.

I shrugged. I didn't like discussing my illness with strangers.

She smiled in a knowing way and then started to play with

the baby. I folded my arms across my chest and closed my eyes. I'd just rest for a couple of minutes and then go back in for the rest of the service.

WHEN I OPENED MY EYES, Miriam and the baby were gone and people were streaming out of the shed. I quickly stood and straightened my dress.

"Sophie!" Jane Berger hurried toward me, holding little Owen, who was now sleeping. Jane was smaller than I remembered, but her eyes were still a deep, vibrant brown. "How are you?"

"All right," I answered. "How are you?"

"Good." She shifted the baby to her shoulder. "I heard you already met Owen."

I nodded. "And Miriam."

"They're staying with me."

That's right. I remembered that Dat had mentioned Jane had a young single mother staying with her. It all made sense now.

Jane dropped her voice. "I'm sorry to hear about your health."

"Who did you hear about it from?"

"Dorothy Mast. Who heard it from her next-door neighbor. Who heard it from Ezra Keim, who—"

"Who heard from my Dat." Of course Dat, not Mamm, would be the one to let others know I'd come home.

Jane nodded. "Anyway, you have been in my thoughts."

Knowing Jane, that meant I had been in her prayers too. "Denki."

Suddenly, a familiar voice called out, "Jane!"

Jane shaded her eyes and turned. It was Derek. He wore barn

pants, a forest-green shirt, and a black hat, which was quite a different look from the baseball hat he wore while driving his truck the day before.

"Sophie? Is that really you?" he said as he joined us.

"Jah, it's me," I answered. "Hallo, Derek."

He smiled. "I don't know why I'm surprised, after hearing you were back and all. But I am. Especially seeing you in a dress."

"I saw you in your truck yesterday afternoon," I said. "So now I'm just as surprised to see you dressed Amish too."

He shrugged. "I keep meaning to take the class and join . . ."

"But?"

He smiled and shrugged. "Are you home for good?"

I wrinkled my nose. "Can I plead the fifth?" I said, using a phrase I'd learned from my roommates.

He laughed and then turned to Jane. "Jane, I wanted to ask you how your garden is doing."

She groaned. "My great-niece took a job as a mother's helper. We had planned for Miriam to run a roadside stand, but that hasn't worked. I'd wanted to start a canning circle, but I've done absolutely nothing with that since April, when I got a license for a commercial kitchen and had my brother build a deck on the side and back of my building." Jane shook her head. "My garden is an absolute disgrace. I was going to work on it Saturday but got distracted by other things."

Derek smiled and stepped closer, towering over Jane. "Need some help?"

"Jah, as a matter of fact I do. When can you stop by?" Her voice had a bit of sass in it, which surprised me. "Last time you offered was a month ago, and you said you would help me the next week."

"I'm sorry." He grimaced good-naturedly. "I can't come by tomorrow, but I should be able to on Tuesday—"

"Perfect," Jane interrupted. "If I don't do something, I'm going to waste a lot of food that someone could use. I don't think the squash is getting enough water, even though I water all the time. Also, I'm thinking I need to put down some sort of ground cover to help with the weeds. What do you think?"

My mind wandered as I tried not to think about how the community garden was doing back in Elkhart, but then I noticed Mamm motioning for me to follow her into the Lehmans' house.

I complied, waving at Derek and Jane as I walked away. They were so engrossed in their conversation that they didn't notice.

The meal was typical post-church fare: pickles, pickled beets, sliced ham and cheese, freshly baked bread, and peanut-butter spread. Mamm helped in the kitchen, and I joined her, filling glasses with water and making pots of coffee. I was exhausted by the time we left and couldn't wait to get home so I could sleep.

What people didn't understand about an autoimmune disease was that during a flare-up, I could never get caught up on sleep. I always felt tired. They also didn't understand that taking an analgesic wouldn't help the pain in my joints. And that essential oils or supplements or chiropractic adjustments or some other treatment wasn't going to magically cure me. There was no cure, which was the other thing people didn't understand. Once a flare-up abated, even I could trick myself into thinking that I was done with lupus. But that would never happen.

Usually, I could coach myself through a flare-up and talk myself out of feeling despondent about my future. But I was having a hard time with this one, especially since I was under my parents' roof again. Could I support myself for the rest of my life? Would I ever marry? Ever be able to have children? If my kidneys failed, carrying a child would be unlikely.

Finally, both Mamm and Dat were ready to leave. Once we were on the way back home, I leaned against the inside of the buggy and closed my eyes. A few minutes later, I heard Dat call out, "Whoa!" and the buggy began to slow.

I opened my eyes. A big silver pickup was stopped in the middle of the road ahead of us. The door opened, and a man jumped down.

Lyle. He wore jeans, a button-up shirt, and cowboy boots. He headed toward Dat's side of the buggy. As he neared, he seemed even taller than he had from afar, and more muscular. His usually sandy hair had blond streaks from the sun, and his face was tanned. He looked so normal.

Perhaps he'd changed.

"Sorry," he called out. "Oh, David, it's you."

"Hallo, Lyle."

"I have a flat I need to fix—a blowout. I couldn't get to the shoulder. Sorry. I'll look for traffic coming the other way so you can go around me."

"You need to put out some reflective triangles," Dat said. "You're not visible coming around the curve."

Lyle shrugged. "I don't have any."

"I do," Dat said, "in the back of the buggy. Go ahead and grab them. You can return them later."

"All right . . ." Lyle headed to the back of the buggy while I ducked my head. He unfastened the back, grabbed what he needed, and then refastened the canvas.

"Denki!" he called out.

I raised my head. Lyle was placing one of the triangles several feet behind his pickup.

Then he jogged up a ways, motioned for Dat to go ahead, and placed the second triangle on the pavement. As we passed the truck, I looked into the cab. A woman sat in the passenger seat, turned so she could see Lyle. I didn't recognize her.

Lyle waved at Dat as we passed by. I was relieved he hadn't seen me.

Ahead was Mill Creek Farms, where both Lyle and Derek worked. There was a large, sprawling house, a big white barn, and several outbuildings. There were orchards, vegetable fields, and berry patches that were u-pick, and then there was a market where the produce, along with other products, was sold.

Mill Creek Farms was owned by a man by the name of Hank Barlow. He had the reputation of being a curmudgeon, but Dat had said one time that he had a kind heart and did more good in our community than most people would ever know. Dat had mentioned that Hank was ill, but I couldn't recall what else Dat said. I shook my head, too tired to try to remember the conversation.

In the distance were fields of soybeans and corn. In one field, several workers were working on the irrigation pipes. At the edge of the property, near the creek, was a collection of cabins where the workers lived. It was called "the village" when I was growing up. Some were employed year-round, although most were seasonal.

When we reached home, Mamm asked if I'd help her get ready for the cookout that evening.

"For the what?"

"Your brothers and sisters and their families are all coming over. We're going to have a cookout in the front pasture."

"Oh." I wished she'd mentioned it earlier. "I'll help, but I need to rest first." And brace myself for the reactions of my siblings. I hadn't seen a single one of them in the last three years. But I'd received their scathing letters about the state of my soul, about where I'd go if I died "tomorrow," and about how cruel I was being to Mamm and Dat.

Jah, I knew exactly what my brothers and sisters thought of me. I couldn't help but wonder what they'd actually say to my face.

CHAPTER 4

❖

Mamm and Dat must have told my siblings that I was home because none of them seemed surprised.

"So, the prodigal has returned," my brother John whispered, sliding up to me with a baby in one hand and a big bowl of potato salad in the other. John was four years older and the closest-in-age sibling to me. "The wayward child. Mamm and Dat should have stopped with me, while they were ahead."

I didn't reply, not really knowing what to say. I couldn't defend myself. Then again, his voice sounded like he was joking. Kind of.

The volume of his voice increased some. "Did you get my letter?"

"What letter?" I teased.

"You did," he said. "I think it was rude of you not to answer."

I lowered my voice. "I thought it was rude of you to send it."

He shrugged as he slid the bowl onto the counter. "I was just following directions, doing my duty." He stepped closer and leaned toward me, catapulting his boy into my arms. "Luke, meet your *Aenti* Sophie."

The boy gave me a sour look but didn't cry. He had wavy

blond hair and hazel eyes. He looked to be about ten months old.

"I'll be back in a minute with Lester. Luke's twin."

Luke began to fuss as John left, until Mamm, who was squishing ground beef into patties, said, "Luke, stop."

He pouted for a half second and then obeyed his grandmother.

"Put him down," Mamm said. "He knows where the toys are." She'd always been a no-nonsense mother—and grandmother.

I did as she said, and Luke crawled off to the living room.

"Now, slice the tomatoes," Mamm ordered.

A half hour later, we'd carted everything out to folding tables set up in the pasture, where Dat had a fire burning in a brick-lined firepit.

John was setting up a volleyball net, and my older nieces were bumping a ball back and forth. My sisters, Ruth and Beth—the first set of twins in the family—stood with their arms crossed at the end of the table. I'd said hello to them when they arrived, and they'd both nodded in response. But that was all. They'd headed straight out to the pasture after that.

Dat and my oldest brother, Timothy, were cooking the patties on a grill over the flames. When they finished, Dat called us all to gather around, and he led us in a silent prayer. Then the mothers began filling the plates of the youngest children. Eventually, everyone had gone through the line and was settled in groups on blankets and lawn chairs. Luke and Lester crawled off their blanket and sat in the grass, pulling at it.

I wasn't sure which group to join and wished I could go back to the house.

My oldest niece, Lydia, patted the blanket beside her. "Sophie," she said, "come sit with us."

I did, feeling self-conscious. She was Timothy's daughter. Would he be afraid I might corrupt her? She was fifteen and would soon start her Rumschpringe. I was sure she was wearing lip gloss and mascara.

As I sat down, two people started toward us. The sun was low in the sky, and it was hard to see who it was. I couldn't think of anyone who was missing.

I squinted just as John walked over to them. "Hey, Lyle! Good to see you."

Lyle waved, the setting sun glinting off the two reflective triangles Dat had loaned him that afternoon.

Lydia pivoted toward them. "That's his girlfriend, Delia. I heard they're getting married. She's Mennonite. Everyone says he's going to join her church instead of ours."

"Is that right?" My voice shook a little.

My next-youngest niece poked Lydia, who squealed, "What?" And then, "Oh! I forgot." She looked at me with her hand over her mouth. "Sorry."

I ignored her and took a bite of my hamburger, turning my head as John, Lyle, and Delia walked by. Timothy and Philip, my middle brother, gathered around them while Lyle made a big show of returning the triangles to Dat.

"Go ahead and put those back in the buggy," Dat said. "On your way out." Was Dat hinting that Lyle should leave? If so, Lyle didn't oblige. He had his back to me as he and my brothers stood around and talked, although I couldn't hear what they were saying. Clearly, Lyle hadn't seen me.

Once I finished my burger, I decided to slip back to the house. Clouds were darkening the sky, and I doubted the cookout would last much longer anyway. A storm was definitely rolling in.

As I turned to go, Lyle said to John, louder than he needed to, "Why didn't you tell me Sophie was back?"

"I just found out," John replied.

"And you didn't think to tell me?"

I quickened my step, not wanting to hear anymore. But the crash of thunder that came next would have drowned out Lyle's words anyway. Lightning flashed, followed by another crash of thunder. As the rain started, Lyle and Delia ran past me, holding hands. Neither he nor his girlfriend acknowledged me or even looked my way.

He hadn't changed a bit. I was sure of it.

For a moment I considered turning back to help haul food to the house, but then decided my sisters and sisters-in-law could help Mamm clean up. They didn't need me.

Lyle was backing his truck out of the driveway when I reached the house. He gave me a fleeting look as I walked up the back steps. Soaked, I headed to my room, changed into my pajamas, and collapsed into bed. Jah, I'd slept all afternoon, but I'd done too much.

Well, seeing Lyle had been too much. Hopefully that wouldn't happen again.

Just before I fell asleep, Dat knocked on my door. "How are you feeling?"

"Tired."

"I hope you'll get a good rest," he said. "*Guti Nacht.*"

"Guti Nacht."

I'm not sure if it was Dat's kindness or something else, but I slept well and felt surprisingly rested in the morning. At breakfast, Mamm said she was going to Plain Patterns for the quilting circle.

"Could I come along?" I asked.

"But you don't like to quilt."

True, because I had such a hard time sitting still. But Mamm had still forced me to learn how to quilt when I was young, so I knew how. "I'd like to go," I said. "I'd like to see Jane's garden too."

Mamm hesitated and then asked, "Won't that be too much for you?"

"It will be a whole lot less than yesterday," I answered. "I can come home and rest afterward."

She pursed her lips. Was she embarrassed by me?

Dat piped up. "I think that sounds like a good idea. Jane would like to see Sophie again, and I think the other women would too. Isn't Dorothy Mast part of the quilting circle? And her granddaughter Savannah?"

"Jah and nee," Mamm answered. "Savannah does not attend anymore."

"Savannah?" I asked. "Dorothy's Englisch granddaughter from California?"

"Jah," Dat said. "She moved here last January."

"Wow." I remembered Savannah from when I was little. She was five or so years older than I was and always came to visit her grandmother in the summer. I found her fascinating, although I never actually talked with her or spent any time with her. I doubted she would remember me. However, Dorothy would. Like Jane, she'd always been kind to me.

"Dorothy has been ill," Dat said to me.

"Just like that," Mamm added. "A few months ago she seemed as healthy as could be and then all of a sudden she's so frail."

"What's wrong?" I asked.

"They're not sure yet," Dat said. "She's been losing weight, so they've been doing lots of blood tests."

That didn't sound good. Dorothy was most likely in her eighties by now, so even something minor could become serious.

I washed the dishes while Mamm watered the garden. She'd already done the wash that morning and had it on the line to dry. After doing laundry for a big family for so many years, washing just her and Dat's clothes—and my sheets and dresses—must seem like a dream.

By 8:30, we were in the buggy on our way to Jane's. Again, we drove by Mill Creek Farms. Lyle's silver truck and Derek's white truck were both parked by the barn. The fields were full of workers, who were moving pipes and picking produce. There were several cars in the parking lot but not as many as the day before. It was Monday, I reminded myself. People were back to work and school.

Mamm didn't say anything as we rode along. Even though the slow pace of our travel was hard for me to adjust to, I loved the rhythm of the horse pulling the buggy and the clippity-clop of the horse's hooves. It reminded me of my childhood and falling asleep in our buggy on the way home.

When we reached Plain Patterns, Mamm and I unhitched the horse. "Water her," Mamm said, "and then put her in the barn."

There was a trough on the left side of the gate. Once the horse was in the barn with hay to eat and the door was shut and fastened, I paused for a moment, trying to make out the sound in the distance. It had to be Mill Creek. I hadn't realized that it ran through the Bergers' property.

I walked back toward the building. When I entered Plain Patterns, I could hear voices in the back but couldn't see anyone. I scanned the quilts displayed, with their distinctive splashes of colors and patterns, along the walls. My gaze then fell over the bolts of fabric—there were solids of maroon, forest green, and sapphire blue; a collection of small-scale flower prints in muted colors; and then the more typical Englisch prints in bolder and brighter colors.

I stepped into the back room, noting the kitchen area in the very back, and then the quilting frame and the women sitting around it, including a woman in a wheelchair.

"Hallo, Sophie!" Jane stood. "Welcome." Jane spoke in English, most likely because there was an Englisch woman also sitting around the frame.

The other women all turned toward me. I saw a few familiar faces besides my Mamm's, of course, including Miriam's. She was standing with Owen in her arms. And Phyllis Raber, Derek's mother, along with Wanda Miller, whom I remembered from my childhood too.

"Come sit by me," Jane said, patting the seat next to her.

None of the women said anything as I moved across the room. Was it up to me to break the silence? I stared at the quilt, a checkered garden pattern. It was bright as a garden—pinks, reds, blues, purples, lavenders, yellows, and teal. I counted quickly. There were forty-nine blocks, and each block was made of forty-nine squares.

"Who pieced the quilt?" I asked.

"I did," Jane answered. "But everyone contributed fabric."

"It's so summery," I said. "Will you sell it?"

"No," Jane answered.

"Who is it for?"

She shrugged. "We don't know yet."

Miriam chimed in, "The last one was for me. A hearth-and-home pattern."

"Cool," I responded. Then my face grew warm as I realized how extra-Englisch I must sound.

Jane alarmed me with her gasp. Had I offended her?

But, much to my relief, she said, "I don't know where my manners are. I just realized you don't know everyone, Sophie."

She nodded around the circle. "You met Miriam and Owen yesterday."

"Jah," I said, concentrating on sounding as Plain as I could while speaking English.

The woman in the wheelchair was Regina Smucker, and the young woman next to her was her daughter, Tally. I vaguely remembered Tally from a district away. I guessed she was two or three years younger than I was.

"Nice to see you again," I said. "How are you?"

"Good," Tally answered as her mother said, "I've been better."

I guessed Regina was just being honest.

Jane continued with her introductions. "And this is Betty Krueger." She was the Englisch woman.

I said, "Pleased to meet you."

"And this is Arleta, Miriam's mother." Jane nodded to the floor, where a baby I hadn't noticed was sleeping in a car seat. She appeared to be eight months or so. "And her baby, Ruby."

I smiled. Miriam and her mother had babies nearly the same age. Yet Miriam was an unwed mother, and still all of the ladies present seemed to accept and support her. Had the community changed that much since I'd left? I exhaled sharply. Or had I misjudged them?

Next Jane introduced me to Wanda and Phyllis, both of whom I remembered, and they nodded in greeting. Mamm sat next to Derek's mother, Phyllis, who chuckled and said, "Welcome home, Sophie."

I smiled at her kindness. I'd always gotten along well with her and her large family, especially her daughter Liza.

"We have a couple of other quilters running late," Jane said to me.

All the women already had needles in their hands. I picked up the one in the fabric in front of me and started quilting, using the tiny stitches I'd been taught so long ago. It seemed stitching, like riding a bike, was something one didn't forget.

The women were quiet for a few minutes, but then Arleta asked Jane what topic she was currently researching for her monthly newspaper column.

"The Chicago Fire," Jane answered. "The idea came to me on Friday."

"How fascinating," Betty said.

I'd gone to Chicago last year with Ivy and Bri. We'd driven over for a day and had gone to The Bean, the reflective sculpture in Millennium Park, and walked along Lake Michigan. We'd also walked the Magnificent Mile, with its high-end shops, restaurants, and hotels. None of us had money to actually buy anything, but it was fun to look.

"Jah, I've just started the research and find it very intriguing," Jane said to Betty.

"Can you tell us about it?" Arleta asked.

"I will soon." Jane smiled. "Once I have more information."

The conversation then shifted to Jane's garden. Jane said that Derek planned to stop by tomorrow to take a look at it.

Phyllis shook her head. "I hope he'll come this time."

"I know he's been busy," Jane answered graciously. "I'm afraid I was overly optimistic about what I could get done. I was going to work more on it this weekend but ended up doing research instead."

Some of the women offered some advice. Then Mamm said, "It's not that hard. A half hour in the morning and another in the evening is all it takes."

"Ah, but that's only if your garden is already as orderly and tidy as yours, Catherine," Phyllis said.

Jane yawned, quickly covering her mouth, as she listened. Owen began to cry, and Miriam walked him to the front of the store.

The bell over the front door dinged, and it sounded as if Miriam greeted someone. A couple of minutes later, Dorothy and Savannah Mast stepped into the back room.

Dorothy was far smaller than I remembered. Her hair was completely white under her Kapp, and she was slightly hunched over. She held on to Savannah's arm as she walked. Once she saw me, she gave me a warm smile. "Hallo, Sophie. I'm glad to see you here." She turned to Savannah, who held her purse and a water bottle in her free hand. "Savannah, do you remember Sophie?"

"Hi." Savannah smiled. Dressed in sandals, a skirt, and a blouse, she looked like the epitome of summer and good health.

"I'm Catherine's daughter," I said. I was pretty sure she didn't remember me.

"Oh, that's right. I've heard about you." She blushed.

I guessed what she'd heard was gossip.

Savannah shot me an awkward glance. "It's good to see you."

I nodded. "You too."

She glanced around the room. "I wish I could stay, but I need to get back to work." Savannah stepped to her grandmother's side and handed her the water bottle. "Tommy will give you a ride home. He'll be here at noon."

Dorothy looked up at her granddaughter. "Denki."

Savannah gave her a hug. "I'll see you after work. Don't forget I'm cooking tonight!"

Dorothy smiled. "I will let you. Denki." It sounded as if Dorothy needed someone to take care of her too.

A FEW MINUTES before noon, Tommy Miller showed up to take Dorothy home. I remembered him from my childhood too. I also remembered several hushed porch conversations between his Mamm and my father, but Tommy had left the area by the time I was a teenager.

He sported a goatee and was dressed in khaki pants and a button-down shirt. He said hello to his mother and then gave her a sweet smile. He was kind and gentle with Dorothy, making sure she had her purse and water bottle. As he escorted her out of the room and into the shop, the other women stood and readied to leave. I did the same, thanking Jane for the morning. Then I asked, "I was wondering if I could look at your garden."

"Oh, I am embarrassed for anyone to see it," she said. "It is in such disarray."

Surprising me, Mamm said, "I will watch the shop while you two go out."

"*Wunderbar*," Jane said. "It won't take long. Sophie will take one look and want to turn and run."

I smiled. I doubted that.

"Let's go out the back door," Jane said. I followed her into the kitchen area and then outside into the bright—and hot— sunshine. A walkway led around the side of the building and to the back.

The garden space was large and in a nice sunny spot, surrounded by a fence. Behind it, on the way to the creek, was a strip of blackberry bushes that weren't entirely out of control. There was a spigot and hose on the right side of the garden and a row of raised beds on the left. Sunflowers and corn grew in several rows in the back.

As Jane opened the gate, Derek stepped around the other side of Plain Patterns. "Hi, Jane! I was able to take a lunch break and decided to come today."

She shaded her eyes. "Hallo, Derek. You just missed your mother." She motioned him over. "I was just going to show Sophie the garden. Come join us."

He waved and then followed us through the gate. A pile of pulled weeds sat in the middle of one pathway, and the other paths were covered with weeds that needed to be pulled. Jane's tomato plants were heavy with fruit, and the ground was covered with rotting tomatoes. She had beans, cucumbers, yellow crookneck squash, and zucchinis that all needed to be harvested. A row of spinach had bolted, but the next row was okay, so long as it was harvested soon.

"I'll bring two or three hay bales over," Derek said. "Once we weed, we can spread it around on the pathways and under the plants. It will help keep the weeds down and retain the moisture."

He lowered his voice and grinned mischievously at Jane. "Don't tell my boss I said this, but if you cut Mill Creek Farms' prices, you'll get people stopping by for produce. Plus, you have lots of traffic here for the quilt shop. Your customers will buy it too." He pointed toward the parking lot. "Put the stand in the middle of the lot, not by the side of the road."

"Denki," Jane said. "Maybe Miriam would try to stock it again."

"And just set out a jar for people to put money in," Derek said. "If you're willing to give it away, anything you do make will be gravy."

As Derek and Jane walked through the garden, I followed them. Derek agreed that her squash needed more water. "The hay will help with that," he said.

The sunflowers and corn looked good, and we stopped there. I was enjoying the conversation about gardening and was sad the visit was almost over.

"I should go rescue your mother," Jane said to me. "She probably needs to get home and get dinner ready for your Dat."

"I'll need to go too, then."

"I can give you a ride." Derek smiled at me and then turned toward Jane. "After we come up with a comprehensive plan on how to save Jane's garden."

She smirked. "So, you think it's worth saving?"

"Of course," he and I said in unison.

"I'll tell Catherine she can go on home, then, if that's all right with you, Sophie."

"Sure." A ride in Derek's air-conditioned cab was preferable to going home in the buggy. "But I should go get the horse for Mamm."

"I'll help," Derek said.

Jane started toward the quilt shop while Derek and I headed toward the barn. By the time Mamm came out of the shop, we had the horse hitched for her.

"I'll be home soon." I hoped she wouldn't be angry with me for staying longer.

She smiled at Derek but then frowned at me. Although she said, "Take your time," I could tell she wasn't pleased.

Once she was in the buggy and headed toward the highway, Derek and I returned to the garden. I looked around. Weeding was definitely the first priority.

Derek took out his phone and made a list of what Jane needed. "We can create moat-like basins around each planting bed to keep the water contained."

We?

After a pause, he asked, "Do you think a canning circle is realistic?"

I shrugged my shoulders. "I taught a class on canning at the grocery co-op where I work. I'm imagining we could do something like that but with everyone participating. I think it's a possibility, but it would take some planning."

Derek nodded and jotted something down on his phone. "Spinach, lettuce, and peas could all be replanted for a late harvest." Derek raised his head. "Any chance you can help with this?"

I wrinkled my nose. "Perhaps some," I said noncommittally.

Derek eyed me, concerned. "I heard you're having health problems."

I nodded. "I came home to rest."

"I don't want you to help if it's too much."

"I think gardening might be good for me." It wasn't as if Mamm needed me to help in her garden. "I'll let you know."

We continued walking through the garden, taking each problem and coming up with a solution. After a half hour, Jane came back out. "How about some sandwiches?"

"I need to take Sophie home and get back to work," Derek said.

"You also need to eat," Jane responded.

He twisted a perfect red tomato off the vine. "How about this?"

She laughed. "How about some bacon and bread to go with it? I have some in my little kitchen. It will only take a minute."

Derek threw the tomato up in the air and then caught it. "All right."

"Grab some lettuce," Jane said to me. "You both can tell me what you've come up with as I fix the sandwiches."

We stood at the counter in the little kitchen as we ate our BLTs and came up with a comprehensive list of tasks. As we finished, Jane said, "I think Miriam would be more excited to help if there were other young people involved—if she experienced community in the work."

I thought of Nadine and Yani and how much fun it was gardening with them. "I won't be here very long, but perhaps I can help coordinate that. Maybe Miriam would work with me."

"If you want to work in the evening, after the worst of the heat is gone, I can give you a ride," Derek said. "Do you still have my number?"

I nodded slowly. "I think so."

"Just text me if you want me to pick you up," he said. "If you, Miriam, and I worked for an hour each evening, we could make good progress. We could at least weed and stock the produce stand."

"I could watch Owen during that time," Jane volunteered.

"Wunderbar," Derek said.

As exciting as it all sounded, I was already tired thinking about all the work to be done. I hoped I would be able to participate like I wanted, but I had to remind myself to take it one day at a time.

CHAPTER 5

On the way home, when we neared Mill Creek Farms, Derek craned his neck as he looked over the field for something or someone. "Do you mind if we stop for just a minute? I need to speak with Victor."

"Who's that?"

Derek turned on his blinker. "One of the year-round workers on the farm. He should be foreman—over both Lyle and me—but he's not."

He turned down the road and drove past the barn, shed, market building, and u-pick fields. At the end of the lane were the cabins, just up the bank from the creek.

Derek pulled up to the last cabin, where an older-model Chevy pickup and an old Ford were parked. Derek turned off the engine and said, "Hop on down if you want. I'll introduce you."

As we started toward the house, a boy, probably eight or so, came bounding down the steps. "Hey, Derek. What's up?"

"Hey, Sebastian," he said. "How are you?"

"Good!"

"Is your dad around?"

He nodded. "He just finished lunch." He took off toward the creek.

The screen door opened, and a man stepped out. He was looking over his shoulder at someone who was yelling, "Papa, things are changing around here. ICE wants to open a detention center. Who do you think they're going to fill it with?"

I stepped backward, feeling as if I were eavesdropping.

A young woman about my age stepped onto the porch. Her long dark hair was pulled back in a low ponytail. Catching sight of us, she blushed. "Derek . . ."

"Hi, Karin."

The man turned toward Derek and smiled.

"Sorry," Derek said. "I didn't mean to interrupt." Derek nodded toward me. "This is my friend Sophie. Sophie, this is Victor Lopez and his daughter, Karin."

I stepped forward and shook hands with them both. "Nice to meet you."

"Sorry to drop by unannounced, Victor," Derek continued. "I just have a question about the pump."

"Sure." The two stepped toward Derek's truck.

Karin smiled at me as she headed toward the Ford. "I have to get back to work. Nice to meet you."

I waved as she started the engine and drove off.

Several minutes later, Derek was done, and we climbed back in the truck. As he backed out of the driveway, I asked where Karin worked.

"At a law office in Elkhart," he answered. "She's a paralegal. She went to college in South Bend and then got the job about a year ago."

I thought of Mr. Jasper's kind eyes. "What type of law?"

"Family, I think, but she seems to know quite a bit about immigration law too." He waved to a man standing by the shop. "She's worried about her parents. And her older brother, Mateo."

"Oh?"

"She and Sebastian were born here, but Mateo was born in El Salvador. Their parents fled with him when he was a baby. They've been trying to get legal status here for the last twenty-five years."

I thought of Mr. Jasper again. "ICE is . . . Immigration and . . ." I couldn't remember exactly what the acronym stood for.

Derek helped me out. "Customs Enforcement. There's a rumor about a detention center being built somewhere in Elkhart County." He shook his head. "This county probably won't be okay with an ICE center here, though, not when immigrant labor is necessary for businesses to survive. Farms are dependent on it. RV plants too. So are lots of restaurants and other businesses. I've heard there are ten thousand immigrant laborers just in Elkhart County alone."

"Wow. I had no idea."

"Do you remember how, during the recession, Elkhart County had one of the worst unemployment rates in the nation?" Derek asked.

I nodded. I remembered that well. Most of the RV factories closed. Both Englischers and Amish in the area lost their jobs.

"Things have totally turned around," Derek said. "No one, including Mill Creek Farms, can find enough workers now that the factories are back in business. There are nearly nine thousand job openings in the county, which gives us one of the lowest unemployment rates in the entire country. But if we lose immigrant workers—meaning undocumented ones—we're toast. Businesses will have to shut down. Food will rot in the fields." He paused as the car in front of him slowed to make a turn.

"There's a narrative going around town that the undocumented commit more crimes than citizens, that they collect food stamps and don't pay taxes. None of that is true. Yes, their children do go to public school, but many of those children are citizens." He sighed. "Our system of labor invited workers to come here. It's not right to punish them for accepting that invitation."

I glanced at Derek. He was absolutely sincere. His passion for the people who worked with him touched me—but his words also alarmed me. What would happen to Karin and her younger brother if her parents and older brother were sent back to El Salvador?

I SPENT THE AFTERNOON RESTING — and thinking about Karin and her family. I felt drawn to them, maybe because of my friendship with Nadine and her children. The two families had different circumstances but a shared story of immigration, although one was able to secure documents, eventually, for each member. Three members of the Lopez family had not.

Would Karin's parents and older brother be picked up by ICE? Would it be more likely if there were an actual ICE detention center in Elkhart County?

Centuries ago, my ancestors had fled from Switzerland to the Palatinate area in Germany, searching for religious freedom. Drawn to the New World by the promise of land grants through William Penn, they'd immigrated to Pennsylvania. Over the years, some had moved to Ohio and then on to Indiana. The Amish had been refugees in search of religious freedom. Many were persecuted back in Europe and had fled for their lives.

I remembered reading about violence in El Salvador. What

danger had Karin's parents been in? What had they feared for their young son and future children?

My bedroom was warm, and as the sun shifted toward the west, it grew even hotter. I finally went downstairs, deciding to lie on the couch where it was cooler.

Mamm sat in her rocking chair, piecing together a quilt block by hand, most likely forced out of her sewing room by the heat too.

"What are you working on?" I asked.

"A nine patch for Lydia, for her birthday." The block she was stitching was made of all blue fabric in different shades and prints.

As I gingerly lowered myself onto the couch, she said, without looking up, "You couldn't stay still for a minute your entire life. Now you're napping all the time."

I bit my tongue to keep from replying, assuming she was leading into some sort of criticism of me.

But then she said, "Maybe there's something to this lupus."

Did she actually believe I was sick? I pulled the couch pillow under my head, feeling vindicated.

Until she quickly changed the subject. "You should stay away from Derek."

I lifted my head. "Pardon?" I should have known she couldn't be sympathetic for long.

"Derek. Don't lead him on."

"Why would you say that?"

"I know what you did to Lyle. Everyone does."

That was rich. "What did I do to Lyle?"

When she didn't answer, I sat up, then stood, and walked out the front door to the porch, my blood boiling. I'd worked so hard to forget Lyle.

I walked around the outside of the house and headed toward

the shed. Dat wasn't anywhere in sight. I opened the side door and slipped inside. It was fairly cool, cooler than my room anyway. I slipped into the passenger seat of my car, opened the glove box, took out my phone, and turned it on.

A minute later, when the screen came alive, I had six texts. Four from my roommates responding to my text that I'd be gone for two weeks. One from Yani saying they'd weeded and watered the garden and harvested the tomatoes and cucumbers.

The last one was from Lyle. I'd deleted him from my phone, but I still recognized his number. *What are you doing home? Why didn't you warn me?* I deleted it and then went to my contacts and found Derek's number.

I'd like to go back to Jane's with you tonight, I texted. *I'll be ready by 6:15.* Mamm served dinner at five. That would give me plenty of time to help clean up afterward.

While I waited for his response, I sat in the dim light in my car, reading through social media for a few minutes. I hadn't missed it at all.

Finally, my phone dinged. It was from Derek. *Great! I'll pick you up then. Jane will be so happy.*

"Sophie?" Dat stood in the doorway of the shed. I quickly turned my phone off and stashed it back in the glove box.

"Jah, Dat?" I climbed out of my car and slammed the door. "I was just checking my phone. I put it away."

"Your mother was wondering about you," he said.

"I'm fine," I answered. "I'll go help with supper."

Dat stepped outside. "I'll be in soon."

Mamm didn't say anything more about Lyle, and I didn't say anything about going out later that evening.

I finished cleaning up by 6:10. Mamm and Dat were both on the porch when I heard tires rolling over the gravel. I quickly dried my hands and hurried into the living room. Then I slowed as I walked onto the porch.

"Who is that?" Dat asked.

"Derek Raber." Mamm shook her head as she said his name.

"We're going to help Jane with her garden. But just for an hour." I kept going, hoping neither would say anything.

Derek jumped out of his truck and waved at Mamm and Dat, and then walked around to the passenger side and opened the door for me. I climbed in quickly and fastened my seat belt. As Derek turned the truck around, I waved at Mamm and Dat. He waved back, but she just crossed her arms over her chest and stared.

"ONE HOUR, RIGHT?" Miriam asked dubiously, looking over the jungle of green before us. I'd never seen her without Owen, and she looked even younger than she had before.

"One hour," Derek said, pulling up the timer on his phone. "Ready? Set? Go!"

He hit the Start button and we were off. We'd decided to see how much we could get done working nonstop for an hour. Or, in Miriam's case, for as long as Owen would let her.

Derek was weeding between the first two rows, Miriam was in the next one, and I was in the third, between two rows of beans. Derek and Miriam had met before but had never spoken to each other. As we worked, she told us about moving to Nappanee from Newbury Township almost two years ago. Although she and Derek didn't know a lot of the same people, they knew some, including Tommy Miller and Savannah Mast.

"Savannah saved my life." Miriam stretched her back. "Literally."

"I heard a little about that," Derek said.

Miriam started weeding again. "I bet you did. I'm sure I was the main topic of conversation around here for a while."

Derek's face reddened. "I wouldn't say that."

I grimaced behind my beanstalks. It was probably worse than that.

"I fell in with a bad group of people, including Owen's father, and ended up in Chicago. Savannah and Jane kept searching for me until they found me. And then they brought me home."

Tears stung my eyes. What if someone had come after me?

"I'd heard something similar to that," Derek said, "but your explanation makes it all clearer. I'm glad you came back."

"So am I," Miriam said. "For my sake and Owen's. And then Jane offered for Owen and me to live with her, which has really helped my relationship with my mother. We were in a bad place before."

I blinked, determined that my tears wouldn't escape. Miriam had done the exact opposite of what I'd done—and everything had worked out for her. Or at least, it seemed it had. No doubt, her situation wasn't perfect. She was a single mom—which I knew had to be hard—but she was making it work.

Their conversation shifted to Mill Creek Farms and a few of the young people Miriam knew who worked there. I concentrated on weeding, and I succeeded in keeping my tears at bay by listening to Miriam chatter away about everything from Owen's attempts to roll over to how hot the weather had been. When I reached the end of my row, I started down the fourth, between two rows of tomatoes, swatting at a mosquito as I pivoted.

A car turned into the parking lot of Plain Patterns. An old Ford.

"Is that Karin?" I asked Derek.

He turned and nodded as Karin jogged from the parking lot across the lawn. Her hair was now twisted on top of her head in a bun.

"Derek!" she called out. "I tried calling, but you didn't answer your phone."

He pulled it out of his pocket and glanced at it. "Sorry," he said. "What's up?"

"It's Mateo. He's been taken to the jail in Elkhart by an officer from the sheriff's department."

"What?"

"He was stopped late this afternoon on a county road with Sebastian in the car."

Derek started toward the gate. "Where's Sebastian?"

"He's back at the house. Papa went and got him."

Derek stepped through the gate, leaving it open behind him. "Why did they take Mateo?"

"The officer claimed he didn't signal for a turn, although Mateo said he did. Then the officer asked to search Mateo's car, and foolishly he said yes. The officer found a substance on the floor of the back seat, underneath Sebastian's booster seat. He did an on-site test and said it was meth."

"No." Derek shook his head.

"Exactly," she said. "We all know that's ludicrous. Sebastian was eating a cupcake, and I'm guessing it was frosting. There have been several incidences when a field drug test was wrong. A lab test will prove it wasn't meth, but that could take a while."

"Can you get him out on bail? Do you need money?"

"I hope so, and no. I've been saving for a new car. I'll use that."

"What can I do?" Derek asked. "Go with you to Elkhart?"

She shook her head. "With all that ICE talk earlier, Papa is now worried that the police might come after him and Mama. Could you go to the house and talk with them?"

"Of course," Derek said. "I'll take Sophie home first and then go straight there." He turned toward Miriam. "We'll come again tomorrow evening, as long as everything is all right with Karin's family. Would you tell Jane?"

Miriam nodded. "I'll keep weeding for a while longer."

Derek pulled out his phone again. "Good, because we made it . . . forty-six minutes and seventeen seconds." He grinned at her. "Sophie and I will try to make it the full hour next time."

We followed Karin until she turned onto the highway to go north toward Elkhart. As we drove adjacent to Mill Creek Farms, I spotted the Lopezes' cabin. A light was on in the front, but that was all I could see.

As soon as Derek pulled up in front of my house, I jumped out of the truck. "Let me know how everything goes tonight."

"I will." He nodded solemnly, lifted a hand to my parents, who were still sitting on the porch, and backed out of the driveway.

"What's going on?" Mamm asked as I walked up.

I sat down on the top step and swung around to face them as I explained what had happened to Karin's brother.

Mamm clucked her tongue.

Dat said, "That is too bad."

"Could our church—" I paused. It wasn't *our* church. I wasn't a part of it. "Could the church do anything to help them?"

Dat hesitated a moment and then said, "I can't think of anything we could do."

"And it is not our business," Mamm added.

"Isn't it everyone's business?" I countered. "Our ancestors were persecuted and came here as refugees."

"It is not the same," Mamm said. "We came for religious freedom."

I swatted at a mosquito. "Mr. and Mrs. Lopez and Mateo fled violence. They could have all been killed."

"You cannot know that for sure," Mamm said.

"Why would Derek lie about that?"

Mamm shrugged. She slapped at a mosquito too and then stood and headed for the door. "I am going to bed."

Dat and I sat in silence until he said, "I am sorry for Karin's family. I will pray for them."

"Denki," I muttered, disappointed in my parents' lack of empathy.

CHAPTER 6

◆

I moved from the top step to Mamm's rocking chair and stayed there, swatting at mosquitos as the sun set. My thoughts bounced from Karin and her family to how much better I was feeling. Maybe it was Mamm's cooking. Or the fact I was sleeping sixteen hours a day. Perhaps I could go back to Elkhart earlier than I'd planned.

Then I thought about Jane's garden and the canning circle idea. She had an abundance of cucumbers to pickle and tomatoes to can. And green beans too. Maybe I could get the canning circle organized for her before I left.

Finally, I stood to go in the house, but then headlights appeared coming down the lane. I squinted. It was a truck. Hopefully Derek's. I couldn't imagine who else might be coming.

Lyle. My heart seized.

No, he wouldn't dare.

I sighed with relief as I recognized Derek's hat.

I headed down the steps as he jumped out of the pickup. "Want to go for a ride?" he asked. "I can fill you in on what's going on."

I shook my head, imagining the gossip that would go around if anyone saw us. "How about if we sit on the porch?"

"All right."

We sat side by side on the top stair instead of in the rocking chairs. He kept his voice low as he told me that when Karin got to Elkhart, Mateo wasn't there. "Someone alerted ICE and they took him to a detention center in Michigan, an hour and a half away."

"Wow, that happened fast. What about his deferred status?"

"Jah, he showed them his papers and everything, but because he's been arrested for a crime, they took him."

"Can they deport him before it goes to trial?"

"Karin is trying to find out. They claimed he's a gang member."

"Around here?" I asked, bewildered.

"No, in Chicago, where he went to college. On those grounds, they can deport him right away."

"That's horrible."

Derek nodded in agreement.

"Has Karin found a lawyer yet?"

"She left a voicemail for her boss but hasn't heard back from him. She's guessing she won't until morning."

Again, Mr. Jasper flashed through my mind. I'd Google him in the morning and see what I could find as far as contact information. And I'd ask my roommate Ivy about accessing the officer's dash cam video, since she worked at the Elkhart County Sheriff's Office.

"What's Karin's cell number?" I asked.

Derek took his phone from the holder on his belt and tapped his phone icon and then his contacts. Then he rattled off her number.

"Do you have a pen?"

He pulled one from his breast pocket and handed it to me.

I lifted my skirt and wrote the number above my knee.

He laughed. "Just like old times."

I laughed too. "Jah. Mamm will never see it." I turned toward Derek. "I really appreciate you stopping by. And if there's anything I can do, I'd like to."

"I'll let you know what's going on tomorrow," he answered. "If all is well, I'll stop by a little after six to go to Jane's again. I'll text you."

"Okay. If you don't show up, I'll check my phone."

We said good-night and then I watched the taillights of his pickup until he reached the highway.

As I tiptoed up the stairs, just as I used to do as a teenager trying not to wake up Mamm and Dat, I thought about how apprehensive I was when I moved in with my roommates. I was shocked when my co-worker Bri, who heard I was looking for a place to live, offered to rent me a room in the house she shared with three other girls—and at a price I could actually afford. Once I moved in, I kept to myself, convinced that none of them cared about me.

But they did. It wasn't as if they consciously made a decision to. Or that they felt sorry for me. They simply treated me with kindness and respect. They never judged me, except in fun when it came to the odd things I said or Englisch things I didn't know, but I took it all in stride and it felt good to laugh with them. When glimpses of my personal struggles emerged, they made it clear that they were there for me, but they didn't ask intrusive questions. I didn't get the sense that anyone I shared a home with was gossiping about me or reveling in my failures.

For the first time in my life, I began to feel emotionally safe, something I realized I hadn't felt at home. I went from thinking that all the mistakes I made were my fault—and that I'd never

be good enough—to feeling a hint of God's grace and love. I
began to talk with Him the way I had as a child. Most of the
time, I felt at peace with God—except when I thought of Lyle.

When I reached my room, I knelt beside my bed and said
a prayer for Mateo and for Karin and the rest of their family.

Then I said a prayer for Mamm and Dat and for my health.

Next, I thought of Derek and said a prayer for him. Then,
my mind fell on Lyle. Jesus taught us to pray for our enemies.
I stood, not able to force myself to do that. Not yet.

THE NEXT MORNING, I descended the stairs and snuck out the
front door, heading straight to the shed. Mamm wasn't in her
garden, and I hoped Dat wasn't in the barn. I slipped into the
shed, leaving the door open for some light. Once I retrieved my
phone and turned it on, I Googled *Jasper, immigration lawyer,
Elkhart, Indiana.* A Jasper Benjamin, Attorney at Law, popped
up. I chuckled at the memory of Nadine yelling, "Mr. Jasper!"
I clicked on the link. It was his business page.

I hit the share button and the text icon. Then I lifted my dress
just over my knees and keyed in Karin's phone number that
I'd written on my skin. *I don't know this lawyer, but I've met
him and he represented the son of my friend Nadine, an Iraqi
refugee,* I typed. *If he can't help, perhaps he can recommend
someone.* I hit Send and then started to text Ivy. I doubted she
had any advice for me, especially since Mateo was in a detention
center already, but I thought I'd touch base with her just in case.

I typed a brief introduction to the story and then, *Do you
have any ideas as far as what Mateo's family can do? He swears
he signaled. How can they access the dash cam video from the
police car?* After I sent the text, just as I was ready to shut off

my phone, it pinged. Karin had returned my text already. *Thank you so much! I'll let you know what he says.*

I hoped the information would be helpful. My phone pinged again. It was from Ivy. *I don't have any ideas for you—except you shouldn't get involved. Let the court system figure it out.*

Yikes. Had I offended her?

Sorry, I texted back. *Just thought I'd ask.*

Seriously, she texted back, *stay out of it, Sophie.*

I felt horrible. Obviously, there was nothing I could do to help get the dash cam footage. I shouldn't have expected Ivy to have any ideas. Perhaps her job would be in jeopardy if she communicated with me about the case.

I powered off my phone and stashed it back in the glove box, then slipped out of the shed.

I scanned the garden. Mamm stood at the edge of it, a hoe in her hand. She was out extra early today. Probably because she wanted to avoid me. I retraced my steps back to the front door and then to the kitchen. Dat sat at the table, drinking a cup of coffee.

"*Guder Mariye*," I said as I filled a glass with water.

"Guder Mariye," Dat responded. "It is a beautiful day, and I think, perhaps, a bit cooler."

"Mamm's out earlier than usual."

"Try not to be too hard on your mother," Dat said. "These last three years have been hard on her. Having you leave has been the hardest thing she's ever gone through."

Baffled, I asked, "The hardest?"

"Jah." Dat took a sip of his coffee.

"Harder than when Joe-Joe was killed?"

He nodded.

I felt as if I might vomit. "Excuse me." I shuffled toward the living room. I aimed for the staircase and kept going. I had three brothers living nearby, but I'd had four total. Joe-Joe was by far my favorite sibling. When I was five and he was eleven, he was helping Dat in the field behind the barn and was thrown from the manure spreader when a new horse spooked. It spooked again as Dat yelled, and the horse took off running, dragging the spreader over the top of Joe-Joe. I was playing along the edge of the pasture and saw the whole thing. Dat yelled at me to go tell Mamm to call 9-1-1. I froze. Dat yelled at me again.

Finally, I ran to get Mamm. Instead of going straight to the phone shanty, she ran to the field.

Dat yelled at her to go call 9-1-1 immediately as he performed CPR on Joe-Joe. I stood, paralyzed, as Mamm finally ran to the phone shanty. I'm pretty sure Joe-Joe was already dead by the time the paramedics arrived, but no one ever talked about exactly what happened. Nevertheless, in that short time, he suffered horribly. For a long time, I blamed myself for hesitating before I ran for Mamm and for not being able to communicate clearly with her what Dat had said.

I reached my room and crawled back into bed. Mamm thought my leaving the Amish, even though I'd never joined the church, was worse than Joe-Joe being run over by the spreader and dying such a violent and painful death? Worse than the loss of him?

He'd brought such joy to our family with his joking, laughing, and peacemaking. He always included me in games and fun even though I was much younger. He left a long and lasting hole in our home—and in me too.

I doubted my leaving had left any mark at all. If Mamm's pride weren't so badly injured by my leaving, I was sure she would realize how much happier she was not having me around. I'd been such a hassle for her, such an ongoing source of shame.

I tried to go back to sleep but couldn't. Maybe the extra rest was helping or the new medication was making a difference. Or both. But I didn't feel as if I needed to be in bed. However, I didn't want to hang out with Mamm either.

Perhaps I could take the buggy to Jane's and talk with her about my canning circle ideas. At least then I could feel as if I would be doing something constructive.

I ASKED DAT for permission to use the buggy, which he granted without asking Mamm. Hopefully she wouldn't be upset with either of us, but it was worth it to me to get away. I slipped into the shed and retrieved my phone from my car. I'd promised I wouldn't use it except in Mamm and Dat's shed, but I hadn't indicated I wouldn't use it other places.

The morning was cooler than it had been, but by no means cold. Or even cool. It was simply warm instead of hot. As I turned onto the highway, a fly buzzed through the open window but then back out as the horse picked up speed.

As I passed by Mill Creek Farms, I said another prayer for Karin and her family. I could see Derek's pickup parked along a field but couldn't spot him out among the people working.

When I reached Jane's and stopped the horse by the stable, I powered on my phone. I had a text from Karin, thanking me again for the information on Jasper Benjamin and saying she'd left him a voicemail.

I texted Derek a quick *How's it going?*

It was eight thirty, an hour and a half before Plain Patterns opened. I knocked on the front door and when no one answered, I ventured around to the garden, hoping I wouldn't need to disturb her at home. I didn't want to be that intrusive.

Thankfully, she was in the garden, weeding.

"Jane!" I called out. "Guder Mariye!"

She turned toward me and smiled. "Sophie. What are you doing here?"

"I had some ideas about your canning circle."

"Shouldn't you be resting?"

"I'm feeling good today." I opened the gate and stepped into the garden. "I'll even weed while we talk."

She stood up straight, stretched her back, and then said, "Have you heard any more about Karin's brother? Miriam told me what happened."

"You know Karin?"

Jane nodded. "She and her mother have come into the shop together."

Maybe Karin and her mother, and other women living at Mill Creek Farms, would be interested in the canning circle. Once we had a clear idea of what we were doing, I could let Karin know. On second thought, I doubted she or her mother would be interested now, not with Mateo detained.

"How are you doing?" Jane asked. I was aware she didn't ask me how I was feeling.

I met her eyes. Did she really want to know?

"I'm doing better," I answered. It was hard to explain my flare-ups and how one day I could be feeling horrible, and then feel better in a few days, and then feel worse again a day after that. "It could be the medicine or that I'm getting more rest."

"Wunderbar," Jane said. "Now, how *are* you doing?"

Tears welled in my eyes. "It's just hard being home, that's all," I finally answered.

Jane clucked her tongue. "I imagine it would be."

For a moment, I wondered what she knew. I was tempted to

ask her, but then decided to concentrate on the canning circle instead.

"Enough about me." I bent down to pull a clump of weeds. "Let's talk about the canning circle. We'll need to collect jars to use. I think we can probably borrow enough camp stoves to do the canning outside. Will that work with your kitchen license?"

"Jah," she answered. "It's the same idea as a barbecue place that cooks outside. I have all of the paperwork and the instructions."

"Great," I said. "We can set up tables and use the hose to fill the baths. I know Mamm has a few folding tables and two camp stoves, along with a canner and a pressure cooker. I'm guessing we can borrow equipment from my sisters too." As long as Mamm asked them and not me. "I'm thinking we should be able to can beets, chow chow, beans, carrots, peppers, and tomatoes. We can also pickle onions and cucumbers, along with making kraut."

"Goodness," Jane said. "You've really thought through all of this."

I nodded.

"When I originally had the idea, I put the word out for jars. That's a biggie," Jane said. "And more canners to borrow. I think working out here is a good idea, although we could set up a station inside in the kitchen too. When should we do it?"

"How about a week from Saturday?"

"Perfect. I'll make a sign for the shop and get a notice in the paper. Too bad I didn't include it in my last column."

As we talked through the details, Savannah came walking across the lawn. "Jane, I thought I might find you out here." When she saw me, she added, "Oh, hello, Sophie! How are you?"

"Good." I shaded my eyes.

"Jane, do you still need jars for a canning circle? I have two boxes from Mammi that have been rattling around in my trunk for a while."

"Doesn't she need them?" I asked.

Savannah shook her head. "She doesn't can much anymore, and she has a lot."

"How is Dorothy today?" Jane asked.

"Okay." Savannah yawned. "Sorry, I worked as a doula on a birth last night, so I decided to take today off from my regular job. Mammi has another appointment this afternoon in Elkhart."

Jane gave Savannah a sympathetic glance. "Let me know how it goes."

"I will." She nodded toward Plain Patterns. "Is the back door unlocked?"

"Jah," Jane said. "Just put the boxes inside. Or you can leave them by the front door and I'll carry them in."

"Thank you," Savannah said.

Jane shook her head. "No. Thank *you*."

As Savannah disappeared around the corner of the building, Jane said, "She's been working with her cousin, who is a midwife, as a doula. Savannah trained in midwifery when she was younger, but for now she's content to be supporting mothers during their labors and deliveries and taking care of them and their babies afterward." Jane turned and faced me. "It's been such a blessing to have her living in the area. Just as it's a blessing to have you here too."

When I didn't answer, she said, "Somehow I feel like you don't believe that's true."

"I'm fine, really," I said. "I just don't feel as if I belong here. I never have."

"You know," Jane said, "I've been researching a relative who lived on this farm over a hundred years ago and who felt the same way. I found notes I wrote down from when my great-grandfather told me about his aunt, which brought his story back to me, plus I've filled in the blanks through research at the library. She was born in 1852, and her name was Mary."

"Is this the story that has to do with the Chicago Fire?"

"Jah," Jane said. "It happened when she was nineteen. She was the youngest child of Emma and Judah Landis. Would you like me to tell you some about her while we weed?"

"Sure." Maybe a story about the past would distract me from the present. "I'm all ears."

CHAPTER 7

❖

Mary Landis

October 6, 1871

Mary Landis lifted the last of the wooden crates of produce into the bed of her Dat's *Vauwa* and then turned toward the morning sun. She'd been working since before dawn, getting everything ready for her Dat to drive to Elkhart and then put the cargo on the train to Chicago. He had an acquaintance who managed the Grand Hotel in the *Shtatt* of Chicago who needed the produce. Dat was taking a load of flour too. The wheat harvest wasn't as good as they'd hoped it would be, but Dat had done well enough to have extra flour to sell, between his own and the wheat others paid him with for milling theirs. Chicago was a long way to travel, but with the months-long drought throughout the region, he thought he could get a better price in the city from his friend.

Dat's farmhand, Lemuel, was going with Dat. Each would drive a freight wagon to Elkhart and then travel along with the goods to Chicago and deliver them in person to the hotel. Dat didn't want to take any risks when it came to any of it being "lost" along the way. Mary had heard him say several times, "We need the income to get through the winter."

Chicago. Mary sighed as she leaned against the crate-laden wagon. She would love to go. She went to Elkhart once with Dat a few years ago and saw the train station for the first time. She could only imagine riding the train on to Chicago, to the big Shtatt that she'd heard about her whole life. Dat had gone to Chicago to buy their farm when she was a little girl. He'd told stories about the river running through the middle of the city and building after building all made from wood. There were hotels and restaurants and shops and banks. Acres of livestock and slaughterhouses. People from all over the country and even the world had moved there to start new lives.

However, as a nineteen-year-old Amish woman, her chances of seeing that for herself were zero. Everyone else in her family was content with their life in Elkhart County, but she'd never felt as if she fit in with the girls she'd grown up with. They all longed to marry and have children, while Mary longed for adventures. She longed to board a train and see what she could of the world.

When she asked if she could go with Dat this time, he said he'd already asked Lemuel. She doubted if he'd let her go even if that wasn't the case. In her head, she knew an Amish girl didn't belong in Chicago. So why did Mary's heart long to go?

Mary had become Dat's righthand "man" since her brother Steffen had broken his back when he fell from the hayloft a month ago in an accident. She much preferred farming to cooking and cleaning. In fact, Mary had always been a tomboy. Instead of just tending to the *Goahda*, she had been harvesting wheat, bucking bales, dragging the *Feld*, picking produce, and now plowing. She felt like she could never get the hay dust out of her lungs, even though she tied a scarf around her face, or the soil out from under her fingernails. It didn't matter. She loved every minute of farming.

Mary's eldest sister, Mathilde, had married a decade ago and lived in Ohio with her family. Her next oldest sister, Olive, lived a few miles away, toward Goshen. But, thankfully her other sister, Sarah, still lived at home. Though it was a silly and selfish thought, Mary secretly hoped Sarah wouldn't marry. If she did, Mary would be expected to take over her duties, along with helping their Mamm, who worked as a midwife and caregiver to the sick and infirm.

"Mary," Dat said, "Lemuel and I are ready to go. We need the food Sarah put together for us."

She glanced toward Lemuel, who was adjusting the harness on his team of horses. He'd only recently moved to Elkhart County from Ohio. Dat had hired him frequently since Steffen's accident. Lemuel seemed quiet and, honestly, a little dull. Mary guessed he was a year or two older than she was.

Mary hurried to the house to grab the *Koahb*, which was now filled with chicken, biscuits, and apples for their dinner and supper, and cheese and bread for their breakfast the next morning, along with jars of water.

When Mary returned, Dat had just finished hitching the horses to the second wagon. Lemuel sat on the bench of the first.

She handed Dat the basket, and he put it under the wagon bench. "I was hoping your Mamm would be back before we left. Tell her good-bye for me." He paused, looking over the fields. "Any questions about taking care of things around here while I'm gone?"

Mary shook her head. "Michael, Vyt, and I can handle it." Steffen and his wife, Hanna, were also living in the big farmhouse with them. They had two boys, Michael and Vyt, who were ten and six. Both were hard workers. Vyt was especially impressive, considering how young he was.

Dat tipped his hat and turned the team away from her, toward the road. Mamm had trimmed his gray hair and even his beard, which she didn't do very often, the night before. Dat was getting older, that was for sure. He'd been the bedrock of the Landis family for so many years, with his good sense and stamina. But at fifty-four, his age was starting to catch up with him.

It didn't seem to be true of Mamm though. At fifty-two, she still traveled throughout Union Township and even over to Jackson Township to deliver babies and doctor the sick. She set bones, cared for those with diseases, and prepared the dead for burial. Her work was unpredictable, but she always rose to the challenge.

She'd lost a little boy, a baby girl, and a husband before she'd ever married Dat, and she had lost two babies since then too. Most of the time Mamm carried on, but every once in a while, it seemed she struggled with some unseen force. After a few weeks though, with Dat's gentle and patient encouragement, she would pull through and carry on with her life and work.

When the wagons were almost out of sight, Mary headed to the shed. Dat had taken the eight workhorses to pull the two freight wagons, but Mary could use the oxen to finish the plowing.

She worked until it was time to go in for dinner. Dat had moved the kitchen back into the house from the summer shed, but the warm day had left her sister Sarah with a red face and sweaty brow, although not as bad as Mary. Her entire body dripped with sweat.

She went around the front of the house and through the door. Years ago, the house had been divided in two—with two front doors, two parlors, and two staircases leading to two upstairs wings. The original owner had shared it with her daughter and son-in-law. But when Mamm and Dat bought the house, they opened up both the downstairs and the upstairs, closed off one of the two doors, and demolished one of the staircases.

Mary cleaned up in the basin in her room and then went downstairs for dinner. Sarah had chicken, baked squash, and greens ready. Steffen hobbled to the table and sat for a short time, but Mary could tell that he continued to be in a lot of pain. Mamm was certain he would heal and not be crippled forever, but she'd said he would most likely walk with a limp for the rest of his life.

After they'd all eaten, Mary helped Sarah clean the dishes. The two sisters were seven years apart but very close.

"Do you need help with the milking?" Sarah asked.

"Jah," Mary said. "Perhaps Hanna can fix supper."

"Hopefully so," Sarah answered.

"I finished the far Feld, so I'm going to start plowing the close-in one," Mary said.

"Ach, but it's so hot."

"It's not bad." Mary was used to the heat. She'd always been hardy and resilient when it came to physical work, whereas Sarah was thinner and tended to get sick more easily.

But before Mary had left the barn with the oxen, Sarah came running toward her. "There's been an accident," she called out. "Dat's been injured. Titus is here to take you to the Weavers' place. Mamm is there and sent for you."

MARY WASHED UP QUICKLY, rewound her bun at the nape of her neck, and put on a clean dress, apron, and Kapp. Then she grabbed her cloak just in case it was late by the time they came back. Titus, who was thirteen or fourteen, didn't talk much on the trip back to his parents' farm.

Once they were on their way, Mary asked, "What happened to my Dat?"

Titus shrugged. "He's hurt."

"Badly?"

"Somewhat."

Mary guessed Dat wasn't dying but couldn't be sure from the boy's terse answers. When they arrived, Lemuel was out front with the horses, who were still hitched to the wagons. Mary thanked Titus and scrambled down from the buggy while the boy continued on to the barn.

"What happened?" she asked.

"A half mile back from here, three mangy dogs ran between your Dat's horses and spooked them," Lemuel explained, his expression full of concern. "He got them calmed down, but the dogs spooked the horses again and Judah was thrown off the wagon when the horses bolted. He landed on his arm when he fell and also ended up with a gash on his forehead."

Mary winced. "His bad arm?" Dat had been shot when he was a young man by another Union Township farmer, something Dat didn't talk about very often.

Lemuel nodded. "Your Mamm did the stiches first. I held him down for that, but then he sent me outside. Now your Mamm is setting his arm. I heard him holler a couple of times, so I'm guessing she's about done."

Mary was sorry she hadn't arrived in time to help. "Are you going ahead without Dat, then? Just taking the flour?" That load had the most value. Maybe Mamm had sent for her so she could drive the second wagon home.

Lemuel shook his head. "He says he's going."

"Can he?"

Lemuel shrugged and then smiled a little. "I'm guessing if anyone can, it would be your Dat."

He could be stubborn at times, but Mary doubted traveling to Chicago with a broken arm was a good idea. He had to be in horrible pain.

"I'll go see what Mamm says." Mary headed up the front steps of the Weaver home. The door was open, and she stepped inside. Dat, his face as pale as she'd ever seen it, sat at the table. His hair was pushed back from his forehead, showing the stitches Mamm had just put in, plus bruising. He held his right arm closely to his chest.

"Sorry I didn't get here in time to help," Mary said.

Mamm tore a piece of fabric in half. "I didn't expect you to." She held the two pieces of fabric up and then dropped one on the table. "The muscles stretched, and I was able to set it." She took the other piece of fabric and threaded it around Dat's back and then under his arm. Then she tied it up by his shoulder.

"What did you need me for, then?" Mary asked.

Mamm answered, "To go to Chicago."

Dat groaned.

Mary tried to hide her excitement as she asked Mamm, "Really?"

"Jah," Mamm said. "You can drive the team into Elkhart and then help in Chicago. Your Dat is going to be in too much pain to drive the team, and he won't be able to do any lifting."

"Emma," Dat said, "Lemuel and I'll be sleeping in stables. Mary can't go with us."

"You're not sleeping in germ-infested stables, not with that gash on your head." Mamm had been studying germ theory lately. "You'll have to stay in a hotel. Make sure to choose one cleaner than a stable."

"Should you go at all, Dat?" Mary asked.

"Well, I'm not going to send you alone with Lemuel. And the two of you wouldn't get a fair price out of Russ Keller, anyway."

She wondered what kind of man Dat was doing business with.

Mamm checked his stitches and then turned to Mary. "I'll send along a bottle of carbolic acid. Apply it two times a day." She picked up her small traveling bag off the floor and showed the bottle to Mary. She pulled out another bottle. "This is a tincture of feverfew. Mix it in water and give it to your Dat four times each day." She lifted the second piece of fabric from the table and stuffed it in the bag too. "Here's an extra sling."

Mary must not have been containing her excitement because her father teased, "Don't look so happy. Your old Dat could have been killed."

Mary couldn't help but smile. "I'm so glad you weren't."

"Jah." Dat grimaced. "Because if I had been, you'd be taking my body home instead of going to Chicago, which is where I know you want to go."

Mary didn't answer, fearing her excitement would be too obvious. Still, there was no use denying this was a dream come true.

BY THE TIME they left the Weavers' farm, it was midafternoon. It took nearly three hours for the trio to reach Elkhart. The town had a population of around three thousand residents, and the crowded streets were much different from the country roads Mary was used to. She used both hands to hold the reins. The horses weren't used to so many other wagons, buggies, animals, and people either.

Dat looked like he'd been in a fight, with his bruised and

stitched face and his arm in a sling. He'd pulled his straw hat down as much as he could to hide the wound, but the side of his face was swollen and had turned a blotchy purple.

When they stopped across the street from the train station, Dat gingerly and a little awkwardly climbed down from the wagon while Mary stayed on the bench, the reins in her hands. She turned around and gave Lemuel a wave. He simply nodded.

Dat headed inside the station, limping as he walked. He had to be sore all over after being thrown.

A saloon about a block in the other direction from the train station caught Mary's attention. Men were frequently coming in and going out. Before she could stop herself, Mary wondered what it was like inside, and then her face grew even warmer than it already was from the long, dusty trip. She shouldn't have those sorts of thoughts.

It wasn't as if she wanted to live that life, but at the same time she often felt she didn't belong in her Amish community. She was different, that was for sure, and that made her curious about other people's lives. That was all. But it seemed no one else shared her curiosity.

The brakes of the locomotive coming from the east shrieked as it came to a stop at the station. Maybe it had come from New York City. Mary's favorite subject as a scholar had been geography, and she loved to dream about all the different places and people. Behind the passenger cars were boxcars, and men had started unloading one of them. Maybe the other cargo was going farther west, perhaps also to Chicago.

Hopefully there was still time to get their cargo on this train. Dat had made arrangements for the produce and flour to be loaded an hour ago. If they were too late, they'd have to spend the night in Elkhart and go in the morning.

Behind the station and the westbound train, the rest of the

train yard bustled with activity. Men loaded and unloaded freight trains. Locomotives switched from one track to another. Men scurried around, looking under passenger cars and boxcars.

Mary turned her attention toward the people around her. A couple around her age strode by arm in arm. The woman wore a bustle, an overskirt, and a fitted jacket. Her hair was piled high on her head, with a little golden hat perched on top. The man wore a suit and a top hat and carried a cane. She smiled at that. He couldn't be more than twenty-five, and he didn't walk with any sort of a limp. But he did look quite debonair.

The woman and man turned the corner. Did everyone in Chicago dress that way? Would everyone stare at her in her simple clothes? She looked down at her own dress and apron, which were coated in dust.

She didn't care. She was going to Chicago. She would be there soon. She wouldn't care for one minute what other people thought of her.

Dat came out of the station, accompanied by a man sporting a fancy mustache. He pointed to a freight car on the westbound train that was stopped along a loading dock. Dat said something to the man and then motioned to Lemuel and Mary. "We have a small enough load that they can fit it on this train. We have a half hour until it leaves, so we'll need to unload the cargo and get the horses to the livery in that time."

Mary turned her team around and Lemuel followed as they pulled up along the loading dock. Men appeared and started quickly unloading the cargo. Lemuel jumped down to help, but when Mary started to, Dat shook his head.

The men finished unloading their wagons just as dusk fell. The man with the mustache returned with a piece of paper for Dat to sign. After he did, Dat struggled back up onto the wagon bench and they headed to the livery stable. Dat winced again as he climbed down, but he was able to move a little more quickly than the first time. Mary guessed he was just gritting his teeth harder.

Again, Lemuel and Mary stayed in the wagon while Dat made the arrangements. Two boys came and took over the wagons. Mary brushed as much dust from her clothes as she could and then grabbed the food basket, her cloak, and Mamm's bag. As they walked toward the train station on the boardwalk, Mary stomped her feet, trying to knock the dust from her boots, but to no avail.

When they reached the station, Dat bought three tickets at the counter. The whistle blew, and they had to run to catch the train. They boarded just as the wheels started to roll.

Dat took off his hat once they reached their seats. His wound was red and swollen around the stitches and his bruise was turning yellow now, mingling with the purple. He looked exhausted, and he put his head back against the seat and closed his eyes. It would take three or so hours to get to Chicago.

Lemuel kept his eyes on the station yard while Mary turned toward the street. The train lurched, which made her smile in anticipation. The whistle blew and then the train chugged down the tracks. As it picked up speed, it swayed a little from side to side. The scent of coal smoke filled the train car and turned her stomach. She took shallow breaths until she adjusted. Once she did, her enthusiasm returned. They left Elkhart behind and entered an eerie darkness. Every once in a while, Mary could catch a glimpse of a lamp in a farm window, but that was all. Lemuel looked over at her, and she grinned. "Isn't this fabulous?"

He nodded. "First time on a train?"

"Jah."

He grinned back, and excitement filled his voice as he said, "Mine too."

Maybe he wasn't as dull as she'd thought.

CHAPTER 8

❖

Dat awoke when Mary opened the basket of food. There were a few pieces of chicken left, five biscuits, and several apples, besides the cheese and bread for the morning. Dat led the three of them in a silent prayer, and as they ate, Mary asked him about his friend in Chicago.

"Well, I wouldn't call him a friend, exactly," Dat said. "More of an acquaintance. I met him two different times. First in the early forties. I'd just moved to Indiana and went out to Chicago to see what it was like. At the time, it had just been incorporated and was nowhere near the size it is now. Russ peddled food on the street, and we struck up a conversation. He was a big man and had the reddest hair I'd ever seen. He was loud and friendly and the sort of person you didn't forget."

The second time he went to Chicago, Dat explained, was about fifteen years ago, to buy their farm from Harriet Burton. Her mother, Lenora, who'd owned the farm and hired Dat to run it, had left the option for him to buy it in her will. "To my surprise, Lenora had invested in a hotel Russ operated. It took me a half second to place him when I saw him. He was at the house too, to settle things with Harriet. We got to talking, and when he found out I was farming in Indiana, he said he was looking for suppliers. We kept in touch throughout the years, and from time to time I've shipped him loads of flour. I got a letter from him last month saying he needed more flour, and this time produce too. He said the drought had dried up one of his supply chains."

Mary had always marveled over Dat's life as a young man. He had traveled more than most in their community. "How did Russ go from peddling food to operating a hotel?"

"He headed out West during the Gold Rush and made money—not a fortune but a significant amount—by feeding people out in California," Dat explained. "He came back to Chicago with what he'd made and rounded up a group of investors to finance a hotel." Dat paused and took a bite of his biscuit. "In his last letter, he said he'll pay top dollar. I'm hoping to figure out what he needs and then come up with a regular shipping plan. I'm hoping he'll buy more flour and produce from farmers in our area. Once we can work out the details, then I can just haul loads to Elkhart and put them on the train."

That sounded like a good idea to Mary. Once they finished eating, they cleaned their hands on the rags Sarah had packed, and Mary closed up the basket. Gradually, more and more lights appeared in the darkness to the left, but the right was solid black.

Dat pointed that way. "Lake Michigan is over there."

Soon, on the left side, buildings with tall smokestacks appeared—factories, she guessed. There were shacks and other buildings along the tracks too, all made from wood. Some appeared to be homes, while others looked like businesses.

And then came a horrible stench.

Concentrating on not gagging, she asked, "What is that smell?"

"The Yards," Dat said. "Chicago slaughters more animals, including hogs, than anywhere else in the country."

Mary held her cloak to her nose. "Does the entire city smell this way?"

Dat smiled. "No, just around the railroad, here in the southern part of the city. The livestock is shipped in and then slaughtered nearby."

The shriek of the brakes signaled they were approaching the station. As the train slowed, people began to stand. But Dat waited. When the train had come to a complete stop, he stood, and Mary and Lemuel followed.

Once they reached the platform, Dat found an agent who told him what warehouse the cargo would be stored in overnight. "You can rent wagons in the morning to deliver it," the man said. He wrote up a receipt for Dat that included all the needed information.

"Can you recommend a hotel nearby?" Dat asked.

"There's the Station Hotel several blocks west of here."

"Thank you," Dat said. Mary knew he had to be exhausted, but he didn't complain. As they walked under the gaslights suspended on poles above the sidewalks, Mary smelled the Yards, gas, and sewage, all mixed together. But then she caught a hint of smoke.

"Is there a *Feiyaha*?" she asked.

"I read there have been more than usual here," Lemuel said. That sounded ominous. "But they have a good fire department, the best in the country. They'll put it out quickly."

Dat changed the subject. "We'll rent freight wagons first thing in the morning, deliver our cargo, make arrangements for further shipments, and then get back on the train by tomorrow evening. The sooner we're home, the better."

When they reached the hotel lobby, Dat approached the man

at the counter. There were several straight-back chairs in the room and a settee, but the furniture was simple. The walls were covered in paneling with no decoration.

Dat asked for two rooms.

"I only have one," the man said.

"Any room in the stables?" Dat asked.

The man nodded.

"I'll take the room for my daughter. My farmhand and I will sleep in the stables."

"No, Dat," Mary said.

Dat held up a hand, a signal to be quiet. She grasped Mamm's bag tighter. He couldn't sleep in the stable, not with his wound. She needed to treat him soon with the carbolic acid and give him the tincture.

Once Dat had completed the transaction, he stepped back to where Mary and Lemuel were standing. "I'll be all right, Mary."

"Judah," Lemuel said, "you should stay with Mary."

"I don't want you out in the stable by yourself," Dat said. "If anything happened to you, what would I tell your folks?"

Lemuel shook his head. "I'll be fine."

Dat smiled and turned to Mary. "I'll walk you up to your room and you can treat my head and give me the medicine your Mamm sent. Lemuel, I'll be right back."

Fifteen minutes later, Dat insisted, as he readied to leave the room, that Mary lock the door and then pull the bureau in front of it.

"It's okay," she said.

He stood in the doorway. "Humor me."

She did as he said, even though she thought locking the door would be plenty. She'd always thought of herself as fearless—and she still did.

Now she was in Chicago. Her dream had come true.

THE NEXT MORNING, Mary rose before dawn and washed from the pitcher and basin in her room, eager for her adventure to continue. She twisted her hair into a bun, slipped on her Kapp, and secured it. Then she grabbed her bag and the food.

As she started down to the lobby, she saw Lemuel walking up the stairs toward her.

Alarmed, Mary blurted out, "Where's Dat?"

"Speaking with a man in the stables who owns freight wagons. He sent me to come fetch you."

A sense of relief filled her. She'd been so caught up in her excitement about being in Chicago that she'd almost forgotten how injured her Dat was—and how quickly something could go wrong.

She followed Lemuel out onto the sidewalk and into a cacophony of sounds—the hooves of horses pulling streetcars, wagons, and buggies; the rattle of wheels; and the ringing of bells. In the distance, train whistles blew. Plus, there was the pounding of hammers at a building site kitty-corner from the hotel.

People scurried up and down the sidewalks and dashed across the streets, seemingly risking their lives as they did. Something brushed against her from behind. Mary turned. A girl, probably around ten, held a toddler with a dirty face and glassy eyes. The girl held out a skinny arm, palm up. Mary's heart lurched. She dug in the basket for an apple and handed it to the girl. A boy appeared behind her. Mary had half of her biscuit left over from last night. She gave that to him.

Lemuel touched her arm. "We should go." He was probably afraid she'd give away their bread and cheese too.

As they walked away, Mary said, "Where are their parents?"

"I don't know. Perhaps they're orphans. There are probably a lot of others like them throughout the city."

Mary followed Lemuel around the side of the hotel and down

a block to a livery stable. Dat was talking with a young man outside. The man was muscular with a clean-shaven face. He wore trousers with a vest over his white shirt. His cap was plain and black. As they approached, Dat said, "I'll be done with the wagons by late afternoon. I can meet you back here."

The man frowned. "I'm worried about you finding your way when you're not familiar with the streets in the city."

"We'll manage," Dat said.

"With that broken arm? And can you even see with that injury near your eye?"

"My vision is not affected."

"I can drive one of the wagons," the man said. "And your farmhand can follow us."

Dat shook his head. "We'll manage." Dat saw Mary approach and introduced her to the man and then said, "This is Kit Matson."

"Hallo," Mary said.

Kit gave her a nod and then turned back to Dat. "Let me guess," he said, "your daughter's going to drive the other wagon."

Dat smiled kindly at the man. "I assure you we will take good care of your wagons and teams."

Kit shook his head. "No, no, no." He gave Mary an apologetic glance. "I mean no offense." He focused on Dat again. "No woman is going to drive one of my wagons through the streets of Chicago. I'll drive it myself, for just a small added fee."

"There's no reason for that," Dat said. "She does as well as any man."

"This is a city," Kit said. "Not a country town. If you'd rather, I'll just rent you the one wagon."

Dat tugged on his beard. "That won't do." After a long pause, Dat said, "I'll take you up on your offer."

"You won't be sorry," Kit said. "I know Chicago. Your time

here will be shorter with my help." He pointed toward the livery stable. "My wagons and horses are here. We can go straight to the warehouse and then on to the Grand Hotel."

KIT'S TWO WAGONS were old and rickety, and his horses seemed sluggish, as if they hadn't had enough to eat.

Dat must have thought so too because he said, "Do you need me to pay you a portion of what I owe you before we get started?"

Kit's face reddened.

"I'd like to do that," Dat said.

"All right." Without even pausing, Kit added, "I do need to feed the horses before we go."

Dat handed Kit several bills and then turned to Lemuel and Mary. "There's a saloon across the street. Let's see if they're serving breakfast."

Mary held up the Koahb. "We have bread and cheese, Dat."

"Let's save that for lunch."

Mary had never eaten in any kind of restaurant before—and especially not a saloon. She smiled. Another new experience.

Dat led the way through a crowd of men to a table in the back. A man wearing an apron wrapped around his waist approached with three mugs and a pot of coffee. "We have hotcakes and sausages," he said.

"Then that's what we'll have," Dat answered. "And the coffee."

Mary couldn't help but stare at the people around her. Some men were wearing suits and appeared to be businessmen. Others wore trousers and shirts with suspenders. Some had full beards while others sported handlebar mustaches. Mary imagined they were drivers or shopkeepers or that sort of thing. She guessed that none of them were farmers.

After they ate, and Dat paid for their meal, they headed back across the street. Kit had both of the wagons ready to go, and the horses looked refreshed. Dat told Mary to ride with Lemuel while he rode with Kit. Mary stashed the basket and her bag underneath the bench, and then Lemuel gave her a hand to climb up to the bench. "Watch the basket and bag," Lemuel said, "so no one takes them."

Mary nodded. She wouldn't have thought of that.

As they followed Kit and Dat over streets paved with blocks of wood, they headed northwest, toward the heart of the city. Mary's head turned from side to side, taking it all in. There were more streetcars and buggies and carriages and wagons. People rushed one way or another, going into shops, stopping at vendors, and hopping on the streetcars. Some women wore wide skirts and fancy hats. Others were dressed in ragged clothes. Mary couldn't help but notice more children begging.

The walkways in front of the buildings were made of slats of wood, which were crowded with people carrying shopping bags and parcels. More wagons and buggies flooded the streets. Hotels were on nearly every corner. At each one, Mary kept expecting Kit to stop his team, but they kept going.

"I've never seen anything like this," Lemuel said.

"Neither have I." In all the years she'd longed to see Chicago, Mary couldn't have even imagined such a place. It was like a different world. She thought of her Mamm and siblings back home. Of Sarah cleaning up after breakfast. Of the peacefulness of the farm. It was like night and day. The pace of the city energized Mary in a way the farm didn't.

They crossed the bridge over the Chicago River and continued west. After several more blocks, Kit stopped along the side street of a hotel. The sign read *Grand Hotel*, but it didn't appear to be very grand. Neither was the neighborhood. Dat climbed down from the wagon, and then walked back and took Mary's hand with his good one and helped her down.

She followed him to the front of the hotel. The lobby was fancier than the hotel they'd stayed in, but the sofa and chairs were worn. The man at the counter frowned as they approached.

"I have a delivery for Russ Keller," Dat said.

"All deliveries go to the dock, at the back of the hotel." The man's nose turned upward. "Check in at the kitchen."

Kindness filled Dat's voice. "Thank you."

As they walked past Kit and Lemuel, Dat said, "Take the wagons to the back of the hotel. I'll find Russ."

Mary continued to follow Dat. As they climbed the steps to the loading dock, a thin woman with her blond hair in a bun and a large white apron wrapped around her body stepped outside of a large door and gave a loaf of bread to a little boy, who was maybe five. When the woman saw Dat and Mary, her face reddened, and she waved the child away.

"Hallo," Dat called out to her. "I'm looking for Russ Keller."

"He's not here."

"Where can I find him?"

The woman shrugged. "The chef might know." She held the door open and motioned to Dat and Mary.

The kitchen was vast, with a large number of workers inside. Some were chopping meat or vegetables, and others were cooking on the tops of stoves. Others carried plates filled with food out toward the front of the kitchen.

The woman told them to stay where they were. Several minutes later, a man wearing a white hat approached them. "Looking for Russ?"

"Jah," Dat answered.

"He's out procuring meat. If you have a delivery, I can do the paperwork, but you'll have to come back for payment."

"When do you expect Russ to be back?" Dat asked.

"By early afternoon, I expect."

Dat nodded. "We'll come back then. When he returns, would you tell him Judah Landis needs to complete our deal by mid-afternoon?"

The chef frowned a little but said, "I'll tell him."

A big burly man wearing a suit stepped around the end of a long counter. He wore a cap and stood with his legs spread apart and his arms crossed. "Everything good?" he asked the chef.

"It's fine, Mort," the chef said. "I don't need you."

As Dat and Mary left the kitchen and headed down the loading dock stairs, she noticed the boy with the bread cowering beneath the steps.

Once they were on the wooden sidewalk, Mary said, "Are you concerned Russ Keller might not show up this afternoon?"

"I'm aware of that possibility, but I'm leaving it with the Lord," Dat answered. "There's nothing more I can do."

CHATPER 9

Sophie

As I drove the buggy back home, I thought of Mary riding the train to Chicago and then of my trip to the city with Bri and Ivy. I'd found the city fascinating too, although it was much different now than it had been in 1871. I didn't remember any smell from the feedlots or slaughterhouses. I guessed that Mary, her Dat, and Lemuel got off at a station in the southeast part of the city.

The Chicago Mary had seen was much different from what I'd seen, but I knew how the energy of the city must have felt to Mary, who'd never been out of Elkhart County before that. I'd felt the same way when I'd visited the city—alive and invigorated. Honestly, I'd felt the same way when I'd left home and moved to Elkhart.

The day stayed a little cooler, in the eighties instead of the nineties, and a breeze blew, which also added some relief. When I arrived home, Dat was sitting on the porch with an Amish man. I waved and headed for the barn. Most likely Dat was counseling the man, although I didn't recognize him. I unhitched the horse, brushed him down, and then fed him.

When I entered the kitchen, Mamm wasn't anywhere in

sight, but there was a turkey sandwich on the table and a glass of milk. I felt the glass. It was still cold. Had she just filled it when she heard the buggy?

I poked my head into the living room, expecting to see her at her quilt frame, but she wasn't there. I ate my sandwich, drank my milk, and then headed up to my room. I opened the window to let in the breeze, hoping maybe I could rest. I could hear Mamm in her and Dat's bedroom. It sounded as if she were moving furniture. Perhaps she was cleaning.

I took a small notebook out of my purse and jotted down the ideas that Jane and I had talked about. Then I pulled one of my books out of my duffel bag, one on canning. It had all sorts of information on preserving everything from jam to soup. For the canning circle, we would concentrate on vegetables.

Most importantly, I wanted to make sure I had the procedure right for each vegetable and that everything we canned would be safe to consume. Mamm—and probably Jane too—had a pressure cooker we could use for the beans and tomatoes. For the canning instruction I did at the co-op last year, I'd made cards for the times and special instructions for each item. It would be easy enough to replicate those for Jane's event.

Safety was our biggest concern. Then education. And community. I wrinkled my nose. How odd I planned to promote community in a place I'd never felt accepted.

I dozed off and didn't wake up until five, according to the windup clock beside my bed. I rolled out of bed and headed downstairs, determined to help Mamm with supper. She wasn't in the living room nor in the kitchen. I stepped to the back window. She was working in the garden.

I ventured outside and stopped at the edge of the lawn. "Could I get something started for supper?" I asked.

She shook her head. "Your Dat has a meeting at the Lehmans'. They're all going to eat there. I don't plan on cooking."

"Oh," I said. "Would you like me to make you a sandwich?"

She shook her head again. "I'll make one when I'm ready to eat. Or I may just eat an apple and some cheese."

"Okay." I took a step backward. "Derek is going to pick me up at 6:15."

She raised her head and met my eyes. "Do you plan to join the church? Because from everything Phyllis says, he does."

"Mamm, I'm not courting him. I'm just going to work in Jane's garden for an hour."

"You don't have a good reputation, Sophie. You shouldn't tarnish his."

Her words stung, and I turned around and headed toward the house. My hand brushed against my apron, and I realized I still had my phone in my pocket. I wouldn't bother to return it now.

I went into the kitchen and scrambled some eggs instead of making a sandwich. Then I sliced a tomato and cucumber, which were on the counter, and sprinkled salt on them. I took everything out to the front porch, as far away from Mamm as possible, and sat down in her rocking chair.

Ivy was best friends with her mother. They texted every day and talked on the phone often. They had brunch together on Saturdays and went shopping on Sunday afternoons. They shared boots and sweaters and books and Netflix and Hulu accounts. Never in a million years would Mamm and I have such a relationship.

But I knew of Amish girls who had close relationships with their mothers too. Instead of sharing boots, they shared recipes. And instead of going out to brunch, they cooked together. They enjoyed each other and were close.

Mamm didn't have that sort of relationship with my two older sisters either, though. Neither had stopped by since I'd been home, except for the cookout, even though they only lived a few miles away. Sadly, neither had ever been close with me, although they were close with each other.

I ate my eggs and then the tomatoes and cucumbers. A yellow barn cat jumped up onto the porch and scampered in front of me. I put out my hand and whispered, "Here, kitty, kitty."

He stopped, licked my hand, and then dashed away.

I had a lot of good memories growing up here. Playing with Joe-Joe. Planting the garden every spring. Selling flowers, produce, and jam in the little shed where our lane met the highway.

Going to school and playing games.

Dating Lyle.

But there was so much heartache woven through those good memories. Joe-Joe dying. My sisters and brothers leaving.

Dating Lyle.

Feeling like I didn't belong. Fleeing in the middle of the night.

I snuck a look at my phone. 5:50. Twenty-five minutes and Derek would pick me up. I hoped I could survive that long.

AT 6:05 I got a text from Derek. *Change of plans. Karin just called. I need to go to the village instead of Jane's. Want to go with me?*

Yes, please, I texted back. When he arrived twenty minutes later, I didn't tell Mamm good-bye. I simply slipped out the front door and jumped in Derek's pickup. He was just ending a call on his phone.

After he said hello to me, I asked, "What's up?"

"There's a broken pipe in the village. I tried to get ahold of Lyle, but he didn't pick up."

"Did you let Jane know?"

He nodded. "I stopped by her place before coming to get you. I'd already gone home."

Coming to get me was out of his way, but I was thankful he had.

A few minutes later, he turned into Mill Creek Farms and headed down the road toward the village. A group of men had gathered in the Lopezes' front yard, but all eyes were on the cabin next to theirs.

Older children played in the street, kicking a soccer ball back and forth, and a group of little kids played with toy trucks in the dirt across the street.

Derek parked his pickup, jumped down, and then opened the door for me. As I climbed down, someone called out my name.

I turned toward the Lopez home, where Karin stood on the porch. "Hi!"

I waved.

"Why don't you hang out over here with me while Derek saves the day?" she called.

Derek shook his head and laughed. "Go ahead," he said to me. "This might take a while."

"All right," I answered. As I approached Karin, I asked, "Any updates on your brother?"

"I drove up to the detention center today, but they wouldn't let me see him. But on my way home, Jasper Benjamin called. He'd been in court all morning. I'm going to talk with him tomorrow."

"Great," I said. "Are you taking time off work?"

"I took today off, and I'll take at least a half day tomorrow." She leaned against the porch rail. "My parents are on edge. Every time a car comes down the road this far, Mama thinks it's ICE."

I exhaled. "I'm sorry."

She nodded. "We all are." She gestured toward the open door. "Come on in and meet my mother."

The smell of tortillas frying filled the house.

"Mama," Karin said, "Sophie is here."

A woman who appeared to be in her forties or early fifties turned toward me. She had a long black braid trailing down her back. "Hello," she said. "Welcome. My name is Rosibel."

"Pleased to meet you."

Sebastian was in the living room, watching TV. I said hello to him and he gave me a little wave, but his expression remained somber.

Quietly, Karin said, "He's afraid to leave the house."

I thought of the way I felt after Joe-Joe had been killed. I wanted to spend all my time in the garden, as far away from the farm machinery as possible. Sebastian had witnessed Mateo taken away. Of course, he was afraid the same might happen to him—or to his parents.

"Come dish up," Rosibel said. "We have tortillas, rice, beans, and pork."

Sebastian scampered into the kitchen and grabbed a plate.

"No, no, no," Rosibel said. "Our guest goes first."

I'd just eaten, but I didn't want to refuse Rosibel's offer. I would have rather followed Sebastian to see the protocol, but I wasn't going to intervene in a mother teaching her son manners. I dished up beans and rice, a little pork that was cooked with peppers, and then a tortilla.

"We'll sit at the table." Rosibel gestured as she poured glasses of lemonade for everyone.

I sat down at the table, which sat five, and Karin joined me a minute later. She didn't touch her food, so I didn't touch mine either. Soon, everyone was crowded around the small table.

Rosibel and her children bowed their heads and then she prayed, out loud. "Bless us all as we gather here today, and let us live happily in your love. Hear our prayer, loving Father, for we ask this in Jesus' name. Amen."

Karin and Sebastian said, "Amen," and then dug into the food. I did the same, warmed by the prayer and being included in the family's supper.

A phone began to buzz. I clutched at the pocket of my apron, but it wasn't mine.

Karin pulled hers from the back pocket of her capris. "It's the lawyer." She quickly answered it, stood, and stepped into the small living room.

I watched as she answered mostly yes and no and then said, "He's in the Mid County Detention Center." Then she asked, "Do you want me to go too? I can take the day off work, if needed."

There was a pause and then she said, "Call me if you need any more information. And please let me know how things go."

After another pause, she said, "Thank you" and then "Goodbye." As Karin returned to the table, she said, "Mr. Benjamin is going to see Mateo tomorrow." She sat down. "Hopefully, he'll have some good news for us soon."

AN HOUR LATER, Derek and I left, but not until Rosibel had made him sit down for supper as well.

"We capped the pipe, but we couldn't get it fixed. I've called Lyle multiple times and texted him too," Derek said as he drove, "but I haven't heard back."

"How is Mr. Barlow doing?" I asked. "Is he back home?"

Derek shook his head. "No, he's had more complications. I sure wish he'd get well enough to come home—not just for his health, but for selfish reasons too."

"What's going on?"

Derek shrugged. "I don't want to say too much. I'll just mention that Lyle and I don't see eye to eye on a lot of things."

That didn't surprise me. Derek was a person of integrity. Lyle wasn't.

As we turned into the driveway, Mamm was still working in the garden. She shook her head as Derek stopped the pickup.

"Is your Mamm all right?" Derek asked.

"It's hard for her to have me home."

"It's not hard for me," Derek responded.

"Then you probably didn't hear what others said about me when I left."

"No, I did," Derek said. "I just didn't believe them."

I wasn't sure what to say because some of what he'd heard was probably true. It was just hard to explain the parts that weren't, especially when I didn't know specifically what he'd heard.

"Well," I finally said, "no matter what, I'm the outlier. My other siblings were all perfect. Then there was me."

Derek laughed. "Their sins just didn't find them out. Maybe they were more secretive. Less reactive. Or didn't get caught. You're not the odd one out, believe me."

I wondered if he was speaking generally or about my family specifically. Still, the less I said to Derek—or to anyone—the better. I'd be gone soon anyway. But I was enjoying getting to know him again in the meantime, and he was making being home a lot more bearable.

I grabbed the door handle.

"Sophie?"

I turned toward him.

"I really am glad you came home."

Tears stung my eyes, and I swallowed hard. "Thank you." I was sure that he and Jane were the only two who felt that way.

I climbed down and started toward the shed to return my phone, when Mamm called out to me. I veered toward the garden. She didn't say anything more until I was at the edge of the lawn. "I told you not to lead that boy on. Jah, he has an Englisch job, but he's never run around, not like some people."

My eyebrows shot up.

"He plans to join the church—and soon," Mamm said. "Unless you plan to do the same, leave him alone."

"He's not interested in me."

"Then why does he keep coming around?"

I shrugged. "We're friends. That's all."

She shook her head. "I know more than you think."

When I didn't respond, she continued, "Lyle never got over what you did to him. He was ready to join the church, but you destroyed him. You're the reason he didn't join. His parents came out from Ohio and tried to convince him. All his siblings tried too. His aunts and uncles. But you damaged him beyond repair. His entire family is devastated. You will not do the same thing to Derek."

I didn't even know where to start with what she'd just said. Lyle never got over what I did to *him*? I destroyed *him*? I damaged *him* beyond repair? Without answering, I turned and ran toward the shed.

I DIDN'T GO to Jane's on Wednesday morning. I felt tired and discouraged and decided to rest instead. By Wednesday evening, Derek had temporarily fixed the pipe, and he and I weeded in Jane's garden with Miriam again. Miriam seemed happy to see us and was even more talkative than before.

Taking care of an infant all day had to be exhausting, and as much as she seemed to adore Jane, I guessed Miriam probably missed being around people her own age. I liked her, and it seemed Derek enjoyed spending time with her too.

I looked forward to seeing Derek again on Thursday, but when I went to check my texts that morning, I saw that I'd already missed one from him. *I need to work on the pipe again this evening. The temporary fix didn't hold.* I wished he would have offered to have me hang out with Karin while he worked, but I didn't feel as if I should ask him. I knew he was busy. Then again, maybe someone had warned him to stay away from me.

The next text was from Karin. *The lawyer's visit to see Mateo didn't happen. The detention center wouldn't allow it. Jasper is going to try again on Friday.*

I texted her back. *I'm so sorry. Why wouldn't they let Jasper see Mateo?*

Some lame excuse, Karin texted back. *I'm hoping to go on Friday too.* I stashed my phone back in my car and returned to the house.

Instead of helping that evening without Derek, I decided to go to Jane's early and help in the garden. When I told Mamm during breakfast, she said, "Quilting circle starts at ten."

"Oh," I answered. "I didn't realize that. I can wait."

"I wasn't going to go anyway," Mamm said. "I have too much to do around here."

"Do you want help? I don't have to go to Jane's. I can stay home."

"No, go ahead."

It dawned on me that it was probably easier for Mamm when I wasn't around. "I'll leave as soon as I do the dishes."

"Go ahead and go now," Mamm said. "I'll clean up."

On my way to the barn, I stopped by the shed, grabbed my phone, and tucked it into my apron pocket. Then I hitched the horse and left for Jane's. As I passed Mill Creek Farms, I kept my eyes on the village as I passed by, hoping I'd spy Rosibel or Victor. Or Sebastian. Or Derek. There were people in a far field, but I couldn't tell who they were. I didn't see Derek's pickup anywhere, but there were fields at another location too.

When I reached Jane's, she wasn't in the garden. After I unhitched the horse and put him in the pasture, I let myself through the gate and started to weed.

A few minutes later, Jane called out my name. "I was hoping it was you when I heard the buggy pull into the parking lot. I'll join you."

"You don't need to. I'm sure you have things to do to get ready for the day."

"No, I want to." She took a pair of gloves from the pocket of her apron. "How are you?"

I told her I was feeling better, and then filled her in on what was going on with Karin's brother. "I don't understand," I said. "Derek seems to support the Lopez family and the other workers, but others don't. How would the farm survive without the workers?"

Jane nodded her agreement. "We've seen more and more fear recently, even here."

I was relieved that Jane seemed empathetic toward the Lopez family.

"What's happening now reminds me of Mary's story," Jane said.

"How's that?" I asked. There hadn't been any immigrants in the story, not that I could remember.

"Mary meets quite a few people in Chicago. Let's see . . . Where did I leave off?"

"Mary, her Dat, and Lemuel had arrived in Chicago and then met Kit. The four of them had just arrived at the Grand Hotel, looking for Russ Keller."

"That's right," Jane said. "Russ wasn't there, and Judah decided to wait. . . ."

CHAPTER 10

❖

Mary

Dat told Mary and Lemuel that they could go for a walk while he and Kit stayed with the wagons at the hotel. "Just be back in two hours," he said.

"Let's go down to the lake." Mary turned north, toward the bridge they'd just crossed.

"It's five blocks to Madison Street," Lemuel said. "If we go east on it, we should reach the lake soon. I don't think it's more than a mile."

Mary agreed. That wasn't far to walk. They'd have plenty of time.

They retraced their route along the wooden sidewalks and then over the bridge. Halfway across, they stopped and stared down at the water. There was a sheen on the top, and a barrel drifted along. There were a few rowboats in the river and a barge. A foamy substance floated along the shore and trash bobbed up and down, here and there.

"I wouldn't drink out of that water," Lemuel said.

Mary agreed. "Let's keep going."

When they reached the end of the bridge, they continued east along Madison Street. The hotels they passed appeared nicer than the Grand Hotel, and the shops seemed to cater to wealthier people.

Gentlemen walked past with well-dressed women on their arms. Buggies with taxi signs dropped off people and then picked up others. Lavish carriages pulled by beautiful horses zipped by.

Mary squeezed past a group of men. Lemuel grabbed her hand and pulled her closer to him when one of the men stepped in front of her. The man laughed, but Mary marched forward, her head high.

She smelled the lake—a breath of fresh air—before she saw it. Waves lapped against a sandy beach. A train trestle was built above the water, yards out from the shore. People strolled along the sand, carrying their shoes. Some waded out in the water. Beyond the trestle, as far as the eye could see, was the vastness of the open water.

Mary had never seen the ocean, but she'd read about it. Now she had an idea of what it looked like. "Let's keep walking." She pulled off her boots as she spoke and then her socks. "To the end of the trestle."

Lemuel took his boots and socks off too, and they walked along the edge of the water. Mary held her dress up with her free hand as she relished the feel of the water on her feet.

As the end of the trestle came into sight, a train came toward them. It was a passenger train, going to the downtown station. Mary could see faces in the window, staring at them.

She waved and smiled while Lemuel laughed at her. They crossed the train tracks, where they veered back onto land. Mary dropped her boots in the sand, lifted her dress higher, and waded out into the water. It was surprisingly warm. The breeze, on the other hand, was hot and strong and blew against her face. Sailboats flew across the water, and ships full of cargo aimed toward the ports that Mary guessed were north of the train trestle. Dat had told her once that Chicago had the largest inland port in the United States.

The waves came in, one after the other. Mary pulled the hem of her dress up to her knees and stepped out farther while Lemuel stayed behind. Mary took another step, and the next wave soaked her hem. If only she could submerge herself in the water.

She turned south and continued to walk in the water, stepping toward the shore when a bigger wave came in. Lemuel walked along, parallel to her, but on the edge of the sand.

Finally, he said, "We should go back."

Mary nodded and turned around, walking back in the water until she reached her boots. She grabbed them and turned to Lemuel. "I don't think I've ever had so much fun in my entire life." She headed across the train track again and Lemuel followed. "Though it would be better if I could swim in the lake."

Lemuel shook his head. "I can't swim."

"Well, neither can I," Mary said. "But I wish I could."

When they reached Madison Street, Mary and Lemuel both put their boots back on and headed toward the Grand Hotel.

When they reached it, Dat said Russ hadn't shown up. "Go get yourself something to eat." He handed Mary a few coins. "There's a kitchen wagon a block that way." He pointed west. "I got Kit something there."

"What about you?" she asked.

"I ate some of the bread and cheese."

When they returned again, after eating bratwursts, Kit and another young man were unloading the flour and produce. Dat stood with an older man on the sidewalk, talking. The man had reddish-blond hair with streaks of gray. He was stocky compared to Dat.

As Mary and Lemuel approached, Dat smiled and said, "Russ, I'd like you to meet my youngest daughter, Mary, and my farmhand, Lemuel."

Russ extended his hand and shook both of theirs in turn. "It's a pleasure to meet you." He turned to Mary. "I've known your Dat since he was practically a boy."

Mary smiled at the man, relieved that he'd shown up and seemed eager to buy their goods.

He turned back to Dat. "Let's talk about the payment."

Lemuel began helping Kit and the other man unload the wagons. Mary stepped over to help too, but then remembered Dat hadn't wanted her to help at the train station, probably because it wasn't very ladylike.

She stepped to the wagon that Lemuel was driving and stroked the horses' forelocks, taking turns with each one. She guessed Dat would need his money from Russ to pay Kit the rest of what he owed, but she wasn't sure. Dat didn't speak much about finances. But she knew he was worried with the drought going on for so long.

Mamm brought in some money midwifing, but mostly she was paid in goods. A bag of potatoes. A couple of hens. A ham. She mainly worked to serve others, but any payment helped.

Mamm often said there would always be good times and hard times in life, and what mattered was that they trusted the Lord no matter their circumstances. Mary had seen her family do that over and over, including during the war.

Her middle brother, Paul, had lied about his age and enlisted in the Union army when he was seventeen, much to her parents' despair. Then, when the army came through looking for supplies, Dat ended up selling to them. Amish neighbors criticized him, as did the bishop, but Dat said that although he didn't agree with Paul, he wasn't going to let him, or other soldiers, starve.

When word came that Paul had been killed at Shenandoah, Mary had been devastated. Many in the community weren't very sympathetic, considering he'd chosen to go off to war. Their judgment made the loss of Paul so much harder on Mary. Her parents seemed to ignore it.

Mamm often quoted the Gospel of John: "In the world ye shall have tribulation: but be of good cheer; I have overcome the world." She said tribulation appeared in all sorts of ways. No one could predict it or escape it.

Mary, at times, wanted to believe that wasn't true. If people didn't go off to war, if they did the right thing, if they followed Christ's teachings, then maybe somehow tribulations wouldn't come. That was her hope, even though she knew it wasn't true.

A raised voice alarmed Mary. She turned toward where Dat was standing. Russ was yelling at the woman who'd given the boy the loaf of bread earlier that morning, and the child was running down the street. "If you want to keep your kids, do what I say!" Russ yelled at her.

The woman turned away and scurried after the boy.

Russ threw up his hands. "We pay her well, and yet she keeps sneaking food out of the kitchen for that little brat."

Dat shifted from one foot to the other, appearing uncomfortable. "I'd like to make the next train, so I'll need the payment now."

Russ took a paper out of his breast pocket and followed Dat to the back of the first wagon, which was empty.

Mary stayed with the horses but watched the men. Dat held the contract with his free hand, read it, and then said, "Good." Then he read, out loud, "Payment upon receipt. I'll take the money, and we'll be settled."

"Here's the thing," Russ said. "I don't have the money right now. I wasn't expecting you until Monday."

"I wrote that I'd be here today."

Russ raised his eyebrows. "I was sure you wrote Monday."

Dat shook his head.

"Well, no matter. I'll have the money by tomorrow morning."

"I need to return home tonight."

Russ shrugged. "If you want your money, you'll have to come back tomorrow."

"Then we'll need to reload the goods."

"There's no need for that," Russ said quickly. "Look, I'll give you my watch and ring as a guarantee that I'll pay you tomorrow."

"I have no idea if your watch and ring are worth anything." Dat looked directly at the man. "I thought I could trust you."

"You can. We've been friends for years. I won't cheat you, I promise."

Much to Mary's surprise, Dat put out his good hand and said, "I don't want your ring or watch. I simply want your word."

Russ shook Dat's hand vigorously as he said, "Of course you have my word. I promise I'll have the money tomorrow morning."

Mary shoved her hands in the pockets of her apron. She hoped Dat hadn't just made a huge mistake.

AS THEY STOOD around the empty wagons, it was obvious Kit wasn't happy that Dat couldn't pay him the rest of the money, and Mary knew it pained Dat not to be able to.

"I'll be honest with you," Dat said to Kit. "I promise I'll pay you, but right now I don't have much more than enough money for food and two more nights of lodging."

"Two?" Kit asked.

"We can't travel home on the Sabbath," Dat said. "We'll have to wait until Monday morning."

Kit shook his head, puzzled.

"If we can find cheaper lodging, I can pay you enough to feed your horses and board them for the night. And I'll feed you, along with Mary and Lemuel."

"All right." Kit motioned to his left. "I have a cousin who has a boardinghouse not far from here. I can also stable my horses there, as long as I can pay."

"Let's go see what your cousin has available," Dat said. Then he added, "Things will work out, one way or the other. I'm old enough to know that much."

Kit didn't respond.

Again, Mary rode with Lemuel while Dat rode with Kit. As they traveled, she noticed there was even more of a mix of businesses, houses, and shanties, all built close together, with small pastures with horses, cows, and sheep grazing here and there. There were a few pig lots too, which put off much more of a stench in the crowded city than they did back home. Much to Mary's relief, they passed a firehouse. The pungent smell of smoke became more pronounced the farther they traveled, and a hazy sheen hung over the buildings to the west.

"Do you think there's a Feiyaha over there?" she asked Lemuel.

"Possibly," he said. "I'll be relieved when we're headed back home."

Mary didn't respond. The smoke was unsettling, but she was enjoying every minute of the trip to Chicago. Wading in Lake Michigan had been her favorite experience, and the energy of the city was something she'd never experienced before. Plus, there were so many different types of people—from begging children to women dressed in fancy clothes and everyone in between.

It wasn't long until Kit stopped his wagon in front of a two-story wooden house on a large corner lot. The house was treated wood and unpainted. There was a stable in the back and a small pasture where two horses grazed. Mary guessed it was about a five-minute trip from the hotel.

Kit and Dat climbed down and headed up to the porch while Mary and Lemuel waited. A few minutes later, they stepped out of the house, followed by a woman who appeared to be in her early thirties. She stayed on the porch as Kit ran down the steps, Dat limping behind him. Dat called out to Lemuel, "We're going to go unhitch the horses."

It seemed to Mary that four more horses on the small pasture would be too much, but she supposed it was the best that could be done. Life in the city was certainly different from back home.

As the men unhitched the wagons, Mary collected the food basket and her bag and put them along the fence. Then she helped brush the horses down as Kit watered them at the trough. Next, he gave them each a bucket of grain and put them out into the pasture.

Mary picked up the bags and basket and then followed the men toward the house. Lemuel waited and walked with her.

Once inside, Kit introduced his cousin to them. "This is Ellen Smith," he said. "Her mother and my mother were sisters."

"Pleased to meet you," Mary said.

"Welcome," Ellen replied. "My home is humble, but you are welcome here."

"Our home is humble too," Mary answered. "We're grateful to lodge in yours."

Ellen smiled, her blue eyes lively. "You'll need to sleep in my room," she said to Mary. "The men will have the one that's open upstairs."

"Thank you."

"I have supper ready to serve. Ham and potatoes. You can wash up in the rooms." She pointed to the staircase for the men. "Kit will show you." Then she pointed down the hall for Mary. "It's the last door on the right, before the kitchen. You can leave your things there."

Mary found the right door. There were two single beds in it, a bureau, and a washstand with a basin and pitcher. She washed her hands and face, used the towel on the stand, and then continued down the hall to the kitchen, which had a large table in it. There were three men already seated around it. Dat, Lemuel, and Kit arrived a moment later. Dat motioned for Mary to sit down and then he sat beside her.

Mary looked around. It appeared all the boarders were men. She was used to working in the Felda with Dat and her brothers, and more recently, Lemuel. But this was a strange new world to her—one she would soon be leaving behind. Would her adventure in Chicago make her more thankful for home? Or even more restless than before?

AFTER SUPPER ENDED, Ellen warned the boarders not to leave a lamp burning when they went to bed. "And don't light any candles," she said. "We've had fire after fire here in Chicago over the last few months." All the men acknowledged what she'd said.

Mary helped clean up after supper, and as they worked together, Ellen shared that her husband had died three years ago from a high fever. He had inherited the house from his parents, and it was all she had to make a living now. "Running a boardinghouse is hard," she said, "but I'm grateful. Kit looks in on me weekly and refers travelers passing through town. I prefer long-term boarders, but I'm glad it worked for all of you to stay a couple of nights." She smiled warmly.

Mamm often encouraged Mary to count her blessings. Being able to stay at Ellen's place was one of them. And even though Kit seemed harsh earlier by not letting her drive a wagon, she was now grateful for him too. They would have been in a real bind without him. Now, if only Russ Keller would follow through with the money.

Mary was also grateful to share a room with Ellen. The bed was comfortable enough, and Ellen talked some more about her life as they settled down for the night.

Her parents had emigrated from London and settled in New York City, where Ellen was born. They'd moved to Chicago when she was fifteen. Her husband had fought in the Civil War, serving under General Grant. "He never talked about the war much," Ellen said. "I met him after he returned."

Mary was tempted to tell Ellen about her brother Paul, about his death at Shenandoah, but decided not to. The woman had lost her husband not that long ago, and that wound was still fresh.

"It feels as if it's been one thing after another," Ellen said. "Now it's all these fires. It's been so dry, and the winds have been blowing off the lake. There are so many immigrants and shanties, and everything—even the mansions—are made of wood. Some are covered with masonry, but it's mostly wood. There are no building codes like other cities, such as New York, according to what my pa used to say. This whole city is a tinderbox."

Mary shuddered.

"Nevertheless," Ellen said, "I make do. God has given me this house—I'd be out on the street without it. All I can ask is for my daily bread, and I must be thankful for what the Lord provides."

Ellen's words warmed Mary. That was exactly how she needed to feel about Russ Keller paying Dat. The Lord would provide. She recited the Lord's Prayer as she fell asleep.

The next morning, Mary gave Dat the tincture, and then he sat on a chair on Ellen's back porch while Mary treated his head wound. It was red and looked infected. She put the carbolic acid on it and covered it with a piece of cloth. She knew Mamm would be alarmed by the filth in the city. The open sewage. The smoke. The dust. Jah, the sooner Dat could get home, the better.

"Perhaps we should travel today anyway," she whispered to Dat. "And get you back to Mamm so she can treat this."

He shook his head but didn't say anything.

As Mary put the bottles back in her bag, she noticed movement at the front door of the shanty, one in a long row of them, on the property across from Ellen's pasture. The woman from the hotel the day before and two boys walked along the fence line. The youngest was the little boy who had received the loaf of bread. By the size of him, she guessed the older one was maybe eleven, but he wore a cap and his back was to Mary, so she couldn't see his face. "We need to hurry," the woman said. The older boy picked up the younger one and swung him up onto his shoulders.

"Dat, look." She pointed as the woman and children headed toward the street. "It's the woman and boy from the hotel. There's an older boy too."

Dat tilted his hat back. "So it is." He smiled up at Mary and then stretched his good arm and stood. "I'm anxious to get home too. I miss your Mamm, and I need a good rest. But for some reason the Lord had us stay longer here." He opened the back door for her. "Now, let's get some breakfast and then go back to the Grand Hotel and finish up this business with Russ."

CHAPTER 11

❖

After bowls of porridge, Kit, Lemuel, Dat, and Mary told Ellen good-bye and drove the wagons back to the hotel. Dat climbed down gingerly and headed to the kitchen door.

The little boy Mary had seen that morning was standing on the street corner across from the hotel. He had a loaf of bread in his hands. Mary climbed out of the wagon and told Lemuel she would be right back.

She crossed the street and approached the boy.

"Will you buy my bread?" the boy asked.

"Jah," Mary answered, taking a coin Dat had given her the day before from her pouch. "I saw you this morning," she said as the boy handed her the bread and she gave him the coin. "I was staying at Ellen Smith's, in the house across the pasture from your home."

"Oh."

"Was that your mother with you?"

The boy nodded.

Mary gestured toward the hotel. "She works in the kitchen here?"

He nodded again.

"Who was the older boy with you?"

"My brother, Patrick. He's twelve," the boy answered. "I'm Colum."

"What is your mother's name?"

"Honora."

Mary smiled. "What a beautiful name."

"Ma is beautiful," Colum said solemnly.

Mary nodded in agreement.

Colum added, "Our last name is Sullivan. From our pa, but he died when I was a baby. He drove a wagon and was crushed under the wheel in an accident."

Mary shivered, even in the heat. "I'm sorry." Her own Dat could have been crushed under the wheel of his wagon when he was thrown the other day.

"My name is Mary." She held up the loaf of bread. "Thank you."

Colum grinned and then started across the street with Mary following. He headed back toward the kitchen, most likely to get another loaf of bread to sell. Mary hoped Honora wouldn't get in trouble for her money-making enterprise.

As the boy turned the corner toward the kitchen door, Dat came around it, heading the other way, with a frown on his face. Mary had seldom seen Dat look discouraged.

She kept walking toward him. "What's wrong?"

"Russ Keller isn't here," Dat answered. "He sent a message that there was a fire near his house last night. His family fled but were able to return this morning. He said he'll come to the hotel as soon as he can."

"What will we do?" Mary asked.

"Wait." Dat looked toward the west, where a haze still hung over the city. "This city is like a tinderbox."

"But they have firefighters," Mary said. "And Russ's house didn't burn."

"But it sounds as if other homes did." Dat pressed his lips together. "I'll be glad when we're on that train and headed home."

Mary nodded in agreement, although she would be sad to leave the city.

At noon, Mary divided the loaf of bread between the four of them. Three hours later, Dat gave Mary more money and sent Lemuel with her to buy sausages. When they returned, Colum appeared and Mary waved him over. She lifted him into the wagon and then shared the rest of her bread and her sausage with him. Dat gave him pieces of his food too.

After Colum had eaten, he curled up in the wagon. Mary put her cloak over the boy and he soon fell asleep.

"How much longer do you plan to wait?" Kit asked Dat.

"As long as it takes if we all want to make any money off this endeavor," Dat answered.

A breeze blew through the tops of the trees as Mary climbed up into the wagon and sat down by Colum. Soon she was curled up beside him, drifting in and out of sleep.

She awoke as the sun, an orange ball in the hazy sky, began to lower. Soon, the streetlights came on and the wind turned from a breeze into what felt like the beginning of a gale.

The chef approached Dat. "Russ sent another message. He wants you to go to his house for the payment." The man handed Dat a piece of paper.

"You shouldn't go alone," Lemuel said to Dat.

"I'll go with you," Kit said. "It will take less time."

"All right." Dat turned toward Mary, holding up the piece of paper. "Memorize the address in case you need it."

205 South May Street.

"Russ also wanted me to send food with you and feed your daughter and hired hand while you're gone." He gave Dat the parcel that was in his other hand.

Mary climbed out of the wagon quickly, not wanting the chef to see Colum. The chef nodded toward her. "You come with me. I'll give you food to bring out here."

Mary motioned toward Lemuel to stay with Colum and followed the chef into the kitchen and then to a small dining area with a large table. A few people, servers she guessed, sat around it, eating quickly.

"Sit," the chef said, pointing to the far end of the table.

Mary obeyed. Fifteen minutes later, Colum's mother appeared with a tray.

"Hello, Honora," Mary said.

The woman took a step backward. "How do you know my name?"

"Colum told me."

Her eyes grew wide. "Shh." She handed Mary the tray. On it were two sandwiches, a wooden plate of boiled potatoes, and two wooden cups of water. "Leave the tray by the kitchen door when you're done."

"Will you start home soon?" Mary whispered. "Colum is in the back of one of the wagons we've been using."

Honora's face reddened. "Hopefully so. But—"

The chef began to yell, and she scurried away without completing her sentence.

Mary left with the food. When she arrived at the wagon, the wind had picked up. Colum was awake, and she and Lemuel shared the food with him. When they finished, Colum thanked them and said, "I better go home."

"What about your Mamm?"

"She told me to go home before dark."

"But it's past that," Mary said. "Shouldn't you wait for her?"

Colum shook his head. "Sometimes she works late."

"What about your brother?"

"He works late too." The boy started to climb over the side of the wagon, and Lemuel helped him down.

"You could give him a ride," Mary said. "I'll stay here. If Dat comes back before you do, we'll wait."

Lemuel shook his head. "I'm not going to leave you here."

"Then I'll walk him home."

"Mary . . ." His expression was tense.

"We can't send him by himself."

"He goes home by himself all the time," Lemuel said.

"But not in the dark." Mary pursed her lips together. "And what if there's a fire on the way? With all the smoke and fire engines going by, he might get turned around."

Lemuel shook his head. "I don't think that's likely as it's not that far to his house."

Mary crossed her arms.

"All right. I'll take him." Lemuel lowered his voice. "Grab your cloak and stay by the kitchen door. I'll be back as soon as I can."

Colum was thrilled to sit on the bench of the wagon and waved at Mary as Lemuel urged the horses forward. As they left, a church bell began to ring. Nine times.

Mary stepped to the back of the hotel. As she waited, another fire engine raced by. Several men followed it on foot, running down the middle of the street. She couldn't see any flames, but the smell of smoke was growing stronger.

There was more commotion on the street. "Where's the fire?" someone yelled.

"Which one?" someone else asked.

How many fires are burning? Mary wondered.

The big man, Mort, who was in the kitchen earlier passed by, running up the stairs to the kitchen door. As he flung the door open, he shouted, "There's a fire headed this way! It started near Diovan Street."

Mary gasped. That was where Ellen lived. Honora and her children too.

And it was right where Lemuel was heading.

Mary hesitated and then started up the stairs. The man bumped into her as he rushed down again. She stumbled but caught herself from falling. As people started rushing out of the kitchen, Mary ran up the last three steps and pressed herself against the outside wall of the building, keeping her eye on the door.

When Honora appeared, Mary yelled out her name.

The woman rushed toward her.

"My friend gave Colum a ride back to your home," Mary said. "We'd better hurry."

Without speaking, Honora grabbed Mary's hand, pulled her down the stairs, and began to run.

THE STREETS were filled with people. In no time, flames became visible over the tops of the buildings. Gusts of wind played with the sparks, shooting them across the sky and over the rooftops. New fires started up blocks away from the main fire. The ringing bells of more fire engines filled the air, along with the call of whistles and the shouts and screams of people.

"This way." Honora took Mary's hand again. They ran down an alley, past a group of men passing around a bottle, and then onto another street that wasn't as crowded. But Mary wondered if Lemuel might be on the main street, coming back toward her. She would have to make her way back to the hotel after they found Colum. Surely Lemuel and Dat would be waiting for her there.

If they could make it.

Honora turned down another alley, which led them to De-Koven. The flames were burning a couple of blocks away, casting an eerie glow over the street, and the wind was howling now. Ahead was a fenced pasture and the back of the shacks where Honora lived with her children.

"Colum!" Honora shouted. She squeezed between two of the shacks, with Mary following her. Up ahead was Ellen's house, and there were flames behind it, only a hundred yards away. Another fire engine sped past them.

Mary started yelling, "Fire! Fire!"

A few shack doors flew open.

"Get out!" Mary yelled.

Honora threw open the door to her shack as she shouted "Colum!" again. Mary followed her into the shack. It was a single room with one bed, a wooden box, and a few garments hanging from pegs.

"He's not here." Honora rushed out the door and started running toward the street, screaming for her son.

Mary grabbed her arm. "Honora. I need to go check on Ellen Smith." She pointed toward the house. "Maybe she'll know something about Colum."

Honora fell to her knees in a daze. Mary pulled her up. "Come on."

In an instant Honora was on her feet. Mary marveled at the woman's strength. When they reached Ellen's house, Mary banged on the door and then opened it. "Ellen!" she yelled, stepping inside. The house was dark except for the flickering light from the flames down the street. One of the boarders came running down from upstairs, carrying a suitcase.

"Is anyone else in the house?" Mary asked.

"I don't know," the man said.

"Have you seen a boy of five or so? He lives in one of the shacks."

"I haven't seen no kids." The man brushed past them and out the door.

"Let's go." Honora headed for the door.

"Give me a minute," Mary said. "I'll be right back." She ran down the hall to Ellen's room and threw the door open. There was a figure on one of the beds. "Ellen!"

Ellen started to sit up. "What is going on?"

"Fire!" Mary grabbed Ellen and pulled her from the bed. "We've got to go." Ellen staggered to her feet. "Grab your shoes and dress."

Ellen handed Mary her boots and then pulled a dress over her nightgown. As they headed down the hall, she took her boots back and pulled them on. Then she gasped. "I need to go back."

"No!" Mary turned to grab her, but she kept on going. Mary rushed after her and saw Ellen snatch a pouch from the top drawer.

"Come on!" Mary grabbed her again. They stumbled back down the hall. Honora wasn't in the entryway, but Mary expected her to be out on the porch. But when they made their way through the door, no one was there.

"Honora!" Mary yelled. Where would she have gone?

Mary squinted. Coming down the street was a wagon. Was it Lemuel? Or maybe Dat and Kit? Perhaps it was someone else. It didn't matter. "Come on," Mary said, grabbing Ellen by the hand. Maybe Honora had found Colum and was headed to find her older son. Mary felt desperate. She needed to help them all.

On the left, sparks landed on a wooden shack. In a split second, it exploded into flames. The fire roared as if it were a monster, consuming all it could. A wandering cow began running down the street just as a horse jumped the fence out of Ellen's pasture. Mary feared for the animals, but she knew she couldn't save them.

She urged Ellen on. The smoke grew thicker as they ran. Through the haze a figure came toward them. "Lemuel?"

"It's me. Kit."

"Where's my Dat?" Mary choked on her words.

"In the wagon."

"Have you seen Lemuel?"

"No," Kit said. "I thought the two of you would still be at the hotel."

Mary tried to speak but started choking on the smoke again. She continued to cough until they reached the wagon. Kit helped Ellen climb into the back of the wagon while Mary climbed in on her own. She then crawled to the front of the bed, asking Dat if he was okay.

"I'm fine." But he didn't sound fine. His voice was weak and shaky. "Where's Lemuel?"

"I don't know." As Kit climbed up onto the bench, Mary quickly told them what had happened. "And now I don't know where Lemuel and Colum are—or Honora. We need to find them."

"We need to get out of here," Kit said, "and across the river as soon as we can."

"We need to at least go back to the hotel," Mary said. "Lemuel might be there."

"No," Kit said. "We need to get out of here. I know a faster route that doesn't go by the hotel."

"Dat!" Mary called out, expecting him to correct Kit.

"Your Dat is ill," Kit said. "He can barely breathe."

"Take him to the train station," Mary said. "I'll meet you there."

Kit snapped the reins. Mary jumped before the wagon picked up speed, and then yelled, "I'll go to the hotel and find Lemuel. We'll meet you at the station."

As Mary ran back to the hotel, she held her cloak over her mouth and nose against the caustic smoke that burned her lungs. She tried to backtrack the route that Honora had used, looking in every doorway for them. Halfway there, she lost her way but then found the main street, which was even busier with people carrying bundles and pushing carts full of household goods. The hotel was only a block away, but Mary darted down an alley, trying to get ahead of the crowd. As she came out on a parallel street, she heard her name.

"Mary!"

Ahead, in the back of a wagon, Honora was on her knees, waving her arms. Mary ran to her. The woman extended her hand and pulled her up. The two women crawled to the front of the wagon. On the bench sat Lemuel with Colum at his side. Both had dish towels from the food basket tied around their mouth and nose.

"We're headed to the hotel." Lemuel spoke loudly. "To meet your Dat."

Mary gasped for air and pulled in smoke instead. Coughing, she shook her head and then managed to say, "They're headed to the train station. We need to get across the bridge as soon as possible."

Honora directed Lemuel to turn to the right. "I know the

back streets. We should cross the river at Van Buren. It's clos-est."

The sooner they got to the train station, the better. She nod-ded toward Lemuel and Colum. "How did you find them?"

"While you were in that house, I ran back to our shack to gather up what I could." She nodded toward a carpetbag. "As I came out, I saw the wagon on the street. I wanted to run back for you, but if I didn't go right then, I would have lost them."

"Of course," Mary said.

"We couldn't get around to Ellen's house, so I told Lemuel to go back to the hotel, and hopefully we would meet you there."

Honora took two pieces of fabric from her carpetbag and handed one to Mary. "Tie it around your face."

Mary obeyed. They all looked like bandits.

As the wagon slowed for a turn, a man lifted a child into the bed and then helped a woman climb in before jumping in himself. Honora glared at the man, but Mary touched her arm. "Focus on directing Lemuel toward the bridge."

Honora pursed her lips but then nodded and turned toward the wagon bench. Colum clung to the side as the team took a sharp turn.

"Keep your eyes out for Patrick," Honora said to Colum. "Hopefully he isn't coming toward the fire, but I imagine he's doing all he can to reach us."

Two older boys jumped into the wagon. Then another man tossed in a bundle of belongings and climbed in too. Soon the wagon was full. Mary knew the extra weight would slow them down, but there was nothing she could do. They couldn't refuse to help those in need.

After a while, the two older boys jumped down and started running, but the others stayed in the wagon. Mary kept her eye on the fire as the wind continued to blow. More sparks flew over the buildings and over the sea of fleeing people.

As they neared the bridge, the traffic slowed to a crawl. "This is the closest bridge." Honora's voice was muffled by the cloth over her mouth. "We'll have a longer wait if we go to the next one."

Lemuel nodded. As the wagon came to a stop, Mary stood, hoping to catch sight of Kit, Dat, and Ellen, but all she could see was a mass of people, horses, wagons, and buggies. A spark fell onto her cloak. She swatted it out quickly. Below, a rowboat near the edge of the water burst into flames. A man screamed and jumped into the water.

Despair rained down with the sparks. Hopefully Dat was at the train station. She hoped he wasn't too worried about her and Lemuel.

Mary grabbed the two watering buckets in the wagon. "I'll be right back."

"Where are you going?" Lemuel asked nervously.

She held up the buckets. "To fill these." For the second time, she jumped down from a wagon, but this one was only inching along. She feared they wouldn't be able to outrun the fire, but she hoped they could still survive it.

CHAPTER 12

❖

Sophie

Jane took a watch out of her apron pocket. "Uh-oh, it's
time to get ready for the quilting circle."

"I'll help you," I said.

"Denki."

While hosing off my hands, I remembered that I'd been to
DeKoven Street when I went to Chicago with Ivy and Bri. Ivy—
who was interested in becoming a firefighter—had wanted to
stop by the Chicago Fire Academy, which was on the grounds
where the fire had started. That was all I knew of the fire until
Jane's story.

I thought of Mary and the mad panic in Chicago. She was
adventuresome and enthralled with the city, but it must have
been so frightening to flee a fire in a city she didn't know and
to not know if her Dat had made it to the train station. And
yet, from Jane's story, Mary seemed fearless.

I followed Jane to the back door, which was unlocked. I
slipped out of my shoes and walked into the shop in my socks.
Then I went into the restroom and scrubbed my hands.

When I came out, I asked Jane, "What can I do?"

"Would you put the folding chairs around the frame? They're in the closet."

Once I had the chairs set up, I asked Jane if she wanted me to put produce and flowers out in the roadside stand to sell during the quilting circle. "If I set it up, maybe Miriam can check on it later."

"If you'd like," Jane said. "I've got some index cards we could use to make little signs and a jar for donations in the kitchen."

As I gathered them, Dorothy and Savannah came through the side door. "Hello!" Savannah said. "We're on our way home from a doctor's appointment, but Mammi wanted to quilt today."

Dorothy grinned.

"Tommy will pick her up at noon and take her home."

Before Savannah could sneak back out the side door, Miriam and Owen came through it.

"Aww," Savannah said. "Could I hold him for just a minute?"

"Of course." Miriam shifted the baby toward Savannah, who scooped him up in a sweet embrace.

"How are you, little fella?" she asked.

He met her eyes and smiled just a little. Again, I sensed warmth and love in the room. Did Miriam have any idea how fortunate she was? If I'd felt that sort of support before I left for Elkhart, would I have chosen to stay instead? How had Jane inspired such a sense of loving community?

I put the stack of index cards and a pen into a glass jar, then headed to the front of the store and out the door. Over the next hour, I picked produce, made signs, and arranged everything in the little stand Derek had pulled into the parking lot the other day.

Once I'd finished my tasks, I slipped back into Plain Patterns. Jane was just finishing waiting on a customer and Miriam was walking a fussy Owen while the other women quilted.

"I'm going to go ahead and leave," I said to Jane. "Miriam, do you mind checking the stand a little bit later?"

Miriam smiled and nodded.

"Denki," Jane said. "For everything."

"Thank you," I said. "You're a bright spot for me. I'm very thankful."

Once I had hitched my horse and was ready to go, I checked my phone. It had died completely. I hoped next time I saw Derek, I could charge it in his pickup.

Again, as I neared Mill Creek Farms, I slowed. This time I did spy something familiar. Karin's car. I wondered if she'd taken off work for most of the week.

I turned to the right, down the road toward the farm, and then right again. As I entered the village, Sebastian ran down the middle of the road toward me.

"Whoa," I called out to the horse.

Sebastian ran around to the passenger side and opened the door.

"Hop in," I said.

He climbed up, a grin on his face. "I've always wanted to ride in a buggy."

I smiled back. "I'm happy to oblige."

A few minutes later, I parked the buggy by Karin's car. She must have heard the horse because she stepped onto the porch.

I jumped down and waved.

Karin pointed at Sebastian and laughed. "Are you an Amish boy now?"

He nodded vigorously.

"My phone died," I said to Karin. "I stopped by to let you know in case you were trying to get ahold of me."

She shot me a confused look.

"I won't be able to charge it for a while," I explained. "My parents don't have electricity or any kind of charger." Some Amish would keep a car battery in the barn to charge a phone for a friend or relative, but I was sure my parents wouldn't do that for me. And I didn't trust my car battery enough to charge it without running the engine, which Mamm and Dat wouldn't approve of.

"Oh, that's right," Karin said. "I forgot about that." She stepped to the horse and petted her forelock. "I'm glad you stopped, then. Did you get my last text?"

"I don't think so."

"I was wondering if you were free to go with us tomorrow morning to the detention center," Karin said. "Mama doesn't feel comfortable with me traveling alone with Jasper."

"You're driving there together?"

"His vehicle is in the shop."

"Oh." I imagined, as a lawyer, he drove a BMW or a Lexus or something. But fancy cars had to be maintained and fixed from time to time too.

"What time will you leave?"

"I'm going to meet him in Elkhart at 7:30. We'll leave from there."

I wasn't sure if I should go. "How about if I think about it and then call you from the phone shanty later this afternoon." I stepped back to the buggy, grabbed my purse, and pulled out my notebook and pen. "What's your number?"

Karin rattled it off and grinned again. "If you go with me, you'll be able to charge your phone in my car."

"That alone would be worth it," I joked.

With a final wave to Sebastian, I climbed back in the buggy, turned it around, and headed for home. As the horse clopped along, I couldn't help but think about what all Karin and I had in common. We both grew up in conservative homes with protective parents. And we both had jobs in Elkhart, although she lived with her family. In fact, she seemed very attached to her family—in a healthy way.

Part of me wanted to go with them so that Rosibel would feel all right with Karin riding with Mr. Jasper. But as shallow as it sounded, my main concern was seeing him again. Would he remember me from the day I fainted at the store? Maybe not if I wore my Amish clothes.

That, in itself, was a dilemma. Did I dress Englisch? Or Amish?

Those thoughts stayed with me even when I arrived home. Finally, after I took a long afternoon nap, I awoke and knew I'd go. How could I not? Why would I not help the Lopez family if I could?

And I also decided that I would dress Amish. Maybe Mr. Jasper wouldn't recognize me. If he did, I'd have to swallow my pride and confess that I was the girl who fainted at the grocery store.

I told Dat and Mamm what my plan was during supper that night as we ate a beet salad and squash soup.

"You certainly are gallivanting all over the place for being ill," Mamm said.

"I'll rest in the car tomorrow," I answered. "Besides, I'm feeling better."

Mamm gave me a sideways look. "So soon?"

I sighed. It wasn't her fault she didn't understand about lupus. Most people didn't. And obviously, I hadn't done a very good job of explaining. "The disease is unpredictable," I said.

"And I think the steroid injection and all the rest and good food have made me feel better."

Mamm actually rolled her eyes.

"Do you think I'm faking it?" I asked incredulously.

"No," she answered. "Not exactly . . ." Her voice trailed off as she waited for Dat to lead us in a silent closing prayer.

He shrugged when I glanced at him, and then we all bowed our heads.

WHEN KARIN ARRIVED five minutes early the next morning, I was more than ready. As soon as I climbed into her car, she nodded toward her charger. "It's all yours."

"Thanks." I plugged in my phone and placed it against my thigh on the seat.

"Nice farm," Karin said as she headed toward the lane. Her tone was sincere.

"Thanks," I said. "My great-great-grandparents settled on it over a century ago."

"That's really cool," she answered. "We had land that was in our family for generations, but my grandparents lost it during our civil war."

I felt embarrassed that I didn't know what she was talking about. "When was that?"

"From the late 1970s until the early 1990s."

"What happened?"

"It was between the military-led government and the Liberation Front," Karin said. "There were death squads, and a lot of people simply disappeared, including my grandfather. Then his land was seized. Soon after that, in 1991, my parents fled north with Mateo."

"Has any of your family gone back?"

Karin shook her head. "There's nothing left for us there anymore. All of our relatives are either dead or in the US."

"Oh." With what the Lopez family had already faced, it had to be terrifying for all of them to have Mateo arrested the way he was. I was filled with fresh determination to do anything I could for the family.

"So, tell me about Derek," she said, changing the topic. "Are you two dating?"

"No," I answered emphatically. "We've been friends since we were little."

"Do you know Lyle too, then?"

"We all grew up together."

"What do you think of him?"

I grimaced without meaning to. The last thing I wanted to do was talk about Lyle.

Karin shot me a look but then focused on the road again. "Sorry. I'll just say Papa really appreciates Derek."

I nodded. No doubt Victor Lopez was a good judge of character.

Fifteen minutes later, Karin pulled up in front of an office building in downtown Elkhart.

"I'll get in the back," I said, unplugging my phone from the charger.

Karin shook her head. "No, stay in the front." She pulled her phone from her purse and sent a text. A second later it dinged. "Jasper said he'll be right out."

But it was another ten minutes before he finally arrived, carrying a briefcase stuffed to the gills. Karin and I stepped out of the car to greet him.

"Hello, Mr. Benjamin," Karin said as she shook his hand.

"Please, call me Jasper," he said amiably.

She smiled and nodded to me. "This is my friend Sophie."

"Nice to meet you," he said.

I nodded and kept my head down to avoid meeting his eyes.

"Thank you again for taking Mateo's case," Karin said as we got back into the car.

"I'm happy to," Jasper said. "I happened to have a case close unexpectedly, so the timing worked out."

"The case ended well, I hope," Karin said.

I caught a look at Jasper's face in the rearview mirror. "Sadly, it didn't." He looked as if he might cry.

Karin gripped the steering wheel and kept her gaze straight ahead. "Oh."

Jasper sighed. "Thank you for letting me have the back seat. If you don't mind, I'll work on the way."

Once we left Elkhart, Karin turned up the music. We chatted a little, but I don't think either of us felt comfortable talking about anything important in front of Jasper.

Then again, we probably shouldn't have worried about it. He seemed engrossed in the papers he was reading, marking up, and shuffling around.

I smiled. He hadn't recognized me.

AFTER WE'D REACHED the detention center and started walking toward the building, Jasper glanced at me. "You look familiar."

"Oh?" That hadn't lasted long.

"Have we met?"

"Technically no," I answered. "But we have seen each other before."

"Sophie is the one who recommended you," Karin interjected.

"Really?" Jasper had a quizzical expression on his face.

I nodded. "I'm friends with Nadine. You represented her son." I felt as if I knew much more about him than I was letting on, due to how much Nadine had prattled on about him.

"Nadine Awad?"

"Jah," I said. "I work with her at the community garden. I've seen you walking by there before."

He shook his head a little, perhaps because he walked by the gardens often, or maybe because he was trying to clear some cobwebs from his head. "I don't remember seeing you there. Have I seen you somewhere else?"

"At the co-op." I paused.

He tilted his head.

"I'm the worker who fainted last Friday."

He stepped in front of me, then turned around and faced me. He smiled, seemingly in recognition. "But you weren't dressed Amish then."

"Right. I grew up Amish. I'm staying with my folks for a little while."

"Oh." He shook his head a little, as if something was clicking into place. "Fascinating. Are you feeling better after . . . ?" His voice trailed off.

My face warmed as I remembered Bri blurting out about my condition. "Yes, much better. Thank you."

He turned forward and led the way to the detention center. He seemed familiar with the place. "This is also a correctional facility," Jasper said as he held the door open for us, "although immigrant detainees and prisoners are housed in separate areas. Everyone here is male." He told me to sit in the waiting room while he and Karin checked in at the front desk. Both had to

LESLIE GOULD

show their identification and answer several questions. Then they came and sat beside me.

Other people checked in after them, some dressed in suits and professional clothing and others in casual clothing. Twenty minutes later, Jasper's and Karin's names were called.

I pulled my charged phone from my purse. I didn't have any texts. I surfed social media for a few moments and then became distracted by a woman and two boys who sat down across from me.

"Don't tell Daddy we're living with Grandma now," the woman said to the older boy. "We don't want him to worry more than he does."

The boy looked up at her solemnly. "Is it so you can afford a lawyer?"

The woman sighed as she nodded. "Now I just need to find one." She appeared exhausted.

The younger boy, who appeared to be around two, began to fuss, and the mother pulled him onto her lap. He began to scream.

Impulsively, without thinking through what I was doing, I reached out my arms to the little boy. "Is it all right if I hold him?" I asked his mother.

The woman nodded gratefully, handing him to me. I lifted him across the aisle onto my lap. Surprisingly enough, he seemed happy to see a new face. He reached for the ties on my Kapp and began to pull on them. After a while, he stuck one in his mouth and leaned against me. Soon, he closed his eyes, and I leaned back in the chair and relaxed.

"I couldn't help but overhear," I said to the mother. "What kind of lawyer are you looking for?"

"An immigration one."

"Where do you live?"

157

"In Indiana, west of Goshen. Do you know somebody?"

"Yes. I'm not sure if he's taking on new clients, though. He's seeing one now, and I can introduce you when he comes out if you're still here. If he's not taking new clients, maybe he could recommend someone."

"That would be wonderful." She took a book out of her bag. "I'm Vanessa, by the way, and this is Tony." She nodded toward her older boy and then across the aisle at me. "And Ryan."

Tony tugged on her arm, and she began reading quietly to him. He snuggled against her.

I gazed down into Ryan's peaceful face, and my heart lurched inside my chest.

A half hour later, Karin and Jasper returned. Karin did a double take at seeing me with a sleeping child in my arms.

"Jasper," I said quietly, hoping I wasn't putting him in an awkward position. "Vanessa is looking for an immigration lawyer. Vanessa, this is Jasper Benjamin."

"Hello, Mr. Benjamin." Vanessa closed the book she and Tony were reading and stood to shake his hand. "I'm sorry to put you on the spot like this, but my husband has been here for a month. Before he was arrested, we thought everything was in order. But he missed a court date, one we weren't informed about."

Jasper took a small notebook from his briefcase. "What is your husband's name?"

"Anthony Gonzalez," the woman said.

"I'll go check if I can see him today. If not, I'll schedule a time to see him next week when I come back."

"That would be wonderful, Mr. Benjamin. Thank you." She smiled gratefully at him, and he smiled back kindly and then headed to the front desk.

Karin sat down next to me and leaned over to smooth Ryan's sweaty hair away from his forehead.

"Vanessa, this is my friend Karin." I didn't want to say anything about Mateo or why we were here, in case Karin was uncomfortable with that.

Jasper returned. "I can't see him today." He extended his business card to Vanessa. "Tell your husband about me. I'll be back next week—probably Tuesday—and I'll hopefully see him then."

The woman took the card and nodded. "I appreciate it."

I stood and slid the sleeping child back into her arms.

"Thank you," she said, "for everything."

I smiled at her. "Thank you for sharing your precious boy."

As we walked out to the parking lot, I asked how the visit went.

Karin just shook her head. Jasper patted her shoulder and said, "It's hard to see someone you love incarcerated."

When we reached the car, I asked her if she wanted me to drive.

"Would you mind?" she asked.

"Of course not."

Jasper climbed in the back again and had his briefcase open before I'd even started the engine. He and Karin both seemed lost in their thoughts.

"Mateo has always been such a protective big brother to me and Sebastian," Karin said, breaking the silence. "And because he became fluent in English before my parents, he felt responsible for them too. I think even now, he's more concerned about all of us than about himself. I doubt he's thought about what his life would be like if he gets deported."

"Oh, I bet he has," Jasper chimed in. "He just doesn't want to burden you with his worries about that too."

Karin sighed. "You're probably right." Then she turned toward me and said, "We did find out a new piece of information."

"Oh?"

"There was an Explorer in the car with the officer."

I shook my head. "What's an Explorer?"

"Someone interested in a career in law enforcement," Jasper explained. "It's a program for high school students."

"I see." Obviously, it wasn't something Amish kids did.

"I'll contact the sheriff's department and try to get a statement from her," Jasper said. "But I doubt the department will cooperate."

His mention of the department reminded me of Ivy. "Is there any chance you can get the dash cam footage?"

"I've put in a request," Jasper said. "Of course they're saying the footage would be irrelevant, but I'll keep pursuing it."

"What about a body camera?" Karin asked. "Was the officer wearing one of those?"

"No," Jasper answered. "The cost is too high to implement a program here—yet."

"What if the officer planted meth?" I asked.

Jasper hesitated before saying, "Are you suggesting they tampered with the evidence?"

"Could it be a possibility?"

"At this point," Jasper said, his voice perfectly calm, "I'd prefer to think this is all a mistake due to poor field-testing capabilities."

We descended again into silence. I flexed my fingers around the steering wheel. They were starting to stiffen up. But knowing what the Lopez family was going through made my own problems seem petty.

Jasper didn't say another word the rest of the trip to Elkhart.

Every time I looked in the rearview mirror, he was jotting down notes on a legal pad, or looking something up on his phone, or reading from a binder. Karin was quiet too, occasionally sending a flurry of texts, but that was all. Mostly she stared out the passenger window.

When I pulled up to the front of Jasper's office, his head flew up. "Are we here already?"

"Yes," I answered.

"Thank you." He met my eyes. "This is the first time I've ever been chauffeured by an Amish woman."

I corrected him. "A woman dressed in Amish attire."

"Yeah, I'm still a little unclear on all of the details." He grinned. "It's been nice to see you again, Sophie." He reached over and touched Karin's shoulder. "And it's been good to meet you and Mateo in person. I will be in touch soon. Call or text if you have any questions."

After Jasper gathered his things and climbed out of the back seat, I asked Karin if she minded if we stopped by my house. Now that I was feeling better and thinking more clearly, I wanted to grab another book or two on canning from my room.

"Sure," she said. "I took the whole day off, so I'm in no hurry. I already texted my parents about the visit. I'll fill them in when I get home."

I drove by the community garden on the way. Everything looked good. Nadine and Yani must be watering like they said they would. The gardens looked weeded, and although there was some visible produce, they'd been harvesting too.

When I reached my house, Ivy's car was in the driveway. She had an erratic schedule, so that wasn't surprising.

"Come on in," I said to Karin. "I can at least offer you a glass of water."

"Sure," she said.

When I opened the front door and stepped inside, Ivy called out a hello from the living room and then exclaimed, "Sophie!" She jumped up from the couch. "What are you wearing?"

I laughed. "An old dress I found."

"Did you convert?"

"No. I'm just dressing this way while I'm home." I gestured toward Karin. "This is my friend Karin from Nappanee."

"Nice to meet you," Ivy said.

"Likewise." Karin smiled.

"What are you two doing in town?"

I wasn't sure what to say, suddenly hyperaware of my last texts to Ivy. Would she think I was trying to manipulate her?

Karin spoke up. "My brother is in a detention center up in Michigan. He got arrested for allegedly failing to use his turn signal, then charged with possessing meth. Now he's fighting not to be deported." I admired Karin's transparency. "Sophie found an immigration lawyer for him and went up there with us today."

Ivy's eyes grew large, and she darted a quick glance at me. "Oh."

"I just stopped by to get some books," I said quickly. "And some water."

"I made bread from the zucchini you left." Ivy pointed toward the kitchen. "It's on the counter. Have some of that too."

"Thanks," I said. "I have a doctor's appointment on Monday. I'll stop back here then."

Ivy nodded but her eyes were on Karin. Was she thinking about the dashboard cam? I hoped so.

CHAPTER 13

I rested most of Saturday, except for doing the dishes and preparing the noon meal. I made a large salad with hard-boiled eggs and sliced chicken breast, dressed with a vinaigrette made from vinegar and olive oil.

I also read the books I'd grabbed—another one on canning and then one on Iraq, which Nadine had loaned me. Like Mary from Jane's story, there was so much about the world that I wanted to know.

On Saturday evening, Derek stopped by. He parked his truck and then started toward the house. He wore a backward baseball cap, a pair of boots, a denim shirt, and his work pants. I was sitting on the porch with Mamm and Dat. As he approached, he said hello to all of us, and then asked if I'd like to go on a walk.

"Sure." I didn't bother to glance at Mamm, sure her expression would show her ongoing disapproval.

"Thank you for helping Karin yesterday," he said as we walked toward the lane. "The entire family really appreciates it."

"I'm glad I could go," I said. "I hope Jasper Benjamin will be able to help Mateo."

"So do I."

When we reached the lane and turned left, so we'd be facing the traffic, he asked if I'd like to go to church with him the next day. "It's a Mennonite church, the one Karin and her family go to."

"I didn't realize they're Mennonite."

"They're not really, but they've been going to church there. It's closer than the church they used to attend over by Goshen."

"I'd like that." It was Mamm and Dat's off Sunday. Perhaps they would visit one of my siblings or some friends.

"The service starts at nine, so I'll pick you up at eight thirty," he said.

The next morning, Karin and her family were already in the church when we arrived. Derek led the way down the aisle to the pew right behind them. Rosibel turned around and took my hand, squeezing it.

I was surprised by the variety of people in attendance. A few women wore cape dresses and Kapps, like I did, although theirs were in prints instead of a solid color. Some of the men had beards and wore barn pants and suspenders. A few men wore suits, but most wore slacks and dress shirts. A few, like Derek and Victor, wore jeans. And even a few women did, although Rosibel and Karin both wore skirts and blouses. It seemed every kind of clothing was acceptable.

The pews had backs to them and were padded—a dream compared to Amish church benches. The singing was accompanied by a piano and led by a woman with a beautiful alto voice. Just as the opening song came to a close, Lyle and his girlfriend started down the aisle on the other side. I must have bristled because Derek whispered, "Sorry. I don't know what he's doing here. They usually go to church in Bremen with Delia's parents."

The sermon was about the parable of the sower, one of my favorites. But I was tired, and I had a hard time concentrating. Still, the length of the service—barely an hour and a half—was much easier to sit through than the three-hour Amish service.

After the service, Derek and I walked toward the foyer. "Want to get a cup of coffee before we go?"

"Sure." Caffeine sometimes aggravated my condition, but it might be worth taking a chance. I couldn't stop yawning.

I was surprised to see Savannah and her boyfriend, Tommy, in the fellowship hall.

"Sophie!" Savannah gave me a hug. "What are you doing here?"

"I came with Derek. Do you know him?" I nodded over to where Derek was filling two Styrofoam cups with coffee.

"Phyllis's son?"

"Jah. Derek and I were in school together."

"Oh, that's sweet." She touched Tommy's arm. "Do you know Tommy Miller?"

I nodded and said hello to him. "Tommy and I saw each other at Plain Patterns when he was picking up your grandmother."

"Oh, that's right."

"I knew you when you were about this high." Tommy lowered his hand to a few feet off the ground.

I laughed. "I was always the tagalong. I'm surprised you remember."

"Of course I do." He grinned. "I also remember your family's place. I spent a good amount of time on your front porch."

I smiled at the subtext. I knew his Mamm had several visits with Dat while Tommy was a rebellious teenager, but I wasn't surprised he had too. Probably long after I was asleep.

This time it was Savannah who was yawning instead of me.

"Excuse me," she said. "I worked as a doula on a birth yesterday, through last night."

"You're doing that along with your day job, right?"

She nodded. "I only take on a client every other month or so, but the last one was late and this one was early. Hopefully I can keep juggling both jobs for a while."

Derek joined us then, along with the entire Lopez family. I introduced Karin and her family to Savannah and Tommy. As they all exchanged pleasantries, I was distracted by a familiar voice. It was Lyle, talking with an older man.

"I agree," Lyle said.

"It only makes sense to have a detention center in Elkhart County. It would bring both construction and enforcement jobs to the area," the older man replied. "Not to mention reduce crime."

"That's right," Lyle answered. "We have a Constitution founded on God's principles. Why shouldn't we enforce it?"

My jaw dropped.

Karin turned around, fire in her eyes. "Lyle, what are you talking about?"

The older man, ignoring Karin, said to Lyle, "Absolutely. Illegal immigrants don't have the same values we do."

Karin took a step toward Lyle, but her father caught her arm and said, "Not here."

Lyle turned toward them, a sneer on his face. "We only want to follow the laws of the land."

"Yeah? Well, I'm a citizen," Karin replied as her father hustled her toward the door.

Lyle laughed. "Are you sure?"

"You're despicable," I said.

Derek stepped between Lyle and me. "Let's go, Sophie."

LESLIE GOULD

"Who are you with today?" Lyle asked Derek. "Karin or Sophie?" He smirked. "Or both?"

Derek hooked his arm through mine and walked right by Lyle.

"What was that all about?" I could hear the older man ask. "Why are they defending immigrants who don't pay taxes? Who collect welfare benefits?"

I took a step ahead of Derek and tried to pull away from him, hoping to lunge back at Lyle and the man, to tell them how misinformed they were. But Derek didn't let go.

BY THE TIME we got to the parking lot, Victor, Rosibel, Karin, and Sebastian were all in their car. I wanted to go talk with them, but Derek said, "Let's drive to their home and talk there. We shouldn't draw any more attention here."

Once we were in Derek's pickup, I asked, "Are there others in the congregation who feel the way Lyle and that other man do?"

"I can't say for sure," Derek said. "But I wouldn't be surprised."

"What's going on with Lyle?"

"I don't know. He has some weird ideas."

"He knows he has workers who are undocumented, right?"

"Of course."

"Does he not want them to work on the farm? And if so, what's his long-term plan as the foreman?"

Derek shrugged. "I can't get a straight answer out of him. I know Mr. Barlow doesn't feel the way Lyle does. He's gruff, but at the same time he's always been fair, especially to Victor and his family. I think he'd be horrified if he knew what Lyle was talking about—and at a church of all places."

167

"Do you know who the other guy was?"

"That's Richard Weber. He's been spouting off like that for years. He thinks ICE should partner with the local law—"

"Like they did with Mateo?"

"Exactly." Derek gripped the steering wheel tighter. "He's one of the people pushing for a detention center to be built in Elkhart County."

"Do you think it's going to happen?"

"There's a rumor that it's being considered, but I haven't read anything official about it in the news or on the Department of Homeland Security website."

"Have you checked lately?"

"Yeah, I keep up with it pretty regularly."

I was impressed. It sounded like Derek stayed well informed.

We rode in silence the rest of the way to the farm. When we reached the Lopez home, the family was climbing out of Karin's car.

I jumped down from Derek's pickup, but all of a sudden I felt afraid I was going to say the wrong thing. I settled on saying, "I'm sorry about what happened back there. That wasn't right, not at all."

Karin crossed her arms over her chest and looked away.

"Don't give it another thought," Victor reassured me. "I don't take Lyle seriously."

Derek rolled down his window. "Call if anything comes up or if you need anything."

"We're fine, really," Victor said. "But thanks."

Derek nodded. "I'll see you tomorrow."

"Bye," I said to Karin.

She gave me a little wave. I climbed back into the truck. I didn't say anything until we reached the edge of the village. "That was awkward."

Derek sighed. "I probably just reminded them of everything they're going through and that there is a significant number of people in this county who aren't supportive."

"No," I answered. "If we hadn't come by, they might have thought we agreed with Lyle."

Derek shook his head. "They know I don't, but I guess it's good to say it out loud."

As Derek turned onto the highway, he cleared his throat and said, "Tell me if I'm out of bounds to ask this."

"Ask what?"

"No, never mind. I shouldn't have said anything."

"Derek," I said, "you can ask me anything you want to. If I don't want to answer it, I won't." Hopefully he wouldn't ask me about the one topic I wanted to avoid.

"What exactly happened with you and Lyle?"

He did.

"Maybe I don't know as much as I assumed," he said.

When I didn't answer, he looked over at me. "Sorry I asked."

"No, it's all right . . ." I replied. Or was it? "What did you hear?"

Derek shook his head. "I shouldn't have brought this up. It's not my business."

"You're my friend. My only one here, in fact, besides Jane. I appreciate you and don't want you to be wondering about me. But it would help me know where to start if you tell me what you heard. I can handle it."

He inhaled sharply, exhaled, and then finally said, "I heard you were pregnant, but it wasn't Lyle's baby."

I spoke slowly and purposefully. "And who did you hear that from?"

"Lyle."

I spoke slowly again. "Did he say who the father of the baby was?"

"Some guy from Illinois, who was out here partying. A one-night stand." He winced. "The term he actually used was 'half-hour stand.'"

That stung. "Anything else that Lyle said?"

"First he said you'd had an abortion," Derek said. "Then that you'd given the baby up for adoption. And then that you'd kept the baby. That was why you'd moved to Elkhart."

"Was alcohol involved during any of these tellings?"

"As a matter of fact, jah," Derek said. "Alcohol was involved in all three of them."

When I didn't answer, he asked, "Does that mean he was lying each time? That none of it was true?"

The sky was a perfect baby blue, without a cloud in sight. So different from the tempest raging inside my soul.

"Sophie?" Derek's voice was so sweet and quiet that it made me want to cry.

"I was pregnant," I finally said. "It was Lyle's baby. When I told him, he swore it was someone else's, but it couldn't be. I hadn't been with anyone else. It was well into the second trimester that I finally accepted I was going to have a baby, and I decided I would do whatever I needed to keep it. I couldn't bear the thought of giving it away. But then I lost it." I paused. "Lost her."

I quickly continued, "At nineteen weeks, I realized something was wrong. I ended up in the hospital because I thought that by going to the ER they could stop it. But there were complications, and I ended up staying for two days. I didn't have health insurance." I knew I was telling Derek more than he wanted to know, but I couldn't stop. "I ended up owing over twelve thousand dollars—and that was after they gave me a discount. I just paid it off last month."

I stopped, but when Derek didn't say anything, I kept going. "The only person I'd told that I was pregnant was Lyle. He told me that if I ever told anyone the baby was his, he'd deny it and say I was lying." I folded my hands in my lap and looked down. "I made a big mistake to ever be with him, and it sounds as if he's only grown worse."

"I'm so sorry," Derek said, compassion in his voice. "For all you went through."

"Denki," I whispered. I appreciated his empathy, but I felt vulnerable and exposed. The way I used to feel in front of Lyle. I just wanted to go home and crawl in my bed. But which home? Mamm and Dat's? Or my place in Elkhart?

AFTER DEREK DROPPED ME OFF, I slipped into the house and went straight up to my room. Hot and weary, I slumped across my bed.

When I woke up, my sisters were standing over me.

"Are you okay?" Ruth asked.

"Jah." I sat up. "Why?"

"It's after five." Beth took a step away from me. "Mamm is fixing supper in the kitchen by herself."

"Is everyone coming over tonight?" I thought that was once a month, not every Sunday.

Ruth responded, "Just our families."

"Oh." I stood. "Mamm didn't tell me."

Beth crossed her arms. "She said you've been up here all afternoon."

Feeling light-headed, I sat back down. I hadn't had any

lunch, nor had I drunk any water since morning. That was foolish of me.

They both put their hands on their hips, eyeing me critically.

I guessed they thought I was faking being ill too. "I'll be down in a minute."

Once they'd left, I felt in my apron pocket for my phone. I had one text, from Karin. *Thank you for coming by today. That was kind of you. Jasper texted me. The sheriff's department refused to release the dash video of Mateo's arrest, but Jasper said he'll petition the decision. Thank you again for recommending him.*

I texted back, *You're welcome.* Loneliness swept over me. It would only be worse when I went downstairs. *Any chance you want to hang out tonight?*

Karin texted right back. *Sorry, I need to stick around home.*

I was tempted to text Derek. But part of me was afraid that he'd text back that he had plans too. I guessed my truth was more than Derek could handle. Sure, he wanted to know, but without meaning to, he would most likely distance himself from me now.

All of those same feelings of anxiety and being trapped rose up inside of me, just like the night I had fled to Elkhart.

I stood slowly, slipped my phone back into the pocket of my apron, and shuffled to the door, which my sisters had left wide open. I couldn't go downstairs. I just couldn't.

I had a doctor's appointment in Elkhart the next day. I could just go back tonight. Check on the community garden. Sleep in my bed. Go to the appointment in the morning and then return to Nappanee in the afternoon. Maybe I'd be doing well enough that I wouldn't need to. Maybe I'd just stay in Elkhart.

But then I wouldn't find out what happened to Mary and her Dat, Lemuel and Ellen and Honora and her two boys. Or what happened with Mateo. Well, I guessed Karin would text me and let me know. But Jane couldn't.

For all my angst about coming home, I had found some community back here. Jane. Derek. Karin. Was I ready to give it up already?

I started down the stairs to the living room, my feet feeling heavier with each step. I turned around. Maybe I wasn't ready to give up the community I'd found here, but I was definitely going back to Elkhart for the night. I stopped in the bathroom and grabbed my toiletries, then stepped back into my room and quickly packed my duffel bag.

I didn't say much to Mamm, Beth, and Ruth, just that I had a doctor's appointment soon and it would be easier to go back to Elkhart tonight. "I'll be back tomorrow afternoon." *Or maybe not.* If I decided not to return, I'd leave a message on the machine in the phone shanty.

Mamm simply said, "Oh." My sisters both scowled at me.

Dat, who was drinking a cup of coffee at the table with my brothers-in-law, said, "I'll go open the shed door for you."

"Denki," I replied.

When we reached the backyard, he took my bag from me. "I'm glad you're coming back tomorrow," he said. "I'm not ready for you to be gone again for good."

I fought back tears as I said, "That's nice to hear." Honestly, it was one of the kindest things either of my parents had ever said to me.

CHAPTER 14

❖

I arrived in Elkhart wearing my cape dress and Kapp. All my roommates were home. Ivy and Bri were watching TV in the living room. The volume was up way too loud. Paige was cooking in the kitchen, with her music turned up high, and Haley sat at the kitchen table with two bongo drums, pounding along to Paige's music.

After I said hello to everyone, I walked to the end of the living room, to the table under the window where my plants were. I'd forgotten to check them on Friday, and it didn't appear anyone had remembered to water them in the week that I'd been gone.

After I changed my clothes, I filled a jar and a spray bottle with water and went to work on my plants, watering the spider plants, Christmas cactus, Chinese evergreen, and tricolor hoya, and then spraying all of the succulents.

"Are you back for good?" Ivy asked as I left the living room.

"Just for the night," I answered without thinking. Had I just decided to return to the farm?

Already drained by all the noise and activity, I grabbed my purse and keys and headed for my car, wanting to get to the garden before the sun set. Perhaps being away from the chaos of the house was helping me get better after all.

When I arrived at the garden, Nadine and Yani were closing the gate behind them.

Yani waved. "Sophie!"

"Hello!" I called out, excited to see them. I started across the lawn, focused on the two of them, when someone behind me said, "Sophie?"

I turned around. Jasper was on the sidewalk.

"You don't have your dress and bonnet on," he said.

"Kapp," I corrected.

"Kapp?"

"Jah." I laughed.

"I'm confused," he said. "You look different every time I see you."

I simply smiled.

Nadine and Yani reached me. "You two know each other?" Nadine asked.

"Jah," Jasper said teasingly.

I laughed.

Nadine shook her head. "I'm confused too."

Yani grabbed her mother's arm and said, "We need to get home. Good to see you, Sophie! And you too, Mr. Jasper!"

Nadine followed Yani down the sidewalk toward their Oldsmobile, glancing over her shoulder a few times, but finally waving.

"Are you out for a walk?" I asked Jasper.

"Yes," he answered. "How about you?"

"I came to check on everything since I've been gone for a while." I gestured toward the garden.

"Could I walk with you?" Jasper asked.

"Sure." I led the way toward the gate and Jasper walked

beside me. "Karin said the sheriff's department refused to release the dash video of Mateo's arrest, but that you're going to petition the decision."

He nodded. "These things, unfortunately, usually take months—and sometimes years."

"What about the Explorer? Any information from her?"

He shook his head. "I've asked to speak with her, but that request hasn't been granted either."

We passed the bed of dahlias. The orange ones had bloomed in full while the lavender ones were fading. Jasper stepped in front of me and opened the gate. Someone had spread fresh straw along the paths.

"Do you garden?" I asked Jasper.

He chuckled. "No."

"How about your parents?"

He shook his head as he smiled. "I grew up in New York City. My mother had a few houseplants, but that was all."

"New York City?" I stopped and stared at him. "What brought you to Elkhart, Indiana?"

"Fate, I suppose." He shrugged and smiled playfully at me again. "What brought you here?"

I laughed. "I grew up twenty minutes down the road, outside of Nappanee. The chances of my ending up in Elkhart were much higher than your ending up in Elkhart."

"Really? Because I dress the same whether I'm in New York City or Elkhart, Indiana—meaning I don't change, culturally, between the two." He grinned. "Whereas you seem to appear different, depending on"—he paused—"I'm not sure what it depends on."

I laughed. "It really just depends on where I get dressed. If it's in my parents' Amish farmhouse, I wear a dress. If I get dressed in my house here, I wear jeans and a T-shirt."

"You said the other day that you grew up Amish?"

"I did."

"I've never known anyone who's Amish. I've seen them around and find the whole living-a-different-culture-in-the-twenty-first-century thing fascinating," Jasper said, "but I've never had a chance to listen to an Amish person's story."

"Well, it's not like you'd ever represent anyone who is Amish. Our citizenship is a given."

"You mean no one new is immigrating here?" he teased.

"It's been at least a hundred fifty years—or more—since any Amish arrived from Europe. A group of Swiss Amish ended up here in Indiana, in Allen and Adams Counties, in the mid-1800s. Maybe some Mennonites from Russia or Ukraine came after that, going to Kansas or Nebraska. That sort of thing."

"Fascinating." Jasper pointed to the row of beans. "I know farming is a preferred way of making a living."

"Jah. Farming has been a part of my family for generations. One of my Dat's sisters has traced our roots back to Switzerland in the 1400s. Some great-great-great-great ancestor farmed on the edge of the Alps way back when."

"Fascinating," he said again. "Obviously at some point they immigrated here."

"Fled," I clarified. "For religious freedom. They were first allowed to go to what is now Germany. And then they continued on to America in the mid-1700s."

"I see," he said. "Part of the Anabaptist movement, right? During the Protestant Reformation?"

"Yes," I answered. "That's right." Not a lot of people who weren't Amish or Mennonite knew the history of the Anabaptists, and it made me wonder what Jasper's background was.

But he didn't offer that information. Instead he said, "So, you come by your interest in plants and gardening genetically?"

"Nature or nurture," I said. "It's always hard to know." I reached down and pulled the first weed I'd seen. Nadine and Yani were doing an amazing job. I couldn't help but think it was because, along with caring about the garden, they cared about me.

I stood, the weed in my hand, unable to resist asking a little bit about him. "How about you? How did you come by your interest in immigration law?"

He hesitated a moment and then answered, "I'm Armenian. My great-grandparents on my father's side fled the genocide in Turkey in 1919. They were part of the diaspora that settled in New York City. The trauma stayed with my family. My grandmother was terrified to have me leave and move so far away from home." He smiled. "She has a deep faith in God, but it is balanced, tenuously, with a deep worry. Or, as my grandfather says, she has a gift for fretting."

I thought about the trauma the Lopez family had with their fleeing from El Salvador, and it gave me a new respect for them—and for Jasper.

"A hundred years ago seems like a long time," he continued. "But in the course of a family, it's not that long. Trauma has a way of hanging around. But faith and redemption also have a way of hanging around. True, my grandmother frets, but she also taught me to pray and to trust. Even though she still worries."

I smiled. I liked that. She hadn't conquered worry, but she did her best to keep praying.

Jasper was silent for a long moment and then stopped walking. "Do you mind if I ask you something?"

I hesitated a moment, wondering what it might be. But his face was so earnest that I went ahead and nodded.

"What made you interested in the Lopez family?" he asked. "Why did you want to help them?"

"Oh, that's easy." I smiled. "Well, first of all, my favorite Bible verse is from Micah, the one that starts with 'He hath shewed thee, O man, what is good.' It goes on to say that the Lord requires us to act justly, love mercy, and walk humbly with God. Then, getting to know Nadine and her family made me realize how vulnerable some people in this world are." *And how vulnerable I had been with Lyle.*

"Anyway, just like the Awad family, the Lopez family struck me as strong but vulnerable." I met his eyes. "And then it made me think of you."

He smiled.

Feeling a little uncomfortable with the connection I already felt with the man, I bent down to pick another weed. "What made you decide to go into immigration law? Your grand-mother?"

He shook his head. "Growing up, her stories seemed so long ago. I was sure the world had changed. But then September eleventh happened. There were a few kids from Pakistan in my high school, and they were scared. A boy was afraid his family would be deported. A girl stopped wearing her hijab. I thought of my great-grandparents fleeing to New York and finding safety, while these immigrants were in New York and didn't feel safe at all. Suddenly, my grandmother's stories didn't seem so long ago."

I was confused. "So, just like that you decided to go into law? How did you even know you could help immigrants by going into law?"

"Well, I already knew I wanted to be a lawyer."

"Oh."

"My mom is a lawyer—family law."

I smiled. I didn't expect that. "What about your father?"

"He's an elementary school principal," Jasper said. "He had his own ideas for my future—like my being a teacher in our neighborhood school, where he worked."

"Aww, that's sweet." We started walking again. "My neighborhood school had forty students all in one room."

"Through the eighth grade, right?"

I nodded. He didn't seem condescending about it, though. Just matter of fact.

"Education is more than schooling," Jasper said. "I know people with advanced degrees who aren't very educated, and others who dropped out of high school and are some of the most well-read people I've ever met."

I doubted that was true, but I found his sentiment endearing.

I veered off toward the right and pointed toward the eggplants. "How did your object lesson in court go?"

He laughed. "You heard me tell Nadine about that? It didn't quite work out the way I hoped. In fact, my apartment got pretty warm over the weekend, and I left the eggplant out on the counter."

A too-ripe eggplant was bitter. A spoiled one was a complete loss.

He shrugged. "It proved my point—just not in court. I wanted something firm but fragile to show the importance of caring for others. But the eggplant turned out to be more fragile than I'd intended, due to my own neglect." He smiled a little. "The object lesson turned out to be entirely my own."

I smiled back at him, touched at his insight.

He met my gaze. "I figured you'd understand. You're empathetic," he said. "You care about other people. You love your neighbor as yourself."

I shook my head. "I wish I did. I want to. I aspire to." In so many ways I was taught to, although it was never modeled to me personally.

Well, that wasn't true. Jane modeled it and now Derek did too. I shrugged. "It's a harder command than it sounds."

He chuckled a little. "Sounds like you're honest too."

I looked to the west, into the dimming evening light. A hint of orange, the same color as the dahlias, spread across the horizon. For a moment I felt at peace, a feeling I hadn't experienced in years. I enjoyed talking with Jasper Benjamin.

My eyes fell to the rosebush I'd planted late one night eighteen months ago, in my baby girl's memory. I kept expecting the groundskeepers to pull it out, since I hadn't asked permission to plant it, but it was still there. They'd pruned it last month, and now it was in bloom—a perfect pink rosebud.

I SLEPT POORLY that night. The light from the streetlamp shining through my window bothered me, along with the laughter from the living room. Then the back door slammed. Then someone took a shower after midnight. At five a.m., I heard Bri getting ready to go to work at the co-op. Usually, she'd be vying for the bathroom with me. Whereas I'd be wide awake and cheerful, having been trained by years of doing early morning chores on the farm, she'd be cranky and bleary-eyed.

But I was no longer the morning person I once was. I was bleary-eyed and cranky too.

I arrived a little early for my appointment with Dr. Jones. I yawned as she entered the room.

"Good to see you, Sophie," she said. "How are you?"

I smiled. "Tired right now but better overall."

"Have you been getting more rest?"

I nodded. "I've been staying on my parents' farm. It's quiet as can be. Plus, my mother has been cooking for me."

"Sounds perfect," Dr. Jones said.

I nodded again, even though it was far from perfect. But that would be hard to explain. Apparently, it was the right environment for my health, although it wasn't ideal for my soul.

"What's going on with work?"

"I plan to take another week off."

"Great. Keep doing what you're doing—getting as much sleep and rest as you can, exercising, eating well, taking the new meds." Her eyes were kind. "Come see me after you've been back at work for a week and we'll evaluate how you're doing then and also do blood work for another kidney check."

"Thank you," I said.

After she left, tears stung my eyes. In just two appointments I felt more cared for by Dr. Jones than I did by my own Mamm.

I headed back to the house to change into my dress and grab my bag. Ivy was in the kitchen, getting ready to fry a couple of eggs, when I arrived.

"Want some?" she asked.

"Sure," I answered. "I'll make toast." I still had a loaf of whole wheat bread in the fridge. And it would give me a chance to have an honest conversation with Ivy.

As I pulled two slices from the bag, I said, "I wanted to apologize about that text that I sent, the one about the dash cam. That was out of line."

"Yeah. . . . It's not like I have anything to do with any of that. And I'm not supposed to talk about cases." She cracked an egg and dumped it into the hot pan. "But I'm sorry about your friend's brother. That's terrible."

"I know, right? It's been pretty intense." I popped the bread into the toaster.

Ivy cracked another egg. "Has the lawyer been able to help?"

"He's hoping the Explorer who was riding along with the officer will give a statement, but that hasn't happened yet. He's also trying to get the dash cam, but he said it can take a while."

"It usually does." She cracked two more eggs into the pan.

"Have you heard anything about a detention center going in around here?"

"Yes, but I think they're just looking into it. Nothing's been decided." She shrugged. "Some people would say only those who have committed crimes will end up in the detention centers, but that doesn't seem to be likely."

Her statement took me by surprise. I'd assumed because Ivy worked at the sheriff's department that she'd be in favor of a detention center in Elkhart County. But maybe that wasn't the case.

I buttered the toast as she slipped the eggs onto two plates. "Do you work today?" I asked.

She shook her head. "I have three off in a row. I'm going shopping with my mom. We haven't had a chance to hang out lately."

"That sounds like fun."

We chatted about nothing in particular over our brunch, and then we each got ready to go on with our day.

After I changed back into my dress, I drove home toward my own Mamm, who clearly didn't like hanging out with me.

Perhaps I'd been a disappointment to Mamm from the beginning. After Joe-Joe died, she changed even more. She was quiet sometimes after that. Other times angry. I avoided her as much as possible.

As I turned down the lane to the farm, a pickup turned the corner into our driveway. A big silver one.

I slowed to a crawl.

Why would Lyle be stopping by the farm? He turned toward

the house, but I kept going to the shed. Dat saw me coming and opened the door for me. By the time I shuffled out of the shed, Lyle was walking across the lawn toward us.

Dat closed the shed doors. "Do you want me to take your bag to the house?"

"*Nee*," I answered, holding it in front of me like a shield.

"David," Lyle said. "How are you?"

Maybe Lyle had come to talk to Dat, and I just happened to come home at the same time. But what did they have to speak about? Was Lyle going to tell my father what a horrible person I was?

Dat walked toward Lyle, and the two began to chat. I managed to take a step and then another. I followed the driveway toward the house, still holding my bag in front of my chest.

When I reached the garden, Lyle called out my name. I kept walking. He yelled a second time. "Sophie, wait!"

Mamm popped her head up from between two rows of squash. She glanced at me and then Lyle and shook her head, as if disgusted with me.

A second later, Lyle was at my side.

I kept walking.

"We need to talk," he said. "In private."

I ignored him.

He whispered, "I need us to get a couple of things straight."

I still didn't answer him. When I reached the house, he dashed up the back steps and planted his body in front of the door. Facing me, he said, "I need to know what happened."

"With what?"

He cleared his throat. "The baby."

I walked backward down the stairs, then sprinted around the side of the house toward the front door.

"Sophie!"

For claiming the baby wasn't his, he seemed awfully worried about it. Most likely, he didn't want someone who shared his DNA finding him someday.

Well, that would never happen. I wouldn't give him the satisfaction of knowing the truth, not when he'd treated me the way he had. Not when he continued to treat me—and others—badly.

I dashed through the front door as he reached the porch. I locked it behind me and then raced through the house to the back door and locked it too—just in time. He was standing at the bottom of the stairs.

I stepped to the window, which was open a foot.

"Sophie!" he yelled. "You need to tell me!"

No matter what I told Lyle about the baby he wouldn't believe me. He especially wouldn't believe the truth—that I'd miscarried.

And he wouldn't believe that I hadn't told anyone at the time, not even my parents.

Dat was walking toward the house from the barn. For a moment I considered going out and talking to Lyle, just so he wouldn't worry Dat.

But then Mamm started toward the house from the garden. Her eyes locked on mine for a long moment as I stood at the window. Then she shifted her gaze to Lyle.

He turned toward her. "You know how she can be."

I expected Mamm to commiserate with him, but instead she said, "Go home, Lyle. It's obvious that she doesn't want to talk to you."

Surprised, I took a step backward, although I could still see all of them.

Lyle didn't move.

Dat reached Mamm and said to Lyle, "Do as Catherine instructed."

Something seemed to have changed in Mamm. Was it something in Lyle's tone? Or how fast he ran to try to get in the house?

Maybe I'd never know, because true to how we always dealt with things, we wouldn't talk about it. As soon as Lyle drove away, she headed back out to her garden.

AROUND MIDNIGHT, after Mamm and Dat were in bed, I heard a vehicle. I had fallen asleep after ten, but then woke up around eleven thirty, my mind going over and over the interaction with Lyle.

I tiptoed to the landing window. Lyle had stopped his big truck in front of the house. I held my breath. I didn't want him to wake Mamm and Dat, to involve them in his drama any more than he already had.

I held my breath as I peeked around the plain white curtain. He revved his engine and then put the truck in Park and climbed out. "Sophie!" he yelled. "You need to talk to me!"

I stepped away from the curtain, hoping the headlights from his truck wouldn't illuminate my silhouette in the upstairs window.

"Sophie!" he yelled again. Then he turned toward his truck and hit the hood—hard—with his open palm.

It had to have stung his hand. I wasn't sure if it would dent the truck or not, but it seemed like a stupid thing to do. Maybe he realized that because he climbed back into the driver's seat and drove away, his tires spinning out as he did. I held my breath as his taillights bounced down the lane and then finally disappeared.

As I turned around to go back to my room, Mamm startled

me. She stood outside her bedroom door with one hand on the landing rail and the other clutching a flashlight. "Who was that?" she whispered.

Their door squeaked open, and Dat's face appeared. "What's going on?"

I wished I could lie to them, but I couldn't. "It was Lyle."

"Oh." Mamm gave Dat a look.

Dat said, "Is he gone?"

I nodded.

"Are you all right?" Dat asked.

I nodded again.

Dat stepped back into the bedroom.

"I'm sorry," I said to Mamm.

She just shook her head and stepped back into their room too.

I continued on to mine, but it was at least an hour before I fell back asleep.

The next morning at breakfast, Mamm asked me if I wanted to go to the quilting circle with her. I was tired and almost said no, but then I thought of her driving past Mill Creek Farms. What if Lyle saw our buggy and thought I was in it? Would he follow Mamm and harass her? Or try to get information from her?

Both of Lyle's tantrums yesterday reminded me of the times he grew angry with me when we were dating. There was no stopping him once he started obsessing about something.

"Jah," I said, "I'd like that."

As I did the breakfast dishes, Mamm went upstairs to change her apron. The back door cracked open and Dat came in with something in his hand. As he approached me, I realized it was my phone.

"Put this in your apron pocket," he whispered. He didn't

say anything else, but I knew he was implying, *Don't tell your Mamm.*

I tried not to be obvious about glancing over at Mill Creek Farms when we passed. Mamm didn't though. She stared out the passenger window the entire time.

No doubt she'd mourned when I'd broken up with Lyle. She'd had such high hopes that he and I would join the church and marry. I'd often felt she held Lyle in higher esteem than she did me. She believed he was the good influence, that he would rescue me. My wild ways would be tamed and I would settle down and have a family. Her work as a mother would be done, successfully.

I knew she hadn't forgiven me for ruining her success, for failing her. I doubted she ever would.

But maybe, just maybe, Lyle's behavior yesterday gave her a glimpse of him that she hadn't expected. By the way she dismissed him, maybe she was seeing that there was a different side to him.

I shivered, even in the heat. He bullied me yesterday the same way he bullied me three years ago. The same way he tried to bully Karin at church.

I didn't have a voice back then, and I didn't seem to have one now either. If I couldn't even speak my own truth, how could I support Karin and her family in their truths?

I stole a glance at Mamm. No. I couldn't tell her about the hardest thing I'd ever gone through.

When Mamm and I turned into the parking lot of Plain Patterns, I saw the little roadside stand was filled with vegetables and flowers. I guessed Miriam had done it.

As we reached the shop, I told Mamm I would unhitch the horse and then work in the garden while she and the other women quilted. But when I went inside to say hello to Jane, she said I didn't need to weed.

"Derek was here yesterday evening. He and Miriam worked for hours," she said. "It's completely done. And they stocked the produce stand. Doesn't it look nice?"

I nodded. That was great Derek and Miriam did all that work, but I couldn't help but note he hadn't called me to join them. Was he avoiding me, just as I feared he would now that he knew the truth about Lyle and me?

"Join us, won't you?" Jane asked, shaking me out of my morose thoughts. "I'll tell more of Mary's story."

"That would be great," I said, taking a seat beside Mamm. Jane sat down too. "Where were we?"

"Chicago was on fire and Mary was fleeing with Lemuel, Honora, and Colum."

"That's right," Jane said. "Mary had just filled the two buckets in the river, right?"

CHAPTER 15

◆

Mary

When Mary returned to the wagon after filling the buckets with water and soaking her cloak, it had moved only a few feet. She draped the cloak over Colum. "If you see sparks coming, duck your face under the cloak too," she told him.

Slowly, the wagon inched over the bridge. When a spark landed on the side of the wagon, Mary filled her hands with water and quickly put it out.

She kept the cloth over her mouth and nose, but still the smoke seeped through. The fire smelled of filth and oil and debris, not like a woodfire or slash fire back home. The wind gusted, and a storm of ash swirled all around. Burned fragments of homes and businesses. And worse. She shuddered.

Another fire engine slowly came across the bridge from the other direction, fighting against the mass of people. When sparks landed on the bridge, the firefighter put the fire out quickly with water from the hose. But as more sparks rained down, Mary doubted the bridge would last long.

A spark landed on Lemuel's hat. Mary snatched it, dunked it in the bucket, and then put the soaking wet mess back on his head. He chuckled. "You may have saved my life."

As they continued on, another boat caught fire in the river, illuminating people who were attempting to swim across. Mary leaned forward, as if she could reach out to them, and then pleaded quietly, "Lord, please help."

They'd reached the halfway point of the bridge when the wind picked up again and a commotion behind them turned Mary back around. A building had caught fire across the street from the west end of the bridge. Someone screamed. A horse bucked. Hot embers fell down like red snow, causing fire after fire to explode as the sparks hit dry wood. Mary gasped as she forced herself to turn away from what seemed to be a vision from hell.

Ahead, traffic slowed to a stop, but then it lurched forward. Finally, they were making progress. More sparks rained down. "Pull the cloak up," Mary ordered Colum.

People on foot began to shove those in front of them. A child fell, but the man beside him jerked him up. The pace increased. They were soon three-quarters of the way across the bridge. The end was in sight, but more sparks were falling on them. Mary swatted at one on her sleeve. When she removed her hand, there was a hole in her dress and her palm stung. Another spark landed on her Kapp, and she swatted it out too as the smell of burnt hair reached her nose. She shuddered.

Colum, his head still covered by the cloak, must have given in to exhaustion because he had collapsed in a heap, with only one foot sticking out. Mary pulled the cloak over the top of it. The fabric was still wet.

By the time they neared the end of the bridge, two more boats had caught on fire. Mary was relieved Colum had fallen asleep and wasn't hearing the screams coming out of the water. Each time someone fell into the river, she had the urge to jump out of the wagon and off the bridge into the water. It was a useless urge. She didn't even know how to swim.

Dear God, she prayed, *please save us, save us all.*

A man yelled to a woman, "Keep going, all the way to the lake. We won't be safe until we reach it."

Mary glanced to the west again. The flames were continuing to rage forward. Then she turned back toward the east. Would they not stop until they reached Lake Michigan?

Finally, the wagon rolled off the end of the bridge and onto the street. Mary had lost track of time, but she guessed it had taken them an hour and a half to get over the bridge. Honora told Lemuel to turn right.

"Shouldn't I go straight and then south to get to the train station?" Lemuel asked.

"I need to check on my oldest son, Patrick. He works at a stockyard west of the station, near here. Besides, it will get us away from the crowd."

"Oh." Lemuel glanced over his shoulder at Mary.

She shrugged, not sure what they should do. Dat was ill, and they needed to take the first train possible. He wouldn't go without them; even if he did, he couldn't get home from Elkhart without her.

But she hated to think of Patrick alone in the city, trying to find his mother and brother. Although Mary guessed finding the boy would be like finding a needle in a haystack.

Once they were back on the woodblock street, Lemuel turned right. "Let's try to find Patrick," he said. "If he isn't there, we'll head straight back to the train station."

"Thank you," Honora said.

The others in the back of the wagon gathered up their things and jumped down once it became clear Lemuel was headed to a stockyard. The traffic wasn't as bad on the east side of the river, but it was still thick and slow. The smell of the Yards mixed in with the pungent smoke, and Mary could smell it long before they reached the feedlots.

When they reached the one where Patrick worked, Honora jumped down from the wagon, yelling for her son. "Patrick! Patrick Sullivan!"

"He left," a man called back. "A couple of hours ago."

Hopefully he wasn't trying to cross the river back to their shanty. He had to be sick with worry about his mother and little brother.

Honora rushed back to the wagon.

"Come on," Lemuel said. "Let's get to the train station."

Honora directed Lemuel to head east again. Smoke filled the air, and when Mary turned to the west, she could still see the flames leaping from building to building and hear one explosion after another. But they'd put enough distance between them and the fire that sparks were no longer raining down. She touched her cloak, which still covered Colum. The heat from the fire had dried it.

As they turned onto the street for the train station, they merged into a surge of people. Some were in carts loaded with furniture, but most were on foot, carrying bundles of belongings.

Just as they reached the train station, someone yelled that the fire had jumped the river. Throngs of people crowded into the depot and around it. The clock on the train station read 11:50. Mary feared they'd never find Dat, but then Kit climbed up in the middle of his wagon and began waving his arms. Soot covered his hands and face.

Lemuel managed to drive the horses through the crowd. When they reached Kit, Mary jumped down. Dat was lying down on the bench, and Ellen was asleep in the back.

"You can get on this next train," Kit said. "Ellen is going with you."

Mary turned toward Honora. "Come with us."

She shook her head. "I can't leave Patrick." She looked up at Kit. "How will you get both of your wagons back to the stable?"

"I'll hire someone."

For the first time, Mary thought of Russ Keller. Had Dat gotten the payment? Did Kit have the money to hire someone to drive his other wagon?

"I'll do it," Honora said.

Kit stared at her.

"I'll drive the wagon wherever you need to go," Honora said. "I have experience with horses. My husband was a driver." She turned toward Mary. "But I want you to take Colum with you."

MARY QUICKLY TOLD Honora everything she thought she needed to know. "We live on a farm in Elkhart County, Indiana, in Union Township, on Mill Creek. Dat has a flour mill. Judah and Emma Landis are my parents. You can only take the train to Elkhart, then you'll have to get a ride from there. Ask a family for a ride, someone who's headed south. Come as soon as you find Patrick."

"I will," she said.

"Kit, will you help her?" Mary asked.

He nodded. "As much as I can."

Mary gathered up Colum, jumped down from the wagon, and handed the boy to Lemuel. Then she grabbed her bag and the basket from under the bench of the wagon and joined Dat and Ellen on the sidewalk. She glanced from Dat to Ellen to Lemuel and then down to Colum. All of them were covered with soot and had burns in their clothes.

Honora gave them a wave and then followed Kit. Mary watched for a moment as the two wagons moved slowly through the crowd. What would they have done without Kit?

Dat handed Lemuel and Mary each a ticket. Ellen already held hers in her hand. It seemed she'd purchased her own. "I have my earnings from last month," she said, holding up the pouch she'd grabbed from her bureau drawer.

"I think, with all of this chaos going on, they'll let you hold the boy," Dat said to Lemuel. He was right. No one asked to see Colum's ticket as Lemuel carried him.

Once they boarded the train, Lemuel handed Colum back to Mary, and Ellen closed her eyes as soon as she sat down. Dat put his head back on the seat and soon closed his eyes too.

"Do you feel okay?" Mary asked him.

He nodded.

"Did you get the money from Russ Keller?"

He shook his head. Russ Keller had swindled him. "I gave Kit what I had left, after I bought the train tickets, to feed his teams," Dat said. "I'll come back and get what Russ owes me . . . someday."

Dat couldn't come back. The city was burning. And who knew where Russ Keller would even end up. Had the hotel burned? Had the man's house? Would Russ Keller and his family survive? Mary shuddered.

"Dat?" she whispered.

He held up his good arm to stop her, seemingly too exhausted—or too sick—to talk anymore.

Mary turned her head toward the east, toward Lake Michigan, and then toward the northwest, looking at the flames coming toward the train tracks. More people, with the eerie light of the fire behind them, rushed toward the station. The whistle blew and the acrid smell of coal smoke replaced the smell of the fire. Then the train lurched forward. Mary turned her head the other way, toward the lake again. There were a few lights in the distance, but otherwise it was pitch-black.

She thought of how peaceful it had been to wade in the water the day before. It felt as if it had been a lifetime ago.

With the weight of Colum against her, Mary slumped back against the seat. "What's going to happen?" she asked Lemuel.

"We'll get him back to his mother."

"Jah, Colum will be fine. But could we have done more?"

Lemuel shook his head sadly. "If the best fire department in the country couldn't put out the fire, what chance would we have?"

"Maybe we could have gotten more people to safety."

"We got ourselves out of Chicago, plus Ellen and Colum. And Honora and Kit are safe too. I think that's pretty remarkable, considering."

Mary looked toward the lake again, closed her eyes, and fought back tears, thinking of all the different kinds of people she had seen during the trip. What would happen to the orphans and widows? To the laborers? To the immigrants?

THEY REACHED ELKHART early the next morning. Dat had slept the entire way. Lemuel took Colum from Mary and then followed Ellen off the train, while Mary struggled to wake Dat. "We're in Elkhart," she said, shaking his shoulders. "We need to get off the train."

Dat opened his eyes and blinked several times. Mary took a look at his forehead now that she was close to him. The bandage had fallen off on the train, and his wound looked inflamed. He was covered with soot and grime and dirt. The stench of singed hair hung around them both.

She slung her bag over her shoulder, grabbed the basket, and then helped him stand. As they shuffled down the aisle, he leaned against her.

"What should we do?" she asked. "Stay here for a bit, or start for home?"

"Let's start for home," Dat said. "If you and Lemuel feel up to it."

Relieved at his answer, Mary said, "We do." She wanted to get him home to Mamm as soon as possible.

As they walked through the depot, a man wearing a cap and carrying a notebook and pencil stepped in front of them. "I'm with the *Elkhart Democrat Union* newspaper. Are you coming from Chicago?"

Mary nodded.

"You escaped the fire?"

She nodded again.

"What was it like?"

"Like a blazing furnace," Mary answered.

"Where do you live?"

"Union Township."

"What's your name?"

Mary just gave him another nod and kept walking with Dat. She didn't want to be quoted in the paper. That would be prideful. Thankfully, a man from Chicago was behind them, and the reporter asked him about the fire. He was eager to talk.

A baggage handler held the door for them, saying, "Looks as if you survived one of those fires. They're all over tonight. Wisconsin has a big one. And Michigan. This dry-as-bones drought has gotten the best of us."

Mary winced, sad to hear there were other fires too. That there were more people who were scared and homeless, some who had lost family and all that they had.

Dat leaned on her all the way to the stable. He'd prepaid for the horses for one night but still owed for the additional two. Mary wasn't sure what they would do, but Lemuel quickly stepped forward and paid the balance.

"Denki," Dat said quietly. "I'll pay you back once we get home."

Once they had the horses hitched to the wagons, Mary settled Colum down in the back of hers and spread her cloak over the top of him. Ellen said she would ride with Lemuel to keep him awake.

Once Dat was settled on the bench of the wagon, Mary treated his wound with the carbolic acid. Puss oozed onto the cloth as she dabbed at it. "How does your arm feel?"

He shrugged, but she could tell by the tense expression on his face that he was in pain. She told him to relax in the bed of the wagon, hoping he'd go back to sleep.

He refused. "I'll keep you company."

Mary and Lemuel lit the wagon lanterns, and then Lemuel led the way. The horses, who didn't seem to appreciate being woken up, plodded along. Mary's eyes grew heavier and heavier until finally Dat asked, "Would you like me to take the reins?"

"No," Mary quickly responded. "I'm fine."

The light from the lantern flickered over the road and bounced on the back of Lemuel's wagon. The light was so different from that of the fire. It was warm and welcoming. Not like the raging hell they'd escaped.

Mary shuddered, wondering how far the fire had burned. Hopefully it was out by now, but she wasn't sure that would happen without rain.

Ahead, it appeared Lemuel and Ellen were talking, or at least Ellen was. Lemuel nodded every now and then.

The sun started to come up on her left. As they neared home,

Mary grew restless. The road followed alongside Mill Creek now. Overcome with exhaustion, she shifted her weight in the seat.

"Where are we?" Colum asked, startling her. It was the first time he'd spoken since they left Chicago.

"Almost to our farm," Mary answered.

"How will Ma find us?"

"I told her where we live. And we know where to find her in Chicago." At least Mary hoped they did. "It might be a while until you're back with her, but you will be."

He frowned but then said, "Look at all of those cows." Mary smiled. There were only seven.

When they reached the Landis farm and turned along the Feld, Colum gasped. "More cows!" He quickly counted fifteen. "That's a lot of milk."

"It is," Mary said. "We'll have a cup when we get home."

Lemuel stopped the wagon he was driving in front of the house and Ellen jumped down. Then Lemuel headed toward the barn.

Mary stopped too and called out, "Mamm! Sarah! We're home!"

"Stay here," she said to Colum. Mary helped Dat down from the bench as the front door of the house swung open and Mamm came running down the steps, drying her hands on her apron.

"What took you so—?" But then she stopped in her tracks and gasped. Mary was surprised at Mamm's reaction to Colum and Ellen.

But when she followed Mamm's gaze, she saw it was the sight of Dat that'd stopped her.

He was as white as a sheet. His hand suddenly went limp on her arm as he slumped to the ground.

CHAPTER 16

◆

While Mamm attended to Dat, Mary scrubbed her hands, arms, and face as best she could and changed into a housedress. She gathered clothes for Colum and Ellen, and then filled a tub with water for everyone to take turns washing.

By the time Lemuel came in from the barn, Sarah had a breakfast of hotcakes ready, and Mary and Ellen had Colum bathed and dressed in Vyt's old clothes.

Mamm took Dat's breakfast to him in their room, while the others sat at the table. Her brother Steffen seemed to be doing better, and Hanna was more settled, although a little alarmed at the two extra faces around the table.

"How long are they staying?" she asked Mary quietly as they poured glasses of milk.

"We don't know," Mary answered.

In overlapping bursts, Mary, Lemuel, Ellen, and Colum told them what happened in Chicago. It sounded bizarre, like the most imaginative story ever. Mary wasn't sure if Steffen completely believed them, but he would soon read about it in the newspaper.

When Mary took a good look at Lemuel, she couldn't help but laugh. He'd washed his hands and face, but his hair was covered in soot and his neck was creased with it.

"You look as if you've been shoveling hot coals," she said when he turned toward her.

He smiled.

Mary laughed again, this time more out of relief and exhaustion.

They had survived. They were home. Everything was going to be okay.

She hoped.

When Lemuel had finished eating, Mary walked him out the back door. "Denki," she said. "You've done so much for us." She gestured back to the house. "For all of us."

He nodded. "I'm just happy God saw fit to use me."

"Me too," Mary said. "I mean that He saw fit to use me too."

"I'll come back this afternoon to help with the chores."

"See you then," Mary said.

But as Lemuel turned to leave, Mamm came out with the money Dat owed him. "Judah wanted me to thank you," she said. "He doesn't know what he would have done without you."

After Lemuel left, Mamm pulled Mary aside. "Where is Colum's mother?"

"Back in Chicago, looking for her oldest son," Mary answered.

"Why did you bring him here? What if you can't get him back to her? Or, God forbid, what if something happens to her?"

"We'll figure that out, if it's the case," Mary said. "But it wasn't safe for him to stay there with her."

"Children belong with their mothers."

"Mamm, you have no idea what life is like in Chicago. Honora, his mother, works in the kitchen of a hotel. Her twelve-year-old son works at a slaughterhouse. Colum was on his own during the day—before the fire. I don't even know if they have a home anymore."

Mamm winced.

"Honora came from Ireland with her family as a child. Her husband was killed in a wagon accident, and she has no one to help her." Mary pursed her lips together. "Immigrants aren't treated well in Chicago, at least not poor ones."

Mamm sighed. "I'm worried about the boy is all. I don't think anyone will think you kidnapped him, but it all appears a little unbelievable."

Mary laughed softly, the images she'd seen burned in her mind forever. "It's not, Mamm. I promise. I mean, it does feel unbelievable now that we are back here, but it was very real. And don't worry about Colum. Either his mother will come get him, or we'll take him back."

Mamm smiled sadly. "I hope that's what happens, I really do." She paused a moment and then said, "What about Ellen?"

"She's cousins with Kit, who owns the wagons we used. We stayed at her boardinghouse. She barely escaped with her life."

Mamm shook her head. "What a tragedy."

Mary nodded. "I could have never imagined any of it."

After she finally got her turn at the bath, Mary put her house-dress back on and then collapsed on top of her bed.

When she awoke, she heard a voice in the hallway, outside of her open door. Colum. She rolled off the bed and shuffled to the hall.

He looked as if he'd been crying.

"What's wrong?" Mary asked, wrapping her arms around him.

"I had a nightmare."

Mary patted his head. "No wonder."

"And I'm hungry," he said.

"It smells as if Sarah has a ham cooking. I bet she has mashed potatoes too. Let's go wash our hands and see if we can set the table."

A half hour later, they were all sitting around the table again, except for Ellen, who was still sleeping. Sarah appeared exhausted. Mary knew she'd been doing chores and cooking, along with starting the laundry that morning.

As they ate, Mamm walked into the kitchen with an empty mug in her hand.

"How is Dat doing?" Mary asked.

"He's running a fever."

"I'm sorry," Mary said. "I tried to take care of him. . . ."

"You did." Mamm turned to face her. "His wound is infected, jah, but I'm afraid he caught something in Chicago."

Mary thought of the raw sewage in the streets and the poisonous smoke of the fire. Dat needed to get well so he could go get his money from Russ Keller. And, more than anything, Mary wanted to go with him.

Besides reuniting Colum with Honora and Patrick, she longed to see the city again. It was dirty and crowded and now ravaged by fire. But there was something about the place that appealed to her. As much as she loved farming, there was an energy in Chicago that enticed her. And a desperation in the people that called for her help.

MARY CLEANED UP after dinner and then weeded in the garden so Sarah could work on the quilt she was making. It was a skill she'd learned from one of their neighbors, whose family had recently emigrated from England. Sarah cut squares from the scraps of the shirts and dresses she made for family members and then sewed them together into a topper. When she was done, she quilted it to a large piece of fabric, with batting in between. It made a warm and appealing bedcovering. Sarah was one of the first in their community to learn how to quilt and had been teaching others.

The weather had grown significantly cooler than it had been, and there were clouds on the horizon to the west. Vyt and Colum helped Mary weed. After a while, Ellen came and helped in the garden too. When it was time to do the milking, Ellen supervised the children while Mary and Michael went to the barn.

Lemuel appeared right on time. He was cleaned up and seemed to be rested, at least partially so.

As they fed and milked the cows, Lemuel asked Mary if it all seemed like a dream.

"Jah." Her heart raced. "I can't stop thinking about all of those people fleeing the fire. Did they make it to the lake? Did they survive?"

Lemuel exhaled. "When I closed my eyes to sleep this morning, all I could see was the city on fire and the people running for their lives."

Mary nodded. She couldn't shake the images either.

"I can't help but wonder how many people died," he said, "and what's going to happen to the ones who survived."

After they finished the milking, Lemuel headed home, while Mary and Michael started toward the house. As they did, Mary's sister Olive and her husband, Abel, arrived in their buggy. Abel helped Olive down and then climbed back into the buggy and continued toward the barn.

Mary waved at her sister.

"Thank God you're back," Olive said loudly. She held up a newspaper in her hand. "There was a horrible fire in Chicago that, as of this morning, was still burning. It must have started after you left."

"Nee," Michael yelled back. "They barely escaped with their lives!"

Olive clutched the paper to her chest, her face pale.

Mary hurried toward her sister and lay a comforting hand on her shoulder. "What does the article say?"

Olive held up the paper. "By Monday morning, large parts of Chicago had already burned to the ground. Some reported walls of fire one hundred feet high."

Mary put her hands to her face.

"Wooden buildings turned into piles of ash," Olive said. "Brick buildings turned into ruins. The fire is still raging, and it's feared that hundreds have already perished." She flipped the page. "And there was a fire in Peshtigo, Wisconsin. Nearly the whole town perished. Over a thousand people."

Mary gasped.

"And there were fires in Michigan—in Holland, Port Huron, and Manistee," Olive said. "Hundreds of people were killed in those places as well." She folded the paper. "Fire crews from Milwaukee, Indianapolis, Detroit, and Cincinnati all traveled to Chicago, but the pumping station was damaged, and there's no water to fight the fire."

Mary felt as if she might be ill. How long would it take for the fire to burn out?

Olive met Mary's gaze. "I'm so relieved you're all safe."

Mary sighed. "Dat's ill."

"Mamm said he broke his arm and hurt his head."

"That was before we left. But now Mamm thinks he fell ill in Chicago. He's feverish."

"Oh dear," Olive said. "I hope the money he earned was worth going."

Mary wasn't about to tell Olive that Dat hadn't earned a cent from the trip—yet. Instead, she said, "There are so many people who don't have anything now. We need to help them."

"What can we do?" Olive said. "We're a hundred miles away. Surely there are people closer who can help."

Mary didn't say anything more. Except for Lemuel, no one else seemed to understand.

As they walked toward the house, the clouds on the western horizon grew darker. Were they finally going to get some rain? And Chicago too?

Soon after supper, just after Olive and Abel left, the rain started. It came down hard, and Mary and the children ran outside and lifted their faces toward the sky, opening their mouths to the gift from heaven. It kept falling long into the night. Mary prayed it was raining in Chicago too.

The next morning, Dat was delirious from his fever. Then, late in the afternoon, after the chores were done, Olive came by with the latest newspaper. "The fire nearly burned out from last night's rain. They extinguished the rest of the flames this morning," she said. "Guess how it started?"

Mary shrugged. "I have no idea."

"An Irish woman's cow kicked over a lantern in her barn." Olive glanced down at the paper. "A Mrs. O'Leary, an Irish immigrant. On DeKoven Street."

"That's close to where Ellen's house was."

Olive had a look of disgust on her face. "Maybe she knows Mrs. O'Leary."

Mary didn't respond, but she found it notable that the fire was being blamed on an Irish woman. On an immigrant.

Olive opened the paper again. "Like I said yesterday, hundreds have died. Now they're saying that over fifteen thousand buildings have burned."

"I wonder how many are homeless," Mary said.

"Practically the whole city, I'd guess."

Mary felt overwhelmed by just the thought of it.

ELLEN KNEW the name *O'Leary*. "They live two blocks down from me," she said. "They have—or had—several cows and sold milk. Their house was a lot like mine, wooden with a barn in back. I think they rented out the front part of the house to another family. They had a fairly good reputation for an Irish family."

Mary winced at the compliment embedded in an insult. "Olive read that a cow kicked over a lantern in the barn and that's how the fire started."

"Well, Mrs. O'Leary and her kind might not be the brightest . . ."

Mary winced again.

Ellen didn't notice. "But she certainly seemed sensible enough. I truly doubt she'd leave a lantern burning in the barn." Ellen frowned. "And she wouldn't have been up that late. People with cows go to bed early and get up long before dawn."

Mary knew exactly what she was talking about. Ellen, who didn't have any cows to milk, was sound asleep that night by nine because she had to get up early to start breakfast for her boarders.

Ellen exhaled. "Anyway, she wouldn't have left a lantern in the barn. She likely wouldn't have taken one in at all. The whole city has been on edge for months because of the drought and the fires. All of us were careful with lanterns, lamps, and candles."

Mary remembered how adamant Ellen had been with her boarders about not leaving anything lit.

On Wednesday morning, Mary took over care for Dat. Mamm had been called to a birth, and Mary promised she would send for her if anything happened.

Mary couldn't believe this could be the end for Dat. He'd always been so resilient. For her entire life, it seemed there was nothing he couldn't do. Mary sat by the head of the bed and mopped his forehead with a cloth.

She thought of Russ Keller and the money he owed their family. If Dat couldn't return to Chicago, she would. Perhaps the man couldn't pay. If so, that would be the Lord's will for her family. But if he could pay, he should.

Dat's eyes fluttered. Then his eyes opened and he croaked, "Mary."

"Dat," Mary said, relieved.

"You should be doing the milking."

She couldn't help but laugh. That was her Dat all right.

His gaze landed on her. "We need to go back to Chicago."

She nodded. "I agree, Dat."

"And take wagons of food and flour and bedding . . . help them while they rebuild. We need to go as soon as we can."

Relief rushed through Mary. He was thinking the same thing she was.

Dat threw off the bedcoverings.

"Not just yet, Dat." Mary tossed the bedcoverings back over him. "You've got to get better first."

The exertion must have slowed him because he didn't protest. Instead he looked at Mary and said, "I'll be well enough to go soon." He closed his eyes and soon fell back to sleep.

Mary was thankful that her Dat was going to be fine—and that he was wanting to help the people of Chicago as much as she did. Her head spun with plans and ideas until Mamm came back from the birth and relieved her.

Mary slipped out of the bedroom and headed out to the barn to finish shoveling the manure from the morning milking. Soon, Michael and Vyt joined her, and then an hour later, they were called in for dinner. Neither Mamm nor Dat came to the table.

Sarah seemed spent after serving everyone, so Mary sent her to the living room to quilt while she and Ellen did the dishes. Steffen, with Hanna's help, limped out to the Felda to take a look at what all needed to be done. Mary braced herself for his criticism when he came back inside, but instead he complimented her. "You and Lemuel have been doing a good job," he said. "Hopefully I'll be able to help with planting the winter wheat."

She hoped so too. Mostly, she hoped she and Lemuel could get to Chicago and back before it was time to seed.

That afternoon, it was too wet to finish the plowing she'd started the week before, so Mary worked in the garden. Colum and Ellen joined her.

Ellen seemed to enjoy being on the farm and the activity with Mary, Sarah, Hanna, and the boys. Ellen was a hard worker and knew what needed to be done. She was maternal and kind to Colum. Still, Mary sensed Ellen was feeling the loss of her home.

But as they worked in the garden, Ellen surprised her by saying, "I'm so thankful I'm not in Chicago. It wouldn't be a good place for me right now."

Late that afternoon, as they did the milking, she told Lemuel what Dat had said.

"He's right," Lemuel said. "We have to go back."

"I'm sure Mamm won't want him to."

"Then we'll go. We need to find Kit and Honora anyway. If we're going, why not take supplies?"

"Dat mentioned flour and food. Maybe Sarah would like

to send the quilt she's finishing up, and I think we have a few extra blankets we can spare. Hopefully Mamm would send medical supplies. But do you think others in the community would donate additional supplies for us to take?"

"Maybe," Lemuel said, "but they would have to care enough about the people of Chicago to give. Do you think they will?"

Mary shrugged. "I'm not sure, but we have to try."

Someone needed to help the immigrants and the poor, the widows and orphans. Who better than Amish farmers in Indiana?

CHAPTER 17

·◆·

Sophie

The next morning as I washed the dishes, I thought about Mary's hope that her community would contribute to the victims of the Chicago Fire. Dat had initially said there was nothing the Plain community could do to help the Lopez family, but I had to wonder if that was true. Without Mateo's income and with the costs of hiring a lawyer, I imagined the family was scrambling to make ends meet.

After the kitchen was clean, I made a blackberry cobbler from the berries I'd picked at Jane's yesterday after the storytelling. I hated making pies—they took too much time. Cobblers and crisps had always been my specialty.

I then spent the rest of the morning helping with the housework. In the afternoon, I rested and read a library book of Mamm's about pest control in organic gardens. Chickens and ducks were one of the best ways to cut down on slugs in the garden. Mamm had chickens who roamed free during the day, which I think certainly helped her with slugs, along with cutworms and beetles. But I seriously doubted the parks department in Elkhart would let us have chickens in the community garden. Essential oils were also mentioned. Hot pepper sprays and garlic concoctions were other ideas.

I'd kept my phone in my apron pocket, just in case Lyle showed up again. When it buzzed, I realized I hadn't turned the vibration off. Thankfully Mamm was outside. I slipped upstairs to my room to read the text.

It was from Karin. *Are you busy? I'm on my way to your house. Is that okay?*

Sure, I quickly texted back. *I'll wait for you on the porch.* I slipped my phone back into my pocket, grabbed my water bottle, and headed back down the stairs. I filled my water bottle in the kitchen and went out to the front porch.

Karin arrived a few minutes later. I started down the steps of the house toward her as she parked her car. As she climbed out, she said, "Can you come over to our place for a little while?"

I glanced toward the garden. Mamm was in between the squash and the tomatoes, staring at us. I didn't speak until I reached Karin. "What's up?"

"Jasper did a TV interview this morning. Hopefully it will be on sometime during the five o'clock news."

"The South Bend station?"

She nodded. "I was on my way home from work and thought I'd text you to tell you to watch it. But then I remembered you don't have a TV, and I wasn't sure if you could stream it on your phone or not."

I was a little surprised she was thinking of me in the midst of all her troubles, but I was touched that she was. "I wouldn't miss it," I said. "Do you have time to meet my mother first?"

"I'd like that," she answered.

We started toward the garden. Mamm shaded her eyes and then made her way to the lawn. Dat must have heard Karin's car because he was on his way from the barn by the time we reached the garden. I waved at him. "Come meet my friend."

When we reached Mamm, I introduced Karin to her. Dat reached us as I finished, and I introduced Karin to him too. Then I said, "I'm going to go with Karin to her folks' place for a little while."

Mamm pursed her lips.

"What is it?"

"Do you think you should be going to Mill Creek Farms?"

I grimaced and then asked Karin, "Do you know if Lyle is around today?"

"I believe he's working over at the other property."

Mamm wrinkled her nose. Was she concerned about me? Or was she concerned about more rumors about me?

"I'll be fine," I said. "I'll be with Karin and her family." For a moment, I wondered if my presence could make more trouble for them, as far as Victor's job. But if Lyle wasn't at the Mill Creek property anyway, he'd never know.

"Don't be late," Dat said.

I wanted to roll my eyes but I didn't. I could be offended that I was twenty-three and they were treating me as if I were fifteen, or I could assume he was concerned about Lyle. "I won't be late," I answered.

"I'll have her back soon," Karin said.

Mamm and Dat both told Karin it was nice to meet her and then we headed toward her car. Once we reached it and climbed inside, she asked, "What was that all about?"

"Lyle showed up here drunk the other night. And yelling."

Karin cringed. "That sounds scary."

"Jah," I said. "It was."

"No wonder your parents are worried."

Were they worried? Or were they more afraid I'd bring more

shame to them? I wasn't sure. I supposed if it was the latter, they'd see it as worry. I saw it more as pride.

WHEN WE REACHED the Lopezes' home, Sebastian came up from the creek. When he saw me, his face fell.

"What's the matter?" Karin asked as she climbed out of the driver's seat.

"I thought Mateo was going to be with you."

She shook her head. "What made you think that?"

"Mama said the TV station was going to talk about him. Why wouldn't the detention center let Mateo come home if the TV people are going to tell everyone what really happened?"

Karin put her arm around him. "Hopefully having the TV station tell Mateo's story will help, but there are no guarantees. And all of this takes time. It's a slow process." She pulled him close. "Go turn on the TV, okay? The news starts in five minutes."

He started up the stairs, his head down.

Once the door closed behind him, she turned to me and said, "I'm worried about him. I think he blames himself."

"Why would he?"

"Because the frosting on the floor of the car was from his cupcake."

I knew kids often blamed themselves for a tragedy in the family. I certainly had when Joe-Joe had died. If only I hadn't gotten mad about him teasing me that morning, perhaps he wouldn't have begged to help Dat in the field. His last words to me were *"Stop being a whiny brat."* He'd grinned and ran off to help Dat.

And then I didn't make Mamm understand she needed to

go call for help immediately, not go to the field. The memory put an ache in my heart. Jah, I felt for Sebastian.

I followed Karin up the steps and into the cabin. The TV was on and blaring loudly.

"Sebastian," she said, "turn it down, please."

The boy sat on the coffee table, staring at the TV. It was as if he hadn't heard her. Karin grabbed the remote and reduced the volume.

"Mama?" she called out. "Sophie and I are here."

"Coming," Rosibel answered from down the hall. She appeared a minute later and greeted me warmly.

"Where's Papa?" Karin asked.

"Working. There's a problem with the pump. He and Derek are working on it. Sophie, can I get you a glass of lemonade?"

I held up my water bottle and said, "I'm fine, thank you."

She turned back to Karin. "There's some good news around here for a change."

"What is it?"

"Hank Barlow is home from the hospital. I'll go up to the house this evening to help, but Papa says he's doing better."

Karin smiled. "That is good news. Have you seen Lyle around at all today?"

"No," Rosibel said. "The first of the soybeans are ready."

"This early?"

Rosibel nodded. "Because of the hot weather. It will be a few weeks until the first fields are ready over here though, at least that's what your papa says."

We settled onto the sofas in the living room as the intro to the five o'clock news played. The first story was about the expectation that the federal government would end DACA, the program that protected undocumented immigrants who came to the United States as children. I held my breath through the segment. Neither Karin nor Rosibel commented on it.

After the segment ended, the news anchor said, "We have a story about one of those Dreamers in our own backyard. Mateo Lopez was arrested outside of Nappanee when he was pulled over by an officer in Elkhart County for not signaling. When the officer searched his car, a crystal-like substance was found, prompting the officer to use a field kit to test the substance for methamphetamines and MDMA. It came back positive. However, Lopez's attorney, Jasper Benjamin, claims the test isn't reliable."

The shot switched to Jasper, standing outside his office, where a reporter wearing a blue dress with cap sleeves said, "Mr. Benjamin, what are your concerns as far as the field test applied to the substance in Mateo Lopez's car?"

Jasper looked at the woman as he spoke. "There's a record of field kit tests registering a false positive. We need the state crime lab to test the material immediately. It will show that the substance isn't meth, but rather frosting that fell from a cupcake." Jasper appeared calm and earnest as he spoke. "This is a case of a Dreamer being profiled and targeted strictly because of his race and then because of his desire to be beyond reproach. The officer claims Mateo didn't signal. Mateo says that he did, and yet the sheriff's department won't release the dash cam in support of its officer. Mateo, in good faith, allowed the officer to search his car, and he also revealed he's a Dreamer when the officer asked about his documentation. Even though Mateo's little brother held a cupcake in his hand that matched the frosting on the floor, the officer insisted on doing a field kit test. Again, Mateo, in good faith, knowing he was innocent, didn't protest."

The news anchor came back on, saying that the officer turned the case over to ICE and Mateo Lopez was being held at a detention center in Michigan. "In an update to this interview conducted earlier today, Mr. Benjamin later informed us that another person who was riding with the officer confirmed Mr. Lopez used his turn signal, which goes against the officer's statement."

Karin jumped to her feet. "What?"

The news anchor ended with, "We'll keep you updated when we have more information on this case. Stay tuned for your seven-day weather forecast, coming up after the break." A commercial came on.

"What does that mean?" Rosibel asked.

I frowned. "That it's the Explorer's word against the officer's." I wasn't nearly as encouraged as Karin seemed to be. I wondered what my roommate Ivy knew about this situation.

Karin's voice was full of hope. "But maybe they'll be more likely to release the dash cam now."

"Maybe . . ." My voice trailed off.

Rosibel sighed and stood. "I like that Jasper Benjamin."

"I do too," Karen agreed.

"I don't," Sebastian said.

"Why not?"

"Because Mateo isn't home yet." Sebastian put his head in his hands. "He's not doing enough." His shoulders began to shake.

"Come here." Rosibel reached for Sebastian and pulled him toward her, over the top of the coffee table. She then pulled him onto her lap, holding him like a baby. She kissed the top of his head and then whispered, "Have faith. We have to trust the Lord, okay?"

Sebastian cried even harder.

AROUND SIX THIRTY, just as Karin was getting ready to take me home, Sebastian pressed his face against the front window.

"What's going on?" he asked.

Afraid Lyle had shown up, I stepped onto the front porch. Coming down the lane toward the village was a TV station van, with a cloud of dust billowing behind it. Through the blur, I could make out a mint-green pickup following it.

The van pulled in beside Karin's car, while the pickup truck parked across the street. Jasper climbed out of the pickup. "Did Karin get my text?"

"I don't think so." I turned back toward the house.

Karin was right behind me. She pulled her phone from her back pocket and read, "Heads-up: A news van is heading toward your house." She looked up. "Yikes. And I missed your three calls too." She stepped back into the cabin. "You go out," she said to me, "while I call Papa and get Mama in the back. Then I'll come out."

Sebastian slipped out the door with me. "You should go back in," I said.

He shook his head.

Jasper was at the bottom of the steps now.

I introduced him to Sebastian.

Jasper extended his hand. "I'm pleased to meet you."

Sebastian crossed his arms.

Jasper pulled his hand back and gave me a puzzled look. I wrinkled my nose and mouthed, *Give him some time.*

A man wearing jeans and a T-shirt stepped around from the back of the van. "Hi." He had on dark glasses and his hair was down to his shoulders. "I'm Dillon Scott, a producer working on the Mateo Lopez story."

"Hello," I said. "I'm Sophie Deiner. A friend of the family."

"Are they around?"

I nodded. "Karin Lopez will be out in a minute."

"And who's this?" Dillon asked, directing his gaze toward Sebastian.

When he didn't answer, I said, "Sebastian Lopez."

"Mateo's little brother?"

I nodded, hoping he wouldn't ask to interview Sebastian.

He didn't. He probably needed parental permission to do that sort of thing.

Instead Dillon turned his gaze toward me. "Could we interview you?"

I looked to Jasper.

He smiled. "If you want to, it might be helpful."

I wasn't sure how it would help, besides giving Karin a few more minutes to get ahold of her father.

I answered Dillon with a nod.

"How long have you known the Lopez family?" he asked.

"Not long. I recently met them through a mutual friend."

"Do you mind sharing your thoughts about Mateo?"

"I've actually never met him," I said. "I'm friends with his sister."

Dillon wrinkled his nose. "Okay," he said. "Do you have an opinion about all of this?"

I nodded. Of course I had an opinion. I'd also watched enough local news back in Elkhart to know that they wanted me to be the "woman on the street" character. I was happy to oblige. I'd always wanted to be on TV, although I never imagined doing so in a cape dress and Kapp.

Another man was setting up a camera, and a woman wearing a blue dress and black flats was standing with her back to the creek. I recognized her as the reporter who had interviewed Jasper earlier.

"Come over here." Dillon motioned toward me and then toward the woman.

I followed him. Jasper trailed after me, but Sebastian stayed on the porch.

Dillon introduced me to the woman, saying I was a friend of the Lopez family, and then said to me, "This is Chelsea Reynolds."

The woman transferred the microphone to her left hand and then reached toward me with her right. I shook her hand.

"Are you Amish?" she asked. "Or Mennonite?"

"I was raised Amish," I answered. "But I haven't joined the church."

"Is that important?"

"Actually it is," I said. "If I'd joined the church, I wouldn't agree to be filmed."

"Okay," she said. "I'll clarify that."

They did a sound check and then Dillon stepped beside the cameraman. "Ready?"

I nodded.

Chelsea turned toward the camera. "I have Sophie Deiner with me. A woman who grew up Amish but hasn't joined the church. She's friends with the Lopez family." She turned toward me. "Sophie, tell me what you think of the situation with Mateo Lopez."

"Well," I said, "as far as his arrest, I believe the Elkhart County Sheriff's Department should release the dash cam from the car immediately, especially in light of the witness recalling that Mateo did signal. As far as Mateo's status as a Dreamer, his parents brought him here from a violent country as a child, hoping for a safe place to raise him. He graduated high school and attended college. He has a job and pays taxes. His situation makes me think of my ancestors, who came to this country in the mid-1700s. They fled violence and also sought a safe place and religious freedom to raise their families. True, the situations aren't identical. But the needs of my people back then were the same as the Lopez family's were twenty-five years ago—a place of safety to build a life. And the contributions Mateo and the other Dreamers make benefit our country, the same as my family."

"Cut." The cameraman took a step back.

I expected that the take wasn't good enough, but Dillon said, "That was great. Thanks." He turned toward the porch, where Karin stood next to Sebastian. "Are you Mateo's sister?"

She nodded.

"Could we ask a few questions?"

"Sure." She put her arm around Sebastian and directed him to walk along with her. He cooperated. I guessed she'd cleared her plan with her parents.

I stepped back to where Jasper was waiting. As Karin stepped by me, she whispered, "Thank you. That was perfect."

Jasper patted my shoulder. "It really was."

The camera started to roll. Karin introduced herself and Sebastian and said, "We were both born in the United States and are citizens." Then she talked about the civil war in El Salvador, the United States's support of the oligarchs and generals, their relatives who disappeared and were murdered, and their parents' dangerous journey to the US with Mateo, who was just a baby. "They had no choice," she said. "It was either be killed or flee." She told about how her parents applied for asylum, which was denied, as it was for ninety-seven percent of the million-plus people who also fled El Salvador during the civil war. "My parents found help through a sanctuary church and eventually found jobs. There was never any reason for them to return to El Salvador—only the threat of death. They've done their best to give back to their new home, to the United States.

And they raised their children to be law-abiding citizens. Mateo did not have meth in—"

Sebastian interrupted her. "It was frosting from my cupcake. I dropped it. Mateo bought me the cupcake at the grocery store when we finished shopping for Mama. I . . ." His voice faltered.

Karin pulled Sebastian close just as someone yelled, "Hey! You don't have permission to be on this property."

At the sound of Lyle's voice, I spun around.

He was walking quickly up the lane. "You need to leave— now!"

CHAPTER 18

◆

Jasper stepped into the lane toward Lyle and said, "Hello, I'm Jasper Benjamin, an attorney from Elkhart."

"I don't care who you are," Lyle snarled. "You and this news crew have no right to be on this farm."

"I'm afraid I do. I'm representing the Lopez family."

As Jasper spoke, Karin slipped behind me and started up the lane after Sebastian, who had taken off when Lyle began yelling.

Lyle stopped inches from Jasper's face, towering over him by at least half a foot. "This isn't the Lopez family's property."

Jasper didn't seem fazed. "This is certainly their home and has been for the last thirteen years."

Lyle took out his cell phone. "I'm calling the sheriff."

"Good idea," Jasper said. "I was just thinking I'd do the same."

Dillon stepped forward and introduced himself to Lyle. Then he said, "And who are you?"

"The foreman of Mill Creek Farms."

"And who is the owner?" Dillon asked, making a note.

"Hank Barlow," Lyle answered. "But he's ill. He can't be disturbed."

Jasper smiled again. "We'll have to wait until an officer arrives."

As Lyle placed the call, I hoped the same officer who'd arrested Mateo wouldn't show up.

I started to walk toward the lane, hoping to see where Karin and Sebastian had gone.

Lyle ended his call and sneered at me. "What are *you* doing here?"

"Hey now." Jasper turned to him with a look of surprise at the malice in Lyle's tone. "What's going on?"

Lyle's eyes narrowed.

"Ignore him." I kept walking as my heart raced. I didn't look back at Lyle. Up ahead, I could see that Karin had nearly reached the shed. A couple of minutes later, she turned off toward the main house. Was she going to get Hank Barlow?

Ahead, a pickup truck was coming toward me. Derek. I waved, hoping to get his attention. Of course I didn't need to. He couldn't miss me. I was in the middle of the lane, wearing a cape dress. As he neared, I could see Victor was in the cab with him.

As Derek slowed the truck, Victor lowered his window. "Is everyone all right?"

I nodded, catching my breath. "Reporters are here, along with Jasper. Lyle showed up, told everyone to leave, and called the sheriff."

Victor's face reddened. "Where's my family?"

"Rosibel is in the cabin. Sebastian ran up this way and Karin followed."

"Climb in," Derek said. "Let's go see what Karin says."

"I don't want to involve Hank," Victor said.

"He would want to be involved," Derek answered.

Victor opened his door and scooted over. I climbed into the

cab, and Derek turned the pickup around. When he turned toward Hank's house, we could see Karin on the front porch. Then the door opened, and she stepped inside.

Derek parked his truck and jumped down. I climbed out and Victor climbed down too and followed Derek. I stayed by the truck.

A couple of minutes later, they all poured out the front door of the house. Hank Barlow went straight to one of two utility terrain vehicles parked beside the porch. He climbed onto it, and Sebastian climbed in on the other side. Then Victor climbed in the other UTV, and Karin joined him.

"Come on," Derek said to me.

I climbed back in his truck.

"What's going on?" I asked.

"I hope Hank's fed up with Lyle," Derek said. "But Hank's so mad, it's hard to tell."

The news crew was still milling around when Derek parked his truck behind Lyle's. By the time I climbed down, Victor had stopped the UTV he was driving by the cabin, and Hank had stopped his UTV about an inch away from Lyle.

Victor and Karin stepped to the side of the cabin.

Rosibel was on the porch. She called to Sebastian, who clearly felt conflicted between wanting to obey her and staying with Hank.

"Go to your mom," Hank said. "Make sure she's okay."

Once Sebastian was out of hearing distance, Hank climbed out of the UTV and poked Lyle in the shoulder. The older man was nearly as tall as the younger.

"Who put you in charge here?" Hank barked. "Do you own this property?" He cursed and then said, "Why would you want the worst for Victor's boy after everything the Lopez family has done for me? For this farm?"

Lyle squared his shoulders. "Mateo's a drug dealer and should be deported."

"Is that what you want? And for Victor and Rosibel to go with him? And then what about Sebastian and Karin?" Hank was practically spitting his words. "What are they going to do?"

Lyle shrugged. "That's not my problem."

"You better bet it is," Hank responded. "You know as well as I do that Mateo didn't have meth in his car."

"No, sir," Lyle said. "I don't know that."

Hank stared him down and then said, "You're a bigger fool than I feared."

I thought of Lyle tripping the boy at school all those years ago and then acting as if the boy had stumbled. Hank saw right through that act.

"Go on. I'll deal with you tomorrow," Hank said to him. He looked around. "Derek!"

He was standing beside me, on the other side of Lyle. "Right here." Derek stepped around Lyle to face Hank.

As he did, Jasper stepped to my side. Lyle bumped into Jasper intentionally on his way to his truck.

Jasper lifted his hand to his shoulder.

"Are you hurt?" I asked.

"No," he whispered. "But that guy's a big dude."

"Derek," Hank said, "you talk to the newspeople. If I try to, I'm bound to lose my cool. Besides, no one wants to watch a sick old man try not to cuss. You tell them how much we appreciate the Lopez family. Say that I have alien labor certification, that I'm the sponsoring employer, and it's only a matter of weeks until Victor and Rosibel get their green cards—and we're working on one for Mateo too."

"Yes, sir," Derek said.

"Dillon," Jasper chimed in, "you can speak to Derek. He works here on the farm."

Hank sighed as he watched the news crew spring into action. "I should have done this years ago."

Did he mean dealing with Lyle or getting green cards for the Lopez family?

Hank turned toward the porch. "Rosibel, would you help me back at the house?"

"Of course."

"Sebastian, how about you come for another ride on the UTV?" Hank added.

The boy nodded and ran down the steps.

Hank turned toward Jasper. "I'll call the sheriff's department and tell them not to bother."

Jasper thanked him.

Rosibel, on her way to Hank, stopped at the bottom of the steps and reached for Victor's hand. He took hers, squeezed it, and let it go.

Sebastian climbed in Hank's UTV, and Jasper and I quickly stepped out of their way as the contraption lurched forward. Rosibel took off after them in the second UTV as Victor slowly walked up the steps and into the house.

Karin joined Jasper and me, while Dillon led Derek to where Chelsea stood, microphone in hand. She asked him his name and a few other questions, and then they started the interview.

"Thank you for coming," Karin said quietly. "I'm sorry that it turned in to such a mess."

"How is Hank?" I asked.

She shook her head. "He's better—well enough to come home. But he's not doing well." Her eyes grew misty.

I wondered if her parents and Mateo could still get their green cards if something happened to Hank, but I didn't ask.

As Derek relayed to Chelsea what Hank had told him to say, I whispered to Jasper, "Do you think all of this news coverage will put pressure on the sheriff's department?"

He shook his head. "I'm guessing they'll sit on it as long as they can."

"So, what's the point of all of this?"

"The truth." Jasper turned his head toward me, conviction shining in his bright eyes. "Hopefully it will be a step toward justice too."

By the time Dillon and Chelsea finished up, Victor had come back outside. Dillon asked if he would say a few words.

Victor shook his head, waved his hand, and started up the lane to the main house.

As the news team packed their van, Karin said she'd give me a ride home. Just as Jasper started to say something, Derek interrupted, "I can take her. It's on my way."

"Thanks." I looked over at Jasper, expecting him to repeat what he had started to say. But he just waved and made his way to his pickup, calling over his shoulder, "See all of you sometime . . ."

Would I see him again? Of course I would—at the community garden or the grocery co-op. But I'd have no other reason than that.

DEREK TURNED ONTO THE ROAD, and right away a silver truck turned and followed us.

"It's Lyle." Derek glanced in the rearview mirror several times.

I looked in the side mirror. I could see the truck, but not his face. When we reached Mamm and Dat's farm, Derek turned and Lyle accelerated, flying past us.

Derek just shook his head in disgust. "He's getting scary."

"Believe me, I know." I filled Derek in on what Lyle had done the night before.

"Wow," Derek said when I'd gone silent. "I'm really sorry he did that. That's so wrong. What can I do to help?"

"Nothing," I answered. "If you brought it up to him, I think it would only make things worse."

Just like how I feared I'd made things worse when I brought up the dash cam with Ivy and now it was going to be all over the news. "Let's not talk about Lyle anymore. Can I get your opinion on something? One of my roommates is a dispatcher at the sheriff's office in Elkhart." I told him about offending her by asking if she knew how to access the dash cam. "But with this news story, I'm wondering if she's heard anything around the office about releasing the dash cam or about the officer who pulled Mateo over or the Explorer who verified Mateo did use his turn signal. I won't ask her directly again, but maybe she'd bring it up if she saw me. Do you think I could get some information from her, in person, and help the case?"

"Or maybe you'll just make things more awkward."

"That's true." I pursed my lips. "But I'd still like to speak with her." As Derek stopped his truck, I asked, "Do you want to go to Elkhart with me? Maybe I could talk with Ivy, and we could get something to eat."

He smiled. "Do you feel up to it? You've had a long day."

"I'm fine." Perhaps I'd been invigorated by all the drama, or maybe I really was feeling better.

"Then sure." He grinned. "You almost sound like your old self. I'm game."

"Great! I'll just run in and change."

Derek nodded toward the porch, where my parents sat. "Should I wait here? Or be polite?"

"Suit yourself." I opened the passenger door.

He opened his too and then followed me up to the porch.

"Hallo," I said. "I'm going to change and go out with Derek."

Mamm shook her head but Dat smiled.

I hurried through the door and up the stairs. The landing window was open, and I could hear their voices below.

"How are things over at Mill Creek Farms?" Dat asked.

"Hank came home from the hospital, so hopefully things will be better. We're getting ready to start the soybean harvest over on the South Farm."

"Seems early."

"Jah," Derek responded. "All that spring rain and then the heat . . ."

Ten minutes later, wearing jeans, a black T-shirt, and sandals, with my phone tucked inside my purse, I stepped back onto the porch. "We won't be very long."

Derek stepped backward. "Nice to see you," he said to Mamm and Dat.

"You too." Dat's voice was kind.

Mamm didn't say anything.

When we reached his truck, Derek said, "Do you mind if we stop by my place? I can shower in five minutes, promise."

"Sure," I said. "Where are you living?"

"With my folks."

"Really."

He nodded.

"Your Mamm never mentions you at quilting circle."

He shook his head a little. "Well, you know kids on their Rumschpringe aren't a favorite topic of conversation."

Oh, how I knew. Maybe if mothers commiserated a little with one another, it would do all of them some good.

When we reached Derek's house, I opened my door and jumped down. Derek was the oldest of eight, and every one of his siblings was on the porch, hanging out with their parents.

He laughed as he saw them craning their necks to see who had arrived with him and then waving like mad once they saw it was me. "Have fun."

"Sophie!" His sister Liza ran toward me, her bare feet flying across the thick grass. She didn't stop until she'd tackled me to the ground. She'd always been feisty and fun.

She wore a cape dress and Kapp, but I hadn't heard that she'd joined the church. I hadn't seen her at church the Sunday before last. Maybe she had a boyfriend in another district.

"Careful, Liza," Derek said as he walked past our sprawled bodies. "Don't hurt her."

"I haven't seen you in years," she squealed. "You just disappeared. Poof. Gone."

I sat up, brushing the cut grass from my hair.

"Are you back for good?" she asked. "Are you going to court Derek?"

I gasped. "Liza!"

"What? I always hoped that would happen."

"I'm only home for a few more days."

Liza frowned and shook her head. "You're breaking my heart."

"How about you? Who are you courting?" I asked. "When are you going to join the church?"

"Shh." She glanced back toward the porch and lowered her voice to a whisper. "I haven't told Mamm and Dat yet, but I'm getting married in November."

"You'd better tell them. They might want to start getting ready."

"He's not Amish."

"Oh."

"We're going to elope."

"Liza. Are you sure?"

She nodded vigorously. "But don't tell anyone, all right? I'll tell Derek soon, I promise. I just don't want to tell the whole family yet." She jumped to her feet and offered me her hand. I took it and she pulled me up.

Why did I feel bad about her not joining the church and not marrying an Amish boy? I certainly had no plans to. Was it because I'd once felt like a big sister toward her? I felt a twinge of guilt. Was that how my older siblings felt toward me?

When I reached the porch, everyone told me hello at once. Phyllis told Sweet Pea, the youngest girl, who had been stuck with the nickname since she was a baby, to let me sit in her chair. She obeyed her mother and climbed onto her lap, even though she was at least eight years old.

"Nice to see you outside of the quilting circle," Phyllis said.

"Nice to see you too." I grinned.

Derek's father, Fred, gave me a quick hello. Both he and Phyllis were quiet people, unlike their oldest daughter. Most of the other kids were pretty rambunctious too. In fact, Derek was probably the calmest of them all.

I'd only been on the porch a few minutes when he came out the front door, his hair wet, his clothes clean, and a biscuit in each of his hands. "Do you want one?" he asked.

My mouth watered. "Of course." Phyllis's biscuits were legendary.

"I'm driving Sophie into Elkhart to talk to a friend," Derek said. "I won't be very late."

I was sure I detected a shadow of concern pass over Phyllis's face. Amish moms, just like most moms, seemed to have multiple worries when it came to their children—young adult children in particular.

After promising I'd come by again, I told everyone good-bye. Once we were back in the pickup, I washed down the last of my biscuit with a drink from my water bottle.

"Hey, can I have a drink of your water?"

"Sure." I handed it to him.

"You're not contagious or anything, are you?"

"I told you it's an autoimmune disease. You can't catch it."

He took a swig and passed it back.

I yawned.

"Rest, if you want to," he said. "I'm not tired."

"Thanks." I wasn't feeling quite as well as I had been earlier. I closed my eyes and the next thing I knew he was slowing for the Elkhart city limits.

"Where to?" Derek asked.

I directed him to my house, but when we arrived, Ivy's car wasn't there. "I'll call her," I said.

She didn't answer until the seventh ring, just when I was ready to hang up.

"Hey, Sophie," she said. "What's up?"

"I came into Elkhart with a friend. Where are you?"

"At the sports bar on Main. I'm having a drink with Brody. Want to join us?"

"Sure," I answered, relieved she'd extended an invitation.

A few minutes later, we arrived and found them in a large booth in the back. I'd met Brody, who worked with Ivy, at a party at the house and wasn't that impressed with him. He seemed self-centered, interrupting others and talking about himself a lot. I ordered a seltzer, and Derek ordered a beer and a burger. After the waiter left, Derek said to me, "Did you stop drinking?"

I nodded. "It's a health thing." The truth was, I didn't drink that much before I was diagnosed with lupus. I'd been wild enough without alcohol.

We made small talk as we waited for our orders. I hoped Brody might go play pool or something—or leave early. But he stuck around. I couldn't bring up the dash cam in front of him, and now that I was here, I was getting cold feet about bringing it up at all. I'd already put Ivy in an awkward spot once. Why had I thought she'd feel better talking about it in person?

I knew I was motivated in hopes of helping Karin and her family, but perhaps I'd been blinded by my good intentions. The waiter brought our drinks and Derek's food. While he ate his burger, I stole several of his fries.

A baseball game was on TV, but at ten o'clock, the news came on. The teaser was footage of Karin.

"Hey," Ivy said. "Isn't that your friend? The one I met on Friday?"

"Yes," I said, feeling hope welling up inside. "She was interviewed this afternoon. So were Derek and I."

"Really?" Ivy nudged me playfully. "You're going to be on TV?"

I laughed. "I don't imagine I made the cut."

A couple of commercials followed, but when the news anchor said, "We have new developments following our earlier interview with Jasper Benjamin, the attorney for Dreamer Mateo Lopez, who is incarcerated at the Mid County Detention Center in Michigan."

Brody kept talking, but Ivy shushed him as more footage of Karin came on. Of course her long response had been edited to a few lines, but she still sounded poised, passionate, and intelligent.

Then the shot switched to me.

"Sophie! There you are, in your dress! And bonnet!" Ivy said. Brody had a puzzled look on his face as he looked at me, then back at the screen, as if he wasn't quite tracking I was the same person.

But when Derek came on, Brody looked straight at him. "Dude! Is that you?"

Derek nodded.

"Shush," Ivy said exasperatedly.

I hadn't heard any of Derek's interview, but he did a great job explaining the situation, that Hank Barlow had alien labor certification and that it was only a matter of weeks until Victor and Rosibel would get their green cards.

"I hope they don't get picked up in the meantime," Brody said.

"Shush," Ivy said again.

When the segment ended, Ivy looked from me to Derek. "You both did so well. And your friend too."

Brody nodded in agreement.

Ivy asked, "What's going to happen to her brother?"

"We don't know," I answered.

"Has his lawyer had any luck with the dash cam?"

I shook my head. "An Explorer riding along with the officer said Mateo signaled, but that might not mean anything. Jasper thinks it could be a while before the dash cam is released."

Brody shook his head. "Why don't they just release it now? Sooner or later, they'll have to."

Ivy pursed her lips and then said, "They probably hope the publicity will all die down before they have to."

"What's the point of having dash cams if the footage doesn't help tell the truth?" Brody asked, his voice getting louder with each word.

"Brody." Ivy glanced at the table beside us. "If anyone hears you talking like that, it might make it back to the department."

He frowned. "I'm not going to shut up. If it's up to me, this is going to be all we talk about tomorrow."

I suppressed a smile. Jasper was right. You never knew what might happen by talking to the media. And I was wrong about Brody, as far as my first impression. He definitely didn't seem as self-centered as I'd originally thought.

"Still," Ivy said, "they came here illegally."

I leaned closer to her. "What would you do in the same circumstance?" I asked. "Would you stay in a violent, war-torn country? Especially if you had a child?"

Brody opened his mouth, then closed it. There was an awkward pause. Then he said, "I'm pretty sure I would do the same thing they did."

Ivy pursed her lips again.

"I have a question." I looked from Ivy to Brody. "For both of you."

Ivy groaned.

"It's harmless, I think. I just want your opinion."

Ivy rolled her eyes, but Brody said, "Shoot."

I must have looked confused because he laughed and said, "Not literally."

I smiled and then said, "Why would an officer see a substance on the floor of a car and guess it was meth, especially when there's a boy in the back seat eating something with frosting on it?"

Ivy sighed, but Brody leaned forward. "Maybe the officer had a similar incident happen before. Maybe he stopped someone who had meth in the car—and a child in a car seat. Elkhart

County has quite a few meth labs around that endanger a fair number of kids." Brody shrugged. "Or maybe Mateo—is that his name?"

I nodded.

Brody continued, "Maybe Mateo looked like someone the officer had pulled over before who was running meth. Or maybe the officer is biased and looking for trouble." He shrugged again. "But my guess is that he had some sort of previous experience that made him suspicious."

"You're just speculating," Ivy said. "There's no way to know without him testifying."

"Well, hopefully the truth will come out before someone gets deported," Brody answered.

"But it's not our concern." Ivy crossed her arms. "We're dispatchers."

"No, Ivy. As citizens, it's a concern for all of us." Brody stood and dropped a twenty-dollar bill on the table and gave Ivy a pat on the shoulder. "See you tomorrow." Then he turned toward Derek and me. "Good luck with your friends. I hope the universe is kind to them."

"Thank you." I'd definitely been wrong about Brody.

Ivy stretched. "I should get home too."

Derek stood and shook her hand. "Nice to meet you."

"You too," she said.

"I'll be home in a few days," I said. "I'll text and let everyone know when."

After Ivy left, I finished my water while Derek finished his fries, and then we paid and left too. As we exited, and turned left toward Derek's pickup, I nearly ran into someone walking on the far edge of the sidewalk, going the same direction.

"Sorry," I said, just as I registered the man was Jasper, still wearing his suit.

He grinned. "Sophie. What are you doing here?"

My face grew warm. "I was just hanging out with a few friends. We happened to catch the ten o'clock news too."

Derek stepped to my side. "Hello, Jasper."

"Hi." Jasper shook Derek's hand.

I asked Jasper, "What are you up to?"

"Walking home, hoping to clear my head."

"Do you always work until past ten?" I wrinkled my nose.

He laughed. "An unexpected trip to a Nappanee farm and an unfortunate shoulder injury took up part of my evening." He gripped his shoulder in an exaggerated manner, where Lyle had bumped into him.

I couldn't help but laugh too.

"Nice to see you," he said to both Derek and me. But then he focused on just me. "Twice in one day. The same person—and yet, again, so very different." He smiled.

I shook my head a little as I smiled back.

Jasper took off, his steps long and quick. As I walked with Derek to his truck, I wondered if I was the same person no matter what I was wearing.

I supposed I was, but it didn't feel like it. Especially when I was around Jasper.

THE NEXT MORNING, during breakfast, I asked Dat if I could take the buggy to Jane's. "We plan to have the canning circle on Saturday." If I could help Jane pull off the canning circle event, and then return to Elkhart on Sunday, I'd feel better about leaving Nappanee. "I wanted to talk with her about it more and start setting up. I didn't have a chance to yesterday."

"I'll go with you," Mamm said.

I felt puzzled and must have shown it by my expression.

"I forgot to get thread yesterday," she said simply.

I doubted that. She had hundreds of spools of thread. Had Mamm and Dat heard about how Lyle had acted at Mill Creek Farms? I wasn't sure who would have told them, but news traveled fast around here.

As Mamm and I passed Mill Creek Farms, Lyle's truck was parked by the office building. And so was Derek's. Hopefully Hank had put Lyle in his place for good the day before.

I wondered if Lyle still drank as much as he had when we dated. Perhaps it was because I was young and rebellious myself, but I never put pressure on Lyle not to drink, even though it bothered me. There were quite a few times, in fact, when we fought when he was drunk. But I didn't feel it was cool to confront him.

We were horrible for each other. I could see that now.

Mamm kept her eyes on the farm as we drove by. She didn't relax until we reached Plain Patterns.

I tied the reins to the hitching post instead of unharnessing the horse. We wouldn't be long.

Mamm led the way to the shop. The door was locked. "Let's try the side door," I said.

That door was locked too.

"We're a little early," Mamm said. "Let's go work in the garden until she's open."

"Good idea," I said. No matter how much work Derek and Miriam had done, there would be more weeds growing already.

As we weeded, I took a mental inventory of the produce. I would need to come over tomorrow and harvest as much as I could. There were plenty of pickling cucumbers. I pulled up one of the beets. It was a perfect size. The tomato plants hung heavy, and there were plenty of cabbages to start a whole mess of kraut and chow chow. There were plenty of green tomatoes, bell peppers, and yellow onions for the relish too. There was also a plethora of green beans and pearl onions.

My mouth watered at the thought of all the good food and the idea of sharing it.

We'd been weeding for at least a half hour when we heard Jane come to the gate. "Hallo! Sorry, we had a rough night. Owen was fussy for most of it."

"How is Miriam doing?" Mamm asked, which surprised me.

"Probably tired," Jane answered. "I know I am, and she took the brunt of it." She stopped at the fence. "Denki for weeding."

"Of course," I said. "I wanted to talk with you about the canning circle on Saturday."

"And I need some thread," Mamm added.

"Come on in," Jane said.

We followed her into the shop.

After Mamm and I washed up in the bathroom, I took my notebook out of my purse and set it on the counter. "We have four folding tables and three camp stoves we can borrow from Mamm and my sisters." I'd checked with Mamm and left phone messages for my sisters and they'd all agreed—likely because it was for Jane, not because it was a favor for me. "They will also loan us stockpots to cook what we need to first."

"Great," Jane said. "I have two more tables from my sister-in-law and another camp stove, plus a canner from her and my own canner too."

That would give us four stations for the canning, plus extra tables for the prep. "We should ask everyone to bring their own paring knife," I said. "We'll need to make sure the bathroom is stocked with soap and paper towels and also have hand sanitizer outside, along with an outside hand-washing station too."

Once we'd talked through most of the details, Jane invited us to stay and quilt. "I can tell you more of the story."

"Oh, I think we need to get home. Right, Mamm?"

She shook her head. "I left a salad and sandwich for your Dat. I'd love to hear more of the story."

So would I, and I was running out of time to hear it. "Thank you," I said to Mamm. Then I turned toward Jane. "That sounds great."

"Let's go unhitch the horse and put her in the pasture," Mamm said.

"Good idea. I'll do it."

When I returned, Jane asked, "Where were we, as far as the story?"

"Mary and Lemuel were both determined to help the people of Chicago, but they were afraid their community wouldn't be willing to contribute anything."

"That's right," Jane said. "Mary wanted to speak with the bishop . . ."

CHAPTER 19

❖

Mary

Mary preferred to have Dat come along when she went to speak with the bishop, but he was hardly leaving his bedroom, let alone the house. On Friday morning, Mamm left for a birth and Dat dressed and joined them at the table for dinner. Colum was having fewer nightmares and seemed to be settling into life on the farm a little more. But he was wary of Dat, who probably reminded him of that horrible night. But after Dat joked around a little, Colum relaxed.

As soon as Dat led them in a final prayer, he asked to speak with Mary privately. She followed him to the living room. "We should plan to go back to Chicago at the end of this week. Probably Thursday."

"Will you feel up to going?"

He shrugged. "Let's plan on Thursday. We'll see how I feel." Then he retreated back to his bedroom. Mary went to check on him after she cleaned the kitchen. He was asleep but tossing and turning.

Mary finished plowing the Feld, and then before Lemuel

came to do the milking, rounded up Ellen and the children to help her harvest squash and cabbage. The produce would keep for a week or more until they could go to Chicago. After they'd loaded everything into wooden crates, she dug up a few potatoes. She'd harvest the rest the next day.

Lost in her thoughts, she barely heard the sound of her mother clearing her throat. Mary knew that sound well.

"What do you plan to do with all of those crates?"

Mary stood. "Take them to Chicago."

"Your father is not well," Mamm said. "Don't be encouraging this."

"I was hoping you could spare some medical supplies. Every little bit will help."

"Mary, we can't save the whole world."

"Mamm, Ellen lost everything she had. So did Colum's mother. And so many others."

"I understand," Mamm said. "And I appreciate your desire to help others. But we won't be able to help anyone if we can't feed ourselves."

"The Lord will provide for us."

Mamm raised her eyebrows.

"Mamm, this is what Dat and you have taught us our entire lives—to care for others. You told us stories about your friend Mathilde and about caring for the Irish women and going to Michigan to help Native women."

"Jah, and we'll continue to do that sort of thing. Here. We can't care for an entire city."

"I know that." Mary clasped her hands behind her back. "But we can care for a few in that city."

Mamm exhaled slowly. "We needed that money from Chicago to buy seed for the winter wheat. Now we'll need to sell as much of our produce as possible to pay for it."

"That's another reason why we need to go to Chicago—to get our money from Russ Keller."

Mamm crossed her arms. "I think it's pretty clear that is a lost cause."

"We still have more wheat to mill for others," Mary responded. "That will bring in some money."

"Neither your Dat nor Steffen is in any shape to mill."

"I can do it," Mary said. "With Lemuel's help."

Mamm shook her head. "We can barely pay Lemuel as it is."

Mary didn't say any more about the matter. "I need to go get started on the milking."

"Fine," Mamm said. "But forget the idea of going to Chicago. I thought we were going to lose your Dat. I don't want you to make this worse."

"I understand." As Mary turned and headed toward the barn, tears stung her eyes. Mamm couldn't see that even a few heads of cabbage and some blankets in a city as big as Chicago could make the difference for a few people, a few families. That was all she wanted.

When she reached the barn, Lemuel, Michael, and Vyt were already bringing in the first of the cows to be milked. She was silent as they worked. Lemuel talked with the boys for a while, and then turned to Mary and said, "What's wrong?"

She shook her head.

"Why are you so quiet?"

She glanced toward her nephews. She didn't want to speak about going back to Chicago in front of them. She knew Steffen wouldn't want her to.

When they were almost done with the milking, Lemuel told the boys to go ahead and wash up for supper. "Mary and I'll finish up out here."

They raced out of the barn, jostling each other as they did.

"So, what's going on?" Lemuel turned the last cow toward the pasture door.

Mary followed him. "Dat wants to go to Chicago, but Mamm says he's not strong enough."

The cow lumbered out the open door, which Lemuel then closed. "I heard that over three hundred thousand people fled their homes the night of the fire."

Mary's eyebrows shot up. She couldn't comprehend that many people, even after seeing so many of them herself.

Lemuel added, "And now over one hundred thousand are homeless."

That meant some had homes to go back to. But she doubted Ellen or Honora did. "We also need to take Colum back to Honora," Mary said.

"I agree," Lemuel said. "The more I think about it, the less likely I think it is that she would ever be able to travel out here. If the hotel didn't survive, she'd need to find another job, save the money, and then have the time to come here. And if the hotel did survive, I doubt Russ Keller would give her the time off to make the trip."

Mary rubbed the back of her neck. She hadn't thought of all of that. Even now, she didn't think it was wrong that they took Colum, at Honora's request, but she did feel it was their responsibility to reunite him with his mother and brother. But what if they were homeless and living on the street?

Lemuel led the way through the barn.

Mary asked, "Could you mill more wheat?"

"Sure."

"I can help tomorrow." Mary stopped. "We need to talk to the bishop tomorrow too, with or without Dat. And then ask everyone at the service on Sunday for help. Mamm doesn't understand what kind of impact we could have, but Dat does.

He thinks we should return to Chicago on Thursday. I know crop yields are down, but even a little bit from everyone, plus household supplies, would help."

"I could go talk to the bishop in the morning after we milk and before we do the milling," Lemuel said.

Mary inhaled sharply. He would probably have more of a chance of convincing the bishop without her. She hadn't joined the church yet, and, as a young woman, her opinion wouldn't be taken into account anyway. She hoped that Lemuel, as a young man, would be listened to. If only Dat wasn't so ill.

LATE SATURDAY MORNING, when Lemuel returned to do the milling, he reported on meeting with the bishop. "He says there are concerns closer to home to address."

"Will he allow us to ask the community for help?"

Lemuel shook his head.

Michael overheard them and said, "Dat doesn't think you should go back to Chicago either. He says if Colum's mother doesn't return, Ellen should care for him or else he should go to an orphanage."

Mary gasped. "He is not going to an orphanage." If it came to that, she'd raise Colum herself.

Michael shrugged and Mary and Lemuel continued down past the Goahda and through the Feld toward the creek.

The grist mill was a two-story building about ten years old and painted white. Dat had built a dam on the creek and then dug raceways to move the water to the mill and then back away from it.

Lemuel adjusted the locks and redirected the water over the wheel while Mary went into the mill and cleaned out the hopper. Then she began pouring grain into it. The two quartz stones began to turn, crushing the wheat and then forcing the flour into the elevator below.

Lemuel took over dumping the wheat into the hopper, while Mary began pouring the flour into the twenty-pound bags Sarah sewed during the winter months. They'd grind enough today for a wagonload.

They worked all afternoon until the wheat was ground, bagged, and stacked in the warehouse room. It was time to do the milking by the time they finished. "We can bring the wagon down along the creek and load it later," Mary said.

After supper was over and the dishes done, Mary bathed Colum and then put him to bed. Colum begged Mary to stay with him. "Whenever I close my eyes, all I see is fire." Mary stayed until he fell asleep.

Then she went down the stairs, slipped out onto the front porch, and sat down on the top step. There was just the hint of lingering light on the horizon. She took a deep breath and then said a prayer, asking for the Lord's guidance about going back to Chicago.

As she ended her prayer, she heard her parents' voices from their open bedroom window. She stood, not wanting to eavesdrop, but then she froze when Dat said, "Mary is right. We need to help where God has called us to."

"Jah, we need to help Steffen and his family. We need to look to our finances and sustaining our farm and the work we're doing here."

"All we have comes from God, and He doesn't want us to hoard it. He'll provide what we need when we need it."

"We need it now—to survive," Mamm said.

"Emma, remember that girl who put someone else first instead of returning home to Pennsylvania?" Dat asked. "Remember

how brave she was?" If Mamm had returned to Pennsylvania
instead of helping her friend Mathilde, Mamm and Dat would
have never married.

"I wasn't brave," Mamm replied.

"You were. And Mary reminds me of you."

"Mary's nothing like me. She's fearless. And strong. She
could do to be a little more timid."

"That's not how God made her."

"Jah," Mamm said. "She's much more like you than me."

Dat laughed. "I'll take that as a compliment. Jah, you were
fearful back then but you still acted courageously—just as you
have all these years since."

Mamm laughed too. "I wouldn't call it living courageously.
I've simply done what I believed God wanted from me."

"That's all any of us can do, and that's why I agree with
Mary." Dat's voice grew serious. "She and I saw the pain and
anguish. God put us in Chicago for a reason, and I owe a young
man there money. I've never not paid a debt. I don't want to
start now."

Mary realized she was definitely eavesdropping, even though
she hadn't meant to, and decided to tiptoe around to the back
of the house instead of going back into the living room. It
was completely dark now, but Mary could see a lamp lit in the
kitchen. Through the window, she saw that Sarah was sitting at
the table, working on her quilt and talking quietly with Ellen.

Ellen must have said something funny because Sarah laughed.
Mary marveled at how resilient Ellen seemed. She'd lost so
much and yet she seemed to be trusting that God would meet
her needs.

Mary trusted God to meet her own needs too, but was that
because she had the security of her parents and her home?
Without that, would she really trust God? Perhaps the bigger

question was, could she trust God to meet the needs of others, or did she feel as if it was up to her to help them?

If she defied the bishop and asked the community to help and they refused, could she trust God with that answer?

She wasn't sure, but she'd find out tomorrow.

ELLEN WAS EAGER to accompany the Landis family to church the next day. "The service will be in Pennsylvania Dutch and German," Mary warned. "You won't be able to understand it."

"I'd still like to go," Ellen answered.

Colum, overhearing the conversation, asked, "Are we going to Mass?"

Ellen quickly explained that it would be different from what he was used to. "And it will be different from what I'm used to also, but we'll still worship God together."

Steffen stayed home because he couldn't sit or stand that long, and so did Dat, at Mamm's insistence. But the rest of them piled into two buggies and made their way to the Engel home.

Colum sat with Michael, Vyt, and Lemuel on the men's side, while Ellen sat with Mary and Sarah. Hanna and her mother, along with Mamm, sat in the very back of the Engels' shed, where the service was held. Mary hoped Colum would be able to sit still through the three-hour service.

Bishop Gerber led the congregation in a prayer. Ellen listened intently, although Mary was sure she couldn't understand a single word.

Toward the end of the service, Mary's heart began to race. Bishop Gerber, before he ended the service in a final prayer, mentioned that Dat was home ill after a harrowing trip to Chicago. "We should pray for his recovery," the bishop said.

Mary wanted to stand and speak out, but it was forbidden. She said a silent prayer, asking for God to intervene. She didn't realize Lemuel had stood until he said, "I have something to add to that."

Bishop Gerber opened his mouth, but before anything came out, Lemuel rushed ahead. "We're collecting food, bedding, and medical supplies to take to Chicago, to those who have lost their homes to the fire. Anything will help. If you have even the slightest amount to contribute, get it to the Landis farm by Wednesday. Let me know—"

Bishop Gerber interrupted. "I've not encouraged Lemuel or anyone to ask for anyone to contribute."

A voice behind Mary said, "We only hope you will ask God to guide you."

Mary didn't have to turn around to know it was Mamm.

"I plan to send medical supplies," Mamm continued. "Can you imagine what it would be like to be injured in a city where one hundred thousand people have become homeless in a single night? Where the landscape is now ashes and rubble? People the Lord loves are hurting, and we are close enough to help."

Bishop Gerber shook his head. "Emma—"

Mary heard the shed door open and a deep voice from the back called out, "She is speaking for me. All we ask is that you seek what the Lord would have you do."

Mary refrained from turning around on the bench as she continued to stand, but she soaked in Dat's words.

"People are hurt and without resources," he said. "Many are immigrants, just as our people were over a hundred years ago. If you have food or other resources to share, we thank you. If not, so be it."

There was a murmur through the congregation.

Finally, Bishop Gerber nodded. "We'll keep your words in mind." He exhaled sharply and then said, "Let's pray."

A half hour later, as Mary sliced bread while other women served soup for the meal, no one talked with her about what she, Mamm, and Dat had requested. She tried not to despair.

How could Bishop Gerber preach about helping others but have no interest in the thousands who needed it and were only one hundred miles away?

CHAPTER 20

Sophie

The sound of the front bell ringing and then the door slamming startled me. Mamm was on her feet before I registered what was going on.

As the sound of heavy footsteps came toward us, Mamm rushed to the front room of the shop. Jane followed her as I struggled to my feet.

"Where is she?" It was Lyle, and he sounded angry.

I found my footing and hurried toward the front room, but Jane stopped me with her arm stretched wide. "Get out of view."

"I need to help Mamm."

"If you want to help her, then go. Slip out the back door. Now."

"Get out of my way!" Lyle bellowed at my mother. His words were slurred, like he had been drinking.

"Go," Jane hissed, sounding as passionate as I'd ever heard her. "I'll take care of your Mamm. I promise."

I did as she said, and I could feel the weight of the phone in my pocket as I ran outside. As soon I reached the deck along the back, I dialed 9-1-1. I rattled off the address of Plain Patterns and said that a drunk man was threatening a fifty-five-year-old woman. "Hurry," I said and then hung up.

I slunk along the outside of the building. Lyle yelled, "She cost me my job! Where is she?" A thud came from inside.

Had he hurt my mother?

I rushed around to the front door. His voice grew louder and louder. I couldn't wait any longer. I flung open the front door.

A rack had been tipped over, scattering bolts of fabric across the floor. Mamm stood behind it with her arms crossed. Her face fell when she saw me.

Lyle spun around, facing me.

"Hi, Lyle." I spoke as casually as I could, even though my knees shook. "What are you doing here?"

"You. That's what I'm doing here."

"Come on outside." I held the door wide open. "I'm sure we can sort this out."

His eyes squinted as he stared me down.

I stepped back outside, the door closing behind me. I walked purposely away from his truck and the produce stand, where I could be seen from both the road and the driveway to Plain Patterns.

Finally, he stumbled out of the building.

I smiled, or at least tried to. "So, what's going on?" My voice shook but maybe he wouldn't notice.

"I got fired." He glared at me. "Hank let me go."

"Wow," I answered.

He shook his head as he stepped toward me. I took a step backward.

"You did this," he said. "You put Hank up to this."

"I don't even know Hank." I spoke slowly, hoping it would

help my voice stay calm. "Yesterday was the first time I've ever seen him."

"You know what I mean," Lyle snarled. "It was your influence over the Lopez family. They never would have put Hank up to this if you hadn't come around, trying to get back at me."

"Get back at you?" I stammered.

He took another step toward me, and I took two more steps backward. My heart began to race. How long would it take for an officer to arrive?

"I'm sorry you lost your job," I said. "Really. I didn't say anything to anyone in the Lopez family about you, and I certainly wouldn't have advocated that you lose your job."

"I don't believe you," he snarled. "You haven't changed a bit. Once a liar always a liar." He lunged toward me and reached for my wrists, but missed. As I stepped away, my right foot fell in a pothole. I went down in a heap, just as a patrol car cruised into the parking lot.

Lyle cursed at me and then started toward his pickup. The officer lowered his window and yelled, "Hey! Stop! Remain where you are."

Lyle jumped into his pickup and started the engine. Then, staring straight ahead and not acknowledging me or the officer, he sped away toward Mill Creek Farms.

THE OFFICER was probably in his early thirties and concerned about the scrape on my elbow. But when I said that Lyle hadn't pushed me, that I'd stepped into a pothole, he didn't seem as worried.

Mamm and Jane both pleaded with the officer to find Lyle and question him.

"At least go by Mill Creek Farms," I said. "He just lost his job and he's a disgruntled ex-employee."

"Has he verbally threatened anyone who works there?"

"Not that I know of," I admitted. "But if he does something and you didn't do anything to prevent it . . ." I paused, racking my brain for something to make the officer take this seriously. "I'll light up social media about you not taking any action."

He made a scoffing sound. "You're Amish. You're not going to light up social media."

"I'm dressed Amish." I pulled my phone from my apron pocket. "But I'm as Englisch as they come, I assure you."

I almost dropped my phone when Mamm smiled at me.

The officer glanced toward the road. "Fine," he said. "I'll check in at Mill Creek Farms and make sure he didn't go there." He took down my phone number and Jane's too, then climbed in his car and headed back toward the road.

My voice quavered as I said, "I'm really sorry."

Mamm's eyebrows rose. "What are you talking about?"

"Lyle. He came here because of me. And I involved you. And Jane."

"It's not your fault," Mamm said. "It's his fault. Don't you try to take any of the blame on yourself."

Had I hit my head and not my elbow when I fell? My Mamm had never said anything so kind to me. As we walked into the shop, I asked, "What changed in how you see all of this?"

She glanced at me and then shook her head. "I've been doing some thinking . . . putting some things together." She pressed her hand against her chest, and it heaved a little.

Concerned, I asked, "Is everything okay?"

Mamm nodded and then turned her head away from me. What was going on with my no-nonsense mother?

I put a hand on her shoulder. "Are you sure?"

She nodded again and then said softly, "I'm just glad you're safe. . . ." Her voice trailed off. But a half second later she turned toward me, completely composed, and said, "Let's get you cleaned up." She was back to her pragmatic self.

After she washed and bandaged my elbow, she said, "I don't know if we should take the buggy home. What if Lyle is waiting for you along the road? Maybe I should call for a driver."

"I can order a ride share," I said, holding up my phone again. Mamm smiled. "That would be a new experience for me." I grinned. "Then let's do it."

Fifteen minutes later, I sat in the back seat of our ride share with my Mamm as we passed by Mill Creek Farms. The patrol car was in the parking lot of the main building, and Derek and Hank were talking with the officer, which meant he had been there for close to a half hour. The officer had spent all of five minutes talking to me.

Mamm must have been thinking the same thing because she said, "Well, I'll be. He'll talk to the men until the cows come home, but he couldn't be bothered to talk with you for more than a few minutes?"

I patted her leg in gratitude.

When we reached the house, Mamm plopped down at the kitchen table and started telling Dat what had happened. Still feeling shaky, I snuck upstairs to my room, needing to be by myself for a while.

I couldn't get over the fact that Mamm had stuck up for me. For the first time in my life—or at least that I could remember—she had seemed to care more about me and my well-being than about how something might look to others. Something had shifted.

I couldn't bear it if Lyle harmed my parents. I needed to leave. Now.

I never should have come back here. The sooner I left, the better. But as I stood, intent on packing my bag, I heard the crunch of tires on gravel. I rushed out of my bedroom and to the landing window. A sigh of relief exploded out of me. It was Derek.

I hurried down the stairs and opened the door for him.

"Are you all right?" he asked, already halfway up the porch steps.

I nodded as Mamm, followed by Dat, hurried into the living room.

"Did Lyle go back to the farm?" I asked.

Derek nodded. "But then he saw the officer coming and he took off down the back roads."

"The officer didn't follow him?"

Derek shook his head. "He said he doubted he'd catch him, and a chase might put other drivers at risk. But he mentioned that Lyle had confronted you at Plain Patterns and blamed you for him getting fired."

I pressed the palm of my hand against the side of my face, not sure what to do. I turned toward Mamm and Dat. "I think I should go back to Elkhart. I don't want to bring trouble to the two of you."

"But we have the canning circle on Saturday," Mamm said. "You don't want to miss that."

"Jah," I answered. "I do if it means protecting the two of you."

"If Lyle is going to try to intimidate us, he'll do it whether you're here or not," Dat said. "And we'd rather you stay. It's been good to have you home."

"Go with Derek now," Mamm said. "Go for a drive or something. Dat and I will hire a driver and go get the buggy. He won't dare confront your Dat out on the road."

I wanted to give them my phone, but I knew they wouldn't take it—or know how to use it. "Will you go to the shed and call for help if he shows up here?" I asked Dat.

"Jah," Dat said. "If needed, I will. Go with Derek."

"Come on," he said, tugging on my hand. "Let's go get something to eat."

BEFORE DEREK TURNED onto the highway, I asked, "Do you mind if we go to Elkhart? I have cards there from a canning circle I did at the co-op last fall. I was going to re-create them tomorrow before the event on Saturday, but it would be easier if I didn't have to. And if I end up leaving tomorrow, I can give them to Jane before I go."

"Sure." Derek turned toward Elkhart.

We drove in silence for a while, but then I asked, "So did Hank fire Lyle for wanting undocumented workers deported?"

"Well, that did tick him off, but it's more than that. It turns out that before Hank went into the hospital, he told Lyle he wanted Victor to manage South Farm. Guess what happened after that."

"Lyle never told Victor?"

"Or anyone else." Derek accelerated a little too forcefully. "That really upset Hank. When Lyle would go to give him updates in the hospital, Hank would ask why Victor wasn't coming too, and Lyle just made one excuse after the other."

"So how bad is Hank's health?"

"Pretty bad," Derek said. "His daughter lives in Denver, and she's arriving sometime today. The doctor recommended starting hospice. They'll check on him and oversee his care, but Hank asked Rosibel to do the actual caregiving. She nursed his

LESLIE GOULD

wife, who died two years ago, when she was sick. Rosibel took a CNA class so she could do everything right."

"Wow." No wonder Hank felt bad he hadn't done everything he could for the family sooner. "What happens . . . ?" My words trailed off.

"If Hank dies before Victor's and Rosibel's green cards come through?"

I nodded.

"I don't know," Derek said. "I've been afraid to ask."

We ate at a diner on the edge of town. By the time we left the restaurant, the sky had turned gray. We hadn't had a thunderstorm for a week.

Derek waited in the pickup for me while I went inside the house to get the cards. For once, no one was home.

I had the urge to stop by the community garden next, but not just to check if it had been weeded and watered. Perhaps it was from seeing Lyle, but I was feeling the loss of my baby intensely, and I wanted to go see the rosebush in the garden. But at the same time, I didn't want to share that with Derek.

As we turned onto the highway back toward Nappanee, the rain started. First it was a few drops on the windshield, but then it turned into a deluge. Buckets of rain poured down from the sky. Derek turned on his lights and slowed, straining to see the road.

A streak of lightning flashed across the sky to the south. Seven seconds later, the thunder crashed. The electrical storm was near Nappanee. I thought of Jane's garden and all the produce ready to be harvested. Hopefully it wasn't getting too battered.

Derek gripped the steering wheel. "I hope the workers are in from the field."

"Me too."

The rain came down even harder and Derek slowed more. The windshield wipers were going at top speed but the rain still flooded over the glass. Derek eased to the side of the road.

"We'd better wait it out for a few minutes." He turned on his emergency flashers.

Finally, the rain slowed just a little. Before he could pull back onto the highway, his phone rang. He answered and a quick minute later said, "I'm on my way."

He slipped his phone back into the holder on his belt. "That was Victor. There's a flash flood on the farm. The creek is rising fast—right by the village."

CHAPTER 21

❖

By the time we arrived, several pickups were parked along the cabins and women were carrying out cardboard boxes and clothing, shoving them in truck beds, which were covered by tarps, as the rain continued to fall. However, there was no activity at the Lopez house, and I didn't see any vehicles or people around.

"Where's Victor?" Derek shouted as he climbed down from his pickup.

The neighbor yelled back, "Sebastian's missing. Victor and Rosibel are looking for him."

I jumped down. "How about Karin?"

"She's on her way."

"Where are they looking?" I asked.

"Along the creek."

Oh no. I turned toward Derek, but he'd already taken off toward the bank. I followed, already soaked to the bone.

We reached the creek, which had turned into a river, before we reached the actual bank. The water was definitely rising toward the cabins. Several men were using shovels to build a barrier between the muddy water and the homes.

"Which way did Victor go?" Derek called out.

"Upstream, to Sebastian's fort," one of the men said.

"What about Rosibel?"

"Downstream."

I yelled to Derek, "I'll go that way."

He nodded and turned back toward the truck. "I'm going to drive, and then make my way back down the creek."

I waved and turned to the right. My slip-ons were immediately covered in mud. I stayed as much on the edge of the weeds as I could, as I looked ahead for Rosibel. The visibility through the sheets of rain was horrible. I kept going, slogging through the mud and creek water.

I came toward the beginning of the village and then scrambled up the rise, where the shop and market were, keeping my eye on the creek. Debris pooled around a willow tree on the bank, which was now halfway covered with water. I was continuing uphill, above the creek, toward Hank's house, when I heard someone shout, "Hold on!"

I squinted through the rain. Below, I could see a figure. I scrambled down the hill. I took out my phone and hit Derek's number, trying to make sense of what I was seeing. Up ahead, Hank was coming down the slope from the house, and someone, maybe his daughter, was following him. Someone small—Sebastian, I thought—was in the water. And Rosibel was extending a branch to him.

Out of breath by the time Derek finally answered, I said, "Sebastian is in the creek up by Hank's house. Rosibel is trying to get him out. Hurry!"

"Got it."

I slipped my phone back into my soaking wet pocket, thankful it had worked, and started to run toward them.

"Sebastian! You have to hang on!" Rosibel's voice was full of panic.

As I reached her, I said, "Derek is on his way." I didn't tell her Hank was coming down the slope. That might distract her.

The water had Sebastian pointed downstream, so his back was toward us. I wrapped my hands around the branch, which was about eight inches in diameter and ten feet long, and started to pull. Immediately I could tell the branch was caught on something.

I stepped into the water, squishing down into the mud.

Rosibel gasped. "No, Sophie!"

"I'll hang onto the branch," I said. "Try to keep it steady."

I took another step. "Sebastian, can you turn toward me?"

He turned his head.

I tugged on the branch, but it wouldn't budge. I took another step, this time onto a rock, which I slipped off with a lurch. I steadied myself and then felt along the bottom of the branch to see why it wouldn't move. In my next pass through, I bumped into what felt like a shrub. Then my leg brushed against it. Even in the cold water, I could feel it scratch my calf and dig into my flesh. I wrapped both my hands under the branch and yelled, "Hold on extra tight, Sebastian! I'm going to lift the branch."

I bent down and then raised my arms straight up. Sebastian held on. Then I took a step backward.

Rosibel began pulling again, and there was a big tug on it. Hank was helping Rosibel. Sebastian flew toward me, and I let go of the branch and grabbed hold of his waist. "Keep ahold of the branch."

As I walked with him back to the shore, Rosibel and Hank pulled the branch all the way in.

Sebastian collapsed into Rosibel's arms.

Hank's daughter—or at least I assumed it was she—touched her father's arm. "We need to get you back up to the house."

Hank ignored her. "Sebastian, are you hurt?"

"No, I don't think so."

"Can you stand? Are your limbs all working?"

Sebastian stepped away from Rosibel and moved his arms. "Everything seems fine."

I took a quick assessment of him too. He had scratches all over his arms and legs and a few on his face. He'd probably have some bruises coming on soon, but he seemed okay.

"Thank you," Rosibel said to Hank as she reached for Sebastian.

"Come on, Dad." Hank's daughter tugged on his arm.

"All of you come up to the house," Hank ordered. "You need to get showered and in clean clothes. Who knows what runoff is in this creek?"

When he stumbled on his way up the slope, I stepped to his side and took his other arm. We were making our way up slowly when Victor and Derek appeared at the top.

Victor shouted, "Thank God!"

When we reached Hank's door, Hank motioned me in, but I said that Derek could just take me home.

"No," Hank said. "There's a dairy upstream from us. Plus, fertilizer has to be running off all of the fields. Who knows what you were steeping in?"

"I have clothes you can wear," his daughter said as she smiled at me. "I'm Cheri Barlow, Hank's daughter. Thank you for all your help back there."

"I'm Sophie. Pleased to meet you."

"I'll get clothes for you," Cheri said. "And show you to the guest bathroom. Victor and Sebastian can take the upstairs shower. Rosibel, will you help my father?"

I kicked my shoes off before entering, as did everyone else. Derek paused on the threshold and told Victor he'd go check on their home and move things from their home into his truck, if needed.

"Would you grab some clothes for Sebastian?" Rosibel asked as she took Hank's arm. "He and Mateo share the last room."

"Sure," Derek said.

Cheri led the way into the house. From the outside, it looked like an old farmhouse, but it had been completely renovated on the inside. The living room, dining area, and kitchen were one big room. Victor headed upstairs with Sebastian, and Rosibel walked with Hank down one hall. Cheri led me down another hall into a bedroom that had a bathroom attached. "This is my room when I'm here," she said.

She opened a drawer and pulled out a sports bra, underwear, T-shirt, and a pair of capri pants. Then she stepped to a closet and grabbed a pair of flip-flops. She was probably in her forties, but all of the clothes were stylish. "These are all old things I've left here to wear on the farm. You don't need to get them back to me."

"Oh, I will," I said. "I'll wash—"

"Really," she said, "it's not necessary."

I caught on to what she was saying. She didn't want them back.

"There's a hairbrush in there you can use. And a box of plastic bags under the sink. You can put your wet clothes in there."

I took the clothing, thanked her, and headed into the bathroom. It wasn't until I started to take my apron off that I remembered my phone. It was ruined, no doubt.

After I showered and dressed, I ventured back out into the living room, with my hand wrapped around my phone. Derek and Victor were talking, their backs toward me.

I waited a half second and then took another step, saying a cheery "Hello" as I did. "How is Sebastian?"

"He'll be okay," Victor answered as he slowly turned around.

"How about your home?"

Derek said, "The water reached the cabins. I'd say they're flooded by a half foot or so. We're going to go back down and get more things out. The rain has slowed, but the creek is still rising."

"Where will everyone stay tonight?" I asked.

Victor shrugged. "I'm not sure. . . ."

"How about the school?" I said to Derek. "I could call Dat and leave a message. He could call the board."

"Do you think they'd do it?"

"I hope so," I answered. "I'll call Jane too. She and the quilting circle can collect bedding."

Sebastian started down the stairs, showered and in clean clothes, just as Rosibel, Hank, and Cheri came up the hall.

Derek and Victor told everyone they were going down to the village. "Call if you need me," Victor said to Rosibel, giving her a kiss on the cheek before he and Derek left.

"Let's get you to your chair," Rosibel said to Hank. "And I'll get your medicine."

Hank wore sweatpants, a long-sleeve T-shirt, and a pair of slippers. He coughed as he dropped into the chair. Cheri covered him with an afghan.

He looked around the room, smiled at Sebastian, and then pointed at me. "What's in your hand?"

Reluctantly, I held it up. "My phone."

Hank grimaced. "Did you have it in your pocket?"

"Yes," I answered.

"Sis," he said to Cheri, "get the girl a bag of rice." He turned back to me. "If that doesn't work, I want to buy you a new one."

"No," I said. "I don't expect that."

"Well, I do," he said. Then he focused on Sebastian. "Come tell us what happened, son."

Sebastian stood next to Hank. "I was down at my fort when

266

the rain and the lightning started, so I knew I needed to get home. Before I could get out, the water rushed through my fort. I was trying to climb the bank when it rose even higher and washed me away. I grabbed onto that branch and held on until it got caught by your house. Then I waited, hoping Papa would find me. But Mama did, and then Sophie was the one who pulled me to safety."

Hank put his arm around Sebastian and pulled him close. "Thank God she did. Or I would have waded into the water myself."

AFTER CHERI gave me a bag of rice and I'd placed my phone in it, I called Dat from Hank's kitchen phone. Dat answered on the first ring. He was in the phone shanty making calls, checking up on people in his district after the flash flood and being available in case anyone had an emergency.

I explained what had happened and that the people in the village needed a place to gather and regroup. "They need a meal, clothes, bedding. Their belongings are all soaked. They're also going to need help with cleanup. Do you think our district would be willing to help?"

My heart fell when he didn't respond.

"Jah," he finally said. "I was just trying to think of the best course of action."

"David?" Mamm's voice carried over the line.

"Just a second." I could hear Dat's muffled voice explaining what had happened.

My heart fell again. Would Mamm quash the idea before it ever got off the ground?

But then I heard her say, "Of course we'll help."

Dat came back on the line. "I'll call the school board and

get everything set up over there. We'll appoint a few women to be in charge of a meal. I'll call the Mennonite church to bring over items from their clothes closet."

"And I'll call Jane about bedding," I said.

"Your Mamm can help with that too," Dat said. And then he added, "I'll call the Red Cross. We may need some medical people and other supplies. Plus options for short-term and long-term housing, depending on the severity of the damage." He paused again. "A family can stay with us."

My heart flew out of my chest. "Great," I managed to say, my throat tight with emotion. "Denki."

After I told Dat good-bye, I called Plain Patterns. I hoped the flooded creek hadn't reached Jane's property, and it was unlikely it had. The bank there was steeper, and the creek was farther away from the quilt shop than it was from the cabins. Jane didn't answer, so I left a message. Then I picked up the bag of rice with my phone and turned back toward the living room. Rosibel and Sebastian were getting ready to go down to the village, and I said I'd go with them.

"Let me know about your phone," Hank said to me as I followed Rosibel and Sebastian out the door.

"I will."

"Promise?"

I nodded, although I still didn't feel right about it. The rain had slowed to a drizzle. As we made our way down the road, I could hear a vehicle approaching from behind. As I turned, I braced myself to see Lyle's truck, but it was Karin.

She rolled down her window. "Thank God you're okay," she said. "Get in!"

We all piled into her car, Rosibel in front and Sebastian and me in the back. As Karin accelerated, she said, "Tell me everything."

In the two minutes it took to get to their home, Sebastian pretty much got the whole story out.

"Wow," Karin said. She parked beside Derek's truck, which was full of furniture. Victor and Derek came out onto the porch, carrying a soaked mattress. "We're going to take this load up to the shed and then come back for more," Victor said as we got out of the car. "You could fill Karin's car with anything that's not wet that we can use tonight, and we'll get the dressers and more furniture in the next load."

I told them about Dat gathering supplies and setting up a meal at the school. "We'll pass the word around here," I said. "But tell anyone you see too."

We waded through the yard to the cabin and then sloshed through the living room to the bedrooms. The water was saturating the drywall and had reached the lower drawers of the dressers. Anything on the floor was soaked.

We continued working to get the Lopez home cleared, and then we helped the neighbors. It was after seven by the time we finished. The shed was nearly filled with all the household goods from the ten cabins.

I rode with Derek to the school. The Lopez family led the other families in a long parade of cars.

When we arrived, the parking lot was filled with buggies and the church wagon. When we stepped inside after washing up in the two bathrooms at the back of the school, I could see tables covered with food—meatballs, mashed potatoes, green beans, applesauce, rolls, and pies. I could smell coffee too. Tables and benches were set up, and other tables were covered with nonperishable food, clothes, and bedding, including several quilts from Jane's shop. There were two people wearing Red Cross vests milling around.

"Welcome," Dat said, smiling at me but extending his hand to Victor.

Jane stepped forward, followed by Mamm, to greet the women.

I made my way to a table and slumped into a chair. I hadn't realized how exhausted I was. Derek brought me a glass of water and sat down beside me. "How are you feeling?" he asked.

"Just tired."

After people ate, Victor, Dat, and the Red Cross workers sat together at a table and figured out housing. As I expected, Hank had offered his upstairs rooms for the Lopez family.

But a family with five children needed a place. I told Dat I could go back to Elkhart and the family could use my room too.

"Sophie, come stay with me," Jane said. "I have room."

That actually sounded appealing. "But do you mind if my car is parked outside your place?"

"Not at all," Jane said.

Two hours later, I found myself at Jane's house. Miriam and Owen were already asleep, and although I was exhausted, I was still keyed up.

Mamm and Dat and their church had come through for the Lopez family and the other workers. I could still hardly believe it. I wondered if hearing part of Mary's story and how her mother Emma had come around to caring about the displaced people in Chicago had inspired my Mamm's reaction. I might never know for sure, but I thought the story might have helped Mamm see another point of view.

So much had happened. I doubted I'd be able to sleep for hours.

Jane must have sensed that because she made me a cup of chamomile tea and then said, "How about more of the story?"

"I would love that," I answered. "You left off with Mary asking her church to donate to help the people of Chicago."

CHAPTER 22

❖

Mary

On Monday morning after the milking, Mary stared at the crates of squash and cabbage in the barn, ready to be transported to Chicago. But if this was all she had, along with the flour, it wouldn't be worth the trip.

Here Mamm had given Mary her blessing in front of the entire congregation and yet how could Mary make it happen?

She brushed away a tear. She didn't think she'd cried since Paul had died. Perhaps in a few weeks Dat would pay her some for her work, and she could use the money for train tickets for Colum and herself. If she could find Kit, he would help her find Honora. Hopefully Dat would have the money to pay Kit by then.

She squared her shoulders and then headed to the shed for tools to fix the fence rail that one of the calves had dislodged. She would have to trust the Lord. There was nothing else she could do.

As she started toward the pasture fence, a wagon turned onto the farm. And then a cart. In the wagon was Ben Eby, a nearby neighbor. In the cart was Daniel Yoder, a deacon in their district.

They headed toward the barn, so Mary did too. Ben jumped down from his wagon and called out, "Where do you want it?"

"Want what?" Mary yelled back.

"Supplies. I have some hams, potatoes, a bag of onions, and some blankets."

Mary's heart began to race. "Denki. We'll put them in the barn."

Ben grabbed a box and headed inside while Daniel said, "I have bags of walnuts and one bag of sugar. Plus a box of apples."

Mary thanked him and grabbed the bags of walnuts.

More people arrived throughout the morning with more bedding and food—dried and fresh—along with more sugar, more hams, bacon, and jerky. Some brought clothing, worn but clean, and soap. Others brought tools and nails. Mamm and Ellen came out after a while and helped sort through everything. The next day, Mary dug potatoes while Michael and Vyt picked apples from the orchard to contribute. Then Mamm added strips for bandages and jars of carbolic acid. She also had dried herbs to send too.

Midafternoon, Mary and Lemuel drove one of the Vauwa down along the creek road to the mill and loaded it up with flour. After they returned to the barn, Steffen shuffled out and said Dat wanted to meet with them in the house.

When they'd gathered around the kitchen table, Dat said, "I would like to go with you, but I know I shouldn't. I have money for you out of our emergency fund for your travel and to pay Kit. However, I don't expect either of you to track down Russ Keller. I had faith he would pay me, but it was probably wishful thinking on my part. It won't be worth your time to look for him."

Mary nodded even though she wasn't sure she agreed.

"When you get to Chicago, find Kit. He can help you find a church to help you distribute the supplies. Then check on Ellen's house."

"Isn't she going with us?" Mary asked.

Dat shook his head. "She's staying here. So is Colum."

"But we need to get him back to Honora."

"Nee. We have no idea how bad things really are. Colum could become ill in the city or get injured. Your Mamm thinks that you need to bring Honora and Patrick here, and I agree."

"What if she doesn't have the money for tickets?"

Dat tugged on his beard. "I included money for tickets for them. Bring them back here—then we can figure out what to do."

After Dat had finished talking, Lemuel headed back out to the barn to start the milking with Michael and Vyt. Mary hung back.

"Dat, it won't look right for Lemuel and me to travel together without you," she said quietly.

He smiled a little. "These are unusual times. It will be fine. Once you get to Chicago, you'll have Kit or Honora with you. My bigger fear is that one of you will venture off on your own. There's apt to be con men trying to take advantage of the tragedy. Stay away from anything like that."

"All right." Mary hesitated a moment.

"What is it?"

"I just want you to know that Lemuel and I aren't interested in each other—in courting or anything like that."

Dat smiled a little. "I figured that. And I trust you both. I know you'll do the right thing." His face grew more serious. "And that means not trying to find Russ Keller. I was foolish to trust him. I know he wouldn't try to hurt me, but I don't know what he might try to do to you."

Mary listened to what Dat said, but when he ventured outside, she crept into his room and opened up his travel bag. The contract from Russ Keller and Dat's map of Chicago from 1851 were all that was left inside. She quickly took both and went upstairs, placing the documents in the travel bag of Mamm's that she would use to go to Chicago. Then she went back outside to do the chores.

An undercurrent of excitement ran through her. She was returning to Chicago.

EARLY WEDNESDAY MORNING, Sarah gave Mary the quilt she'd made to give to Honora. It was a nine-patch made with fabric from the family's dresses and shirts, squares cut out of material that wasn't too worn. The back was navy blue.

"It's perfect," Mary said, admiring her sister's work. "I can't wait to give it to Honora."

Then Sarah gave her ten loaves of freshly baked bread wrapped in newspaper. She must have been up half the night. Mary gave her sister a kiss on the cheek. "Denki."

Mary and Lemuel left before the milking with the wagons tightly packed—filled with far more than they'd taken the first trip.

The plan was simply to follow what they'd done before. They arrived in Elkhart before nine, unloaded the supplies at the railroad station, and then took the wagons to the stable and boarded the horses. Soon they were on the train to Chicago. It had been less than two weeks since the last time they'd made the trip, yet it seemed like a lifetime ago.

When they arrived in Chicago around one thirty, they were able to get the supplies unloaded and stored at the station, which was now the end of the line, since the trestle over the lake had burned. They also found out from the railway clerk at the warehouse that the Station Hotel had burned too.

"How about the nearby stables?" Mary asked.

The man shrugged. "The fire skipped around. It's hard to say."

They decided to go there to start their search for Kit. They took off on foot into a gray wasteland. It took Mary a minute to realize nothing was green. The trees, stripped of branches and leaves, were reduced to charred trunks. Half-burned buildings stood like monstrous skeletons next to piles of rubble. The wooden sidewalks had burned, but the woodblock street hadn't, most likely because the wood was treated.

Most buildings along the route had burned too, either partly or completely, but every once in a while there would be a house or store intact, although Mary knew everything inside the building had to be ruined by the smoke. There were men working everywhere, sorting through the debris and shoveling it into wagons. Some buildings were being rebuilt with the framing already up, and both adults and children were scavenging for bricks and placing them in piles to be reused.

When Mary and Lemuel reached the spot where the hotel had been, they found a pile of ashes. The only thing intact was the chimney. But a block away, the stable still stood.

Lemuel and Mary jogged toward it. As they grew closer, it was evident the roof was partly burned and the edges of the pasture were singed, but the green grass must have stopped the fire.

The stables were full of animals—horses, cows, and goats. Mary guessed it was probably one of the few stables in the area that had survived the fire.

Lemuel asked the stable hand if he'd seen Kit Matson. The

boy nodded. "He's out right now, on a job. But he'll be back soon."

Mary noticed that two of his horses were in the stable, in the same stall. She walked over and rubbed both of their forelocks at the same time.

"Thank you," Lemuel said to the stable hand. "We'll wait for him."

Mary took bread, cheese, and two apples out of the bag she carried and handed Lemuel an apple. "The city still has an energy to it, doesn't it?"

Lemuel nodded. "But it's so sad now. I don't know how anyone can stand to stay."

They sat down on a bale of hay, and Mary said, "Oh, I can see why they do. It's going to be rebuilt. Out of the ashes comes beauty, right?"

He smiled a little. "I hope you're right. And I hope the poor are treated better once it is rebuilt."

Mary hoped so too. Just as they finished their food, Kit pulled up in his second wagon. "Hello!"

Lemuel and Mary both stood. Kit appeared exhausted, with dark circles under his eyes.

After greeting him, Mary said, "We have what we owe you. But we also need your help."

Lemuel interrupted Mary, asking Kit, "How are you doing? Are you well?"

Mary took a step backward, embarrassed she hadn't inquired about his health first.

Kit shrugged. "I've been better. Relieved to see you two—and surprised, to be honest. How is Ellen? And Honora's little boy?"

Mary told him that they were all doing fine. "Colum has been missing his mother and having nightmares, but they have lessened some. Ellen likes being in the country."

Kit smiled. "I thought she would. I'm so glad that she—that both of them—went with you. This is no place for a woman on her own right now. Or children."

"Speaking of," Mary said, "how is Honora?"

"I don't know. I lost track of her that night, after we returned one wagon and team of horses here. We did find Patrick, but then they headed for the lake while I helped more people get out." Kit rubbed his shoulder. "The Grand Hotel survived. The fire stopped a block before it, so she may be back there."

It sounded to Mary like she and Lemuel would definitely have to go to the hotel now. Hopefully she would be able to talk with Russ Keller too. "What about Ellen's house?" she asked.

"I drove by the other day. The barn burned, but her house is still there. The roof is damaged but repairable. I'd planned to go by today and see if it's full of squatters." He rubbed the back of his neck. "It never should have happened. It never should have gotten so big."

"The fire?" Mary asked.

He nodded. "The firebox where the first call was placed malfunctioned. It took forever for the first crews to arrive."

"The newspaper said that Mrs. O'Leary's cow kicked over a lantern, but Ellen doubts that's what happened," Mary said. "She thinks Mrs. O'Leary is being blamed because she's Irish."

Kit nodded. "That's the consensus in the neighborhood. The story here is that a group of men had been booted out of one bar and were refused service at another. They congregated outside the O'Learys' barn to drink and gamble. Some think they accidentally started the fire." He shook his head. "No one knows who started the story about Mrs. O'Leary, but she's mortified and has hardly left her house."

"Her house survived?"

Kit nodded. "Same as Ellen's. Her barn burned, but by some miracle her house still stands."

Still, Mary felt sick to her stomach for the woman. How horrible to have the whole country, maybe the whole world, accuse you of something you didn't do—all because of your nationality.

"You mentioned helping more people get out. How did the rest of the night of the fire go for you?" Lemuel asked.

"I picked up folks in that neighborhood and their house-wares, and headed over to the river again. By the time we crossed the bridge, the river was on fire, as well as the ware-houses on both sides. I was foolish to try to get out of it again, although I'm not sorry I was able to help more people. But I put my horses at risk. Thank God we made it." He took his cap off and ran his hand through his hair. "By Monday morning, I made it back to the stable but then, as the fire approached, I had to keep going north. It was a day of hell. Finally, it started to rain. It wasn't until then that I was sure I'd survive."

Mary swallowed hard. They'd gotten out just in time.

"You can't imagine how relieved I was when I returned here," Kit said, "and realized my second team survived too."

"What have you been doing since the fire?" Lemuel asked.

"Hauling debris away from the burned areas," Kit answered, "and in some cases hauling building supplies back to the con-struction sites. You wouldn't believe how quickly people started rebuilding."

Kit's mention of supplies brought Mary back to the present. As much as she wanted to hear all of Kit's story, they needed to establish a plan. "Speaking of supplies," she said, "we've brought donations. Food and bedding, nails and tools, that sort of thing. We hoped that you could give us an idea of where to go and that we could use your wagons to deliver them."

Kit's eyes grew wide. "Thank you. Not only for coming back to pay me, but for bringing supplies too. You didn't have to do any of that."

Mary smiled at him. "No, we felt compelled to. You helped us that night. You saved us and then helped Honora find Patrick. And the donations aren't just from us. They're from many others in our community."

"Then please extend my thanks to them. As far as where to deliver them, there's a Methodist church just south of the burned area, on the way to the hotel, that is coordinating relief. I trust that they will see that the goods go to those who need them the most."

IT TOOK THE REST of the afternoon to collect the goods from the railroad warehouse and deliver them to the church, except for Honora's quilt, which Mary had tucked under the bench of the wagon. After taking the last load inside, Mary noticed several children hanging around the outside of the church.

"They are orphans, most likely," the pastor said soberly, following her gaze. "Either their parents died in the fire or are injured. But at least they will be fed tonight." He turned to look at her. "Thank you."

Mary nodded at him and swallowed hard to keep her emotions under control. After saying good-bye to the pastor and the others, she turned to Lemuel. "Let's go to the Grand Hotel."

"You can take the wagon," Kit said, "but you'll have to go south to cross the river. All the bridges north of here burned. And it's hit and miss as far as the streets. Some are passable, some are still filled with rubble, and some are filled with tents and refugees."

Mary nodded, acknowledging his instructions.

"Meet me at Ellen's when you're done." Kit patted the packet of money that Mary had given him, which now resided in his breast pocket. "Thankfully I can settle my accounts and buy a decent supper."

On their way around the burned area, they passed the feedlot where Patrick worked. Mary found the right one and even recognized the man who had told Honora the night of the fire that Patrick had gone home.

Trying not to breathe in the stench, she jumped down from the wagon and asked the man if he'd seen Patrick Sullivan.

He shook his head. "Not since the night of the fire."

Mary thanked him and then climbed back into the wagon. At least Kit had seen him after the fire. But where had he gone? Maybe he was helping Honora at the Grand Hotel.

Driving to the hotel meant dodging the streets full of rubble and zigzagging their way through the area. Finally, they arrived at the hotel, which was a block beyond the fire line, just as Kit had said. The blocks north and east of it had burned all the way to the river and beyond. The blocks directly south and west of it hadn't.

Throngs of people gathered near the hotel. Men in business suits. Women with children. Men with tool belts around their waists. Several people were begging. Lemuel had to park the wagon across the street from the hotel because there were so many buggies parked in front of it.

As they rounded the corner to the back of the hotel, there were several wagons up against the dock, filled with bags of flour and sugar, along with crates of produce. The big man named Mort from the night of the fire was supervising the unloading.

"Hello," Lemuel called out to him.

He squinted.

"We were here right before the fire."

He nodded slightly, as if he remembered.

"We're looking for Honora Sullivan and her son Patrick."

"And Russ Keller," Mary added quickly.

The man spat off the dock, between the parked wagons. "That Irish woman?"

Mary gasped and then nodded.

"I haven't seen her since the day after the fire," he said. "I have no idea where she is or if she survived." He crossed his arms. "As far as Russ, he's around here somewhere."

"He better be," said an older man who stood on the dock. "He owes me for this load and for the last one too."

Mort barked, "Stop complaining."

A few minutes later, Russ came out and addressed the man. "I'll be with you in a few minutes. You wouldn't believe the chaos around here. I appreciate your delivery. It's just that I need a minute to get the payment."

Mary stepped toward him.

Russ's head jerked back. "What are you doing back here?"

"We came for Judah Landis's payment."

"Well, well, well," Russ said, shaking his head. "Judah didn't look well the last time I saw him. Did he survive the fire?"

"He's fine," Mary said. "Just waiting for his money."

Russ nodded. "I'll attend to your payment too."

"Have you seen Honora Sullivan?" Lemuel added. "And her son Patrick?"

"I haven't seen either of them"—Russ cocked his head—"since the night of the fire. Wait here," he said. "I'll be back with your payment soon."

Mary and Lemuel stayed on the dock, leaning against the wall. Finally, the older man walked to the door to the kitchen and started yelling. "Russ Keller, get back out here with my money," he bellowed. "I have other deliveries I need to make."

After about five minutes, the chef came out. "I'm sorry, Russ seems to have left."

"Don't give me that—"

"Come back first thing in the morning," the chef interrupted. "Russ comes in early."

The old man stomped down the steps, shouting over his shoulder, "Tell Russ I'll get him for this. No one in this city will deliver to him after I'm done."

Mary gave Lemuel a questioning look. It was taking longer than she'd hoped, but she wouldn't leave without finding Honora—and she really didn't want to leave without Dat's money.

Mary reached into her bag and retrieved the map of Chicago. *205 South May Street*. She remembered Russ's address from the night of the fire, when Dat had told her to memorize it when he went to Russ's home.

Why not go by Russ Keller's now and see what they could find?

CHAPTER 23

Sophie

On Friday morning, I woke up under a nine-patch quilt in Jane's bedroom to the sound of a lark chirping outside the window. She'd insisted on taking the hide-a-bed in the living room. I protested, but Jane proved to be more stubborn than I'd expected.

As I stretched out, I thought of Mary searching for Honora and Patrick, and then about the group at the schoolhouse last night. I understood Mary's desire to help those in need, particularly those who appeared to be vilified for being immigrants. It wasn't right. I remembered the verse from Leviticus that I had struggled to memorize in school: *And if a stranger sojourn with thee in your land, ye shall not vex him. But the stranger that dwelleth with you shall be unto you as one born among you, and thou shalt love him as thyself; for ye were strangers in the land of Egypt: I am the Lord your God.*

It warmed my heart, to the point that tears filled my eyes,

that Mamm and Dat and others in their community had done just that in helping the Lopez family and the others who lived in the village.

The smell of bacon frying and a baby crying finally inspired me to crawl out of bed. Everything hurt. I had definitely over-done it the day before. After I dressed, I took my phone out of the bag of rice. It wouldn't turn on. I put it back in but doubted it would do any good. I placed the bag of rice on the top of Jane's bureau.

Jane was holding the baby and Miriam was cooking when I reached the little kitchen. Owen stopped crying and smiled at me. I smiled back and then held out my arms. "I'll take a turn."

I walked with him to the window and looked across the street at the shop, imagining the canning circle the next day.

Over breakfast, I said that I planned to go by the village and then to the schoolhouse.

"You should go with her," Miriam said to Jane. "Owen and I can handle the shop today."

"Oh, that's too much," Jane said. It was a Friday in early September. Chances were they'd be busy.

"Everyone's always so nice about Owen," Miriam said. "If he's fussy, they take turns holding him. If I need to feed him, everyone's always willing to wait. He brings out the best in people. It's easier to spend the day at the shop than here alone."

"All right," Jane said. "As long as Sophie doesn't mind me tagging along."

"Not at all," I said. "I'll get you back here eventually."

"Let me get everything ready first," Jane said. "Then you can take over, Miriam."

It was nearly eleven when we left Plain Patterns. We stopped by the village first. Amish men and boys, along with Victor and Sebastian, were hauling flooring and damaged drywall out of the cabins. Several women and older children were working too. Hank sat on his UTV, watching.

I climbed out of my car and, after greeting him, asked where the other women were. "The ones with young kids are at the schoolhouse," Hank said. "It sounds as if everyone plans to meet there for lunch. Your people are taking care of everything."

Your people. My heart swelled at the words. I might not have joined the church, but they were still my people.

"Is Karin around?" I asked.

He shook his head. "She went to work. She's worried about missing too many days."

Just as I was ready to climb back in my car, Derek arrived. He said, "Can you hold on a minute? I need to ask you something."

I wandered over to Derek's truck while he talked over a few things with Hank and then told Victor he needed his help to get the pump on the creek working correctly again. "The flood really messed with it."

Victor nodded and said he'd be right there.

When Derek finally walked over, he reached out and touched my shoulder. "How are you feeling today?"

"A little achy but mostly okay."

"Have I told you how nice you look in your Kapp and dress?"

I tilted my head. What was he up to?

"Look," he said, "I'm sorry that I was avoiding you. It took me a few days to work through what you told me—as far as Lyle and you and everything. But I have. And now I was wondering what your plans are—"

I realized I was holding my breath and exhaled.

"I plan to join the church next summer. I don't know if I'll be able to keep working here or not. But I hope so. Is there any chance that you'll stay?" Before I could answer, he continued, "Because it would make me so happy if you did."

"Derek!" Hank hollered. "I have a question for you."

Derek took a step toward his boss. "I know it's a lot to spring on you right now with everything going on. But can we talk about this later?"

I opened my mouth, but nothing came out, so I just nodded instead.

Derek grinned and then jogged across the street.

I followed at a slower pace and then climbed into my car. What *did* I want? Living with an autoimmune disorder—and with this flare-up in particular—had forced me to live day by day and not think about the future. Could I stay in Nappanee and join the church for a good man like Derek? Was that what God had for me?

When Jane and I reached the school, the Amish scholars were playing games outside with the preschoolers. Inside, Mamm and my two sisters were making sandwiches and cutting up fruit. Jane and I joined them. As we worked, I asked if everyone was still up to having the canning circle the next day.

"Jah," Mamm said. "But let's plan to serve lunch there. Derek said Hank Barlow wants to sponsor the meal, and several of the wives of the workers said they would like to fix lunch for everyone."

I thought of Rosibel's cooking and my mouth watered. "That sounds amazing."

Just before we were ready to serve lunch, an Amish boy came running into the school. "There's a TV van outside," he said. "And an Englisch guy in an old pickup just pulled up."

I HURRIED OUT the door. Dillon and Chelsea were climbing out of the news van, and, sure enough, Jasper was climbing out of his little truck too. He wore a suit and tie, and his shoes looked freshly polished.

"Hello, Sophie. Did you get my text?" Jasper asked as he came toward me.

I shook my head. "My phone is toast. It got soaked yesterday."

"I'm sorry to hear that. Well, Karin called me about the flood, and Dillon's hoping to do another interview. He wants to ask me a few questions and talk to other members of the community."

"Everyone's gathering here for lunch soon," I said. "But Karin's at work. I'm not sure who would want to be a spokesperson."

"We're going to start with Jasper," Dillon said, joining us. "And then get shots of the kids, if that's permissible."

"We'll have to check with the Amish parents. Maybe the backs of their children would be allowed."

"Could you tell us, on camera, what happened yesterday?" Dillon asked. "And what the response from the community was?"

I hesitated.

"Why don't we start with me?" Jasper said, noticing my discomfort. "And give Sophie a chance to think about this."

"I can speak with Chelsea and tell her what happened," I offered. "She could lead into interviewing Jasper with the information."

"Why were you willing to speak on camera before?" Dillon asked. "What changed?"

I glanced around. "The location. When you interviewed me down at the village, I was speaking for myself. If you interview me now, it will appear that I'm speaking for the Amish community here—and I'm not."

He rubbed the side of his face and muttered, "Whatever."

I ignored him and walked over to Chelsea. Briefly, I told her about the flash flood and the ruined cabins, and then about the Amish community fixing meals, collecting clothing and bedding, and helping to provide lodging. I didn't tell her about Sebastian. That was a story I would leave to the Lopez family to tell, if they chose.

Once the camera was set up, Chelsea did an introduction, recapping most of what I'd told her. Then she said, "We have Jasper Benjamin with us again, the attorney for Mateo Lopez, who's incarcerated in the Mid County Detention Center in Michigan." She turned toward Jasper. "Tell us about migrant labor in Indiana."

"Over thirty thousand Latinos work and live here in Elkhart County." Jasper squinted in the bright sun. "Some of the workers were born here and are citizens, some have been naturalized, some are documented, and some are undocumented. It's not unusual for a family from Mexico or Central America to be a mixed-status family, which means a mix of citizens, documented workers, and undocumented workers. We couldn't survive economically without these workers. In just eight years, Elkhart County went from a twenty percent unemployment rate in 2009 to a two percent unemployment rate today. Overall, in the state of Indiana, farmers employ at least twenty thousand migrant workers per year. In fact, an economic development agency is hunting for job candidates as far away as Puerto Rico. Fifty percent of our entire country's food system is dependent on immigrant work, including farms, food processors, distributors, and restaurants."

"Great! Cut!" Dillon held up his phone. "Breaking news.

According to Twitter, someone in the sheriff's department just anonymously released the video of Mateo being stopped."

"What did it show?" Chelsea asked.

"That he signaled." Dillon motioned to the cameraman. "We need to get to Elkhart ASAP."

"I've got to go too." Jasper gave me a wave and ran toward his truck. "Tell Rosibel and Victor—and Sebastian," he yelled. "I'll call Karin on my way!"

THE LOPEZ FAMILY was overjoyed with the news about the release of the dash cam. Rosibel asked me if that meant Mateo would be immediately released. "I don't know," I said. "Hopefully Karin will have more information."

With the excitement of the news crew gone, the children all washed their hands to get ready to eat. Everyone gathered inside, and Dat led the group in a silent prayer. Then everyone dished up their food. Some ate inside and others ate outside. When the children finished, they started a game of volleyball. I couldn't *not* join in.

But soon I was hot and sweaty and tired. I checked in with Mamm and my sisters one more time to remind them they needed to be at Plain Patterns by eight in the morning with their tables, canners, and stockpots.

"We'll be there," Beth said. "Don't worry."

Mamm nodded in agreement and then said, "You should go back to Jane's and get some rest. You look exhausted."

I didn't protest. I felt exhausted.

Jane was cleaning up, but she abandoned her duties to Mamm and my sisters. When we reached her place, she told me to go rest while she checked on Miriam and Owen.

I awoke to a knock on Jane's front door.

I sat up groggily. Who would come here looking for Jane when Plain Patterns was open?

But the second knock woke me up fast. It had a lot of force behind it. I slid out of bed and grabbed the bag of rice, digging my phone out of it.

I hit the On button, even though I doubted it would work, left the bedroom, and tiptoed behind the front door.

Another knock sounded. "Sophie! Are you in there?"

It was Lyle.

I frantically looked at my phone. It wasn't coming on. I stayed behind the door.

The door opened before I could reach for the lock. I held my breath. Thankfully the door didn't open far enough to hit me.

I froze as I watched Lyle go down the hall. I could hear Miriam's bedroom door open.

I needed to act fast before he came back. I sprinted back into Jane's room, grabbed my keys, and slipped them and my phone into my apron pocket. There was no lock on the door, so I pushed the bureau as hard and fast as I could against the door. Then I rushed for the window, opening it all the way and popping out the screen.

"Sophie!" came Lyle's voice from down the hall. "I just want to talk with you."

I doubted that was all. I scrunched down, lifted one leg onto the windowsill and then the other, and jumped down to the flower bed in Jane's backyard. As I rounded the corner of the house, Lyle appeared and grabbed me.

"Let me go!" I screamed.

"Shut up," he hissed.

I tried to wrench my arm away.

"Stop it." He yanked me closer to him. "You were determined

to ruin my life three years ago, and now you've succeeded." He pulled me even closer. "And now I have you to blame for losing my job too. Where's the baby?"

Instead of pulling away again, I pushed forward into him, using his own momentum and catching him off guard. I wouldn't have time to get in my car and start it, but I might have time to dash across the road. I'd raced Lyle enough times to know that even though he was powerful, he wasn't that fast.

I took off. A car was coming from my right, but I charged ahead. It honked and slowed. I sped up and made it across the street. I glanced over my shoulder. Lyle had slowed for the car.

The front door of Plain Patterns opened and Jane appeared, holding Owen, with Miriam close behind them. "Sophie? Whatever is the matter?" But then she must have seen Lyle because she yelled, "Hurry, child!"

I stumbled past her and Miriam into the store, and Jane slammed the door behind me and locked it.

"All I wanted to do is talk with her!" Lyle shouted, pounding his hands against the door. "She's overreacting!" With a last slam of his fists against the door, Lyle turned and strode back across the street.

Reflexively, without thinking, I let my hand slip into my apron pocket, and I pulled out my phone.

It had turned on.

I had one text from Karin and two from Jasper, in addition to the one he'd sent earlier about the news crew. Karin reiterated what Dillon had said about the video being released. Jasper confirmed it and said he had petitioned the judge who sent Mateo to the detention center. He said he'd let me know when he found out more.

I didn't want to call the police again. I felt defeated by them not taking me seriously the last time. Maybe Jasper could advise me on what I should do.

"Do you mind if I use your back room to make a call?" I asked Jane.

She shook her head. "Not at all. Please don't go outside."

Jasper answered on the third ring. "Hello, Sophie. Your phone is working, I take it?"

"Jah," I said.

"I'd forgotten you said it had gotten wet when I sent the texts." Jasper paused a moment, and when I didn't say anything, he asked, "What is it?"

"I need some advice." I briefly told him about my history with Lyle and how he had harassed me again.

"You need to call 9-1-1," Jasper said.

"Did you miss the part where I wasn't taken seriously before?"

"I hear you, and I know it's frustrating, but you've got to call again," Jasper said. "There are a lot of good law enforcement out there. Believe me."

I was wary, but I knew Jasper was right. I needed to involve the authorities. Again.

"Call me back, would you? And let me know what happens."

Touched, I thanked him and then ended the call. Next, I called 9-1-1 and was told to stay inside and that an officer would arrive as soon as possible. As I slipped my phone back into my pocket, I realized I'd reached out to Jasper instead of Derek. I wasn't sure why. But I thought it was the right thing to do.

I walked back into the shop. Jane was peering through the window.

"He's gone," she said. "He was in my driveway for a while, staring at the building, but he climbed into his truck and left."

A few minutes later, an officer arrived and knocked on the

door of Plain Patterns. Jane invited him inside, and he introduced himself as Officer Pitt. He was even younger than the last officer I spoke with. With my voice only shaking a little, I described how Lyle had harassed me before. Then I rolled up my sleeve and showed him the angry red-and-purple mark on my arm and explained what Lyle had done this time.

The officer took notes, as well as a photo of my arm, and then asked for a description of Lyle's vehicle.

"It's a big silver pickup. A Ford, maybe? I don't know the license plate number."

"Where does he work?"

I explained Lyle had just been fired from Mill Creek Farms. "He blames me for that too."

Officer Pitt took my cell phone number and then looked me in the eye. "I'm sorry this happened to you," he said. "No one should treat you this way. I'll try to find Mr. Stauffer and talk with him, but I'll file a report whether I can find him or not."

I winced. "Will I be expected to press charges?"

"He could be charged with misdemeanor assault whether you press charges or not, but I'll talk with you first before that happens."

I nodded. I didn't know what to do. But Lyle needed to be stopped.

"He's likely to be violent again—with you or another person," the officer continued. "Pressing charges might not lead to any jail time, but it could lead to probation and anger management classes." His eyes were kind and caring. "I'll give you a call and update you on what I find out."

Tears stung my eyes. Officer Pitt took what I'd said seriously and had a plan to follow through. "Thank you," I managed to say.

He gave me a quick nod, followed by a kind smile.

After Officer Pitt drove away, I asked Jane, "What do you think I should do?"

She took my hand and squeezed it. "Pray about it. Give your worries to the Lord."

I nodded in agreement. "We still need to pick the produce for tomorrow, though."

"We can pick in the morning."

"Then let's get over to your house now," I said. "I'll feel safer once we're all home."

I left Jane and Miriam to close up the shop as I stepped into the back room and left a message for Mamm and Dat on the phone out in the shanty. I kept it brief, not wanting them to worry about me but wanting them to be aware in case Lyle went to their house.

Next, I sent Jasper a text with an update, saying the officer was kind and helpful. He replied immediately. *Thank you for letting me know. So grateful to read this.*

Then Jane, Miriam—with Owen in her arms—and I crossed the street. Once back at Jane's, I climbed back through the bedroom window, closed it, and moved the bureau, while Jane firmly locked the front door behind her. It wasn't unusual for Amish folk not to always lock their doors, but Jane would now, at least until the problem with Lyle was resolved. An hour later, after an uncharacteristically quiet supper, Miriam went back to her room to feed Owen.

Still lost in thought, I started running the dishwater. Jane grabbed a towel. "Want me to tell you the rest of the story?"

"Yes, please," I answered. That would be a good distraction. "Mary had decided to go to Russ Keller's house to try to get the money he owed her Dat."

CHAPTER 24

❖

Mary

Mary pulled out Dat's map from her bag and began searching for 205 South May Street. She found where she thought it would be, across from a park. From the map, which she hoped wasn't too outdated, Mary surmised it was only a couple of miles to the Keller residence, and it looked like it was out of the burned area, so the streets would be passable. She directed Lemuel to head southwest.

About a mile from the hotel was a church with a tall steeple and cross on the top, with people lined up on the sidewalk. A table was set up in front of the church with several pots of soup and loaves of bread. There were homeless people sitting on the wooden sidewalks and other people walking with bundles on their backs.

The houses grew larger the farther they traveled. There were even brick houses mixed in with the wooden ones, which were covered with masonry. They reached the park, which was filled with tents. On the other side was May Street. Russ Keller's home was a brick house, wedged between two other brick houses. It wasn't a mansion, but it was a good size.

"Let's go around the block," Mary said. "I want to think about what to say before we knock on the door."

When they turned the corner halfway down the block, Mary saw an alleyway. "Turn here," she said. "Let's see what the back of the house looks like. Maybe there's a place to park the wagon."

The alley was fairly wide, with stables behind the row of houses. However, there wasn't room for the wagon, so Lemuel kept going. As they turned to park on the side street, a tow-headed boy carrying a small barrel on his shoulder turned into the alley.

After they parked, Mary put the map back in her bag and looked down at the contract. To make Russ Keller honor it, she might have to get the law involved. That wasn't something encouraged by her church, and she wasn't sure she could go that far.

After Lemuel helped her down from the wagon, Mary pulled her cloak tight against the chill in the air. When they reached the house, Lemuel raised and lowered a brass knocker several times. Finally, a woman came to the door. For a moment Mary thought maybe she was the mistress of the house, but when Lemuel asked for Russ Keller, she responded, "Mr. Keller is in his office. I was instructed to convey that he's not taking any appointments." Mary realized that the woman was probably the housekeeper. She was dressed plainly, in a gray dress and white apron.

Mary took the contract out of the bag. "We're only in town for today, and Russ Keller owes us money for a delivery from October seventh. We need to collect what we're owed."

After a long pause, the woman said, "I'll let him know. Wait here." She closed the door.

Mary shook her head. "I doubt she's coming back." Ten minutes later, Mary said to Lemuel, "Let's go around to the back door."

As they turned down the alley, the boy they'd seen before was walking toward them.

Mary waved at him. "Do you know Russ Keller?"

The boy stopped and spoke in a hushed voice. "I saw him return a few minutes ago. He's inside his house."

"The housekeeper left us on the stoop," Mary said.

"She does that to everyone who comes to see Keller."

"What do the others do?" Mary asked.

"Bang on the door." The boy shrugged. "Threaten to call the police."

Mary smiled, hoping to put him more at ease. "Does it do any good?"

He shook his head. "The police don't care about things like that now. They have more important things to do." He hesitated for a moment. "But he probably won't come out at all if you keep hanging around here." His voice was practically a whisper as he said, "He usually goes back to the hotel and then returns for a late supper."

"Is he crooked?" Mary asked. "Or just a bad businessman?"

The boy shrugged again and then quickly veered off into the stable.

As they walked back to the wagon, Mary said, "We need to wait until Russ Keller comes out. It's our only hope of finding Honora, and I'd like to at least try a little harder to get the money. Let's wait in the wagon."

"All right," Lemuel said. "And then we'll figure out where to stay the night."

In the dim light, Mary could make out a man driving an open buggy with a bed behind it coming down the alley. Without saying anything to Lemuel, she jumped down.

"Wait," Lemuel called out.

"Shh," she hissed. "And get down. I don't want him to see you." She ran down the alley toward the buggy. Mort drove while Russ sat on the bench beside him.

"Russ Keller!" she yelled. "I need our money. And I think you know more than you're telling me about Honora Sullivan and her son Patrick."

The horses stopped, and a boy riding in the back of the buggy stood. It was the same boy they'd seen in the alley earlier.

Mary gasped. What was he doing with Russ Keller? He'd sounded as if he hardly knew the man.

Russ turned and said something to the boy, who sat back down. Russ squared his shoulders and faced her. "Mary Landis! I'm so happy to see you again. After I saw you earlier, I got to thinking that I could use your family's help." He crossed his arms over his wide chest. "We're feeding half the city—morning, noon, and night. I need more flour and anything else you have. Beef. Chicken. Pork. I'll compensate you for that along with what I owe you from before, all in one payment as soon as you can deliver the next load."

"No. We need our money now," Mary said. "We're returning to Indiana tonight. And we also need to find Honora."

Russ took off his hat and ran his hand through his salt-and-pepper hair. "Like I said, I haven't seen her since the day of the fire. Another foolish Irish woman. Can you believe Mrs. O'Leary leaving a lantern where a cow could kick it over? She should be hung."

Mary bit her tongue to keep from responding.

He shrugged. "I have no idea if Honora or her brats even survived the fire."

"They did," Mary answered. "We were with her and the younger one. She left us to find Patrick . . ."

Russ swatted a hand back toward the boy, who'd stood up again.

"Wait a minute." Mary stepped toward the buggy.

Russ said something to the boy and then turned back to Mary. "Leave. Now."

Mary turned toward him and crossed her arms. "Not until you pay me."

Mort turned toward Russ and said something quietly.

Russ shook his head.

Mort spoke louder. "The cops are on to you, not to mention lawyers representing the companies you owe. How many lawsuits do you want? What we need now are more supplies, and no one is going to sell to us if you keep this up. Word is getting around. Just pay the girl."

As Russ shook his head, his face turned red. But then he climbed down from the buggy and muttered, "I'll be right back."

Footsteps fell behind Mary. She turned to see Lemuel approaching her. "What's going on?"

"I'm not sure," Mary whispered. "I'm waiting for Russ to come back."

"Do you think he will?"

"I hope so." Mary stepped to the bed of the wagon to speak to the boy, but he shook his head and buried his face in his hands.

They waited for a few more minutes. Just as Mary was ready to pound on the back door of the house, Russ came out.

He shoved a packet at her. "Now get out of here." He climbed back up in the buggy.

Mary quickly opened it, finding it short of the contract but close enough. She doubted she could do any better.

"Thank you," she said.

"Like I said, I'll take more supplies from you."

Mary stepped back from the buggy as it lurched into motion. "I'll let my Dat know." But there was no way they'd risk bringing more to Russ. Maybe to some other business in Chicago, but not to him.

Once Mary and Lemuel reached the street and crossed it, Russ's buggy turned right. The boy, who was now on his knees in the back of the buggy, raised his arm and whirled it around his head and then pointed it toward the back door of the Keller house. Then he turned and faced forward as the buggy picked up speed and turned toward the hotel.

"Did you see that?" Mary asked Lemuel, who shook his head. "The boy made a motion." She imitated what he'd done. "Like to go back. I think Honora is in Russ's house."

"The boy?"

"The blond boy, the one we saw earlier. He was in the back of the wagon. I'm almost sure he's Patrick, Honora's son."

Lemuel shook his head. "Did he say that's who he is?"

"Pretty much," Mary said.

Lemuel gave her a puzzled look. "What do you mean?"

"His expression said it."

"Oh." Lemuel stopped at the wagon.

"We should pretend we're leaving," Mary said. "And then come back once we're sure Russ hasn't returned."

Lemuel sighed. "All right." He hesitated and then asked, "Any idea where we should stay tonight?"

Mary didn't have enough money to pay for a room—not even a stable stall. She answered, "Maybe Kit will let us stay at Ellen's when we go back to meet him."

"What if there are squatters there?"

Mary shrugged. "We'll figure it out. The Lord will provide."

TEN MINUTES LATER, when they were confident Russ was on his way to the hotel and not returning, they approached his house for the second time that day. Campfires now burned in the park and people gathered around them. Someone played a harmonica. Others sang. Someone else yelled angrily.

They walked down the alley, and Mary knocked on the back door. When no one answered, she knocked again. Finally, she tried the doorknob. It turned.

"Mary," Lemuel whispered. "Don't."

"Shh," she replied. "You can stay out here if you want."

She slipped inside. Lemuel sighed and followed her.

Mary led the way into a dark entryway. The savory scent of a roast and of freshly baked bread made her stomach growl. Below was the dim glow of a lamp. She took a step forward. There was a staircase leading toward a basement. Perhaps the kitchen was down there.

She grabbed the handrail and started down the stairs. As she reached the last stair, the housekeeper came around the corner.

The woman gasped. Before she could say anything, Mary yelled, "Honora! Are you here?"

"Who's there?" a voice called out as the housekeeper shoved Mary into Lemuel, who caught her.

"Honora! It's Mary. And Lemuel! We've come for you!"

Footsteps came toward them.

The housekeeper turned around and yelled, "Get back in the kitchen or Mr. Keller will hear about this!"

Honora appeared, wearing a tattered dress. "Is Colum okay? He's not here, is he?"

"He's fine." Mary reached around the housekeeper for Honora's hand. "He's back at the farm. We need to go."

The housekeeper shoved Mary's arm away, pushing her backward. Lemuel stepped around the two and grabbed Honora's hand and pulled her up the stairs. The housekeeper lost her balance and fell back against the wall.

"Go, go, go!" Mary called to Lemuel and Honora. The three of them ran up the stairs and burst through the back door. As they stumbled into the alleyway, Mary yelled, "Go to the left!" to Honora as Lemuel led the way.

A minute later, the housekeeper appeared in the alley. "Police! There's been a kidnapping! Someone get the police!"

Fortunately, no one seemed to be paying any attention. Patrick had been right. It seemed the police had more important things to do.

As they ran, Mary asked Honora, "Was Patrick with Russ Keller?"

The woman nodded. "Mr. Keller takes him back there to work late into the night, cleaning up and then baking bread for the morning."

"Why aren't you working at the hotel?"

"Mr. Keller's cook disappeared the night of the fire. He's making me work here and Patrick too, in addition to the hotel."

Mary shook her head and helped Honora into the buggy before climbing up herself. "Why do you agree to do it?"

Honora bit her lip. "My husband worked for Mr. Keller, driving his wagon and horses and picking up deliveries. When my husband was killed in the accident, one of Mr. Keller's horses was too, and the other had to be put down. Mr. Keller's wagon was smashed to smithereens.

"He claimed I needed to work for him to make up for what he'd lost. He rented us the shack, found Patrick the job in the stockyards, and forced me to work at the hotel. We have to work until the debt is paid off, which is hard to do because I have to pay for our lodging out of my wages."

Mary shook her head. "None of that sounds fair."

Honora sighed. "Fair or not, we had nowhere else to go and I had nowhere else to work. Many had it worse, even before the fire. At least we have shelter and food."

Never in her life had Mary had to worry about shelter and food. Jah, Mamm and Dat were both concerned about money in a way Mary hadn't heard them talk before, but they wouldn't starve. Somehow they would figure out a way to buy seed for next year. Perhaps they'd have to sell a team of horses. Or even a few acres. But they wouldn't completely lose what they had.

"On the night of the fire, I wanted to go after you after I found Patrick, but Mr. Keller wouldn't give me any money, and I couldn't buy train tickets without it." Honora clasped Mary's hand. "Thank you for taking care of Colum."

"My Dat sent enough money for train tickets for you and Patrick." Mary squeezed her hand and then reached under the seat for the quilt Sarah had made. "And my sister made this for you."

"Your sister made this?" Honora ran her hand over the quilted material. "Someone I've never met made this for me?"

"Jah," Mary said.

Honora buried her face in the quilt. The strong, no-nonsense woman began to cry. Mary put her arm around Honora's shoulders and listened to her muffled sobs.

When they reached the hotel, Honora took a deep breath, dried her tears on the cloth, folded the quilt, and slipped it back under the bench. She and Mary jumped down before Lemuel parked the wagon.

Russ's buggy was in the stables.

"Should we wait here?" Mary asked. "Or go into the kitchen?"

"Patrick will be in the kitchen," Honora answered. "If we run into Russ out here without any witnesses, well, who knows what he'll do?"

"What might he do?" Mary asked warily.

"He carries a pistol," Honora said.

"The chef seemed fed up with him earlier today. And so did Mort."

"That's good," Honora said. "Maybe one of them will intervene."

"Lemuel, you go in first," Mary said. "Russ might not recognize you as quickly. Try to find Patrick."

Lemuel nodded and slipped into the kitchen.

At first Mary couldn't hear anything, but then there was the sound of someone running toward the door, followed by shouting and a high-pitched yell of, "Stop it!"

"Patrick!" Honora opened the door and ran in, with Mary following her.

Russ Keller held Patrick around the waist and off the ground. When he saw Honora, he cursed and lifted Patrick a little higher. "You owe me. And so does he."

"We've worked for you for three years in exchange for rotten food and a run-down shack. You treat us as if you own us, and now you're holding us captive in your house. We're leaving."

"No," Keller boomed. "You haven't paid me back."

"I'll never be able to pay you back!" Honora cried shrilly. "First it was the wagon and horses. Then the rent. Now it's our lodging at your house." Honora's voice continued to increase in volume. "You'll never let us go."

"That's right," Keller hissed. "You're not going anywhere."

"You can't do this," Mary said.

Russ laughed. "That's not how this works. They owe me."

Honora took a step backward. "I'm going."

Russ put Patrick on his feet but kept his beefy hands on the boy's shoulders. "Fine. But he's not."

Mary stepped forward, her hand gripping the bag slung over her shoulder. "Keller, how much does Honora owe you?"

He scoffed. "More than you can pay."

"That might be." She reached into the bag and pulled out the packet of money. "But what about this?"

"I'll get far more out of Patrick working for me," Russ said. "And both of them—and the rest of their kind—need to pay for what they've done to our city."

The chef stepped into the fray, arms crossed. He glanced from Russ to Mary.

"But you can have the money now," Mary argued. "His work will take much longer to benefit you. Take this. Buy more supplies. You can feed more people and make more money."

Keller tightened his grip on Patrick. Mary extended the packet toward him.

"Let the boy go," the chef barked. "He's the least of your worries."

In an explosive motion, Keller grabbed the packet with one hand and shoved Patrick with the other. "Get out, now!" he bellowed. "All of you."

Honora grabbed Patrick and ran while Lemuel took long-legged strides toward the door.

But Mary stared right at Russ Keller. "I hope you'll find some sort of peace in this life," she said, "and turn from your criminal ways."

The man's face reddened. "You self-righteous brat! You're as bad as your father." He lunged toward her, but the chef grabbed Russ's arm and held him back.

"Get out of here!" the chef yelled to Mary.

Mary turned and calmly walked out of the kitchen. Once she reached the wagon, she saw that Honora had wrapped Patrick in the quilt. She turned toward Mary with a brief nod and a whispered, "Thank you."

A block later, once they reached the burned area where there were no more streetlamps, Lemuel stopped the wagon and lit the lantern. Mary gawked at the destruction all around them in the area she remembered so well. One whole block would be gone, except for a shed in the middle. On another block, a single house stood. On another, only a barn remained in the middle of a pasture. But mostly there was complete devastation. As they neared Ellen's, Mary looked toward where St. Paul's Church with its high steeple should be. It was completely gone.

Ahead, they could see a few houses standing. One was Ellen's, just as Kit had said. Her barn was gone, but the shed stood. The pasture between her house and the barn had perhaps saved her house, along with the ever-changing wind, most likely. Across the street, though, all the shacks were gone, reduced to piles of ash.

Kit had hobbled his other two horses in the pasture. As Lemuel, Honora, Patrick, and Mary climbed down from the wagon, he waved and walked toward them. "Honora! So good to see you." He locked eyes with Patrick. "Good to see you too."

The boy smiled up at him.

Kit turned toward Mary. "It appears you completed everything you set out to do."

"I have," she said. She no longer had the money, but she would trust the Lord to see her family through. Patrick and Honora's lives were what mattered most.

"So, you're headed home?"

"Jah," Mary answered. "In the morning. Is it okay to stay here?"

"It is," Kit answered. "There's no one inside."

"Denki," Mary said gratefully.

"Tell your Dat I have a lead on a hotel that would buy flour from him—and anything else he might have to sell," Kit said. "It's a reputable hotel, not like Russ Keller's operation. He can send a letter to me here, at Ellen's, and let me know if that's something he's interested in."

Maybe, Mary thought, she could return with Ellen and deliver Dat's reply to Kit herself. It might be the answer they needed to earn enough money to buy seed.

But as exciting as farming had been to her, part of her dreaded going back to that when there was so much work to be done here. So many people to take care of. So much she could help with. Still, the right thing to do was to go home and reunite Honora and Patrick with Colum, and to let Ellen know her house had survived.

All she could do was trust the Lord for guidance. But standing blocks from where the Chicago Fire had started, Mary felt her future might be far different from what she'd imagined a month ago. Chicago had won her heart.

CHAPTER 25

Sophie

Jane and I sat on the sofa as she finished the story. "Years later," she said, "a newspaper reporter admitted to having made up the story about Mrs. O'Leary's cow—a story that resulted in a woman being shamed for something she didn't do. She lived the rest of her life mostly as a recluse, shunned by her neighbors and afraid to venture out into society. Sadly, in some circles, that story endures today that Mrs. O'Leary's cow kicked over a lantern and started the Great Chicago Fire of 1871."

I shook my head. "What a travesty. And to think the story was an attempt to blame Irish immigrants for a tragedy that killed hundreds and displaced thousands."

"Jah, a story to harm others."

"Do you know why so many Irish ended up in America?"

Jane nodded. "I came across it in my research. During the potato blight of the mid-1800s, a million Irish starved to death, and another two million fled to the United States. They were poor, and people were afraid they carried diseases. Some

Americans believed they'd take their jobs and strain the local welfare budgets. Most practiced what was considered an alien religion—Catholicism. And many were accused of being criminals."

I took a deep breath and then exhaled. "Just like the accusations against the migrants here, huh?" It seemed to be human nature to fear and blame "the other."

Jane patted my leg. "If it's any consolation, gradually the Irish were accepted into the dominant culture. The prejudices against them are a distant memory or no memory at all."

Only time would tell how long it would take for the Lopez family and others from Mexico and Central America to be fully accepted. "So what happened to Mary?" I asked. "Did she go back to Chicago?"

"She did," Jane answered. "She accompanied Ellen, Honora, and the boys back and worked with the Methodist church for a while, feeding the homeless and distributing supplies. Then she took a position with a children's aid group."

"But she loved farming. She really gave all of that up?"

Jane nodded. "It turned out what she really loved was *doing* something. And helping others. She was a strong woman, both physically and emotionally. God used those gifts to help many over her lifetime."

"Did she ever move back to the Landis farm?"

"She did, when she was old. Vyt, who was my great-grandfather, had the farm by then. Mary lived her last years with him and the family of his daughter, who was my grandmother."

"She never married?"

"That's right," Jane said. "She believed the Apostle Paul's words that she could do more good single than married."

"Interesting." I couldn't help but think about the fact that Jane had never married either. She ministered to many single women in ways that she wouldn't be able to if she were married. I'd grown up expecting that I would marry, but perhaps I wouldn't. Only time would tell that too.

"What happened to Lemuel?"

"He ended up marrying Sarah. They purchased a nearby farm, and their descendants are still in the area."

"Aww, that's sweet."

"In fact," Jane said, her eyes twinkling, "the farm now belongs to your parents."

I sat up straight. "What?"

Jane smiled. "Lemuel and Sarah Deiner are your great-great-great-grandparents."

"Why didn't anyone ever tell me this story, then?"

Jane shook her head a little. "Perhaps it's been lost to time. Your paternal grandfather died when your father was still in his twenties. Perhaps he never had a chance to tell it. Or maybe his father never told him."

I squeezed Jane's hand. "So we're related?"

"Distantly," she said and squeezed back.

I wasn't surprised, though I was delighted. I was sure I was "distantly" related to half the Amish in the county, as was Jane and almost everyone else I knew.

"What about Ellen and Honora and her children? And Kit? What happened to them?"

"Kit and Honora married a few months after the fire and added more children to their family. Ellen continued to run the boardinghouse and remarried a few years later. Mary boarded with her for years and dearly cared for both families."

"No doubt." Mary truly seemed to care for all of them. Her relationships were genuine and sincere.

"Well," Jane said, "we are going to have an early and busy day tomorrow."

I stood. "Jah, we need to get to bed."

"The doors are locked," Jane said. "I sleep like a baby—literally." She grinned. "Meaning, I wake up at the slightest sound. I'll shout if I hear anything, and you keep your phone handy."

Once I was in the bedroom, I checked my phone. I had a voicemail from Officer Pitt. "I tracked down Lyle and questioned him. He admitted to grabbing your arm. Call me when you can."

I decided to call Officer Pitt in the morning. Hopefully I'd know what I should do by then.

Next, I looked at my weather app. It was supposed to be seventy degrees the next day, with possible clouds but no rain. Perfect for an outdoor canning circle.

The next morning, I was up by five, feeling rested and ready to go. I found that helping others energized me, which made me think of Mary again. She was a distant aunt of mine. We shared the same family and culture. Jah, we were separated by well over a century, but her story resonated with me.

Perhaps my interest in both the Awad family and the Lopez family came naturally. Perhaps something from Mary had been passed down to me, or perhaps it came from the Amish and biblical admonition to "love your neighbor as yourself."

After I had showered, dressed, and scrambled eggs for all of us, Jane and I headed over to Plain Patterns, hauling her canner and stockpots, along with her paring knives. Her folding tables were already in the shop.

By the time Mamm and my sisters arrived, all in one buggy, Jane and I had picked the tomatoes and beans and stored them in crates that Derek had brought from Mill Creek Farms. We finished up the cabbage and beets as Mamm, Beth, and Ruth unloaded their things, which also included produce from their three gardens. Miriam arrived with Owen in a front pack and began putting the canning jars on a table to be sterilized. That was the first order of business.

Soon, Dorothy, Savannah, and Tommy, along with his mother, Wanda, arrived with more tables and another canner. I hauled out a folding chair so Dorothy would be able to sit and rest whenever she needed to.

When she went into the shop for a drink of water, I asked Savannah how she was doing.

"She's improved," Savannah answered. "Her iron was low, so taking a supplement seems to be making a difference. We're waiting for some other test results, though."

I gave Savannah a hug and said, "I'll pray for Dorothy."

Savannah hugged me back. "Denki."

Tally and Regina arrived next in their buggy. I hurried to help Tally with her mother's wheelchair.

"I'll get your Mamm," I said to Tally, "while you take care of the horse."

"Denki," Tally said.

"Regina, how are you?" I asked as I positioned the wheelchair by the passenger door of the buggy.

She gave her standard answer. "I've been better."

I smiled and nodded as I transferred her down into her chair. "We put a table in the shade where you can work," I said. "And when you need a rest, we'll roll you into the store."

"We won't be here long," Regina said.

I knew Tally would like to stay longer, but her mother's health had to come first. I rolled Regina around to the front of the shop and then to the deck along the far side. When we reached the deck in the back, Jane greeted her and then my Mamm and sisters did too.

Regina actually smiled, the first time I'd seen her do so. We set Regina up with a bucket of beans to snap and soon Miriam, with a sleeping Owen strapped to her chest, joined her.

We set up the camp stoves, lit them, and began boiling water. My sisters took over sanitizing the jars, while I set up each station and put out the instruction cards.

Before nine, Arleta and little Ruby arrived. Miriam greeted them, and Ruby, in her mother's arms, patted Owen on the head. Arleta seemed reserved and hard to get to know, but she and Miriam seemed to have a good relationship.

My eyes searched out my own mother. After all these years, it seemed as if our relationship was finally getting better. Perhaps that had been the heart of the reason God had brought me home, to experience that healing.

If I'd never left my community, or returned as Miriam had ended up doing, would my relationship with Mamm have started to heal three years ago? If I'd been honest about how Lyle was treating me, would Mamm have been empathetic toward me and willing to support me through my pregnancy? If I hadn't been so stressed, would I have not lost the baby?

Before I could fall into any more introspection, Phyllis and her brood—except for Liza—arrived. Her teenaged boys had agreed to take care of the horses and buggies. Derek hauled Phyllis's table, camp stove, canner, cutting boards, and miscellaneous extra jars in the back of his truck.

Once he had everything set up, he pulled me aside. "A patrol car stopped Lyle up the road from the farm yesterday. Any idea what was going on?"

In the bustle of the morning, I hadn't had a chance to call Officer Pitt back yet. "Lyle tracked me down here. He entered Jane's house and when I tried to run away, he grabbed my arm."

Derek shook his head. "We were afraid of that. Hank's upset about Lyle stalking you. And I've been worried about you too."

313

I smiled at Derek. He was a true friend. "You don't need to worry about me, and tell Hank not to either." I patted my apron pocket. "Oh, and please tell him my cell phone is fine."

"I will," Derek said. "I need to get back to the farm, but I'll see you at noon—if I can find a ride. Karin is going to use my truck to haul all of the food over for lunch."

"Great!" I said. "If you can't find a ride, give me a call and I'll come get you."

He grinned. "Maybe we can talk then."

My heart lurched as I remembered what he'd wanted to talk about the day before. But I would have to put any thought of that off until later, along with the phone call to Officer Pitt. Right now, I needed to concentrate on making the canning circle a success.

WE HAD A NICE MIX of Amish and Englisch women, and we paired experienced canners with inexperienced ones. We had a few glitches. A stove stopped working. A couple of jars didn't properly seal. One broke. But overall, things went smoothly.

Except that Karin and Rosibel, and none of the other Hispanic women, had shown up.

Just before noon, as I watched over a batch of jars in the pressure cooker at the tomato station, Derek returned, carrying two tables from the church wagon.

"What's going on?" I asked.

"Your Dat drove the wagon over from the school and picked me up at the farm." He lifted the tables. "We're setting these up for the food."

"But Karin and the others aren't here yet."

"Yes, they are." He grinned. "They just arrived. And Hank and Cheri came with them, along with Victor and Sebastian."

As he continued toward the grass under the oak tree, Regina motioned to me. "Would you find Tally? I think we should get going."

"Can you stay for lunch?"

Regina frowned. "I don't think so."

"You could rest inside until everything is set up."

"Oh, all right."

I turned my duties over to Beth and wheeled Regina inside. I got her a glass of water and left her by the quilting frame. "I'll be back as soon as lunch is ready," I said.

Once back outside, I saw Hank sitting under the tree in a reclining lawn chair while Cheri helped Rosibel and Karin unpack foil pans of tortillas, beans, rice, meat, and vegetables.

Dat and Derek finished setting up the tables, and then Dat went over to sit with Hank, while Derek sought me out.

"I know you're busy, but I wanted a chance to finish our conversation," he said.

"Jah," I said. "I do too. I'm not sure exactly what you were getting at, but I wanted to let you know that I'm going back to Elkhart tonight. Being home has been a healing time for me. And, honestly, one of the best parts has been reconnecting with you. You've been such a good friend to me. But I don't plan to join the church." Mary's story had helped me realize the next chapter in mine. I couldn't stay in Nappanee. It wasn't what God had for me. "My life, for now, is in Elkhart."

His face reddened a little, but he said calmly, "It's been good to spend time with you too. Thank you for what you've taught me—and for your kindness."

If I could have hugged him, I would have. But that would

have only started rumors. Instead, I held up my fist for a bump. He smiled as our knuckles met.

A few minutes later, I saw him talking with Tally. Derek would find the right woman—and join the church. Or join the church and find the right woman.

Lunch was plentiful and amazing. Even Regina seemed to enjoy it. I looked around for Tally and Derek, but they weren't anywhere near each other. Tally was gathering up plates to wash inside, in the kitchen.

It took me a minute to find Derek. He was on the deck, talking to Miriam, who held Owen. Derek was tickling the baby's bare feet.

My heart lurched. In the long run, once he had a chance to think about it, Derek had gotten over that I'd been unmarried and pregnant. Was there a future for him and Miriam?

If I'd never left home—or if I'd returned with a baby, the way Miriam had—would Derek and I have had a chance back then? I was speculating again, rotating my emotional kaleidoscope turn after turn, guessing at what might have been.

It didn't matter. That hadn't been my destiny. I left, and my life took a completely different turn. I was a different person with a different future because I *hadn't* stayed. The sooner I accepted that, the better.

After the cleanup was complete, Victor loaded the tables back into Derek's truck while Dat and Derek loaded up the church wagon. Hank had just stood up when Sebastian started running across the backyard toward the parking lot. "Mateo!"

I stepped to where I could see. Jasper and another young man were walking toward us, wide grins on both their faces. Sebastian nearly flew through the air into the arms of his older brother.

The details of his release came out in a jumble of words.

316

Once the video was released, Jasper requested a release of the state lab tests on the "probable meth" found on the floor of Mateo's car.

No surprise. It turned out to be frosting.

With that, Jasper pushed for his release, challenging the charge that Mateo belonged to a gang in Chicago. There was no evidence to support it. Hoping to avoid a lawsuit, the state released Mateo that morning.

"It was my idea to surprise all of you," Mateo said as Victor, Rosibel, Karin, and Sebastian all hugged him at once. Hank stood at the edge of the circle, leaning on Cheri.

As tears filled my eyes, I noticed Mamm with her hands to her face, as if she were praying. Dat stepped to her side. A tear escaped and rolled down my cheek at the joy on my parents' faces for the Lopez family. And it appeared absolutely genuine.

THE REST OF THE DAY couldn't compare to Mateo coming home, but it went well. By midafternoon, we'd gone through most of the produce and most of the jars. As we cleaned up, women left with boxes of filled jars, thanking us as they left.

I helped Mamm load her wagon. "I'm going back to Elkhart this evening," I said, "but I'll stop by and grab the rest of my things first."

She met my eyes, and I was surprised at how misty hers were. "I'll look forward to seeing you."

Regina and Tally ended up staying until nearly the end. As they got ready to go, Regina said, "That's the most fun I've had in years."

Tally smiled as she pushed her mother toward the parking

lot. "Denki," she said to me. "I can't tell you how much we appreciate this."

Soon after, I told my sisters thank you and good-bye as they left, and then Jane told me to go too. "Phyllis is going to help me clean up. Go get your things so you can get on the road. You must be exhausted."

"You must be too," I answered.

"Well, I'll soon be able to collapse in my house. You still have a trip home."

I gathered up my things from Jane's and then headed to Mamm and Dat's. My stomach lurched as I arrived. Lyle's truck was parked in front of the house, and he sat on the porch with Dat and Mamm, who must have just arrived home.

I parked my car and considered calling Officer Pitt but decided to see what was going on first. As I headed toward the porch, he stood and came down the steps. "I'm not here to make trouble," he said. "I promise."

I turned sideways, so Mamm and Dat could clearly see us but not hear us.

"I'm sorry for stopping by Jane's yesterday," he said. "I shouldn't have done that."

"No, you shouldn't have," I said. "There are a lot of things you shouldn't have done." I was ready to unload on him when I thought of Jesus telling His disciples to pray for their enemies. I took a deep breath. Could I finally pray for Lyle?

I wasn't sure, but I could pray for myself. *Show me what to say.* I decided I could try to pray for him too. *Show him what you'd have him learn. Heal us both.*

"Lyle, you know the baby was yours."

He inhaled sharply. And then, as he exhaled, he gave me a quick nod.

"I lost her at nineteen weeks. I'd decided to keep her—I had to. I couldn't imagine doing anything else. But then I lost her. I spent two nights alone in the hospital. It's taken me two and a half years to pay off the twelve-thousand-dollar hospital bill. But if I hadn't gone to the ER, I would have died."

His face grew red.

"So, there you have it. The truth. No child of mine will ever come looking for you. But the past will, if you're not honest about it."

He didn't respond.

I wondered how much even registered with him. That there was a baby. That I held her. That I would have bled to death if I hadn't gotten to the ER. That I spent every extra cent I had paying off that bill.

Was the most formative experience of my life just empty words to him? Was he relieved I'd miscarried the only baby I might ever have?

"You should take an anger management class," I said. "And evaluate how much you've been drinking. In fact, you should be honest with Delia about both of those things too, in addition to everything I just told you."

He nodded.

"You can go ahead and leave now," I said.

His face reddened even more, but he did manage to whisper, "I'm sorry. For everything."

I took a deep breath and managed to say, my voice raw, "I accept your apology."

He turned to go and didn't look back as I watched him drive away. He'd accepted responsibility. He'd apologized. Perhaps that was all I could hope for.

As I headed up the steps to the porch, I saw the concerned looks on Mamm's and Dat's faces. "I need to tell you something

I should have told you three years ago," I said, "about Lyle and me and why I left."

WHEN I FINISHED my story, Mamm and Dat dabbed at their eyes. And then both of them apologized.

"I was so worried about what everyone thought about our family that I made your leaving about me," Mamm said. "I felt like such a failure as a mother. And I was. But not for the reasons I believed."

"And I should have asked more questions," Dat said. "I should have gone to Elkhart and found you. I shouldn't have believed the rumors about you."

"And I could have at least tried to talk with you," I conceded.

Dat sighed. "Well, I would like to say we would have listened, but I don't think we would have. I think we had to learn a lesson first."

"And what was that?" I asked.

"Not to care so much about what others think that it gets in the way of loving our own child," Mamm answered. "Because we were more concerned about how things appeared, we were numb to the fact that you had been hurt and lied about."

"Denki," I said. "I'm sorry for how rebellious I was. For how wild I was."

"You were always wild," Mamm said. "Energetic. Full of adventure. You were born that way. I wish we would have found a way to acknowledge that—and direct it."

"Me too." I smiled a little bit. "But I think I'm figuring it out." I stood and stretched. "I need to get going, but I'll come down and visit soon."

Mamm stood too. "I'll get some food packed for you to

take." As she opened the screen door, she said, "Call and let us know what the doctor says, and come down to stay again if you need to rest."

I was contemplative as I drove back to Elkhart. Mamm had had all of my dresses laundered, fresh sheets on my bed, and the room dusted when I arrived, even though my leaving had devastated her. Dat had prayed from the instant I showed up that good would come from my being home.

God had answered Dat's prayers. Not only had I healed physically, but I'd found emotional and spiritual healing too. And I had a better relationship now than I'd ever had with my Mamm. Most importantly, my faith had grown. As I reached the outskirts of Elkhart, I prayed God would grow that faith even more.

Before I got out of the car at the house, I called Officer Pitt and left a message, saying I'd leave it to him whether to arrest Lyle for assault. I explained that I'd seen him at my parents' place, that Lyle seemed open to dealing with his problems, and that I no longer felt in danger. I stated that I certainly couldn't assess if anyone else was in danger or not, and I would certainly be willing to testify against him, if needed. Then I ended the message, gathered up my things, and headed into the house.

I was home.

Ivy was in the living room, watching TV.

"I don't know what happened as far as the dash cam," I said to her. "But thank you."

"I have no idea what you're talking about." She stared at the TV.

"Did Brody—"

"Sophie, stop." She made a cutting gesture across her neck, her eyes still on the TV. "Everything is fine. Once the Explorer came forward that Mateo had signaled, there were a lot of people who were upset about the dash cam not being released. Let's just leave it at that."

"Okay," I said.

Then, as I took another step toward the hall, she mouthed, "You're welcome."

That evening, I walked through the community garden, wearing a sweatshirt and jeans. The weather had changed. Just like that, it was now cool and windy.

The soil was wet, and like before, there were no weeds in sight. I hoped to see Nadine and Yani, but they weren't at the garden.

Someone else, however, was.

"Sophie! Is that you?" Jasper, wearing jeans and a sweatshirt too, stepped off the sidewalk onto the pathway toward the garden. "How are you?"

"Good." I stepped to the garden gate. "How are you?"

"Fantastic!" When he reached the garden, he asked, "I was hoping you would be here. Do you have time for a walk?"

I nodded.

"How about if we go down to the rose garden?"

"Sure," I said. "How is Mateo doing?"

"As well as he can be. He's unsettled, of course, and traumatized—the whole family is—but he's happy to be home."

"Thank you for fighting so fiercely for him."

"Thank you for giving Karin my name and number."

"I'm glad you didn't mind. It's not like you knew me or anything," I said. "If I hadn't fainted at the co-op, you wouldn't have remembered me at all."

"Oh, I would have." He smiled.

Puzzled, I smiled back.

"So, will you be going back to Nappanee?"

"I'll go home to visit from time to time," I said. "But I'm

staying here—it's where I belong." I took a deep breath and then, as quickly as I could, told him about my lupus journey. "That's why I fainted and then went home in the first place, to get some rest."

"I overheard your co-worker say you had lupus that day, but I didn't feel like it was any of my business to ask about it." He rubbed the back of his neck. "But it was always on my mind, and I wondered about you pulling a little boy out of a creek and coordinating a canning bee for thirty women when you were supposed to be resting."

I laughed. "I've never been good at taking it easy. I'm going to try to do better. Although, I've finally made the connection that serving others is energizing for me, although I still need to balance what I do. I'd like to find more ways to help others—people like Nadine and Karin and their families."

"There's a refugee mentor program I could give you some information on," he said. "But I think an obvious place you could help would be with food resources. Several groups, including a Mennonite one, are working on building a center for refugees and immigrants in the area. One of the services they want to provide is a food bank. Perhaps you would be interested in helping coordinate it."

My heart raced at the thought. "I definitely would."

"I'll text you the information," he said, "once I'm in my office." He smiled at me, a little shyly. "As long as you promise to take care of yourself and don't overdo it. I'd hate to lose you to Nappanee again."

Suddenly things felt a little awkward, but then he continued, "I was hoping the two of us could get to know each other better."

Immediately, I replied, "I'd like that."

The conversation turned back to Nappanee. He hadn't been

down there before going to the village for the first time. "It's beautiful countryside," he said. "The farms are impressive. What is yours like?"

I told him about our farm. And then briefly about Mary Landis and her family, who lived on the property where Plain Patterns was now located, and how Mary's long-ago trip to Chicago changed the course of her life. After I told him about how Mary had helped immigrants in the city, I asked, "Did you know that Mrs. O'Leary was blamed for the Chicago Fire because she was an Irish immigrant?"

He shook his head. "I didn't know that, but it doesn't surprise me. Immigrants have long been vilified and falsely blamed through the centuries. As we know firsthand."

I had the feeling I'd tell him the whole story of Mary Landis someday, how her story impacted mine and helped shape my purpose. Perhaps, I hoped, that purpose might intersect with his again someday.

When we came to the edge of the garden, we passed my rosebush. The single pink bloom was gone.

I would tell him that story too, when I was ready. In the meantime, I'd get to know Jasper—and enjoy spending time with him.

But I'd leave the future of my story up to God.

Epilogue

October 8, 2018

Jane juggled a peach cobbler in one hand and unlocked the front door of Plain Patterns with the other, yawning as she did. Owen was now a toddler, running around everywhere and getting into everything. She yawned again and chuckled, wondering why she'd been so tired when he'd been a baby.

However, in a month, she'd be missing him like crazy. Derek and Miriam had both joined the church and planned to marry in November. Derek had kept his job at Mill Creek Farms, where Victor was now the foreman. Rosibel, Victor, and Mateo received their green cards a few months after Mateo had been released from the detention center, and, thankfully, Hank was able to witness the event. He lived longer than anyone expected, and Jane was sure it was due to Rosibel's gentle care.

Before he died, Hank joined in the effort to forcefully speak against building a detention center in Elkhart County. Others followed his lead and took over the movement after he passed away. Finally, the county officials formally and completely abandoned the idea.

Jane shuffled through the quilt shop to the back room, where her desk was tucked into a corner. On her chair was the checkered garden quilt the quilting circle had completed almost a year ago. The circle would be meeting in less than an hour, and they would have a special guest today.

Sophie was coming down from Elkhart.

Jane had seen her a couple of times in the last year. Once at church, when she was visiting her parents, and another time when Sophie had stopped by the shop. Jane had asked her if she still saw Jasper. She blushed a little and said, "We see each other from time to time."

Jane wasn't sure exactly what that meant, but she didn't press her.

Sophie also said her lupus was under control, and she hadn't had another flare-up since the one the previous August. *Thank you, God, for that,* Jane prayed.

For the last year, Jane knew she wanted to give the quilt to Sophie, but she had also wanted the women in the quilting circle to be involved.

Today was the day. Even Savannah would be able to attend, along with Dorothy, who had been diagnosed with non-Hodgkin lymphoma just after the canning circle the year before. She'd grown even smaller, but she'd been holding her own with the treatment. Savannah had moved in with Dorothy to care for her and had ended up resigning from her job at the hospital and increasing her work as a doula. She planned to resume her midwifery training and start her own business in a few years.

Jane moved the quilt to the table next to the frame and then sat down at her desk. Her article about Mary and the Chicago Fire for the *Nappanee News* last October had been such a hit that she'd written a follow-up article about Mary's work with immigrants in Chicago for the latest edition of the paper.

Now she needed to come up with an article for her November

column. However, it would be hard to top Mary's story. She smiled at the thought of the story and how it had encouraged Sophie. The girl had spunk and grit, just like Mary. And it seemed she'd found someone who truly shared her values in Jasper.

The two had spent the last year serving the refugee and immigrant population of Elkhart County. Jasper continued with his legal work, and it seemed he was collaborating with Sophie to add a food bank to a local resource center to ensure that surplus food from stores, restaurants, and farms was directed to refugees and immigrants.

Jane had speculated that perhaps the two were dating after all, and then Miriam confirmed it when she'd looked up Sophie on social media on a friend's phone and told Jane that Sophie had changed her status to "in a relationship."

That warmed Jane's heart too. Sophie could certainly take care of herself, but if the Lord gave her a husband like Jasper, then that would be a blessing too.

As far as Lyle, Sophie never said whether Officer Pitt arrested him or not, but Jane did hear that Delia postponed their wedding and that Lyle was taking anger management classes and had stopped drinking. Six months ago, surprisingly, Victor had hired him back at Mill Creek Farms—not as a supervisor, but as a regular worker. That was true grace in action, and Jane hoped Lyle would prove himself worthy of the second chance.

Jane shook her head a little at her wandering train of thought and refocused on coming up with an idea for her next article. Perhaps one of the stories from the past, from her Gross Dawdi Vyt or her Mammi Katie would work. She sighed when nothing came to mind. Perhaps it was time to read through her childhood notebook again.

She retreated to the kitchen area, started the coffee, and then dished the cobbler onto plates. Then she wandered through the shop, straightening bolts of fabric and reorganizing spools of thread.

At ten, she flipped the *Closed* sign to *Open*.

Miriam arrived first, with a squirming Owen in her arms. She put him down and he toddled to the toys in the back room. Arleta arrived next, with Ruby walking alongside her. The little one joined Owen at the toy station that Jane had put together last spring. Savannah and Dorothy arrived, then Tally and Regina. Phyllis was next. Finally, Catherine arrived with Sophie.

Jane never stopped giving thanks that Sophie's relationship with her mother had been restored during her time back home. That had truly seemed a miracle.

After everyone had said their hellos and caught up a little, they gathered around the frame, where they'd just started quilting a sunshine-and-shadows quilt, a radiating circle of squares—blues, greens, purples, and black. It was a pattern more typical to the Lancaster County Amish in Pennsylvania, but Regina had chosen it and Jane was happy to oblige her.

Once they'd all sat down and picked up their needles, Jane cleared her throat. "Sophie, would you tell us how you're doing and what you've been up to?"

Sophie smiled. "Same old same old, really. Working at the co-op. Winterizing the community garden. Working with the food bank at the center to distribute as much food as we can to those who need it."

Catherine nudged her.

Sophie smiled again and said, "Mamm" in a pleading voice.

"Share your news," Catherine said. "Your big news."

Before she could say anything, Savannah squealed and pointed at Sophie's hand.

Jane hadn't noticed before, but there was an engagement

ring on Sophie's ring finger. Jane never looked since Amish women didn't wear them.

Sophie held her hand up. "Jah, Jasper asked me to marry him. We're planning our wedding for next July."

After the women said their congratulations, Jane stood and retrieved the checkered garden quilt from the table.

"This is a more appropriate gift now than I even thought." She extended the quilt to Sophie. "We want you to have this."

Instead of taking it, Sophie's left hand went to her throat.

"Take it," Catherine said.

"I can't."

"Sophie," Jane said, "remember how Sarah made the quilt for Honora and Mary took it to her?"

Sophie nodded.

"It's a long-standing tradition to give quilts," Jane said. "That's what Amish women do."

"I don't deserve it," Sophie whispered.

Jane nearly dropped the quilt. Sophie still believed she didn't deserve it because of her past? That broke Jane's heart.

But before she could figure out what to say, Catherine threw up her hands in exasperation. "All the more reason to take it, then. Just like God's grace."

The women all seemed to hold their breath until Sophie laughed. "Denki, Mamm. Always the practical one."

Catherine stood and took the quilt from Jane and then placed it, a little forcefully, on Sophie's lap.

"*No one* deserves it more than you," Catherine said to her daughter. "Take it gratefully, just as those who accept your gifts of food do. They show gratitude for your generosity, and that's all you need to do."

Sophie placed both hands on the quilt. "Denki," she said, "to each one of you." She scooped up the quilt with both hands and held it to her face, then lowered it. "Even though I don't live here, I feel valued and cared for by each of you." She looked around the circle. "As if I belong."

Catherine put her arm around Sophie in a rare expression of affection. "You do belong," she said to her daughter. "We all do."

Jane stepped back from the circle for a moment. She too was grateful for the sense of belonging in the group, for the gifts each of these women offered. All had patched-together lives, in one way or another, as checkered as the quilt they had lovingly tended.

A quilt told a story, but only a glimpse. Women, on the other hand, lived and breathed stories that could shape generations to come. Jane knew Sophie's life and her impact on others would one day be passed down to another generation, just like Mary's.

A new chapter had begun.

ACKNOWLEDGMENTS

The Chicago Fire of 1871 has always fascinated me, starting with the childhood song that went something like this:

Late one night, when we were all in bed,
Old Mrs. O'Leary left a lantern in the shed,
And when the cow kicked it over, she winked her eye and said,
"There'll be a HOT time in the old town tonight."

I had no idea way back then that I was helping to spread propaganda that started immediately after the fire and continued through the next century. Learning about the truth of the Chicago Fire was a pivotal moment in my love of history (and made me question what else I'd believed that had been propaganda too—most likely, a lot!).

Another piece of information that fascinated me was shared by my friend Marietta Couch. Her Amish ancestors, who lived in northern Indiana, donated supplies to the refugees from the fire and even helped rebuild Chicago. As I thought more about the nearby Amish in 1871, the three hundred people who died from the fire, and the hundreds of thousands of refugees—

many of whom were immigrants—the idea for *A Patchwork Past* began to come together.

A few of the many research books that helped shape the story are *Days on the Family Farm* by Carrie A. Meyer; *Chicago, America's Railroad Capital: The Illustrated History, 1836 to Today* by Brian Solomon; *The Great Chicago Fire and the Myth of Mrs. O'Leary's Cow* by Richard F. Bales; *Elkhart, Indiana* by Amy Wenger; and *They Call it Nappanee, A History, 1874–1974.*

A big thank-you to Marietta for sharing her stories, brainstorming with me, reading my manuscripts, loaning me books, and encouraging me! Any mistakes are my own. (All of the characters in *A Patchwork Past* are entirely fictitious, except for Mrs. O'Leary and her cows.)

I'm also very thankful for the members of the immigrant and refugee communities in Portland, Oregon, and other locations who have shared their stories with me.

I'm grateful for my husband, Peter, and his support on research trips and his overall positive attitude about life, which is especially helpful when I'm on deadline. I'm also thankful for our four adult children—Kaleb, Taylor, Hana, and Lily Thao—and for all the ways they've made me a better person.

My agent, Natasha Kern, also has my gratitude, as does my outstanding editor, Jennifer Veilleux, and the entire crew at Bethany House Publishers.

I'm also thankful for my readers and for their ongoing encouragement! And most importantly, I'm grateful that God keeps providing stories for me to tell.

Leslie Gould is the bestselling and award-winning author of over thirty-five novels, including the SISTERS OF LANCASTER COUNTY series. She holds an MFA in creative writing, teaches at Warner Pacific University, and enjoys research, traveling, and hiking. She and her husband, Peter, are the parents of four adult children.

Sign Up for Leslie's Newsletter

Keep up to date with Leslie's news, book releases, and events by signing up for her email list at lesliegould.com.

More from Leslie Gould

Dumped by her fiancé a week before the wedding, Savannah Mast flees California for her Amish grandmother's farm, where she becomes unexpectedly entangled in the search for a missing Amish girl. When she discovers her childhood friend, Tommy Miller, is implicated as a suspect, she must do all she can to find the Amish girl and clear his name.

Piecing It All Together
PLAIN PATTERNS #1

You May Also Like . . .

Returning for her father's funeral, Jessica faces the Amish life—and love—she left behind years prior. Struggling with regrets, she learns about the life of a Revolutionary War–era ancestor who confronted some of the same choices she has. Will Jessica find peace during her visit, along with the resolution she hopes for?

A Plain Leaving by Leslie Gould
THE SISTERS OF LANCASTER COUNTY #1
lesliegould.com

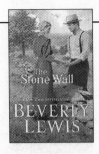

After a disastrous marriage, Elizabeth Kaufman is determined to never be at the mercy of any man again. When Aaron Zook returns from the battlefield, he never imagined the Amish way of life his grandfather had rejected would be so enticing—nor a certain widow he can't stop thinking about. Will he be able to convince her to risk giving her heart away once more?

Softly Blows the Bugle by Jan Drexler
THE AMISH OF WEAVER'S CREEK #3
jandrexler.com

Eager to begin a new chapter as a Lancaster County tour guide, Anna searches for the answers of her grandmother's past and an old stone wall—both a mystery due to the elderly woman's Alzheimer's. And when Anna grows close with a Mennonite man and an Amish widower, she's faced with a difficult choice. Will she find love and the truth, or only heartbreak?

The Stone Wall by Beverly Lewis
beverlylewis.com

BETHANYHOUSE